Ralph Marlowe

by

James Ball Naylor

Dr. James Ball Naylor
Photo courtesy of the Morgan County Historical Society

Ralph Marlowe

by

James Ball Naylor

Reprinted with Additional Material:
Foreword, Afterword, and Addendum

Edited and Annotated
by
Theresa Marie Flaherty

Theresa Marie Flaherty

www.TurasPublishing.com

No part of this publication may be reproduced or transmitted in any form or by any means, electronic or technical, including photocopying, recording, or by any information storage or retrieval system, without permission in writing from the publisher.

Volume arrangement, formatting, and notes
copyright © 2011 by Theresa Marie Flaherty.
All Rights Reserved.

Photo Credits:
Courtesy of the Morgan County Historical Society: Naylor Portraits; D.W. Garber: Figures 1, 16, and 17; Rick Shriver: Figures 2, 3, 7, 9, 13, and 20; Richard Walker, Ph. D.: Figures 4, 5, 10, 14, and 15; James W. Mason: Figures 6 and 8; Jeff Carskadden Collection: Figures 11 and 12.

RALPH MARLOWE

by

James Ball Naylor

Original Copyright
1901 by Saalfield Publishing Company

ISBN-13: 978-0-9832342-7-2

Cover Design: Michael Flaherty
Front Cover Photo: Courtesy D.W. Garber
Back Cover Photo: Courtesy Morgan County Historical Society

www.TurasPublishing.com

Tribute Series

Ralph Marlowe is the second book
in a Tribute Series to
James Ball Naylor

Table of Contents

Foreword vii
Dedication ix
Preface x
Chapter I 1
Chapter II 11
Chapter III 28
Chapter IV 41
Chapter V 57
Chapter VI 79
Chapter VII 99
Chapter VIII 118
Chapter IX 131
Chapter X 155
Chapter XI. 173
Chapter XII 197
Chapter XIII 214
Chapter XIV 231
Chapter XV 253
Chapter XVI 268
Chapter XVII 279
Afterword 292
ADDENDUM
   Book Reviews 296
   Characters Based on Real People. 317
   Locales Based on Actual Locations 318
   Period Photographs. 319
   Writings of James Ball Naylor 329
   Acknowledgments 334

FOREWORD

My husband sometimes refers to James Ball Naylor as the *other man* in my life. Although he died the year that I was born, he has been a part of my life for nearly forty years. My introduction to him came when I began transcribing sixteen years worth of his handwritten diaries for Dwight Wesley Garber, an Ohio historian who had been collecting Naylor's books and ephemera since 1905 or 1906.

As Wesley's amanuensis, the old-fashioned word for secretary that he used to describe me, I began by typing manuscripts for him. Before long I was helping him with various research projects. As my interest in Naylor grew, Wesley involved me more and more until he convinced me that I could write Naylor's biography. After several starts and stops over the course of many years, *The Final Test – A Biography of James Ball Naylor* was published in May, 2011.

I quickly learned that although the biography was finished, I was not *finished* with Naylor. It was not enough that I had written his story. I wanted to bring his works back to life with a Tribute Series. The first was *Vintage Verse*, a collection of his poetry that did not appear in any of his six previous volumes of collected verse. The poems had been culled from old family scrapbooks by one of his daughters in the late 1960s.

This second book in the Tribute Series is Naylor's 1901 best seller, *Ralph Marlowe*. Although not his first novel, I chose it because he *was* Ralph Marlowe, as he confirms in the Preface of the book.

Naylor reveals much of himself in these pages. From my research on Dr. Wesley Emmet Gatewood, on whom the character of Dr. Barwood is based, it is obvious that Naylor's depiction of him was right on the mark. His influence on Naylor was profound and long lasting.

There were many commonalities between Naylor and Ralph Marlowe. Many believed Naylor was agnostic, just as the townspeople in the story believed it of his counterpart. This was not true of Naylor or Ralph Marlowe. In the pages of *Ralph Marlowe* Naylor reveals his deeply held beliefs. Another trait they shared was their willingness and ability to fight, physically and otherwise. From his early years, Naylor was a fighter. So, too, was Ralph Marlowe. Naylor was an original, and often influenced those around him, another trait shared by Ralph Marlowe.

Like the biography, this book has been a journey for me. What started out to be merely the reprinting of one of his books has become another tool in gaining a deeper understanding of this fascinating man.

Theresa Marie Flaherty

To
My Mother

Preface

Ralph Marlowe is the legitimate child of actual experience. Much of the story—the places, characters, and incidents—I have known; a part of it I have lived. The plot is founded on fact; many of the incidents are actualities; the characters are living, breathing entities. The village of Babylon was and is as represented. For its inhabitants I offer no apology; they are as heredity and environment have made them. This is no purpose novel. I have recorded what I have seen and known—that is all. And things are as they are; not as one would have them.

With this brief explanation, I hand over the story to the reading public. If that final critic be pleased with it, my labor—a labor of love—will have been worth the while.

J. B. N.

Malta, Ohio
    January 4, 1901

CHAPTER I

A DREAR[1], sodden October day was rapidly drawing to a close. The thin cold mist that all the forenoon had enveloped wood and field, like a limp and loose cloak of gray, had gradually changed to a snug and heavy garment of cloud and rain. And yet the trees shivered and moaned as the vagrant, shifting wind stripped them of their autumn robes of green and gold and crimson; and the damp leaves fluttered helplessly to the ground and quivered in a seeming ecstasy of terror at the touch of clinging clay. Bleating flocks and lowing herds huddled in the shelter of rocks and fences and looked with longing eyes toward the distant farmyard where, through the pelting rain, the stacks and sheds loomed grim and ghostlike.

The storm grew in force. The gloom steadily deepened; the dim daylight quickly faded. Gaunt night stalked in and held the Muskingum Valley in its chill embrace.

Here a solitary light appeared in the window of a farmhouse; and there a glowing group told of a hamlet nestling at the foot of the beetling cliffs. The drowsy "choog-poof" of a slow-plodding steamboat mingled with the clamorous voice of the gale. Then above all

---
[1] drear: dreary

other sounds rose the hoarse vibrating notes of the whistle, quickly followed by the mellow notes of the clanging bell.

The vast shape of wood and iron slowly turned a bend in the river and majestically ploughed its way onward—a gigantic fiery monster belching smoke and flame from its two black horns. The reflected lights glimmered and danced in the tawny water; two radiating ridges of yellow foam leaped and surged from wheel to shore. And then the asthmatic leviathan dragged itself around another bend of the stream—and was lost in the black shadows beyond.

The wind soughed[2] dolefully among the bare willows upon the banks; and the waves lapped sullenly upon the shelving sands. Then came a lull—the stillness broken only by the baying of a dog upon the hilltops far away.

Again the wind arose, and blew with redoubled fury. The clouds wept torrents. Suddenly an ear-splitting screech split its way through the sheets of driven rain and echoed from hill slope to hill slope. A muffled, grinding roar followed. And presently a blinding glare of light flashed around a headland of rock and shale; and a rumbling, screaking[3] train swept up to a small, barnlike station building clinging to the skirts of a pretty village.

It was the southbound accommodation on the Z. and O. R.—two hours late.

The road is a short line from Zanesville to Marietta; and, to be candid, each train is an accommodation—and more frequently the schedule is broken than kept.

The engine stopped, and hissed and spluttered like an angry thing of life. The cars bumped one another and groaned in unison. "Malconta!" bellowed a smut-faced brakeman, throwing open the door of the rear coach.

The buzzing murmur of many voices suddenly grew to a din; the thunder of the moving train had ceased. A gust of wind and wet swept into the car, laden with the suffocating odor of steam and

---

2 sough: to make a soft murmuring sound
3 screak: to make a harsh shrill noise : screech

smoke. Passengers hurriedly caught up wraps and satchels and sidled toward the door. The wind and rain met and buffeted them. Muttered maledictions[4] mingled with sharp exclamations. Then the platform of the coach was clear—and for a few moments all was quiet within.

Ralph Marlowe lifted his chin from his breast, removed his knees from the plush-covered back of the seat in front of him, and lazily drew himself erect. Then he turned down his coat collar and yawned behind his hand. He had been asleep.

"Hello!" he muttered to himself, "where are we?" And he swept a hasty glance around the interior of the car which now contained but a half score of passengers.

Of a sudden arose the tramp and shuffle of many feet upon the steps and platform of the coach; and wet and bedraggled passengers with umbrellas, bags, and bundles, came crowding and jostling through the door.

Marlowe screwed half around in his seat and curiously watched their bustling entry. They were a nondescript lot: farmers and their wives who had been to market; a nattily dressed drummer; a red-faced lumberman; a pursy, flabby-faced oil man in sou'wester, and slicker; and a sharp-nosed horse jockey in corduroys—the worse for liquor.

With much good-natured banter they secured seats and arranged their manifold parcels and packages. Then nought was heard except the low monotonous hum of their voices, the head-splitting buzz of steam in the engine, and the jarring bump of trunks tumbling from the baggage van.

Ralph looked at his watch—and again yawned. He was a young man of eight and twenty, straight and athletic, with brown hair and eyes and a dark dramatic face—whatever that may mean. His clothing was neat-fitting and stylish, from the patent-leather shoe protruding into the aisle, to the black derby hat that lay upon a gray top coat carelessly flung over the back of the seat.

For the want of something better to do, he turned and peered out of the window. But he could see nothing, although he shaded

---

4 malediction: a curse

his eyes with his strong white hands and flattened his nose against the cool pane. He was on the side of the car opposite the lights of the station, and all without was blackness impenetrable. The glass, backed by the wall of gloom, was a mirror upon which drops of rain, like globules of quicksilver, sparkled and trickled.

"All aboard!" bawled the smut-faced brakeman bounding up the steps and into the car—closing the door with a bang.

A snort—a start—and they were off. The engine coughed and wheezed. The low rumble of wheels grew to a deafening roar and rattle. Dancing lights flew past the windows as the train crossed the principal street of the village, lumbered through the outskirts, and reached the open country. The brakeman shook the water from his cap, and steadying himself against the wood-box swayed with the lurching car. Grotesque shadows—cast by the jiggling lamps staggered drunkenly along the aisle. The conversation of the passengers was a drowsy murmur. The smoke of a vile cigar added pungency to the close atmosphere; the bibulous[5] horseman was openly and willfully violating the rules of the road.

The door opened and shut; and the conductor—his short legs far apart, his cap perched rakishly on the back of his head, and his blonde mustache dripping moisture—stood in the aisle, sniffling suspiciously and scowling. But he skillfully thrust his lantern into his armpit and quietly began to take up the fares.

Marlowe plucked the blue sleeve as it brushed past him, and inquired:

"How far are we from Babylon?"

"Ten miles—next stop but one."

And the uniformed taker of fares savagely punched an old farmer's bit of pasteboard—but kept his eye upon the pimpled face of the puffing jockey.

Slowly down the aisle he moved. The natty drummer smiled across at Ralph, and winking slyly jerked his thumb in the direction of the retreating conductor. Ralph smiled and nodded in return. Other passengers taking in the situation grinned broadly. All

---

5 bibulous: fond of alcoholic beverages,

conversation ceased—the lull before the gale.

"If you want to smoke, go forward into the smoker," growled the conductor as he reached the jockey's side.

"Go where?" returned the horseman, as he straightened up in well assumed surprise and indignation.

"Into the smoker," repeated the conductor in a louder tone. "This isn't the smoker."

The passengers twisted their necks and held their breaths, to catch the reply.

"Naw?" remarked the jockey with a tipsy leer. "No, it isn't."—Angrily.

"Well, who said it was?"—With a fine show of dignity.—"D' you think I ain't onto my job—say? Of course this ain't no smoker; it's a stock car. *I'm* the smoker. See?"

And he nodded his head and pursed his lips contemptuously.

A titter rippled through the coach. The conductor flushed, but manfully controlled himself.

"No nonsense!" he said severely. "Put out that cigar or go into the smoking car."

"This ain't no cigar; it's a stogie."—Puffing vigorously and blowing the smoke into the other's eyes.

"Listen!" thundered the exasperated conductor. "Put out that cigar, go into the smoker, or I'll put you off."

"Say, ol' man, you ain't preachin' no sermon to a deaf an' dumb asylum."

"Do you understand?"—taking him by the arm and shaking him roughly.

"Say?"

"Well?"

"I'm *in* the smokin' car."

"You are not."

"It's a *smokin'* car when I *smoke* in it, ain't it—hey?"

"Don't get gay, now!" the conductor hissed menacingly, placing his lantern upon the floor and pushing up his sleeves.

"Oh!" ejaculated an elderly woman, with a catch of the breath.

"They're going to fight." The other passengers ceased to smile; the comedy was assuming a serious aspect.

"Don't be scared," whispered the red-faced lumberman to the timid lady. "They ain't goin' to fight. One's afraid, an' t'other dassen't."

His words hissed through the car like escaping steam.

"Don't git gay, eh?" sneered the jockey. "I ain't gittin' gay; I'm alluz gay—gayer'n a red ribbon at a county fair."

"The first thing you know, off you'll go," the conductor shouted, grabbing at the fellow who retreated to the end of the seat, farthest from the aisle.

"You say I'll go off?" he asked, with a humorous twinkle in his rat-like eyes.

"Yes you will!"—striving to catch him by the collar.

"Say, pardner, may be you think I'm *loaded!*" A roar greeted the horseman's sally. The big lumberman guffawed loudly:

"Loaded? Well, I sh'uld say! Loaded to the neck! Haw—haw—haw!"

The drummer familiarly slapped Marlowe's knee, and laughing until he was purple in the face, exclaimed:

"Loaded—and likely to go off! That's a good one—eh?"

"He has diagnosed his own case—and correctly, in my opinion," Ralph replied smilingly.

The conductor was furious. Frantically he snatched the offending cigar from the jockey's teeth, and flinging it upon the floor stamped it to dust. Then shaking his fat, ringed finger at the offender, he began in tones hoarse with rage:

"There! It's *out*."

"But *I* ain't *out,*" interrupted the perverse horseman coolly producing another stogie and fumbling in his pocket, for a match.

"Don't you dare to light that?"

"Why—what'll happen?"

"I'll fling you off the train!"

"So?"

"Just try it and see."

"If I *light* this stogie, I'll light on my head and shoulders, in the mud—eh?"

"Yes—you will."

"Say!"—Cocking one eye and smiling—"I guess you're in earnest, pardner. Well, 'nough's enough. Le's kiss an' make up."

And slowly, fumblingly returning the cigar to his pocket, he extended a hand not overly clean.

"Huh!" the conductor snorted, contemptuously ignoring the proffered paw and picking up his lantern.

Without more ado, he turned and hastily left the car.

The jockey got upon his feet, and swaying drunkenly, remarked in injured tones:

"Mad—wasn't he? Right up on the bit—head high an' tail over the dashboard—an' comin' like a wind-broken hoss in a two-forty trot. An' all 'bout nothin'. It's mighty strange what fools some people can make o' the'rselves."

After delivering himself of this bit of sage philosophy, he dropped upon the cushioned seat and lapsed into a drunken sleep.

The train sped on through the rain and darkness.

Up slippery grades the engine coughed and labored; wheezed and panted momentarily on gaining the level; and then—as though bent on self-destruction—plunged headlong down the succeeding slope.

With a great grinding of wheels, and whistle and hiss of escaping air and steam, the train pulled up at a flag station. A number of passengers got off. Marlowe peeped through the smoke-streaked pane and saw a swinging lantern, and under its light a pair of rain-sodden shoes, a water-dripping hat, and between, a humped heap of ragged humanity. Nothing else was visible.

"Two hours late on account of a landslide, and stopping at every pig pen and turkey nest between Zanesville and Marietta," grumbled the natty drummer, flashing his gold watch toward Ralph. "At this rate we won't get into Marietta in time for breakfast. This is the worst rattletrap road in the state, anyhow. 'Twon't be but a year or two till there won't be anything left of it but a few rotten ties and two streaks of rust. There—than, heaven!—we're off again."

Then pleasantly:

"Are you on the road?"

"Yes and no," Marlowe smilingly answered, facing his questioner and coolly surveying him.

"Ah!" ejaculated the commercial man, twisting his small black mustache and fidgeting uneasily. "That's a little hard to understand. I—I—"

"It's like this," Ralph explained, still smiling. "I'm on *this* road—unfortunately; but I am not a knight of the grip."

"Oh! pardon me."

With a deprecatory gesture, his rosy cheeks flushing as red as the carnation in his buttonhole, to the ample bald space extending from forehead to occiput[6].

"A rare specimen of the class—capable of blushing," Marlowe thought.

But he said aloud:

"That's all right. *You* are a traveling man, of course."

With animation: "Yes, indeed. I travel for the Baldy Drug Company of Zanesville."

"You are well acquainted up and down the valley, then."

"Sure! I sell drugs to the doctors, patent medicines to the grocers, liquors to the saloon keepers; carry flowers to the ladies—and give candy to the babies."

Laughing good naturedly, until his plump little body shook and his watch chain jingled musically against the buttons on his vest.

"A jolly fellow, well pleased with himself and all the world—ten years older than I, but looking younger," was Ralph's mental comment.

But to his companion:

"How large a place is Babylon?"

"In square miles or population?" returned the drug man, still smiling broadly.

"Either or both," laughed Marlowe.

"It covers half a township and has about six hundred inhabitants."

Ralph's countenance fell.

---

6 occiput: the back of the skull

"So small?" He muttered peevishly—incredulously.

"Small!" echoed the drummer. "I call that plenty of territory for that many people."

"Perhaps—yes, no doubt," Ralph murmured, his eyes downcast, his foot absent-mindedly tapping the floor.

"You going to stop off there?"

"Yes," replied Marlowe without looking up.

"And you expect to find it a bigger place?"

"I got the impression it was a place of three or four thousand inhabitants."

"Thunder," gasped the drummer. "That's pretty near as many people as there are in the county. You must be thinking of Malconta. No, I've told you the truth. Babylon is a place of about six hundred."

Marlowe looked up and remarked: "It can't be a first-class place for a drugstore, then."

"I don't know about that. I sell old Doc Barwood lots of drugs. He has the only drugstore in the township—sells heaps of drugs and makes money hand over fist. Quakerville and Foxtown are tributary to the place, too. You're not thinking of going into business there? Oh! may be you're an oil man."

"No, I am going to accept a position."

"That so?"

Ralph merely nodded.

"In a store?"

"In a drugstore, or pharmacy—or whatever it may prove to be."

"You don't mean you are going there to clerk for old Doc Barwood?"—with lifted brows.

"I do—I am, yes."

"The—devil—you—are!" ejaculated the drummer.

Then, with dropped jaw and wide open eyes, he sat and looked at Marlowe for a full half minute.

The whistle screeched eerily.

"Is that for Babylon?" Ralph asked.

"Yes," replied his companion rousing himself and extending his hand. "Well, so long. Give my respects to the old doc. I'll be around to see you in a week or so. Try and have an order for me. Here—smoke a good cigar on me. Seldom smoke? I do—and I carry 'em to give away. Matter of business, you know. By the way, I haven't introduced myself. My name's Crider—L. W. Crider—Leonidas Wallingford Crider. How'd you like to carry such a name as that, around in your grip all your life—eh? And your name?"

"Ralph Marlowe."

"Ralph Marlowe," Crider rattled on. "Some sense in a name like that. Short but sweet. Here—let me help you with that overcoat. On she goes. By jocks! That's a nice traveling bag you've got. Wouldn't mind having one like it myself. Here—have a cake of gum. Don't chew the stuff? And so *you're* going to try to clerk for the old doc. I'll be—excuse me. Well, here you are. So long—see you later."

The locomotive was slowing; the bell clanging. Ralph stood leaning against the end of his seat, satchel in hand, waiting for the train to stop and wondering why his new acquaintance had been so surprised at the announcement that he—Ralph—had accepted a place with Dr. Barwood. The final bump came—the coach stood still. The young man edged his way along the aisle, muttering:

"I wish I had asked him what he meant. But then he gave me no opportunity; he talked incessantly. A country village—a place of six hundred inhabitants—a fine outlook, truly! But stuff! Why should *I* care? I'll be lost here—buried alive. It could not be better; I shall be securely hidden from all who ever knew me. But what did that drummer mean by saying—'So *you're* going to try to clerk for the old doc?' No matter. Here I am; and if there's anything amiss, I'll soon have the satisfaction of knowing it."

The last thing he observed as he left the car, was the big lumberman arguing politics with an old farmer and emphasizing his points by thumping the floor with his measuring stick; while the oil man—a rotund heap of lemon-colored oilskins—was fast asleep, and the jockey was rubbing his rat-like eyes and staring confusedly around.

Then Ralph stood alone upon the station platform; and the train was thundering away in the blackness.

* * * * * *

CHAPTER II

THE RAILROAD—that coquets[7] with the winding river from one end of the valley to the other—at Babylon suddenly grows ardent in its wooing, and hugs the stream closely. Only a zigzag row of frame warehouses and lumber piles—perched insecurely upon wooden docks—separates it from the object of its adoration.

The station building, a low, rambling affair, faces the tumble-down warehouses and stares across the track at them, frowning at their brazen emptiness. Back of the station the ground rises rapidly, and dotting the slope and the sandy plain beyond, are the residences and business places of the Babylonians. The town resembles a garden hose—one principal thoroughfare extending westward from the river to the hills a half mile or more away.

Ralph Marlowe stood upon the empty platform and gazed after the rear lights of the disappearing train. The wet rails gleamed in the yellow light streaming from the station window. The express agent—a muffled, indescribable figure—trundled his truck around a distant corner of the building, and was lost to view. The young man was indeed alone.

"I feel as though I had just bid good-bye to civilization and dropped

---
7 coquets: flirts

upon an uninhabited shore," he murmured—a catch in his voice.

Then suddenly becoming aware that the rain was fast soaking his outer garments, he set down his traveling bag, raised his umbrella, and looked about him. A door of the station stood open, revealing a dimly lighted interior. Ralph quickly sought shelter within.

The room was long and narrow, with a rough wooden bench running along one side of it. An upright stove near the center of the floor and a smoky oil lamp suspended from the ceiling, completed the furnishings. In the middle of the yellow wall opposite the long bench, was a small square opening with a meager shelf or ledge at the bottom. To Marlowe's vivid imagination, the whole resembled the blank face, open mouth, and projecting lips of a saffron-tinted ogre. Above the window, in blue-and-gilt letters, were the words: "TICKET OFFICE—*passengers will please procure tickets before boarding the train.*"

Ralph heard the clicking of a telegraphic instrument in the other room, and advancing to the opening, peeped through. A sallow-countenanced, brown-mustached young man, with a green-visored cap pulled low over his spectacled eyes, was bending over the table on which the Morse instrument rested, writing industriously. A tall student lamp with a milk-white shade was at his elbow.

"Good evening," Marlowe ventured.

The operator nodded and moved his lips, but made no reply. Ralph waited impatiently. After a time the operator looked up and remarked questioningly:

"Something?"

"Can you direct me to the best hotel in the village?"

"There isn't any."

"No hotel?"—In surprise savoring of incredulity and bordering on consternation.

"No *best* hotel. There's only one. It's the *worst*—I board there."

"Will you kindly direct me to it?"

"Are you in much of a hurry?"

"I am tired and hungry."

"That's unfortunate—for you. Well, I can't *direct* you to the place; but if you'll sit down and wait a few minutes, I'll *pilot* you to it. I'll finish up things and go along with you. I've done enough work for one day, anyway—for forty dollars a month and board yourself. Drop down on the bench there. I'll be through in a jiffy."

Marlowe retired to the wooden seat, and busied himself with his own thoughts and a closer survey of the barren and uninviting surroundings. He heard the operator moving about in the other room, putting things to rights. Of a sudden the light in the office went out, a key turned in a lock—and the ticket window was a black square in the yellow wall.

Presently the operator entered the waiting room and remarked:

"All ready. Give me your satchel—you carry the umbrella over us. It's darker 'n a tunnel up the street—and still raining like the deluge."

Then as they stood outside and he turned to lock the door:

"You ought to have on overshoes; you'll find it muddy enough up the grade. But we're in for it. Come on."

The street was deserted and black, but outlined by dim lights twinkling here and there in stores and shops. In silence the two young men began to ascend the slope, sinking deep into the soft wet sand at every step. It was like traversing the length of an immense mortar bed tilted at an angle of thirty degrees. At last the operator panted:

"This is tough—on you, especially. It'll try the patent on your enameled shoes. I've been here three years; and it's all mortar in winter and all sand in summer—and not the sign of a street lamp. I'm getting tired of it, too; and I don't mean to stay much longer. It's too slow a burg for yours truly."

Ralph, roused from the reverie into which he had fallen, said with a show of interest:

"This is not your home, then?"

"No, indeed. I came from Parkersburgh. There's a fly town for you. I took this job because I couldn't get a better one at the time. But I'm getting tired of being agent, operator, and general roustabout for forty dollars a month. I'm going to quit soon as something else shows up—*I* am. A fellow of my make-up gets the blues here. A few more years of it'ld kill *me*."

"You do not consider the tranquillity of the place conducive to longevity?"

"How's that?"

"You think the village too quiet—too slow?"

"Slow? That's it—that's the word. Slow! The people here are slower than the wrath of the Almighty—slower 'n promotion on the Z. and O. R. There's no amusements, except an occasional dance. That's where all the young folks are tonight—down at Flat Bottom to a dance. That's the reason nobody from the hotel was at the train. She was two hours late, you know—and all the help had gone to that shindig. Deuce of a dark night, isn't it? Here's the crossing. The hotel's just on the other side of the street. Watch out now—or you'll get mired."

With some difficulty they crossed from one sidewalk to the other, carefully picking their way along a narrow path of cinders. The crossing was dimly lighted by the rays of a large lantern, perched upon a post standing at the foot of the steps leading up to the hotel entrance.

The building was a large and rambling frame with a stone basement, and a veranda running along two sides. Marlowe noted that much, in spite of the darkness.

Following his companion up the steps and through the door, he found himself in a large bare-floored room that did duty as office and, also, served as loafing rendezvous for the village idlers.

The operator placed Ralph's traveling bag upon the floor; and turning toward a group of men, who were playing "seven-up" at a table in one corner, asked quickly:

"Where's the landlord?"

"Tendin' bar," mumbled one of the players, vigorously and skillfully shuffling the cards.

Then he slapped the greasy pack upon the table, and nodding to his associate on the right said briskly:

"Cut 'em."

The player addressed cut the cards. The other took them up and proceeded with the deal, wetting his thumb at frequent intervals, by touching it to his bulbous nether[8] lip.

"I'll go and bring the landlord in," said the operator to Ralph, in a low tone. "I won't be gone but a minute. Just take a chair."

With the words he vanished through a rear door. Marlowe took a seat and glanced ruefully at his muddy shoes and damp garments. The room was empty and chill; and he shivered. The black and yawning grate contained only a few branches of dead evergreen, a bunch of withered dogwood blossoms—summer decorations—and bits of waste paper. A brown earthenware cuspidor upon the hearth was full of tobacco quids, cigar stubs, and half-burnt matches. A single lamp lighted the apartment, having a place of honor upon the dusty mantelshelf. In consequence, much of the room was in shadow. Against a side wall stood a high, spindle-legged desk with a cabinet of pigeonholes overtopping it; and upon its sloping lid lay a number of newspapers, a wet and dripping umbrella, and a small, canvas-bound, blank book—the hotel register.

The odor of moist soot came down the chimney, and mingling with the stale smell of rank tobacco smoke pervaded the close atmosphere.

Marlowe turned his attention to the group of card players. There were four of them. He learned afterward that two of them were oil men—guests of the hostelry[9]—and two of them were villagers. The small, pop-eyed man, with short cropped red hair, was the village cobbler; his partner in the game—a thickset individual with a face like a red full moon—was the bridge-tender. One of the oil men was a prospector, and the other a driller, in the oil fields a few miles back of the town.

They played out their hands, laughing, and bantering one another good-humoredly. It was the cobbler's deal. Holding the cards caressingly in his calloused palm and tapping the bare table with his knuckles, he looked searchingly at Marlowe and remarked:

---

8 nether: lower or under
9 hostelry: inn or hotel

"Bad night out."

"Very," replied Ralph in a tone of conviction.

"Train was late, too."

Marlowe merely nodded. He was in no mood to encourage the cobbler's advances.

The latter persisted:

"Did Clark go to find the landlord for you?"

"The young man who came in with me did—yes."

"That's Clark—good feller, too. I reckon you hain't had no supper, neither."

Marlowe shook his head, uttering a curt negative.

"Come—shuffle up them cards, Crawford," admonished the prospector. "We want to strike some grease this time. Mix them up good. There must be big ones in the deck some place. Me and Roberts is tired o' strikin' dusters. Ain't we, Roberts?"

"You bet," the driller answered with a cavernous yawn.

"Closer 'n a number eight foot in a number six shoe," whispered the cobbler with a nod toward Marlowe and a wink at the prospector.

But he dealt the cards; and the game went on. Presently Clark returned to the room, a foaming glass of beer in one hand and a ham sandwich in the other.

"Charley'll be in in a minute," he announced mumblingly, his mouth full of bread and meat. "He's busy at the bar."

Seating himself, he tilted his chair against the wall and contentedly sipped his beer and munched his sandwich.

Marlowe was hungry. The smell of the food and drink made him ravenous. Consulting his watch he found it marked seven-forty-five. He got upon his feet, and thrusting his hands deep into his trousers' pockets, strode up and down the floor, a scowl upon his handsome face. He was fast losing his temper.

"Just as well to sit down and take it easy," Clark advised, grinning impishly. "I told you this was the slowest burg you ever struck. Just before you die of starvation they'll get you something to eat, though."

The card players looked up and laughed. They were enjoying the stranger's discomfiture. The latter resumed his seat and said nothing. Clark set his empty glass upon the sloping lid of the tall desk, fired a bit of bread at the black grate, and hitching his chair toward Marlowe's, asked in an undertone:

"Going to stay in town long?"

"Not unless I succeed in finding more hospitable quarters," was the snappish reply.

The operator laughed half pityingly as he returned:

"Oh! this isn't half a bad place. I've been stringing you a little about it. Then you've struck it at a bad time—help all away. They'll give you a clean bite and bed. Charley Williams—that's the landlord—is a jolly good fellow, and he'll do all he can to make you comfortable. Here he comes now"—springing to his feet and facing a big man coming through the rear door—"Charley, this is my friend, Mister—Mister—"

He hesitated and cast an appealing glance at Ralph.

"Ralph Marlowe," the latter prompted in a low tone.

"My friend, Mr. Ralph Marlowe," Clark went on glibly. "I brought him up from the train. Nobody there to meet him, you know. He wants supper and bed—supper as soon as he can get it. He hasn't had a bite to eat since week before last. Do the handsome by him, Charley."

The big man smiled blandly. He wore an immense, drooping, black mustache; and there were dark, bladder-like puffs under his eyes. Wiping his large red hands upon the white apron reaching from his chin to his ankles, he remarked in an apologetic tone:

"It's a bad night out, Mr. Marlowe—an' no doubt you're cold an' hungry. I'm sorry I had to keep you waitin'. You've hit us at a bad time, though; the help's all away to a dance an' my wife's in bed with the sick headache. But I'll have you fixed comfortable in a jiffy."

Then to the operator:

"Clark, you'll have to help me out a little. Start a fire in the grate; the room's too damp. You'll find coal an' kindlin' in the closet there. I'll go an' git some one to tend bar; then I'll git the gentleman some supper."

With the words he bustled through the back door—and was gone.

Clark proceeded to build a fire, all the while grumbling whimsically to himself. Soon a genial blaze sprang up in the black grate, effectually dispelling the gloom and dampness of the place and giving a rosy tint to the time-stained walls. Ralph wheeled his chair close to the hearth and stretched his wet shoes to the fire. Already he was much mollified. The world looked brighter—and he hummed the air of a comic opera.

"Feeling better, eh?" Clark questioned, holding his arms stiffly away from his body—his blackened palms turned outward.

"Much better," Ralph smilingly replied.

"Going to stay in town awhile?"—Banteringly.

"Undoubtedly. I came here to take a position."

The card players overheard Marlowe's words; and holding their cards aloft and listening intently, forgot to play.

The telegraph operator showed the surprise and curiosity he felt, as he returned quickly:

"That so? Not going into McDevitt's store?"

"No."

"Bentley's?"

"No. I am a pharmacist; I am going into Dr. Barwood's employ."

"Not going to clerk for old Doc Barwood!"

"I am. But why do you manifest so much surprise?"

Clark shut his jaws with a snap and stared hard at Ralph, as if he questioned the latter's sanity. The card players looked at one another, and silently shaking their heads and grinning maliciously resumed their game.

At last the operator muttered:

"The hell—well, I'll be skedaddled!" And suiting the action to the words, he dodged out the rear door.

All this was not lost upon Marlowe; and his wonder and perplexity increased the more he thought about it. He was silently cudgeling his brain over the affair, when Clark returned to the room.

"Been out to wash my hands," he explained.

"Williams told me to tell you your supper'll be ready in a half minute."

"Very well," Ralph replied, fixing his keen brown eyes upon his companion's pale face. "Sit down here."—Pulling a chair to his side.—"I want to talk with you."

Clark dropped into the seat and squirmed uneasily.

"Now," Ralph continued, "tell me what you meant."

"Meant by what?"

"You know. Why were you so thunderstruck when I announced my intention of working for Dr. Barwood?"

"Well—I—"

He hesitated, fidgeted—and stopped.

"Well?" Ralph relentlessly insisted.

"I—I don't want to say anything against the old doc; he's a good patron of the road. But—"

"Is he insane?"

"No—of course not."

"Idiotic?"

"No!"—In a tone of deep disgust.—"He's smarter'n a patch of nettles."

"What then?"

"I'm not going to say another word; I'll leave you to find him out. He don't like me none too well, anyhow."

The operator said this doggedly, compressing his lips.

"Say, Sam Clark!" the red-headed cobbler cried, throwing down his cards and springing to his feet. "Why don't you tell the gentleman what kind of a man ol' Doc Barwood is? The young man ought to know—he has a right to know."

"Tell him yourself, then," Clark retorted hotly.

"I'm not under your orders."

"And that's jest what I'll do," the cobbler snapped, his short, fiery hair bristling with excitement and anger. "I ain't afraid."

"Here—here, Crawford!" shouted the prospector. "You're

breaking up the game. Set down. Your news'll keep till the young man's had his supper. It'll set better on his stomach then."

And taking the cobbler by the coat tails, the oil man jerked him into a chair.

At that moment the landlord came into the office by a door in the corner near the tall desk, and announced:

"Your supper's ready, Mr. Marlowe. I've fried you some ham and eggs, warmed up some biscuits, and made you a cup of coffee. It ain't very much; but it'll have to do fer tonight. It'll keep soul an' body together till mornin', anyhow. Then we'll try to use you better."

Marlowe desired to hear what the cobbler had to say, but he desired food more; so he followed the landlord through the corner door, into the dining room.

On reentering the office, after finishing his meal, he saw the moon-faced bridge-tender pounding the table with his fist, and heard him exclaiming exultingly:

"High, low, jack an' the game! Six games to y'r five! That's enough fer tonight. Put up the cards and shove back the table."

The other players acquiesced in the bridge-tender's decision. The cobbler placed the greasy cards upon the mantel and pushed the table against the wall. Then, having bitten the end from a long stogie and lighted it, he dropped into a chair and puffed away in silence.

Clark was absent. Ralph wished very much to know Crawford's opinion of Dr. Barwood, and considered how he might obtain it. But the man of the last and awl[10] appeared to have forgotten his avowed determination to express himself; and Marlowe could evolve no plan to set him going.

So the young man sat and dried his shoes by the fire—consulting his watch occasionally and yawning—and listened to the idle gossip of his companions, hoping all the while some turn of the conversation would remind the cobbler of his intention.

The murmur of his companions' voices made Ralph drowsy, so

---

10 man of the last and awl: cobbler (*last* is a foot-shaped block used in making or repairing shoes; *awl* is a pointed tool for making holes as in leather)

he thought. He dropped into a reverie—half asleep, half awake. Of a sudden he heard the prospector say—"Yes, the ol' doc's got an' inter'st in that well, too"—and he was wide awake in an instant.

"In that new one on the Worden place?" the bridge-tender asked.

"Yes," the prospector answered. "Have they drilled in yit?"

"Jest got through the first Cow Run sand yesterday, I understand."

"Where'll they find the grease there?" the cobbler inquired.

"In the second Cow Run, most likely."

"Say!" volunteered the driller. "I heard today they'd jest shot that wild cat well out at Coon Holler."

"That so?"—From the prospector.—"What show?"

"A duster."

"Jest as I expected."—With a sneer.

"But the Climax people drilled in a good one on the Gaddus lease, a day 'r two ago."

"Did, eh? What did she run?"

"Pumped forty bar'ls the first ten hours."

"Purty fair," said the prospector, nodding approvingly.

"An that's in the stray sand, too. There's another well the ol' doc's in on. He has the luck fer sure. He's interested in that whole string o' wells on the Gaddus tract, ain't he?"

"Yes—an' the ol' cuss's gittin' rich," muttered the bridge-tender in an injured tone.

"Gittin' rich!" the cobbler snorted angrily. "He *is* rich—been rich fer years—an' gittin' richer. The ol' hog!"

"You can't say but what he's lucky, anyhow," the prospector said, beaming affably upon the hotheaded little cobbler—and winking slyly at Marlowe. "I've only been here a few months; an' he's made over ten thousan' dollars sence I come. He must be worth over a cool hundred thousan'—from what I can learn. I ain't much of a believer in this section as a deep oil field,—though it's a good shaller one,—but if I had ol' Doc Barwood in with me, fer a pardner, I'd poke a hole down to the Berea grit an' give 'er a hundred quart shot o' glycer'n. A man *might* hit a gusher. Yes, the ol' doc's a lucky dog—an' no mistake."

"Lucky!" snarled the cobbler. "He's luckier 'n four aces 'g'inst a full house. He ought to play poker—*he* had. If he'd draw to a shoestring, he'd ketch a side o' leather. But he's the meanest, contrariest, stingiest, most cantankerous ol' cuss that ever drawed breath. He hain't got a good friend in the town. I don't b'lieve his own fam'ly likes him—I don't see how they can. He wants his own way in ev'rything—an's mad whether he *gits* it 'r *don't git* it."

Marlowe was learning what he wished to know. Crawford took a pull or two at his expiring stogie and went on:

"Yes, he's the most even-tempered man in all creation; got a temper like a rat-tail file—an's raspin' away *all* the time. He's so c'ntrary the hair on the back o' his neck grows uphill 'stid o'down. An' stingy? He'd skin a flea fer its hide an' taller."

Crawford was greatly wrought up. His face was scarlet; his red hair was on end. Rising to his feet and pointing a pudgy finger at Ralph, he shouted:

"Young man, you're in fer a good time—an' I wish you much joy. W'y the ol' scamp's had three clerks in the last year 'r so; an' couldn't keep one of 'em. The first one took to drink; the second one run away an's never come back n'r been heard of; an' the third one went to Cincinnati an' committed suicide. You won't be here a month till you'll be in the notion o' gittin' married 'r doin' some other desper'te thing. The ol' infiddle! Calls hisself an agnorstic—an' brags that he ain't 'fraid o' God, man, n'r the devil. That's what he does. It makes me sick to talk 'bout him."

Crawford collapsed into his chair, and sat there chewing viciously at his cigar stub, and wiping the perspiration from his glowing visage, with the back of his hairy hand.

Ralph was embarrassed; and made no attempt to reply to the cobbler's fiery outburst. He shrewdly conjectured that Crawford had a grievance, real or fancied, laid up to the credit of Dr. Barwood. Yet the cobbler's intemperate accusations might be the true interpretation of Crider's surprised ejaculation and Clark's noncommittal silence. The young druggist was worried. Once more he looked at his watch, and wished some one would come to show him to his room. He desired to be alone, that he might think more clearly.

"Crawford," the driller chuckled, "you remind me of a thirty-quart shot o' glycer'n' with a splutter'n fuse to it. You're ready to explode at any minute."

"Say!" laughed the prospector. "That reminds me of somethin'."

"Tell it," cried his companions, in expectant chorus.

The prospector stretched his long legs toward the fire, produced a piece of tobacco by diving deep into his trousers' pocket, and deliberately ground off a chew. Then he coolly returned the serrated fragment to its usual resting place, and with a few preliminary masticatory[11] movements began:

"You fellers all knows ol' John Lovett out at Bethel—great big man with a red face, an' a voice a cross 'twixt a steam whistle an' a megaphone. His whisper sounds like a steamboat blowin' mud out of 'er b'ilers—an' he talks faster 'n a horse can trot. Well, one wet an' muddy day last winter, George Gifford—that little bald-faced dude that shot the wells on Stringer's Fork—come a drivin' 'long past ol' John's place, goin' down to Dullson to put in a shot. The mud was stiff an' heavy; an' he had fifty quarts o' the stuff in his rig, an' was drivin' slow.

"Ol' John's niece had been visitin' him fer a week 'r two, an' that mornin' was wantin' to git down to Dullson, to take the train fer home. So the ol' man, 'stid o' hitchin' up his own team an' drivin' her down, stood out in the front yard, watchin' fer some one to come 'long, that she could ride down with.

"Well, after while he spied Gifford draggin' his load through the mud; an' rushin' down the path leadin' to the road an' wavin' his hands like a crazy man, bellered at him—like a bull with the whoopin' cough:

"'Say there, young man! Say there! Stop right where you are—stop right where you are, sir. My niece, M'randy—yes, sir, my niece,

---

11 masticatory: grinding or chewing

M'randy, wants to go down to Dullson to take the cars—yes, sir, to take the cars, you understand. You're goin' down there—of course you are—you're goin' down there; an' she wants to ride down with you. She ain't very hefty—she won't make much of a load—yes, sir—yes, sir. An' it ain't but a mile 'r so—jest a mile 'r so. Let 'r ride, eh? Let 'er ride? Of course—of course. I'll run right up an' tell 'er. She'll be all ready in a jiffy—yes, sir, in a jiffy. Won't keep you waitin' but a minute—not more 'n a minute. Jest stay where you are, sir—right where you are.'

"An' ol' John ambled off up the path, like a stepladder with the rheumatiz.

"Gifford hadn't been able to git a word in edgeways; but now he hollered:

"'Say, mister! Wait a minute.'

"'Well—well!' roared ol' John turnin' 'round an' comin' back. 'What is it, young feller? Out with it, sir—out with it!'

"'The young lady's welcome to ride with me,' says George, 'providin' she ain't afraid—'

"'Afraid?' broke in the ol' man madder'n a wet hen, an' a wavin' his arms like a windmill. 'Afraid? Afraid o' what, sir—afraid o' what, I'd like to know? Not o' you—I reckon—you little, insignificant piece o' nothin'ness—not o' you? Maybe you think she's afraid o' y'r bony ol' tackeys? Not much, sir—not much, I say! She's druv better hosses 'n you ever saw, sir—yes, sir—better'n you ever saw. An' I've got 'em right in the stable there—right in the stable; pair o' match bays—not a white hair on 'em—not a hair. But I don't want to put 'em out in the mud, you understand—no, sir—don't want to put 'em out in the mud. Afraid o' what, sir—I'd like to know? Speak right out an' tell me. Afraid o' what?'

"'I thought she might be afraid o' the load I've got,' cheeped George in a scared voice. He thought he'd struck a lunatic.

"'Afraid o' the load you've got?' ol' John fairly snorted. 'Afraid o' the load you've got? I reckon you ain't no travelin' circus with a cage o' tigers an' a box o' snakes, eh? What's the matter with y'r load—what's the matter with it, sir—what's the matter?'

"'W'y,' says Gifford as meek as a lamb, 'I've got fifty quarts o' nitroglycer'n' in the buggy; an' I thought—'

"'What!' exploded the ol' man—like a shot o' the glycer'n' itself. 'Nitroglycer'n'? Drive on, man—drive on! What you stoppin' here fer, anyhow? Hain't you got a mite o' sense, sir—hain't you got a mite o' sense? Drive on, I say—'r I'll have you arrested fer riskin' life an' limb an' property! Drive on! Nobody asked you to stop—no, sir—nobody asked you to stop. Be off with you! Want to blow up all creation—an' me an' M'randy an' the ol' woman, to boot? What'll you 'tarnal oil men be up to next, hey? Git out o' here—'r I'll fill you so full o' buckshot y'r hide won't hold cornshucks! Whip up them ol' crowbaits an' git out o' here. Go, I say—yes, sir—go!'

"Gifford was scared. He drove on down to Dullson an' told his 'xperience—thought he'd met an' ol' luny, sure. The boys had the laugh on him; an' it cost him a nice wad, to set 'em up to the crowd.

"Ol' John tellin' of it afterward, said:

"'No, sir—no, sir—hain't been skeered so bad sence Morgan's raiders threatened to hang me, fer hidin' my hosses from 'em. Fact, sir—honest fact.'"

The prospector was a good mimic, and told the story well; and of course his auditors laughed heartily. Even Marlowe found himself smiling.

"Come on, boys," said the driller, arising and stretching his arms above his head. "Le's go into the bar an' have a drink. Stranger, won't you have somethin' with us?"

Ralph thanked him but gracefully declined the invitation, pleading as an excuse that he meant to retire at once.

"We're goin' to bed some time tonight, too," laughed the driller; "but we'll take a few nightcaps with us."

And together the four passed out at the rear door, leaving the druggist alone.

A moment later Clark came into the office, a lighted lamp in his hand, and said rather brusquely:

"Ready for bed? Williams sent me to show you to your room."

"Ready and waiting," Ralph replied pleasantly, rising with alacrity.[12]

As they ascended the narrow, winding stairs, the agent leading the way looked over his shoulder, to remark:

"I suppose Crawford pumped you full of the old doc's faults and failings?"

"He said many disparaging things of him."

"The shoemaker—I mean Crawford—has a grievance."

"I thought so."

"Yes. The old doc asked him to pay a bill once—a thing Crawford is not in the habit of doing."

"I see."

"The devil's never half as black as he's painted."

"No."

"Doc Barwood's contrary and peculiar; but he's honest. And he has a big practice and makes a heap of money. Well, here's your room. Mine's at the other end of the hall. Here—take the lamp. There's one in my room. You'll find the key on the inside of the door. It's unlocked—go right on in. Good night."

"Good night, Mr. Clark," Ralph returned affably. "But before we part for the night, permit me to thank you for your untiring efforts in my behalf."

"Don't mention it," replied the operator with a wave of the hand, retreating along the hall, in the direction of his own room.

Marlowe stood and gazed after the lithe, fragile form. At his door Clark stopped, half turned the knob, and paused irresolutely. Then he said:

"Can I ask you a question?"

"Certainly," Ralph answered eagerly. He felt under obligations to his companion and wished to retain his friendship.

"How did you come to get the job with Doc Barwood?"

"I saw his advertisement for a clerk, in a drug journal, and answered it."

"Oh! Well, good night."

---

12 alacrity: cheerful eagerness

"Good night."

Marlowe entered his room, locked the door, and placed the lamp upon an old-fashioned bureau that served as a dressing case. The place had a barren and impoverished aspect, but was neat and clean. The bed looked comfortable and inviting. He began to disrobe; but finding the air close, raised a window that opened out upon the roof of the front veranda. The storm had passed; the wet street was flooded with moonlight. The sullen roar of the river dam came distinctly to his ears.

Just as he was crossing the borderland of sleep, he murmured drowsily:

"Out of the old life—into the new. What strange—what eccentric characters—"

Then he slept.

Sometime during the night—he did not look at his watch—he was awakened by some one boisterously singing:

> "Go to the fair an' see the funny fowls,
> The double-headed pigeon an' the one-eyed owl;
> The ol' lame goose with a web 'tween 'er toes—
> She laughs 'erself to death w'en the shanghi crows.

> "Don't you bet y'r money on a shanghi,
> Don't you bet y'r money on a shanghi;
> Alluz put y'r pennies on the pigeon in the pit—
> But never bet y'r money on a shanghi."

Marlowe raised himself upon his elbow and peeped out of the window. He had recognized the maudlin voice; it was Crawford's. In the swimming moonlight, he saw two men staggering down the street, arm in arm—the cobbler and the bridge-tender.

"Drunk!" muttered the young man, in a tone of disgust.

And he turned over and went to sleep again.

* * * * * *

CHAPTER III

THE SUN was shining brightly when Marlowe awoke the next morning. The moist, woodsy odor of fallen leaves came through the open window. The air was sweet and crisp. A catbird flitting about upon the edge of the veranda roof, squawked stridently—scolding a tabby cat perched in the fork of a maple tree in front of the house. The cheer of the bright morning was infectious. Ralph forgot his dismal thoughts and forebodings of the night before, and whistled merrily as he washed and dressed.

Just as he was finishing his toilet, there came a knock at the door; and he heard Clark calling:

"Hello, Marlowe! Up yet?"

"Yes—come in."—Turning the key in the lock.—"It's a nice morning."

"Yes," said the operator.

"A beautiful morning," Ralph added, facing the small mirror and giving a final touch to his tie.

"Ready for breakfast?" asked the agent.

"In a moment."

"Sleep well?"

"I was awake but once during the night."

"That tipsy Crawford woke you up with his caterwauling, did he?"

"Yes."

"He's a drunken nuisance. All ready? Well, come on. I've got to get my breakfast and be off to the station."

Then as they descended the stairs:

"Going up to call on the old doc this morning?"

"I shall beard the ogre in his den."

"Maybe you will—and maybe you won't. He's in the country a good deal; it may be a day or two before you get to see him."

"Does he lock up the drugstore when he leaves?"

"No; leaves Jep Tucker there. Jep's his hostler[13] and man of all work—and a character."

"He knows nothing of drugs?"

"No!—no more than a hog knows of religion. He just stays there and tells people where the doctor is and when he'll be back. The old doc hasn't had a clerk for over two months. You'll find things in a mess."

"Why do you call Dr. Barwood 'the old doc?'"

"Everybody does. Years ago there was a young doctor of the same name here—a nephew of old doc's; and people called one 'old doc' and the other 'young doc.'"

As the two young men entered the office, they noticed it had been swept and dusted. A fire blazed in the grate; and the stone hearth had been scoured to snowy whiteness.

Passing into the dining room, they found breakfast awaiting them. Other boarders had already eaten and taken their departure. A black-eyed girl in white collar and apron served them—tiptoeing noiselessly about the bare floor.

Both ate heartily—as young men have a habit of doing no matter what their perplexities. The biscuits were flaky; the steak was tender. Ralph thoroughly enjoyed his first breakfast in Babylon.

When they had finished, Clark arose and remarked:

"I must hustle for the station; it'll soon be train time. See you at

---

13 hostler: one who takes charge of horses as at an inn

dinner. Hope you'll have good luck and find Doc Barwood at home, and make a good impression on him. The drugstore's three squares above here, up on the level. You can't miss it—a long, low brick building. Keep a stiff upper lip. Ta-ta!"

The operator hurried forth. Ralph took up his hat and sauntered out upon the street, bending his steps in the direction of Dr. Barwood's place of business. He walked slowly, meditating upon the reception he was likely to receive, and cursorily noting his surroundings.

The hotel stood near the summit of the slope leading up from the river; and beyond it lay a level, sandy plain, rolling away to the brown hills in the distance. The main street was broad and unpaved, with sidewalks of foot-pressed cinders. Along it—with ample vacant spaces between—neat frame dwellings alternated with stores and shops. Short cross streets led off to right and left; and the plain was dotted with houses. Far off on one hand, Ralph saw the crumbling walls of a large brick building; and at an equal distance, in the opposite direction, loomed the blackened, smokeless chimneys of a silent factory.

He passed a hardware store, a grocery, the post-office—then came to a sudden stop in front of a one-story brick edifice with a basement of stone. It was long and low, one end facing the street. The narrow front contained two large show windows and a wide doorway. Broad stone steps led up to the entrance. And over all was a weatherstained awning supported upon an iron frame.

"This must be the place," Marlowe muttered as he ascended the steps.

The door stood wide open; and he walked in.

No one was in sight; so he paused and looked about him. It was a drugstore, without doubt; but such a one as he had never seen. The two side walls were lined with rows of shelves. Those upon the right hand were open, and laden with jars and bottles of various shapes and sizes, containing drugs, chemicals, and liquors; and those upon the left were inclosed by glass doors, through the grimy panes of which could be seen a vast array of patent medicines. Two hardwood counters extended the length of the room, almost; and upon each rested one or more showcases containing toilet preparations, brushes, sponges, candy, cigars, *et cetera*—piled in higgledy-piggledy.[14] An upright coal stove with a large sheet-iron drum stood in the rear of the room; and along the wall back of it ran a bench or seat. Just inside of one of the front windows, a high black-walnut desk with slender, tipsy legs—a near relative of the one at the hotel, undoubtedly—had a place. In the rear wall were two doorways, one leading to the basement, the other to Dr. Barwood's private office.

Ralph took in all this at a glance. He noted, also, that there was no prescription case nor screen, that the woodwork, once white, was a smoky, dingy yellow, that dust and cobwebs reigned supreme, and that dirt and general disorder held high carnival.

He heard some one moving about in the basement, and stepped toward the back of the room.

"Be up in a minute," rumbled a voice from the depths. "Set down, if you're tired o' standin'; 'r walk 'round, if you're tired o' settin'. I'm wras'lin' a pesky bar'l o' whisky. Be up—in—a—m-i-n-u-t-e."

The last sentence was uttered in a hoarse, strained voice that indicated the owner was undergoing severe muscular exertion, or was in the last throes of physical torment. Then all was silent.

"The whisky barrel must have got the better of the tussle," Ralph smiled, seating himself upon a stool. "At any rate it has silenced him. No; I hear him coming up the steps. But he has a leg or two broken, judging from his gait."

The owner of the voice was indeed ascending the stairs, shuffling and stumbling painfully—and indulging in a deal of grunting and grumbling. Ralph fastened his eyes upon the doorway and impatiently awaited the fellow's advent. Presently the looked-for personage limped into the room and dropped into a chair.

"Good morning," was Marlowe's greeting.

"That's once you've told the truth, young feller, if you never do ag'in," the man replied in a drawling nasal tone, squinting one twinkling gray eye and narrowly scanning his visitor. "Yes, sir, this *is* a good mornin'."

---
14 higgledy-piggledy: in utter disorder or confusion

"You are not Dr. Barwood?" Ralph remarked tentatively.

"You seem to be in the *habit* o' tellin' the truth," the other answered whimsically. "I am *not* Doc Barwood. I'm Jep Tucker, the ol' doc's hos'ler an' hired hand."

Marlowe regarded the speaker closely. Tucker was about forty-five years old—a lank, loose-jointed frame upon which a leathery skin hung in folds and wrinkles. His hands, feet, and ears were large; his nose, arched and prominent; his hair, scant and light colored. His face was puckered with innumerable fine lines and wrinkles; and a stubby, sandy mustache—like the eaves of a roof of thatch overhanging a wide doorway—projected from his short upper lip. Screwed askew upon the back of his knobby head, was a broad-brimmed straw hat, badly gone to seed. One gallows essayed the utterly reckless task of suspending a pair of baggy plaid trousers, patched with cloth of darker hue at the knees and frayed and stained at the bottoms; and a ragged coat hid all but the checkered bosom of a raggeder shirt. The toe of one of his coarse cowhide shoes was cut away, revealing an expanse of soiled muslin swathed around an injured foot.

His open countenance was as easily read as a page of primer; and told that Jep was of an easygoing disposition. His shrewd and twinkling gray eyes gave a hint of the quaint philosophy and whimsical drollery that was in him.

"Is the doctor in?" was Ralph's next question.

"Yes, he's *in,* in more ways 'n one," Jep drawled, crossing one leg over its fellow and tenderly caressing his sore foot. "He's in business; an' he's in good health. Do you want to know anything more 'bout him?"

"Is he in town?" Marlowe asked, his lips twitching. He realized he had to deal with an eccentric.

"He is," Tucker answered complacently, running a thumb under his one suspender and hitching it along his collar bone, toward his neck.

"Will he be here soon?"

"Can't say—an' tell the truth. Maybe he will; an' maybe he

won't. It all depends on him; he's of age, an' comes an' goes as he pleases. But he'll be in *sometime* ag'in, most likely. He alluz comes in to fill up his saddlebags, 'fore he goes to the country. You a drummer?"

Ralph replied with a negative shake of the head.

"I thought not," Jep went on. "I didn't see y'r grip—then you ain't tonguey 'nough fer a drummer. Honor bright, some o' them cusses can talk the hat off y'r head. An' I never *could* understan' why they call 'em drummers. Don't see why they ain't called *buglers*— they're all the time blowin' the'r *horns.* Ther's one comes here—a little fat runt named Lon Crider, 'spect you never met him—that's a purty fair feller. But he's got more cheek 'n a town sow. An' the funny thing about it is, he blushes like a school miss ev'ry time he tells a whopper. Seems to be ashamed o' his capac'ty fer lyin'. I like him first rate. But he's slick—slicker 'n a peeled sapling;' an' he hangs onto a bargain, like a bur to a cow's tail. So you ain't no drummer?"

Again Ralph silently shook his head. Then he inquired:
"Do you think Dr. Barwood will be in soon?"

"Some time 'fore the resur'ection day," Tucker mumbled, nonchalantly biting off a piece of tobacco and rolling it about in his cheek. "You in much of a hurry?"

"I should like to see the doctor as soon as possible."

"I's a goin' to say it wasn't no use o' y'r gittin' in a hurry in *this* town. I've lived here all my life; an' I've never saw but one feller in a hurry, in all that time. He was hangin' onto a pair o' runaway hosses, an' couldn't help hisself. He wasn't to blame—he didn't mean no harm. No, sir, the people o' this place is slower 'n thick molasses on a cold mornin'. I'm 'bout the only hus'ler round here; an' I ain't what I once was. I'll tell you what's a fact. I hain't never seen but one feller run, in the forty-five years I've lived here; an' that was a boy that ketched a cold an' run at the nose. I b'lieve one feller did start to run fer justice o' the peace once. But s'ciety got so down on him he had to settle down to a walk. You ain't much a'quainted 'round here, are you?"

"This is my first visit to Babylon," Marlowe admitted, glancing up and down the rows of dusty shelves.

"Is that so?" Jep exclaimed. "Didn' come this mornin', 'nless you drove in; ther' hain't been no train yit."

"I came last night."

"Oh!"—Then with sudden animation: "Say! you ain't the feller that was comin' to clerk fer the ol' doc, are you?"

"I am."

Jep quickly uncrossed his legs, bent forward, and putting forth a knotty-fingered hand cried:

"Give us a wag o' 'r paw, young feller! I never was as glad to see anybody, in my born days. What's y'r name?"

"My name is Ralph Marlowe. But why are you so delighted to meet me?"

"Why am I so delighted to meet you?" drawled Jep, a serio-comic expression upon his homely face. "I'll tell you. If you hadn't come fer another month, I'd 'ave been crazier 'n a three weeks old goslin'—that's why. Folks has purty nigh wrecked my intelleck, comin' in here an' askin' fer things with jaw-breakin' names I never heard of. I'm mighty glad you've got here; now I can d'vote my time to somethin' I know how to do. I've felt like a rooster in a millpon', fer the last two months—neither ridin' n'r a walkin'. An' you hain't met the ol' doc yit?"

"No, but I am anxious to do so."

"Well, I'd go up to his house an' hurry him up, if 'twasn't fer two good reasons. In the first place, he don't like to have folks meddlin' with his business—jest comes an' goes as he pleases; in the second place, the sor'l mare stepped on my foot a few days ago, an' I'm crippleder 'n a wagon with a wheel off. But he'll be here purty soon now—never fear. Say! what do you think o' my way o' keepin' drugstore, anyhow?"

This last with a mischievous grin and a wave of the hand at the dust-covered counters and littered floor.

"I think you might have kept the place a *little* cleaner," Marlowe said with great solemnity, rising and walking about the room.

"That's what the ol' doc hinted at sever'l times—said I'd ort to sweep an' dust *once* a month, whether the place needed it 'r not. Well, I took him at his word, an' tried it; but ev'ry time he'd come in he'd make me quit—said I's mixin' things up so he couldn't find nothin', an' was 'feared he'd pizen somebody by givin' 'em salsody fer salts. He likes to have things right down on the counter, where they're handy. You'll find that out."

"I understand," Ralph remarked dryly.

"I hope the ol' man'll take to you," Jep went on. "He's had three 'r four clerks in the last twelve months; an' they've all proved a disap'intment to him. He's a little touchy, of course—but—say! There's one thing 'bout you he won't like; I can tell you that. You dress too nice."

"Do I?" —Still walking up and down the floor and unconcernedly inspecting the stock.

"Yes, you do. The ol' doc don't like dudes—an' you're jest a little dudish. Look at them shiny shoes o' yours—an' then look at mine."

And Tucker assumed a grotesque attitude, thrusting his hands into his trousers' pockets, elevating his shoulders, and extending his feet.

"I observe," Ralph murmured, with a swift glance at his companion. "But your shoes answer the purpose of foot coverings, as well as mine. They are not mates, however."

"No," Jep admitted, shaking his head lugubriously[15], "they ain't *both* mates, that's a fact. *One's* a mate; an' *t'other's* a deckhand. Say!"—In a tone indicative of consternation.—"What you doin' there?"

"I am testing the qualities of this elixir."

"A lick sir?" Tucker chuckled. "When a feller takes a whole mouthful o' anything an' gulps it down, I call it a purty fair-sized lick. You'll git into trouble meddlin' with them medicines—all mixed up like they are. If you're needin' somethin' fer y'r stomach's sake, you'd better come down cellar with me. There's some medicine in a bar'l down there, that'll make y'r hair curl."

---

15 lugubriously: mournful or sad, esp. to a ridiculous degree

Jep winked slyly.

"I thank you for the prescription," Ralph laughed; "But I am not in need of anything of the kind this morning."

"I alluz hate to see a feller nosin' 'round somethin' he don't know nothin' 'bout," Jep went on musingly. "An' that puts me in mind o' the time Sweety Jimson took the smell o' hartshorn. Ever hear 'bout that?

"I think not," Ralph replied, flicking the dust from a showcase, with his handkerchief.

"Didn't? Well, I'll tell you the story. It's a purty good one; an' it all happened right in this store. As I've told you, the ol' doc hates meddlers worse 'n a cat hates smoke. This Sweety Jimson was a youngster 'bout twelve 'r fourteen years old, an' was alluz stickin' his bill into other people's business. He was freckle-faced, hare-lipped, an' had a voice like a screaky wagon wheel; an' couldn't keep his pesky fingers from stickin' to ev'rything they touched.

"He used to come into the drugstore when the ol' man an' the clerk was busy as weevils in a wheat bin, an' pester an' torment 'em 'most to death. It was—'Let me taste that; an' let me smell this; an' let me see the other.' An' ol' doc 'ld git so mad he couldn't see straight, an' chase the meddlesome, pilferin' scamp out o' the place. But the next day in he'd come, as big as Pompey, an' go through the same m'neuvers ag'in.

"Well, one day the ol' man was busier 'n usual; an' Sweety was in here, leanin' over the counter, handlin' this an' that, an' chatterin' like a chipmunk. The ol' doc c'ncluded he'd start him—an' he did. Fer he took down a bottle o' hartshorn—not the wishy-washy kind you sell to folks fer cleanin clo'es an' things. What is it you call that kind that's stronger 'n ackyfortis an' goes up y'r nose like a streak o' double-geared lightnin'?"

"Ammonia fortior," Marlowe suggested.

"Mony a Fortier? I 'spect that's it. It's a good name fer the stuff, anyhow; for it's *forty 'r* fifty times stronger 'n the dishwater kind you sell to folks. Well, soon as the ol' doc took the bottle off the shelf an' set it on the counter, that tarnation boy spoke up as peart as a pet crow, an' says:

"'Let me see that—let me smell of it.'

"'You let that alone,' says the ol' doc, kind o' solemn-like. 'That's the tinckshur o' the chloride o' bumfoozle'—'r some such name—an' it hain't got no smell.'

"'Let me smell of it, anyhow,' says Sweety, grabbin' holt o' the bottle an' twistin' the stopper out quicker 'n you could say—'Jack Robison.'

"An' he stuck his nose over it an' took a good long whiff o' the stuff.

"Well, he didn't try to put the stopper back in—not by sever'l percent on the cost price. He jest screwed up his face till his harelip was on a level with his nose holes; an' kicked an' clawed the air like a cat with paper socks on 'er feet. An' he made the funniest noise, tryin' to git his breath; kind of a 'w-e-e-k'—like a fat hog choked on an apple. Then he took a straight shirttail fer the open air; an' gittin' outside, he leaned up ag'inst the wall an' commenced to cry.

"Some women was comin' 'long; an' one of 'em says to him:

"'W'y, what in the world's the matter, Sweety?'

"'Oh! nothin' much,' he says, wipin' the tears from his eyes. 'I jest went—went to smell o' some—some stuff, an' ol' Doc Barwood stuck—*stuck a stick up my nose!*'

"An the funniest thing 'bout the whole business," Jep concluded, laughing uproariously, "is that Sweety b'lieves to this day that ol' doc prodded him in the nose with somethin'."

Marlowe smiled indulgently, but said in a tone of mild reproof:

"Don't you think that was a rather cruel joke?"

"Joke?" Tucker gasped in mock surprise—his mouth open, his brows elevated. "Twasn't no joke 't all; 'twas a cure fer a bad disease. An' like many another case, the medicine had to make the patient worse 'fore he could git better. It worked like a charm, too—cured Sweety sound an' well; an' he hain't ever had no r'lapse, neither."

Time hung heavily upon Marlowe's hands. For the want of anything else to do, he sauntered into the basement, leaving Jep idly swinging his injured foot and softly whistling to himself.

On reaching the bottom of the stairs, the young druggist found himself in a large, airy cellar extending the whole length of the structure. The floor was of gray cement; the windows were heavily barred with iron. A wide door opened into the alley back of the building. Boxes, barrels and casks, cans and jugs were scattered promiscuously about the floor.

Satisfied with a hasty examination of the place, Ralph ascended the stairs. He found Jep talking with a spruce young man with the reddest of red hair, and with a prominent mole upon his chin.

"Here!" Tucker cried as Marlowe put in an appearance. "Mr. Ralph Marlowe, this is Mr. Airly Chandler, an' he wants to git a toothbrush, an' some perfum'ry, an' such things. I told him you could wait on him. He's a young school teacher; an' has to go trigged[16] up like—to please the gals."

Young Chandler said nothing, but blushed and sidled about confusedly; seeing which Jep coughed behind his hand and winked facetiously.

"I shall be pleased to wait upon you, Mr. Chandler," Ralph remarked pleasantly, "provided I can find the articles you desire. Things are in a state of confusion, as you see."

After some delay, incident to the sad disorder, the young teacher made his purchases and took his departure. Then Marlowe turned to Tucker and said severely:

"You should not make remarks about a customer—especially in his presence. It has a tendency to injure your employer's business."

"I didn't mean nothin' by it—jest wanted to plague him a little," Jep answered contritely. "I ain't in the habit o' doin' such things. It popped out 'fore I thought."

Then his volubility getting the better of him:

"But lawzee! I've knowed Airly ever sence he was kneehigh to a grasshopper; an' he knows me. He won't take nothin' to heart, that *I* say. He's kind o' dudified—but a good-hearted, cheerful boy, fer all that. He's been away from home some, too; went to school in Zanesville a year 'r so ago. Hadn't ever been out o' the county

---

16 trig: in good condition

before. An' I guess he learnt a thing 'r two—I guess he did. Anyhow he wrote home to his mother an' said:

"Dear Mother:

"'If the world's as big a down the other way as she is up *this* way, *she's a whopper.*'

"That's what folks tells on him, anyhow. But he's a smart, cheerful boy; an' I don't b'lieve he ever had but one trouble in his life—an' that's that mole on his chin."

"It's a source of annoyance to him, eh?" Ralph said, stepping to the door and anxiously looking up, and then down the street.

"You might call it that," Jep replied, joining his companion in the doorway. "Anyhow it worries him like sixty."

"Does he fear it may develop into a malignant growth?"

"No, 'tain't that. He's sorry 'bout the situation of the thing; says he wouldn't care, if it was on the back of his neck—that he could button his collar to it then, an' make it *useful* as well's *ornamental*. What do you think of that fer an idee?"

"I think it original—and that you are its originator," Ralph laughed. "You should apply for a patent."

"Have thought some 'bout it," Jep chuckled. "Do you 'spose the gove'nment 'ld ask me to send on a model?"

Marlowe did not reply. He was lost in thought, his eyes fixed upon the tree-bordered street stretching away to the west. Presently he murmured musingly:

"What an excellent site for a large town. Babylon should be a thriving city, instead of a sleepy village of a few hundred inhabitants."

"That's so—you've hit the nail on the head," Tucker assented, nodding vigorously. "An' we *did* think it would grow to a city once. But that was twenty 'r thirty years ago. Then we had five 'r six stores 'nstead of two 'r three; an' saloons an' taverns in pr'portion. Them was the great days fer steamboats on this river; an' Babylon was the best shippin' point 'twixt Zanesville an' Marietta. Quakerville brought in her tobacker an' tanbark: an' Foxtown, her wool and fruit. I've seen the wharf stacked with bales, an' bar'ls, an' hogs 'eads, from one end to t'other. Then we had an oil refin'ry, a big salt furnace, an' a lot o' cooper shops. Them was good times when ev'rybody was makin' money like dirt. See that ol' smokestack standin' over yander?"

"I do."

"Well, that's all that's left o' the ol' salt furnace."

"A monument to a dead industry," Marlowe murmured to himself.

"What's that you say?" Jep asked quickly.

"A monument to a dead industry," Ralph repeated, pointing to the black shaft looming heavenward.

"That's what it is," sighed Tucker, feelingly.

"You can say things mighty purty, young feller, when you try. You can, I swan! No, the ol' town o' Babylon's been goin' back'ard fer years—ever sence the railroad come through. 'Stid o' helpin' us it hurt us—drawed trade away to the two towns at the ends o' the river. Of course the oil business has made things a little better, in the last year 'r two; but I'm 'feared it's only the flash of a dyin' fire. Ol' Babylon ain't what she once was—not by a consider'ble."

"Babylon is fallen," Ralph whispered abstractedly.

He was not thinking of the village, but of his own past—of his dead hopes and aspirations. But Jep caught the whispered words, and slapping his companion on the shoulder, cried admiringly:

"You drove the nail clear in to the head at one lick, that time, young feller. Babylon *is* fallen. That's it—that's it! An' fallen to rise no—" Then with a sudden change of tone and countenance:

"There comes the ol' doc at last. I'll give you a knockdown to him, an' leave you alone to fight it out."

* * * * *

CHAPTER IV

WITH SWINGING stride, Dr. Barwood drew near. Quickly ascending the steps, he stood face to face with Marlowe, eyeing him inquiringly.

Ralph felt his heart quicken its pulsations as he looked upon the man before him; and he longed to hear him speak.

Dr. Ephriam W. Barwood was of medium height and weight, and slightly stooped. His snappy black eyes, set far apart, were over-arched by beetling brows and bulging forehead. His nose was short and slightly bulbous at the end. Through his sparse and straggling beard was revealed a glimpse of heavy jaws and firm thin lips. His iron-gray hair was cropped close to his bullet head. Apparently he was about fifty years old.

His clothing comprised a pair of baggy gray trousers, a shiny black coat and vest—the outer garment a full-skirted frock, drooping at the corners—and a soft muslin shirt with a puffed bosom. A soft broad-brimmed black hat, and a pair of kip[17] boots—red from lack of blacking—completed his attire. A long watch guard of black tape encircled his neck. His forceful, arrogant disposition was stamped upon his countenance.

---

17 kip: untanned hide of a small or young animal

"A born fighter, who has had his way in most matters and desires to have it in all," was Marlowe's mental comment.

But he kept silent, waiting for Tucker's promised presentation.

"Good morning," Dr. Barwood said curtly. "Is there something I can do for you?"

Jep interposed:

"Doc, this is the young feller you sent fer, to come an' work fer you. I s'pose you both know each other's names—seein' you've been correspondin', as I understand. Nevertheless I'll intr'duce you. Mr. Ralph Marlowe, this is Doc Barwood—Doctor Ephr'am Barwood, I should say; an' Doctor Ephr'am Barwood, this is Mr. Ralph Marlowe."

"Huh!" the physician grunted ungraciously, knitting his heavy brows and surveying Ralph from head to foot.

For several seconds the young druggist smilingly submitted to the trying ordeal. Then putting forth his hand, he observed pleasantly:

"I am glad to meet you, Dr. Barwood."

"Yes—certainly," returned the doctor, grasping the outstretched hand and pressing it so hard the tendons showed white and tense upon his own knuckles.

But he did not remove his eyes from Ralph's face; and his rugged features were puckered into a scowl, as he went on:

"Come into the office; I want to talk with you. I'm glad you've got here, at any rate."

Then suddenly dropping Marlowe's hand and turning upon Tucker, who had descended the steps and was moving away:

"Here! where are you going?"

"Goin' to take the gray 'round to the blacksmith's, to have a shoe drove," Jep replied, pausing and squinting over his shoulder.

"No!" the doctor cried sharply. "Put her to the cart and drive around to the hitching rack. I am going to the country."

"But," Tucker objected. "She ain't in no c'ndition to travel, doc. She needs—"

"You heard what I said, Jep?"

"Yes, doc, I did. But—"

"Then you know what to do. And when you have followed out my orders, return to the drugstore. I want to have a private talk with this young man. Come, Mr. Marlowe."

Jep hobbled around the corner of the building, grumbling to himself:

"Ther' never was such a man to have his own way as ol' Doc Barwood. But—if I ain't bad mistaken—he's met his match *this* time. That young feller's harder to move 'n a meetin' house, when he sets his head. You can't fool me. It'll be—kill Dick, kill devil—betwixt 'em. Lordy! won't the fur fly one o' these days? Well, I reckon!"

Ralph silently followed Dr. Barwood into the back room of the building, the latter closing and locking the door behind them.

"Take a chair," the doctor jerked out, with his foot pushing one toward the young man.

Ralph seated himself. Dr. Barwood went to the flat-top desk standing in the center of the room, and carefully sorted and piled a number of medical journals lying upon it. When he had arranged them to his satisfaction, he stooped and replaced the upturned corner of a large fur rug in front of the empty grate. Then, swinging back the corners of his long frock coat and thrusting his hands into his trousers' pockets, he strode restlessly up and down the bare floor, his boot heels clicking loudly. Occasionally he paused before the rear window and looked toward the stables whither Tucker had gone.

Marlowe was interested. He coolly leaned back in his chair—noting every movement of his companion, every fleeting expression of his countenance—and calmly awaited his pleasure. Of a sudden Dr. Barwood dropped into a chair, hitched it close to Ralph's, and leaning far forward—his elbows upon the arms of the chair, his alert eyes half hidden by his corrugated brows—asked coldly:

"When did you arrive?"

"Last evening, doctor," Marlowe answered, unflinchingly returning his questioner's steady gaze." The train was late; and being tired and sleepy I waited until this morning to call upon you."

"You spent the night at the hotel, of course."

"Yes."

"Did you meet Clark, the railroad agent, there?"

"I met him first at the station. He kindly accompanied me to the hotel."

"Oh!"—A world of meaning in the monosyllable. Then after a moment's silence:

"You told him you meant to work for me?"

"I did, doctor."

"What did he say?"

"Very little—nothing of importance."

"Didn't he read my pedigree to you?"—Sneeringly.

"He said nothing of your lineage, doctor—no."

"You know what I mean."—With a show of ill humor.—"Didn't he try to discourage you—to dissuade you from taking a position with me, by telling you what an irreligious, penurious, uncharitable, violent, old scoundrel I am?"

"Mr. Clark did nothing of the kind, doctor," Ralph replied frigidly. "You wrong him. He spoke disparagingly of Babylon, but not of you nor of your business. I believe he did say you were somewhat peculiar. I do not care to discuss the subject further. If you desire Clark's opinion of yourself, go to him for it."

Dr. Barwood reared back in his chair and glared angrily at the audacious speaker. It was a new and unwelcome experience to the irascible medical man; to be pulled up so summarily. His black eyes flashed; his thin lips twitched. Gripping the arms of his chair so tightly his nails turned white, he breathed hard through his dilated nostrils.

Ralph carelessly threw one leg over the other and scratched a speck of dried mud from his trousers. Presently the physician partially regained control of himself and asked with forced calmness:

"Has anyone else favored you with an opinion of me?"

"Yes," Marlowe reluctantly admitted. "I overheard the loafers in the hotel office discussing your predominant traits and characteristics. But what does it matter, Dr. Barwood? You are as you are; their idle talk does not alter the fact. Their expressed opinions have not influenced me. I have no opinion of you—I have yet to form one."

"Was Crawford, the shoemaker, in the company?"

"I believe so—yes."—With a yawn and a shiver.

Dr. Barwood started and said:

"The room *is* chilly, without fire. But I will not detain you long. Before we proceed to business, however, I want to say this: Don't form too hasty an opinion of me. Others have done so—and made the mistake of their lives. I know what you heard Crawford and his associates say of me. They called me an infidel—an agnostic; when they know as little of my belief, as I know myself. They accused me of being greedy, penurious, uncharitable. And I give away each year three times as much as any one of them earns. They informed you of my selfish, obstinate, brutal disposition; and each of them—to a man almost—is in my debt and under obligations to me for services rendered and charities dispensed. Yes, I know well what they said. And the man who was foremost in decrying me—Jim Crawford—has a fancied grievance—"

"So Clark informed me," Marlowe could not help saying.

"Who?" the doctor inquired sharply.

"Clark, the station agent."

"Huh!" grunted Dr. Barwood frowning darkly. "I do not like that young man; he is an impudent fellow."

"Perhaps you have been too hasty in forming your opinion, doctor," Ralph replied, slyly smiling.

Dr. Barwood stared aghast. Could he believe his ears and eyes? Was the young man before him actually laughing at him, while reproving him in a patronizing tone and manner? His impeccability was called in question; his dignity was assailed. Such temerity was unpardonable. He was not used to such treatment; and he would not stand it. He was grievously insulted, thoroughly angry. But for some reason, he felt it would not do to fly into a passion, and rave and storm as he was wont to do on such occasions. So he gripped the arms of his chair, bit his nether lip and manfully strove to gain the mastery of his violent temper. In this he succeeded so well—to his own unbounded surprise—that after a few preliminary fumblings at his watch guard, he managed to say with an outward show of calmness:

"Mr. Marlowe, if you expect to gain and retain my favor, you will do well to keep such suggestions to yourself. I am not in need of an advisory committee to formulate or alter my opinions on any subject."

It was Ralph's turn to show anger. Instantly his lounging, indolent manner and attitude disappeared. Drawing himself rigidly erect—his brown eyes snapping, his nostrils aquiver—he returned hotly:

"I am but returning the advice—in the form of a mild suggestion—you so kindly offered me, Dr. Barwood. Let us understand each other. I have no desire to curry favor. I did not come here for that purpose. I came according to written agreement, to serve you—in the capacity of druggist, to the best of my ability. That I stand ready to do. But you will find in me no cringing underling. I am as independent—as self-willed, as yourself."

A peculiar expression—like a gleam of sunshine breaking through a cloud bank—shot athwart[18] the physician's swarthy visage, sparkled in his black eyes—and was gone. His voice was clear and steady as he answered:

"Let us drop the controversy. You are willing to work for the salary I have offered?"

"I am."—Firmly.

"When do you wish to begin?"

"At once—today."

"Very well, it is settled. But I desire to have this understanding: Either of us may annul the contract at any time. Is that satisfactory?"

"Eminently."

"I am off to the country then," concluded Dr. Barwood rising to his feet. "I have a drive of thirty to forty miles to make, including a number of visits. Probably I shall not be back before some time

---
18 athwart: from side to side; crosswise

tomorrow forenoon, as the roads are heavy—especially in the neighborhood of Black's Mills on Bear Run, where I am going. You may acquaint yourself with the stock and look after whatever you think needs attention. When I return we will consult further about the management of the business."

They had left the office and returned to the drug room. Tucker lay sprawled upon the bench by the stove in which he had kindled a fire. The doctor caught up his saddlebags, his overcoat and gloves from the over-laden counter where they had reposed all the morning, and hurriedly left the room. Marlowe stepped to the one side window, and watched him as he stiffly climbed into his cart and drove away.

"Well, I see you're still alive yit," Jep drawled lazily, rolling his eyes at Ralph, who stood gazing after the cart disappearing up the sandy thoroughfare. "Thought maybe you two hot heads might git into a Kilkenny cat[19] fight an' eat one another up. But you both come out lookin' 's pleasant as a purty woman in a pink sunbonnet. Couldn't 'ave had much of an argyment, I guess. Must 'ave agreed to disagree, an' let it go at that. By the way, there's somethin' funny 'bout people argyin—dogged if ther' ain't! Ever think 'bout it? Say you didn't? Well, sir, it's jest like this: It's purty toler'ble *hard* fer two men to be on opposite sides in an argyment, an' *both* be *right;* but it's most danged *easy* fer 'em *both* to be *wrong.* Ain't that so? Course it is. An' yit people's alluz anxious to stick the'r noses into an argyment. The way they go nosin' 'round fer trouble puts me in mind o' Jack Rosser's ol' sow. Ever hear that story?"

Marlowe shook his head, as he turned from the window and resignedly dropped into a chair.

"Then I'll tell it to you," Jep volunteered with cheerful alacrity, ejecting his quid and stroking his stubby mustache between his thumb and fore finger. "It'll help us to pass the time. You see this Jack Rosser's a plasterer an' painter an' so on; an' two 'r three summers ago he had an ol' sow that run the streets an' tormented ev'rybody. She had a long, slim nose she could poke clean to the bottom of a gallon fruit jug; an' an appetite like the unquenchable

---
19 Kilkenny cat: people who fight relentlessly till their end

thirst o' perdition—alluz eatin' an' alluz grunting fer more.

"Jack used to feed 'er jest outside his front gate—'ld set a bucket o' slop out there an let 'er eat it. Well, one day he'd been doin' some whitewashin' fer ol' Mrs. Britton; an' comin' home to dinner he set down his bucket o' whitewash—'bout two 'r three gallons he meant to use on Joe Frick's cellar that afternoon—jest outside the gate, where he'd been in the habit o' feedin' that ol' sow. He was hot, an' hungry, an' mad—'cause he never did like to do whitewashin', seemed to look at it as b'neath his dignity—an' wasn't thinkin' what he was doin'.

"Well, jest as Jack an' the fam'ly sets down to the'r dinner, 'long comes that ol' sow lookin' fer her'n. An' seein' the bucket, she gives a satisfied—ugh! ugh!'—an' makes a dive fer it. Never stops to c'nsider n'r 'nvestigate; but comin' to the rash c'nclusion the stuff's milk, jest shoves 'er nose into it clear up to 'er ears, an' begins to blubber fer the p'tater peelin's she 'xpects to find in the bottom.

"'Tain't much of a trick to 'magine what happened. She took one gulp o' the stuff—an' it got in 'er eyes; an' givin' an extra kink to 'er tail an' lettin' out a squeal that split the weatherboardin' on the warehouse 'cross the street, she jerked 'er snoot out o' the whitewash an' started on a beeline fer nowhere.

"But the bail o' the bucket—Jack had left it standin' straight up—fell back over the ol' rip's neck; an' she was in a fix. She pawed an' clawed, an' shook 'er head, an' grunted an' squealed—scatter'n' whitewash to the four corners o' kingdom come—till half the people in town was out lookin' at the circus an' nearly dyin' a laughin'.

"Well, finally she fell down an' rolled over the bucket. That jerked the bail off; an' away she went lickety-brindle—like she was shot out of a gun—squealin' like all possessed an' a twistin' 'er tail like a screw pr'peller. Liter'ly run off the edge o' the earth an' disappeared.

"An' she never come back," Tucker concluded solemnly; "an' was never heard of but once. A drummer come into town a week 'r two after—I b'lieve it was Lon Crider—an' said he'd seen a hog answerin' to the description o' Rosser's, 'way down in Meigs County, close to the Ohio. Said it had dried whitewash all over its snoot an' head, an' was runnin' an' squealin' an' screwin' its tail, like it had jest had an interview with a passel o' hornets. Most people didn't take much stock in the story; but I did. I argied this way: The sow hain't come back; an' ther'fore she must still be runnin'. An' if she's still a runnin', she's passed through Meigs County, an' Lon Crider's seen 'er. Anyhow the ol' rip didn't come back to bother 'round no more: an' folks is still blessin' that bucket o' whitewash in the'r prayers, an'—"

Marlowe, seeing no end to the fellow's maunderings, interrupted:

"Jep—if I may call you that—do you wish to help me to work a miracle?"

"You may call me anything you please," Tucker replied yawning, "jest so you don't call me too late fer dinner. But 'bout y'r miracle. Don't want to send me up to heaven in no chariot o' fire, do you; n'r chuck me into no whale's belly?"

"No, I want you to work."

"Well, that *would* be workin' a kind of miracle—to git me to work, would," Jep replied, grinning sheepishly. "What're you drivin' at?"

"I mean to work the miracle of bringing order out of chaos."—With a wave of his hand about the room.

"Oh!" Jep chuckled. "I understand you; you mean to clean up things. Well, it won't be much of a miracle to do *that*. All it'll take 'll be a little soap an' water an' elbow grease. But it *will* be a miracle, if you *keep* 'em clean. I can tell you that."

"Why?"

"Cause the ol' doc won't let you. He'll come in an' throw his muddy overcoat down in one place, an' his saddlebags in another, an' string things 'round to suit hisself—pilin' empty an' mussy bottles all over the counters an' showcases, an' so on. I know *him*. Says he likes to have things handy."

"That is his habit, eh?"

"Yes."

"I shall break him of it."

"What!"—In unfeigned consternation.

"Yes, I shall put the place in order and keep it so."

"You'll have a fuss with ol' doc, 'fore forty-eight hours."

"Probably. Did the other clerks have difficulty with him on the same score?"

"No—not hardly. They jest let him have his own way; an' when they couldn't stand it no longer, they packed the'r kits an' left. I don't say ther' wasn't other troubles between 'em, you understand."

"I understand. Well, you will assist me in the task, will you?"

" Sure pop. When you goin' at it?"

"This afternoon. We ought to have two strong, active women to help us. Do you know where to find them?"

Jep grinned from ear to ear as he replied:

"Might git the woman an' gal where I board. They live on the lot jest 'cross the alley back o' the buildin'. They could heat water there, an' I could tote it over."

"'The very thing. Who are they?"

"Jep Tucker's wife and gal."

"Oh!"—and Ralph laughed softly; "I shall leave you, then, to make all arrangements. It is now ten o'clock. I shall go to the hotel, change my clothing, and get an early dinner. Have everything in readiness by the time I return—say in an hour from now. Have you the keys?"

"Yes."

"All right. Lock the door when you go to your meal."

"That young feller's sharper 'n a bee sting," Jep muttered as Ralph left the store; "an' as set in his way as a blacksmith's anvil. But"—With a dubious shake of the head—"he'll come into a c'lision with the ol' doc, one o' these days, that 'll shake his back teeth loose. I'll live in mortal dread of a blowup from this time on."

And sighing heavily, he hobbled behind the counter and helped himself to the contents of a large black bottle standing upon the lower shelf.

Marlowe returned, to the drugstore at eleven, wearing a pair of heavy russet shoes, a crush hat,[20] and blue overalls and jumper. He found Mrs. Tucker—a wiry little body of forty—and her strapping eighteen-year-old daughter, already on hand and sweeping and dusting vigorously. Jep—according to his own statement given in a wheezy, dust-laden voice—was "reddin' up the lower regions."

Ralph assumed direction of affairs, lending a hand here and there; and the work progressed rapidly. By mid-afternoon the accumulated dust and waste of months had been routed; and armed with mops, cloths, brushes, and hot soapsuds, the whole force made a determined and concerted assault upon the hosts of dirt and disorder.

An hour before supper time—Marlowe was polishing a show case near the door—two young ladies paused upon the sidewalk in front of the building, and looked into the store. Ralph slyly observed them. The older was tall, slender and dark, with jetty hair and eyes; the younger, plump, graceful and fair, with violet eyes and hair of spun gold.

"There he is," murmured the fair one nudging her companion. "And oh, Julia! He's handsome."

"Hush, Dorothy—hush!" cautioned the dark one, in an undertone. "He'll hear you. Come on."

"Doesn't he look cute in that rig?" whispered the blonde, a smile dimpling her peachy cheeks. "Let's go in and make his acquaintance."

"For goodness sake, hush—and come on," gasped her companion in an affrighted whisper. "I shall inform mother of your unladylike behavior, Dorothy. Come."—Plucking her by the sleeve.

"Wait," giggled the younger. "I want to get a square look at him. Wait until he looks up."

"Your conduct is disgraceful, Dorothy," the older said angrily, releasing her companion and walking away.

---

20 crush hat: a hat which collapses, and can be carried under the arm, and when expanded is held in shape by springs; hence, any hat not injured by compressing

Marlowe had heard and seen all; and was greatly amused. His eyes met the mischievous violet ones fixed upon him—and he smiled. The petite blonde blushed; and ducking her head, scampered after her companion.

"Sisters, I presume," Ralph muttered, again turning his attention to his work. "The older is ladylike, reserved, and takes life seriously—fancies she has a mission, and all that. She is attractive but not beautiful. The younger, a mere child—not more than seventeen, is a fairy. Beautiful—but spoilt and willful; and somewhat of a mischievous hoiden.[21] Babylon is fallen"—Smiling—"but is not a waste place of the earth, after all. I wonder who they are."

"Saw 'em, did you?" Tucker drawled in the druggist's ear.

Ralph nodded.

"Didn't know 'em, though?"

"No."

"Them's the ol' doc's two gals."

"Indeed?"

"Yes"—Shaking out the cloth he had just wrung dry—"They're all the children he's got. The oldest one's Miss Julia. She's a good 'eal like 'er daddy—an' looks some like him, too—a well meanin' gal, but hard to git along with. Alluz puts me on nettles to talk to her; she's everlastin'ly findin' fault with the world an' wantin' to reform it. Ain't willin' to let God A'mighty have his own way 'bout things. She's a mighty religious, good gal, though; but kind o' cantankerous an' queer. 'Tother one's Miss Dolly. She looks like 'er ma—an' *is* like 'er ma, in most things. Purty an' good natured—an' sweeter 'n the corncob stopper in a 'lasses jug. But she's got a streak of the ol' Barwood stock in her, too. When the ol' doc gits on his dignity, he thinks Grover Cleveland's overcoat wouldn't make him a vest. An' Miss Dolly's like 'er daddy, in that respeck—wants to use the equator fer a sash ribbon an' the par'lels o' latitude fer shoe strings. She'll be a good friend to you, though, if you git on the right side of 'er. But if you don't—well, look out! She'll make you wish y'r mother'd died 'fore you was born. She's a reg'lar tomboy, too; an'—"

---

21 hoiden: A rude, bold girl; a romp

"Jep," Mrs. Tucker interrupted sharply, "don't stand there gabbin' all day. Come an' help me move this tub; an' then go over to the house fer more hot water. Le's make hay while the sun shines; fer I've got to do Mrs. Alberry's washin' tomorrer."

"Make hay while the sun shines!" Jep grumbled *sotto voce*. "That's jest like that woman. She'd talk 'bout makin' hay while the sun shines, if it was Chris'mas an' the snow was knee deep. They call a woman a man's better *half.* Huh! She's the whole thing in most cases. *That* woman nearly pesters me to death; an' she'd see me work till I dropped dead in my tracks. An' I was jest goin' to tell you a good yarn, too. But"—with evident reluctance—"I s'pose it'll keep."

Still grumbling he went about the task his spouse had set him.

At supper time Marlowe remarked:

"We have done a hard day's work. I think we would better quit now, and finish tomorrow."

"We won't do nothin' o' the kind," Mrs. Tucker answered snappishly. "What me an' Lizy does we'll do tonight. We've got a washin' an' ironin' to do tomorrer. If you want our help, you'll finish up this job tonight. 'Twon't take but an' hour 'r two to finish up the scrubbin' an' scourin'; an' then you can have all day tomorrer to straighten up things to suit you."

Ralph was weary, grimy, and disgusted with the job; but he felt he could not afford to dispense with Mrs. Tucker's efficient help. In his perplexity he gave Jep an appealing look. That worthy, leaning heavily upon his mopstick, drew down the corners of his mouth and feelingly rubbed his back—but said nothing. The lazy, light-hearted fellow was such a picture of abject helplessness and utter dejection, Ralph had to smile covertly behind his hand.

Mrs. Tucker had her will—and got her way.

When they reassembled after supper, Jep managed to sidle up to Marlowe and whisper—an expression of injured innocence upon his wrinkled visage:

"My stomach's emptier 'n the bottomless pit. We didn't 'ave nothin' fer breakfast, warmed it over fer dinner, an' used what was left fer supper. Darn it! That woman o' mine's all right—a mighty good helpmate; but she ain't c'ntent to do a decent day's work. It's go the whole hog 'r none, with her. Her an' the gal's jest alike—six o' one an' half dozen o' t'other. Not but what I think a whole heap of 'em, you understand; but they hain't got no c'nsideration for my feelin's. I'm gittin' thinner 'n a katydid—nothin' left but the runnin' gears. One o' these days I'll jest natcherly dry up an' blow away."

At nine o'clock the work was done—and well done. Chaos still reigned; but it was a chaos of cleanliness. The Tuckers gathered up their things and went home—Jep groaning and complaining under his load of empty tubs and pails. Left to himself, Marlowe dropped upon the bench by the warm stove; and rubbing his aching limbs, cast his eyes over the billows of disarranged shelfware and furniture piled topsy-turvy upon the counters. Then leaning back against the wall, he fell into a reverie.

Presently he was aroused by the sound of footsteps, and looked up to find Clark smiling down at him.

"Hello!" the agent cried cheerily. "Taking a snooze?"

Then, ere Ralph could make reply:

"My! you're a beaut in those togs—you are. You look like a coal heaver on a local freight. Been cleaning up the old den, have you? Well, I should think! I missed you at dinner; didn't run across you at supper; and came to the conclusion you had taken your foot in your hand and hoofed it out of town. This looks like you were going to stay awhile, though."

Marlowe nodded, smiling wearily. Clark took his cue and went on:

"Dog tired, aren't you? Lock up; and let's go down to Charley's and turn in. You've done enough for one day. No use of breaking your heart and your health, the first twenty-four hours. You won't get any thanks for it all, anyhow. So you made a bargain with the old doc?"

"Yes," Ralph answered, arising and putting on his hat.

"How much a month are you to get?" Clark inquired as they passed out at the door.

"Seventy-five dollars," Marlowe replied, turning the key in the lock and smiling to himself.

"Whew!" whistled his volatile companion. "That's a pile and a half. I'll bet old doc broke a heart string when he agreed to give you that. I didn't suppose his old shebang *took in* that much in a month. Another case of knowing it all. You'll have a jolly time spending all that lucre in this burg."

"I have never experienced any difficulty in spending all I earned," Marlowe laughed.

"That so?" Clark laughed in reply. "Well, you're a strange one. Why, any fool can *make* money; but it takes a wise man to know how to *spend* it to the best *disadvantage*. By the way, have you met your employer's daughters?"

"No, I have not *met* them."

"Well, have you seen them?"

"I saw them pass the drugstore this afternoon."

"Didn't get to speak to them?"

"No."—A shade of annoyance in his tone.

"Which one did you think the prettiest?"

"I do not set myself up as a judge of beauty."

"Get out! I want your opinion. Which one's style of beauty do you prefer?"

"I have made no choice."

"I have. I prefer the little one—Dolly—by all odds. She's peaches and cream—she is. I've escorted her home a few times. But the old doc put a veto on the business; and I'm out in the cold."

For some reason he did not try to fathom, Ralph was irritated by his companion's familiar reference to Dr. Barwood's younger daughter, and his voice showed it as he said:

"You should not speak of Miss Dolly in that way, Clark. She is a mere child."

"I didn't mean any harm," the operator replied humbly; "it's just my rattletrap way of talking. There isn't a girl in the town I respect more than Miss Dolly—as you call her. But, Marlowe"— Very seriously—"if you think she's only a child, you're badly fooled. She may be young in *years*—*of* course she *is;* but she's older than Methusaleh in *some* things. You mark my words. Wait until you know her; and you'll—you'll *know* her."

After Ralph had closed his eyes that night—and just as he was dropping to sleep—a vision flitted before his mental sight; a vision of golden hair, pearly teeth and violet eyes.

* * * * * *

CHAPTER V

"*HOW ARE* you this morning, Jep?" was Ralph's breezy greeting to the forlorn-looking Tucker, who lounged into the drugstore—bringing with him the aroma of the stables—and dropped into his accustomed seat near the stove.

"Sick abed an' not 'xpected to recover," grinned Jep, shifting his quid from one cheek to the other, and pursing his lips preparatory to expectorating upon the spotless floor.

"Hold!" Marlowe cried sharply, wrinkling his brows and shaking his fist in mock rage. "There's a cuspidor behind the stove. Use that, please."

"A what?" gasped Jep, peering into the corner indicated.

"A cuspidor."

"Oh! that's jest a new-fangled name fer spittoon, is it? Well, here goes. But I don't know whether I can hit the mark from here. Say, young feller! Do you know what c'nclusion I've come to—after a heap o' thinkin'?"

Ralph shook his head.

"Well, it's this: A woman's like a kicky cow in fly time—more bother 'n she's worth. An' yet we've got to have cows; an' we can't do without women. Take a cow in fly 'time, fer instance. You have to run 'er all over a ten-acre field, to git a chance to milk 'er. Then w'en you're purty near tuckered out, an' are debatin' whether to set the dogs on 'er an' let 'er go, she stands as meek as you please an' gives a brimmin' bucket o' milk. Then jest as you're c'ngratulatin' y'rself that you're in luck an' ain't goin' to have no more trouble with 'er, she cracks you in the eye with 'er stump tail; kicks over the bucket o' milk; starts 'cross the field, bellerin' like ol' Nick seekin' whom he may devour; an' leaves you ponderin' on the hollerness an' vanity o' human uncertainty."

Tucker paused, squinted one eye, and appealed to his auditor, with the words:

"Ain't that right?"

"It may be so—I cannot say," Marlowe answered, smiling at his companion's earnestness and solemnity. "I have had no experience with kicking cows. But go on—make your comparison."

"Well, it's so, ev'ry word of it, whether you've had the 'xperience 'r not," Jep resumed doggedly. "Now, as to women, I'll jest take my ol' woman as a horrible example. Yisterday was fly time; an' she was c'ntrarier 'n all git out. Last night she quieted down; got me a hot supper when we went home—'way after nine o'clock—an' was as good as apple pie with cream on. Then 'way in the night this ol' foot o' mine got to hurtin' an' throbbin'; an' she jumped out o' bed, made a poultice fer it, an' couldn't do too much fer me. Do you see what I'm drivin' at?"

"Yes, but you have not finished."

"No; but I'm gittin' there. This mornin' she made me git up an' build the fire, 'fore daylight—right when I was gittin' the best sleep I'd had all night; an' said the only reason I didn't sleep well was 'cause I'd eat too much 'fore goin' to bed. Sort o' hinted ther' wasn't nothin' ailed my foot, an' that I'd ort to had the poultice on my stomach. What do you think of an unreason'ble human critter like that, anyhow?"

Tucker asked the question in such a lugubrious tone, and his homely countenance wore such a sympathy-seeking expression, that

Ralph burst into a roar of laughter. At which Jep whined:

"Tain't no laughin' matter, young feller, an' you'll find it out, if you ever git spliced. I ain't complainin', though. My frow's as good as the next one—but she's a woman; an' women is like kicky cows in fly time. Say!"—Suddenly brightening.— "You remember I 'lowed to tell you a story yesterday?"

"I remember," Ralph replied, looking at his watch. "But I haven't time to hear it now."

"What?"—Incredulity in voice and manner.—"Hain't got time to hear a good story?"

"Not at present. I wish to put things to right ere Dr. Barwood returns." Jep slowly arose to his feet; and sadly wagging his head, went out muttering:

"Then I might as well go back to the barn an' finish my job o' washin' an greasin' harness. But I'll tell you one thing, young feller—an' that ain't two—you've got a heap to learn yit, 'bout gittin' the best out o' life there is in it. Hain't got time to hear a story! The man that hain't got time to hear a good yam, hain't got time to eat n'r sleep; an' he ort to swap time fer etarnity, an' quit goin' through the motions o' livin'.'"

Marlowe resumed his task of putting things to rights. He rearranged the shelfware, overhauled the contents of drawers and showcases, placed fresh goods and advertising matter in the windows, and put everything upon the counters in shipshape. By eleven o'clock, the apparently impossible job was done; and in silent satisfaction he gazed upon his handiwork.

"It doesn't look like the same place," he murmured admiringly. "But there is much yet to do—that ought to be done, at least. The woodwork should be repainted and varnished; the walls, repapered. Then plants in the windows would help greatly. But I am satisfied; I have made a good beginning."

The noon hour arrived; and Dr. Barwood had not yet returned. In the meantime business had been rather brisk. Quite a number of coins had jingled into the till in the tall, spindle-legged desk. Also, not a few persons had been in to see the doctor. Some had gone their ways, saying they would call again; others had left requests that he would come to their homes on his return. All in all, the forenoon had passed pleasantly and profitably; and Marlowe whistled softly to himself as he sauntered to his dinner.

Coming back he noted that a chill wind was blowing from the northwest and that slaty[22] clouds were marshaling in that quarter.

Tucker—who had discarded his dilapidated straw hat for a cloth cap of equal disreputability—sat upon the edge of the wide top step in front of the drugstore. He was idly swinging his long legs, and amusing himself by holding a bit of straw between his nether teeth and lip, and with spasmodic motions of his lower jaw thrusting the free end of it through his stubby mustache. Meantime he was humming through his nose:

> "Come, love, come! The boat lies low;
> She lies high an' dry on the O-hi-o.
> Come, love, come—an' go along with me,
> I'll take you down to Tennessee."

Breaking off abruptly as Ralph drew near, Jep flung away the piece of straw he had been juggling, and gazing admiringly upon the neat business suit of brown the druggist had donned while at dinner, exclaimed:

"By jeeminy! 'Fine feathers makes fine birds,' 'cordin' to the ol' sayin'. My ol' daddy used to put it—'fine fur makes a fine mink skin'; an', I heard a feller say in rhyme one time:

> "''Tain't what he knows, but what he wears,
> That helps a feller put on airs;
> A stovepipe hat upon his head
> Counts more 'n all the books he's read.'

"May be that's overdrawn a little; but ther' ain't no denyin' that good clo'es counts fer more 'n most people gives 'em credit. You'd look nice in sackcloth an' ashes; but you'd look a darn sight better in purple an' fine linen. But say!"—Rising and following Marlowe into

---

22 slaty: having the color of slate

the drugstore.—"I want to ask you a question, if you won't think me too peart."

"Out with it," answered Ralph, tossing his hat upon the desk and walking behind the counter.

"Well, it's—it's this."—Hesitating and rubbing his husky palms together.—"What's y'r politics?"

Marlowe laughed outright. Then suddenly checking himself and looking sober, he said in return:

"Why do you ask?"

"Well, that's question an' a half," chuckled Jep, albeit a little uneasily. "I ask 'cause I want to know."

"Perhaps I do not subscribe to the tenets of any political party."

"I don't ketch y'r meanin', 'xactly," Tucker admitted, shaking his head. "But you vote, don't you?"

"Sometimes."

"An' when you vote you vote some ticket, don't you?"

"Certainly."

"Then that's jest what I want to know. What ticket do you vote?"

"And again I ask—why do you inquire?"

"W'y the 'lection's comin' on," Jep explained, easing his back against the edge of the counter; "an' both parties is countin' noses. Some o' the fellers was 'round to the stable a while ago, an' wanted me to feel o' you an' find out how you voted. They want to list you on the poll book."

"I see. By the way, what is the political complexion of this community?"

"Oh! what few of 'em ain't Republicans is Democrats; an' what few of 'em ain't Democrats is Republicans."

"That's very clear," laughed Marlowe. "But which party is in the ascendency?"

"Which one has the biggest vote?"

"Exactly."

"Well, it's nip an' tuck—an' sometimes one, an' sometimes t'other. But the Republicans 'll beat this year."

"Indeed? What are you, Jep?"

"Me? I'm a Republican. All good-lookin' fellers is Republicans."

"Why do you think the Republicans will win this year?"

"'Cause they will, that's why. That Billy Bryan couldn't beat nothin'. He couldn't beat a carpet."

"What is Dr. Barwood?"

"The ol' doc? He's the leadin' Republican o' the township. Now what are you?"

"A Democrat. Are there no other parties represented?"

"No, I guess not."—Then with a whimsical grin.—"Ther' was one pro'ibitionist here sever'l years ago. But he jest natcherly argied hisself to death; an' that broke up the party. So you're a Democrat?"

"I am."

"Ever scratch y'r ticket?"

"Seldom."

"N'r me, neither. I'm purty near as bad as ol' Ed O'Neil. Heard him say once he wouldn't scratch his ticket to save Christ from the cross. An' so you're goin' to vote fer Bryan, are you?"

"If I vote at all—yes."

"Think he's a better man 'n McKinley?"

"Both are gentlemen, so far as I know," Ralph laughed. "I am acquainted with neither."

"You're a little like ol' Tomp Nutt, I guess."

"Explain."

"He's all the time growlin' 'cause he ain't a'quainted with the presidential candidates. Says he don't see why they nominate fellers that nobody knows; that they ort to nominate somebody like Hugh McDevitt 'n Doc Barwood. Says ev'ry body knows them—"

Tucker paused suddenly; and leaning toward Marlowe whispered:

"There comes ol' Tomp up the steps this very minute. Now you *will* meet a good one. He stutters like a jig saw; is odder 'n the figger seven, an' fuller o' queer notions an' idees 'n a scrapbook."

Ralph faced the door. It opened and shut; and a grotesque figure slouched toward the center of the room.

Judging from appearances, Mr. Thompson Nutt was indeed a character. He was a deep-chested, round-shouldered man of sixty years, with long arms and bandy legs. He did not walk, he shuffled—his body bent well forward, his arms dangling. His ruddy face—bare from forehead to chin—was encircled by a halo of snow-white hair and beard. His wide mouth sagged grievously at the corners; and his kindly blue eyes were weak and watery. But his whole appearance denoted great physical power and endurance.

As to his apparel, it consisted of a pair of ragged trousers, a chinchilla coat—threadbare in many places and lined with flaming red flannel, an old-fashioned blue satin waistcoat, and a black neckerchief. He wore a white slouch hat; and his feet were encased in well-worn arctics.

"How d' y' do, Tomp," Tucker cried, edging out of the way as the newcomer approached the counter. "How are you today, anyhow?"

"'B-'B-'Bout the s-same, if any d-d-differ'nce," grinned Nutt, throwing back the corner of his coat and diving deep into his trousers' pocket. "H-H-How're y-you?"

"Fair to middlin'," Jep replied, winking at Ralph.

The elderly man fished up the coin he was angling for, and slapping it upon the counter demanded:

"G-Got any f-f-fetty?"

"Pardon me," returned Ralph. "But what is it you want?"

"F-Fetty. G-Got any?"

"Fetty, you say?"

"Y-Yes—d-darn it! F-F-Fetty."

"I fear I don't yet understand what you mean."

Jep came to the rescue with:

"What's the matter with you, anyhow, Ralph Marlowe? Tomp Nutt wants some fetty."—This was Tucker's unique way of introducing the two men.—"You know what the stuff is, if you'll jest think a minute. It's that bad-smellin' truck that folks puts in bags, an' hangs 'em 'round the'r childern's necks, to keep off diseases an' witches an' things. An I hain't no doubt it'll keep off anything dead 'r alive; fer it smells worse 'n a dirty shotgun."

"Oh, I understand!" Marlowe exclaimed, smiling blandly. "Mr. Nutt wants some asafetida."

"That's what you drug fellers calls it, I guess," Jep answered, nodding; "but down in this patch o' clearin' we call it—fetty."

"It d-don't m-m-make no d-differ'nce what you *c-call* it," stuttered Tomp, "jest s-so you've *g-got* it."

"How much will you have, Mr. Nutt?" Marlowe asked pleasantly.

"F-Five cents w-w-worth."

When Ralph had wrapped up the required quantity of the odoriferous drug, he shoved it toward the purchaser, quoting as he did so:

"'Asafetida, the resinous gum
Named from its odor—well, it does smell some.'"

"S-Say that ag'in," stuttered the old man, his eyes flying open like those of a mechanical doll.

Ralph laughingly repeated the couplet.

"S-S-Say!" Tomp exclaimed with candid admiration. "Y-You're a p-p-poet."

"That is not original with me," the young druggist explained; "it is a quotation. Dr. Holmes is the author."

"Doc who?" Tucker interjected with a rising inflection.

"Doctor Oliver Wendell Holmes."

"Don't know him, I guess," Jep observed reflectively. "Never practiced in these parts, did he?"

With an effort Marlowe managed to smother his risibility; and went on to give a brief biographical sketch of the great anatomist and littérateur. Tucker listened attentively; Nutt, absent-mindedly. Evidently the old man's thoughts were elsewhere; for as Ralph concluded he hastened to say:

"D-Do y-y-you know I'm p-purty g-g-good at m-makin' rhymes?"

"Indeed?" Ralph replied with feigned surprise and interest.

"Y-Yes. S-See them two f-fellers 'cross the s-street there?

N-Now "I'll m-m-make a rhyme 'b-'bout 'em. The'r n-names is B-Bob B-B-Brown an' B-Bob J-Jones."

And Nutt pointed to two villagers—their coat collars turned up, their hands in their pockets—occupying a bench in front of the wagon-maker's shop, busily talking.

Then the old man said impressively:

"N-Now l-l-listen:

"Ther' was two B-Bobs s-s-set on a b-bench,

An' they g-got sk-sk-skeered at a h-hornet's n-nest."

"S-Say! Wh-What do you th-th-think o' that?"

The manner in which he said it all—his earnestness, his gravity—was irresistible, Marlowe laughed heartily. Tucker threw himself across the counter, and kicked up his heels and roared. The old man took their merriment as a compliment to his poetical genius, probably. At any rate, he did not take it amiss; but picking up his purchase smilingly shambled out of the store.

"Didn't I tell you he was a good one, young feller?" said Jep—as soon as he could say anything—resuming his lounging attitude at the side of the counter and wiping his eyes with the back of his hand. "Ol' Tomp's funnier 'n a funer'l—he is, by jeeminy! 'Taint *what* he says, but the *way* he says it. Wasn't I right w'en I said you'd strike an odd stick in him?"

"Yes," Ralph admitted—busying himself with the filling of a prescription for horse liniment, that a farmer had brought in before dinner—"but there are others."

"Oh! I know that," Tucker assented innocently, never dreaming himself was meant. "But ol' Tomp's the cap sheaf o' the whole caboodle. Ther's lots o' funny tales 'bout the ol' codger. One spring sever'l years ago, he come to the c'nclusion he'd go into business, 'stid o' workin' at his trade—carpenterin'. So he opened up a kind o' hardware store an' groc'ry c'mbined, in a room in the Gridley buildin'.

"Well, he hadn't more 'n fairly got started, till one sunshiny day in corn-plantin' time, a farmer from back on the hills walked in an' asked fer a pair o' bull-tongues. Say!"—Abruptly.—"Of course you know what bull-tongues is?"

Ralph had to admit that he wasn't certain that he knew. And Jep resumed:

"You wouldn't 'ave been no better off 'n Tomp, then. Bull-tongues is them long, narrer shovels that goes on cultivators. Well, w'en that farmer asks the ol' codger—'Have you got any bull-tongues, Mr. Nutt?'—Tomp thinks the feller's a huntin' somethin' good to eat; an' without waitin' to be sure 'bout it, he blurts out:

"'N-No I hain't g-got no b-bull-t-tongues; b-but I've g-g-got some m-mighty good b-b-b'lony s-s-sausage.'"

Marlowe was devoting his attention to a refractory label he was pasting upon the bottle he had just filled; and he smiled but feebly. Not at all discouraged by his companion's lack of appreciation, however, Tucker maundered on:

"'Nother time the ol' feller got on a pr'tracted spree; an' w'en he went to taper off, done like ev'rybody's likely to do—made the taper end the biggest, an' got drunk ag'in. Aunt Hanner, his wife—a good, religious ol' soul—lectured him 'bout his sinful ways. Says she:

"'Tomp Nutt, you'll die on one y'r drunken frolics some day, an' leave me a widder. An' then w'en *I* die an' go up to heaven, I won't find *you* there; an' how bad I'll feel.'

"Tomp straightened hisself up as stiff as a ramrod, an' answers:

"'M-Mother, if I d-die f-first, I'll l-leave the g-gate o' h-h-heaven open f-fer you. An' w'en y-you g-git in, y-you'll f-f-find m-me up there in all m-my g-g-glory—s-shinin' like a n-new c-c-crosscut s-saw.'"

Tucker's imitation of Tomp's stuttering delivery was perfect, and Ralph felt like laughing. Not caring to encourage the volatile fellow to further effort, however, the young man concealed his merriment by asking quickly:

"Jep, what is keeping Dr. Barwood, do you think?"

"Don't know," answered the eccentric, sauntering over to the side window and peeping out, "'nless he's got *into* one o' them cases that a doctor never knows when he'll git *out* of. I know what you're thinkin' 'bout, though; an' you're goin' to be disapp'inted."

"Of what am I thinking?"

"You're thinkin' that w'en the ol' doc comes back, he'll praise you fer havin' the drugstore all cleaned up. But you're mightily mistaken; he won't do nothin' o' the kind. He'll jest strut in an' let on he don't notice no change—By jolly! Here he is this very minute; an' lookin' sourer 'n an ol' maid's smile. He's hitchin' his hoss to the rack; an' 's comin' in. Now, young feller, watch out fer breakers."

Marlowe did not think it necessary to make reply. A minute later Dr. Barwood strode into the store, his head erect, anger and defiance in his eyes. Without giving the slightest attention to the altered condition and appearance of the place, apparently, he threw his muddy saddlebags and great coat upon the counter and said gruffly:

"I would have been back sooner; but I have been dragged all over the southern end of the county by a pack of scalawags who are always sick—and always penniless. What calls are in, Mr. Marlowe?"

"Here is the list I kept, doctor," Ralph replied simply, handing him a slip of paper.

The physician took the list and hurriedly looked it over. As he did so, his shoulders sagged wearily and a spasm of pain crossed his face.

"You are tired," Marlowe remarked in a matter of fact tone.

Without looking up, Dr. Barwood answered surlily: "Yes, I am tired—and hungry. So would you be, had you been over every crossroad and into every cabin, almost, between here and Bear Run; and had nothing to eat since daylight."

Then meditatively to himself:

"Curston's on the Foxtown road. I can't go there today; must leave that until tomorrow. All the other calls are in town, except the one to Smiley's on Norton Ridge. Jep,"—With startling suddenness—"take the gray mare to the blacksmith and have her shoes reset; and put the sorrel to the cart. I must be off to the country again as soon as I have had a bite to eat and have made a few calls."

Tucker arose lumberingly and started for the door. With the words—"I am going to dinner, Mr. Marlowe; shall be back soon"—the physician also turned to leave the room.

"Doctor, I will hang your things in the entrance to the basement," Ralph said carelessly. "I have put up hooks there."

"No," Dr. Barwood answered shortly. "Leave them where they are."

"But they are in my way."

"I can't help that. Leave them alone. I want them handy."

"I'll get them for you when you want them, doctor."

With the words, Marlowe quietly picked up the bones of contention and carried them from the room. Like a beast at bay the doctor stood and glared after the young man's retreating form. Tucker gasped for breath. Such temerity was unheard of. He felt the air was surcharged with electricity, that the storm he had been expecting was about to break. But he was mistaken. Ralph returned to his place and coolly dusted the counter where the offending articles had lain; and turning on his heel, the physician took his departure—a curious smile flickering about his firm mouth.

Jep followed his employer through the door, muttering under his breath:

"Well, I'll be everlastin'ly bamboozled! I never seen Doc Barwood melt an' leak[23] away like that before. I was countin' on a storm—a reg'lar cyclone an' jimmycane[24] rolled into one; an' ther' wasn't even a puff o' wind n'r a clap o' thunder. Nobody else on earth could 'ave done what that young feller done. The ol' doc 'ld stormed the'r castles in a minute. Huh! Blamed if the ol' man didn't ruther seem to enjoy it. Went out a smilin', by jeeminy!"

It was two o'clock when Dr. Barwood returned to the drugstore.

"I have made my calls," he remarked pleasantly, to Marlowe;

---

23 leak: an opening through which something can escape; to escape or pass through a leak

24 jimmycane: a violent storm that blows in with little or no warning, does a bit of damage, and quickly moves on

"and now I must be off to the country again. But before I start I want to talk with you. Sit down here."

Ralph dropped into a chair near the end of the bench where the doctor had seated himself; and the latter went on:

"I wish to get on pleasantly with you; therefore I would warn you against doing certain things that are objectionable to me, and associating with certain people whom I dislike. To begin with, I will not tolerate drinking nor gambling—"

"I indulge in neither," Ralph interrupted stiffly. Unheeding the interruption, the doctor continued placidly:

"Of the three clerks I had in the last eighteen months, the first was a sot—and neglected my business; the second, a gambler—and systematically robbed me; the third, a consummate scoundrel—who was both and did both. The public does not know this; I am not in the habit of publishing my private affairs. Therefore, I am blamed in the matter. People say these young men could not stand my eccentricities, my arrogance, my brutal temper; and that they left of their own accord. It is not true. I discharged them—just as I will discharge you, if your services do not come up to my expectations."

He paused to note the effect of his words upon his companion.

"You will not have to discharge me, Dr. Barwood," Marlowe said calmly. "If at any time I get an inkling that my services do not please you, I shall resign immediately. More than that, if I find the situation does not suit me, for any reason, I shall promptly quit your service."

That inscrutable smile again lighted the physician's countenance, as he replied:

"I like your spirit, at any rate; and I hope we may not come into conflict. But to proceed with the matter in hand: I know nothing of your past, your antecedents, your record; nor do I wish to know. The recommendations you sent are sufficient. But I would caution you that there are people in this village, with whom you must not become intimate, if you would gain and retain my favor."

Again he stopped, as though expecting his auditor to say something. But the latter kept silent.

"To explain my position," the doctor resumed, " I shall give you a brief sketch of my life. I have traveled a rough road—and planned it with my own brain, and built it with my own hands. I was born in a log cabin; was reared in the backwoods. I literally educated myself. At the age of eighteen I began to teach school. Previous to that, I had worked at hard manual labor—anything I could get to do. The privations I endured while preparing myself for my life's work, no one knows—or ever will know.

"Immediately after I graduated, I married and began the practice of my profession in this village. Armed with good health, pluck and perseverance, I have fought my way step by step. I have made many enemies—and but few friends. My early struggles tempered the metal that was in me, and prepared me for the battle I have had to fight. I was naturally pugnacious; my training made me aggressive. It has been a hard and bitter contest—a contest that has coarsened my finer sensibilities, perhaps. I do not know. At any rate, there was no avoiding it; it was thrust upon me.

"Those who were my enemies when I came here are my enemies today. I have succeeded in spite of their opposition—not by their help. I ask of them no favor; I show them no quarter. Chief among those who have assailed me on every hand—and who have not scorned to take unfair advantage of me when opportunity offered—are the McDevitts, the Gridleys, and the Bentleys. They are called—'the best families'; and no doubt they are good people in many ways. But they are my enemies. I do not patronize them; they do not patronize me. I buy my dry goods in Malconta; they send there for a physician. The condition of affairs is to my liking.

"Besides, I could not trust one of them. George Bentley is grasping. Had he lived in the days of Christ, he would not have cast lots for the Saviour's raiment; he would have taken the whole by force. Hugh McDevitt is deceitful—dishonest. He would steal the tear from an orphan's cheek, if he thought it had a cash value."

Marlowe was startled by his employer's strange but apt metaphor; and his countenance showed it. Dr. Barwood had uttered the last few sentences in a tone of bitter and intense earnestness. But noting the expression upon his companion's face, he smiled and said:

"Does my language shock you? It need not; for they say meaner things of me, I assure you.

"I cannot help but doubt that," Ralph replied, smiling in turn.

"You think they *could* not?"

"That's what I mean—yes."

Dr. Barwood made no reply; but sat silently staring at the floor, for some seconds—the while stroking his thin beard and scowling fiercely.

Marlowe smiled inwardly. He was beginning to understand the irascible physician, to appreciate his strength and weakness. The older man had revealed himself more than he knew; and the younger had caught a glimpse of his true character—and was irresistibly drawn toward him.

"He is a chestnut bur," was Ralph's shrewd estimate; "the exterior all spines and prickles—the interior, all oil and satin. But the frost of age is beginning to crack the pod; and he who will may gain a peep inside."

Of a sudden Dr. Barwood threw up his head and said briskly:

"But to come to the point. I don't want you to become the intimate of any members of the families I have named."

He paused expectantly; and Marlowe replied:

"If they speak me fair, doctor, I shall not reject their friendship."

"You persist in misunderstanding me," the doctor snarled. "I do not wish you to take up my quarrel; nor do I wish you to ally yourself with my enemies. I shall not object to a passing acquaintance—an outward show of civility and friendliness. But you *must not* become intimate with them."

"Why?"—Coldly.

"Because—because they will make trouble between us—will do all in their power to make you dissatisfied with your place and your employer."

"I understand your meaning, doctor. But you will find I am not easily influenced by the opinions of others. I depend largely upon my own observation and experience, in forming my estimate of men and things. If ever I come to dislike you, become dissatisfied with your employ, it will be because of your *usage* of *me;* and not because of what others may *think* or *say* of *you.*"

A gratified expression for a moment softened the hard lines of Dr. Barwood's countenance. But shaking his head, he replied:

"Perhaps—but remember I have cautioned you."

"Would it not be better, doctor," Ralph suggested, "that I should be intimate with both you and your antagonists—if it be possible—and use my good offices to bring about a lasting truce?"

"No!" thundered the doctor springing from his seat, his features contorted with anger. "It is not to be thought of. As you have intimated, you cannot sustain such a position. You *must and shall* make your choice between us. A truce! A truce indeed! Never! I will fight them as long as I live; and hate them at the hour of my death. When I break off a friendship, I burn the bridges behind me, to prevent a return. They have wronged me, maligned and abused me. I will never forgive them—never!"

Marlowe made no effort to reply to this fiery outburst. Dr. Barwood's anger subsided as quickly as it had arisen; and resuming his seat he said calmly—almost sadly:

"No truce with my enemies, Mr. Marlowe; but a truce to the subject. I cannot ask more of you than I ask of my own family. Do what you think right; but do not forget my caution. As I have said, the Bentleys, the Gridleys, and the McDevitts are considered reputable people. They are leaders in the society of the village—so I am told. I never mingle in it; I have neither time nor inclination for such frothy nonsense. But my wife and daughters do—to an extent that I disapprove. Yet I say little; I don't want them to think me *too* tyrannical.

"The McDevitts are Catholics; the Bentleys and Gridleys are Protestants. My wife and older daughter belong to the Methodist Church. My younger daughter—I have but two children, both young women—frequently attends the Catholic Church; but is not a member.

As to myself, I adhere to no creed—attend no church. I cannot accept the absurd and unscientific beliefs presented; and I have had no time to formulate a satisfactory one for myself. I have been too busy looking after the physical ailments of my fellows; and have had to neglect my spiritual welfare—quoting my orthodox enemies. Thus far have I got—and no farther—in all the years that have bowled me onward: I believe in a Supreme Intelligence that made and rules the universe. Matter is inert; it cannot shape nor move itself. It must be acted upon by a power without. That power—that force—is the Supreme Intelligence; is God, if you please.

"Also, I believe the Bible to be a human history, inspired by human intelligence and written by human hands; a book full of mistakes and blunders—of legends that have little or no foundation in fact, and of accounts of miracles that were never wrought—yet a book full of valuable experiences and worthy lessons. In conclusion, I believe that Jesus Christ is the grandest human character that ever graced the pages of history; a son of God, as you and I are sons of God—no more. I believe in the civilization that rests upon his example and teachings. It is his words and deeds that will save the world; not his death upon the cross, nor his blood. Remember I do not say I *know* these things; I *believe* them. I may be entirely wrong."

He stopped, apparently waiting for Marlowe to voice an opinion.

"You have little use for creeds, then, doctor," Ralph said.

"There are creeds and creeds," was the reply.

"One is as good as another, so long as it teaches humanity. I use the word in its broadest and best sense."

"And miracles?"

"There never was one—never will be. A miracle would be a violation of the laws of the Divine Intelligence—of God—which are immutable, inexorable. Sin is a violation of God's law. Should God violate his own law, He would be the chief of all sinners. In no instance has prayer changed His will or modified the inevitable result of His laws. Yet prayer is a good thing—for the individual who makes it."

"And of course you do not believe in a personal devil?"

"I do not. I am too loyal to the Giver of all Good, to believe He has a rival in the universe. Such belief is preposterous—the worst of impiety. There is no prince of evil, because there is no such thing as evil."

"You astound me."

"I will try to make my meaning plain. Light is a positive force, or substance—as you please to consider it; darkness is *not* a negative force or substance. It is not an entity, as is light. It has no existence. The term is relative; and means the absence of so much light. Do you follow me?"

Ralph nodded.

"The same is true of heat and cold; of good and evil. Cold is the absence of so much heat; evil is the lack of so much good. The absence of heat constitutes cold; the lack of good constitutes evil; the want of heaven constitutes hell. For heaven and hell are conditions, not places. There is a god—or intelligent power of heat, and light, and good; but there is no god of cold, and darkness, and evil—for as entities they have no existence."

"Do you believe there is a future life, doctor?"

"Yes."—Emphatically.—"That is, I believe there is a present life that is continuous. Life is a force—the resultant of other forces. It cannot be destroyed; but its form or mode of operation may be modified. There was no conscious existence before physical birth; yet the ego existed in some form or other. And there may be no conscious existence after physical death. I do not know—I scarcely know what I *believe,* even. What we call life is a narrow isthmus, with the black sea of obscurity on one side and the veiled ocean of futurity on the other. Our path lies across it—now steep and rocky, now level and flower-bordered. We have no remembrance of the sea of obscurity whence we came; we have no knowledge of the ocean of futurity whither we are hastening. All that we know is that we left the shore of the one, and that in time we shall reach the shore of the other."

"Your doctrine is not the most cheerful, nor is it the most hopeful, doctor."

"You think that? It is not orthodox, I admit. But that it is not as assuring as any other, I deny. There is naught of faith in it—naught but hard, cold reason. Your orthodox saint prates to me of faith. I ask him, faith in what—faith in whom? And his answer is, faith in my book—in my creed. His witness has never been qualified. And what is creed but the formulated opinion of some man, or set of men? Why should I take their opinions instead of my own? They *know* no more than I, no matter what they *believe.* Do they not differ among themselves; are they not at variance? All of them cannot be *right;* and all of them may be *wrong.* So may *I* be—I lay no claim to infallibility. But one thing is certain. The Divine Architect of the universe—the Intelligent Power of which I have spoken—would not have given me a brain, had He not meant that I should use it in the government of my beliefs and actions. Your creed-makers do that; yet quarrel with me for exercising the same privilege. What of Luther, of Calvin, and Campbell—and hosts of others? Were they not pronounced heretics in their day? Did not Christ himself come preaching a new doctrine? Are not the standard Protestant creeds of today undergoing frequent and radical changes? Have they received any new light upon the perplexing problem since the advent of Christ? Not a scintilla[25]! Has the Bible been altered? The New Testament has been revised; but not an essential precept in it has been modified. No! The reason they do not believe and preach as in years past is because they have done just what they say I shall not do—they have reasoned. And if they be wise, they will continue to reason—will continue to prune and eliminate, to alter and revise. Ignorance and superstition do not make piety.

"But"—Hastily glancing at his watch—"I have talked too long already. Let me say this in conclusion, however. Do not accept my belief. It may not be my belief tomorrow or next year. Think for yourself—do not be afraid to think. No unreasoning and unreasonable orthodox monster stands ready to damn you for it. Thought may not add an inch to your linear stature; but it will add cubic feet to your mental capacity. As a final word on the subject upon which we

---
25 scintilla: a small amount; trace

started, my enemies will—"

"Doctor," Ralph broke in, "did you not say you are a believer in the teachings of Christ?"

Dr. Barwood's features instantly grew hard and tense; and his black eyes snapped. He scented danger, and was steeling himself to meet it.

"I did," he answered unhesitatingly.

"Then you should be willing and ready to forgive your enemies."

"My young friend," the physician answered solemnly, laying his hand upon Ralph's shoulder—and the latter noted the familiar tone and jesture, and was both surprised and pleased, "you have said things to me during our short acquaintanceship I would not have tolerated coming from another. I hardly know why I have borne with you. But do not put my forebearance to too severe a test. I am not given to fulsome praise; but I have not failed to notice what you have been doing in my interest."—With a glance around the room.—"I think we shall get on together—exercising due caution on both sides. As to forgiving my enemies, I find it impossible. It is one thing to accept a precept; quite another thing to act according to its teachings. Then—but why multiply words? Get me my things—as you kindly agreed to do—and I will be off."

The older man smiled cordially as he concluded; and the younger hastened to procure the desired articles. Just as the former was about to leave the store, Jim Crawford staggered into the room, closely followed by Tucker. The doctor stopped suddenly, every fiber in his body stiffening, and pierced the cobbler with his keen black eyes.

The latter presented a pitiable spectacle. His clothing was torn, soiled and awry. He staggered as he walked, trembling in every limb. His red hair was bristling; and a greenish pallor overspread his twitching features—the sickly hue of a tree toad's belly.

"Doc, I'm sick—I want some medicine," he said in quavering accents.

"You've been drunk again, eh?" the doctor returned frigidly.

"Yes, doc, I have been on a little spree."—Shivering and nervously interlocking his tremulous fingers. "An' I'm all knocked out.

My stomach's sick; an' I can't sleep. Give me somethin' to sober me up. Please do!"

"You're a fine specimen of manhood!" roared Dr. Barwood, striding forward and towering over the cowering cobbler. "You get drunk and spend your money; neglect your family and make yourself sick. Then—in your extremity, and without a cent in your pocket—you come creeping and whining to the man you have slandered and wronged. It would be serving you right to kick you into the gutter. You sot! You scoundrel!"—Snarling like an angry dog.—"If you had any sense of shame, you would go and drown yourself."

Crawford tottered and nearly fell to the floor, as he essayed to escape from the irate physician. But clinging to the counter, to steady himself, he huddled into a quivering heap and groaned:

"Fer God's sake, doc, give me *somethin'!* I b'lieve I'm dyin'."

"Same ol' game," Tucker leaned over and whispered to Ralph, upon whose face rested an expression of disgust and pity mingled; "an' it'll come out in the same ol' way, I s'pose. You watch now—an' see if I ain't right."

"You ought to die, Jim Crawford!" Dr. Barwood cried. "You are a miserable, low-lived cur—unfit for the society of decent people!"

But his manner belied his words; and the harsh lines of his swarthy visage relaxed and softened as he spoke.

Turning quickly to Marlowe, he whispered:

"Give him an ounce or two of Bromidia with directions to take a teaspoonful each hour, until he sleeps."

Would I not better combine with it some elixir of pepsin, bismuth, and strychnia, doctor?" Ralph suggested.

"Y-e-s," Dr. Barwood replied slowly, sharply eying his employee, his lips apart. "Make the prescription half and half of each."

The young druggist hastily compounded the preparation. Crawford frantically clutched the bottle and reeled from the room. When the sound of the cobbler's retreating footsteps had died out, Dr. Barwood silently walked to the till in the tall desk and taking out two dollars handed them to Tucker, saying:

"Here, Jep. Take this money down to Pearson's grocery, buy a sack of flour, some meat and potatoes, and carry the whole to Mrs. Crawford. That brute has been drunk for ten days; and no doubt his wife and children are in want. Wait!"—As Jep started to leave.—"If they are out of coal, order them a load from Beckwick; and have it charged to me. And mind you!"—Shaking a finger at each.—"Not a word of this to any one, from either of you."

Without further remark he shame-facedly caught up his saddle-bags and left the place, closing the door with a bang.

The clouds from the northwest had overspread the sky. The heavens were leaden and somber; and a cold drizzle was falling. Marlowe stood at the side window and watched his employer's muffled figure fade into gray mist, as the light cart went careening up the wide street. And as he looked the young man murmured softly:

"An enigma—a bundle of contradictions. Yet I feel that I shall like him."

* * * * * *

CHAPTER VI

THE WEATHER cleared; a week passed. The farmers were busy with their fall work; and few of them came to town. In consequence, trade was dull and things in the village were very quiet.

But Dr. Barwood had a practice that fluctuated but little. No matter the season or weather, he had more patients than he could well attend. Now he was extremely busy; for typhoid fever was epidemic in the country surrounding Babylon, and he scarcely had time to eat or sleep. Many whole nights he spent in cart or saddle; and days passed that he was not in the drugstore at all.

When he did enter his place of business, he was sullen in manner and surly in speech; and he stayed long enough only to renew the plethora[26] of his foxy saddlebags. As though regretting that on a solitary occasion he had given Marlowe a fleeting glimpse of the better side of his nature, he treated his clerk with scant courtesy—apparently determined to obliterate the favorable impression he had made.

One mild, clear morning Marlowe stood upon the steps of the drugstore, drinking in the delights and beauties of the new day. The sun shone brightly; the sky was blue and the air was sweet and cool.

---

26 plethora: superabundance, excess

There was just a hint of frost in the air; and the birds, hopping from limb to limb of the maple trees near the building, fluffed their feathers and twittered plaintively—grieving over the advent of winter.

Down the sidewalk came two young ladies, the taller walking with elastic step and easy carriage, the other tripping daintily. As they drew nearer Ralph discovered that they were his employer's daughters; and instinctively divining that they intended to enter the store, he retreated within and took up a position behind the counter—across which Jep was lolling, idly reading the names upon bottles and drawer-pulls.

"Ladies are coming, Jep," Ralph said shortly. "Withdraw to the rear of the room, please."

"All right," assented Tucker, with unwonted alacrity of speech and movement.

A moment thereafter the Misses Barwood entered. Marlowe noted with surprise and admiration—for he had not expected to meet the latest fashions in the humdrum little village—that both young women were well groomed and stylishly gowned.

Miss Julia—who was twenty-four, and looked it—wore a tailor-made suit and cape of gray cloth. Miss Dolly's dress and jacket were dark blue—a color calculated to enhance her blonde beauty. Upon the head of each rested an indescribable creation of the milliner's art. Neat patent leathers peeped from beneath Julia's sober gown; and Dolly's feet were encased in cloth-topped French kids—the shortness of her skirt enabling the interested observer to make sure of the fact. Each wore gloves to match her gown.

Julia appeared sober—and slightly embarrassed; Dolly, on the contrary, was the embodiment of the morning, with its sunshine in her face and the glint of latent mischief in her violet eyes.

Seeing who they were, Jep quickly emerged from his place of retirement and smiling broadly, cried:

"W'y, good mornin', gals. How are you this mornin', anyhow? I declare but you're both lookin' sniptious![27] Miss Julia's neater 'n a new pin; an' Miss Dolly's purtier 'n a pot o' posies."

---

27 sniptious: attractive, smart, fine

Dolly, her eyes twinkling merrily, smiled at Tucker's effusiveness and said—"What a courtier you are, Jep!"

But Julia disdainfully curled her upper lip and maintained a dignified silence.

Looking straight into the younger sister's bright countenance—and wholly ignoring the scornful expression upon the face of the older one—Tucker went on:

"Gals, let me intr'duce you to y'r daddy's new clerk. Mr. Ralph Marlowe, this is Miss Dolly Barwood—Dolly's the butt end o' Dorothy, you know; an' Miss Dolly, this is Mr. Marlowe. Mr. Marlowe, this is Miss Julia Barwood; Miss Julia, this is Mr. Marlowe. Mr. Marlowe, these is the ol' doc's gals; an' gals, this feller's the new clerk."

Ralph and Dolly looked at each other and smiled—the latter biting her ripe lips and with difficulty repressing her exuberant merriment.

Julia drew down the corners of her mouth, and nodding stiffly murmured—"Mr. Marlowe."

Leaning across the counter the young man warmly shook the hand of each.

"I am pleased to make the acquaintance of my employer's daughters," he said simply.

"Thank you," responded Julia, in a half whisper.

"And we're glad to meet you," Dolly put in animatedly, "for more than one reason. You see papa has had a world of trouble with his clerks, and in consequence has been as cross as a bear—though he's a dear old daddy. So we've all been anxious for him to get a clerk he could depend upon."

"And do you think he has at last secured the jewel of great price, Miss Barwood?" Ralph asked in an amused tone.

"I am sure he has," Dolly answered earnestly, though her mischievous eyes gave doubt of her sincerity. "The old den looks like a new place, already. I feel certain you will suit papa. But oh, Mr. Marlowe!"—Clapping her gloved hands and laughing gleefully.—"You did look *so* cute in that suit of working clothes. Julia and I stopped in front of the store and peeped in at you; and—"

"Dorothy!" the older sister cried reprovingly.

"Well, what now, Miss Prim?" replied the younger, tossing her head and pouting bewitchingly.

Jep chuckled, and clapping the back of his hairy hand over his mouth, turned around and stared hard at the opposite wall. Ralph wanted to laugh—but wisely refrained from doing so.

"You are talking too much, Dorothy," Julia said reprovingly. "What will Mr. Marlowe think of us? Besides, you are not stating facts. I did *not* stop in front of the store and peep in at him; and I tried to keep you from doing so—but could not."

"Now who's telling tales out of school—who's talking too much now?" Dolly asked saucily.

Unheeding the pert rejoinder—though her face flushed slightly—Julia turned to Ralph and said quietly:

"Mr. Marlowe, we came in to get some perfume."

"Why, Julia, what a fib!" exclaimed Dolly, in a tone of mock horror—and actually winking at Ralph. "You *know* we came in on purpose to get acquainted with Mr. Marlowe; you know we talked it over as we came along."

"Dorothy, how *can* you!" the older sister cried plaintively, her face scarlet—yet a smile twitching her lips. "What will Mr. Marlowe think of us and our actions?"

"I think your actions were perfectly natural," Ralph said in a tone of easy indifference, smiling all the while, "and quite proper."

"Thank you," Julia murmured confusedly, placing upon the counter a book she had held in her hand, and peering at the array of perfume bottles in the showcase. "You relieve my mind. Dorothy is incorrigible, and mortifies me greatly."

"Oh, do hush, Julia!" cried the irrepressible Dolly, mimicking her sister's tone and gesture. "I'm not a child—if I do wear short dresses."

This she said with a flounce of her skirt and a roguish, defiant glance at Ralph.

Then quite ignoring Julia's whispered protestations, the minx proceeded:

"But you haven't finished what you started to say, Mr. Marlowe. You've told us what you think of our *actions*, now kindly tell us what you think of *us*."

"Oh, Dorothy Barwood!" groaned her sister.

"I fear to give expression to my opinion, Miss Dorothy"—Marlowe began laughingly.

"Call me Dolly—and be done with it," advised that young lady. "That's what everybody but Julia calls me. I like it best. Now, go on."

"Very well," Ralph assented with assumed gravity. "But, as I started to say, I fear to express my flattering opinion. You might accuse me of being a courtier—as you did Jep."

"No, I won't," Dolly asserted stoutly. "Go on—say just what—"

"Dorothy, I shall surely inform mother of your behavior," Julia interrupted in a tone of severity.

Then to Ralph:

"Mr. Marlowe, please give me an ounce of that violet. We must be going."

"Excuse me just a moment, while I get a bottle." Ralph replied, bowing. "I haven't had time, as yet, to wash a lot and have them ready for use."

He started for the entrance to the cellar.

"I'll come down some day and help you wash them up," Dolly called after him.

"I shall hold you to your promise, Miss Dorothy," he replied a moment later, as he returned to where the sisters stood.

"Much help she would be," Julia remarked sneeringly, "She will not help to wash the plate and china at home, even."

"Is that an exact statement of the facts in the case, sister mine?" Dolly asked soberly. "Remember you are a church member—and must tell the truth, the whole truth, and nothing but the truth."

"Well, you do assist *me* occasionally," Julia answered, smiling in spite of herself; "but it is under protest, usually."

"I thank you for making the correction," Dolly said, pursing her lips and fetching a sweeping bow."

"And *I* stand corrected," returned Julia.

Then all three laughed good-humoredly.

Jep had kept silent—for a wonder—observing the thrusts and parries of the others, and chuckling to himself. Now he advanced to the counter and picking up the book lying thereon, closely scrutinized the title, remarking as he did so:

"Just want to see what kind of a book you've been readin', Miss Julia. I'm some fer books myself. I read one clean through last winter. I don't jest remember what its name was; but it was a crackin' good book. Airly Chandler lent it to me to read. Queer, I can't recollect the name of it. It had a heap in 'bout Injins, an' outlaws, an' wildcats—an' things like that. Well, I'll be doggoned! Miss Julia, you ain't one o' them *new* women, are you?"

"No; she's an *old* woman," Dolly giggled.

"Why do you ask the question, Jep?" inquired Julia, condescendingly.

"W'y, I see you've been readin' politics."

"Politics!" exclaimed both young women.

"Yes, politics," tapping the book with his finger.

"That's not a history of political parties," Julia explained, with more graciousness than she had yet shown; "nor has it to do with their platforms or principles."

"That's all right," Jep interrupted, obstinately shaking his head. "Maybe you can make me b'lieve that; an' then ag'in, maybe you can't. I can tell what's in a jug, by smellin' the cork, 'bout as well's the next one, I reckon; an' I can guess what's in a book, by readin' the name on the back. An' what does it say right there, hey?"—Pointing triumphantly at the gilt title.—"*The Popocrat at the Breakfast Table.*"

"Oh, Jep, you'll kill me!" cried Dolly, convulsed with laughter.

"You've mistaken the contents of the jug this time," said Marlowe, also laughing heartily. "You'd better smell the stopper again."

"I can read just as well as you can, young feller," retorted Tucker, slightly nettled.

"But read it again—read it, Jep," Julia cried insistently, shoving the book under his nose. "It's *'The Autocrat of the Breakfast-Table.'* [28]"

"I don't care what you call it," he answered doggedly, "autocrat, 'r popocrat, 'r plutocrat, 'r 'ristocrat, 'r Democrat. They're all one, anyhow—I reckon I read the papers. You folks is tryin' to fool me—like Miss Dolly done one day last summer, when I was weedin' out the flow'r beds fer 'er mammy."

And Jep grinned inanely.

"What did she do?" inquired Marlowe, anxious to hasten the inevitable.

"W'y, I was tinkerin' 'round the flow'r beds, an' Miss Dolly she was playin' on the pianner in the parlor. It was a kind o' purty rattle-te-bang, ding-a-ling-ling tune; an' I moseyed up to the open winder an' asked 'er what key she was playin' it in.

"'In a minor,' says she.

"'What minor?' says I.

"Then she laughs an' says—'Asia Minor.'

"So I thought I'd show my smartness by sayin' 'no, you ain't; you're playin' it in Babylon.' But it didn't pan out as I 'xpected; fer she downed me by askin' if Babylon wasn't in Asia Minor, an—"

"Do hush, Jep!" Dolly interrupted, stamping her little foot. "It is cruel in you to betray my miserable attempt at pun making. Keep still now—or I'll never give you any more sherbet when you are tired and hot."

"An' will you treat me, ag'in sometime, if I'll shut my fly trap an' keep still?"

"Yes—yes."

"All right—it's a bargain. An' fer fear I might fergit my good resolution, I'll go out to the barn an' go to work. Yum-yum! I can taste that cold stuff yit."

Julia heaved a sigh of relief as the voluble oddity passed through the door. Then picking up her book and bottle of perfume, she said:

---

28 *The Autocrat at the Breakfast Table:* essays by Oliver Wendell Holmes, 1858

"What with Dolly's faults, and what with Jep's inanities and father's eccentricities, I lead a merry and care-free existence, Mr. Marlowe. But come out to church next Sabbath and learn where I get my strength to bear with them all. I attend the Methodist Episcopal Church. In fact; I am a member, and a teacher in the Sunday School. There are but two Protestant denominations here, you know, the Methodists and the Disciples. The Catholics I need not mention; I know you would not attend their services. Our Sabbath School is at nine o'clock; our preaching service at ten-thirty. Come out to both. Will you not?"

"I would rather not promise, Miss Barwood."

"Why?" With lifted brows and inflection.

"Early rising is not one of my virtues. And on Sundays I sleep late—until noon often."

"You are in the habit of consulting your ease and inclination, rather than your duty, then."

"I will not plead guilty to the charge. I try to do my duty when I know it. The whole thing is a matter of individual opinion and preference, it would not be worth our while to argue."

Then turning to the younger sister:

"What church do you attend, Miss Dolly?"

"Occasionally I meet with the Catholics, at Haggart's, across the river," answered that young woman, idly drumming upon the showcase. "I always attend when Father Bede comes down from Malconta. I like him; I believe he's a good man. But I don't pretend to understand all they believe—nor believe all I understand. I'm like daddy—a freethinker. Sometimes, too, I go with mamma and Julia to the Methodist Church. To what denomination do you belong, Mr. Marlowe—if any?"

"None."

"But you ought to belong to church," put in Julia. "You are not living as you ought. No matter how moral you may be, you are setting a bad example. But come, Dorothy—we *must* be going."

As they reached the door, Dolly turned and said archly:

"Do you dance, Mr. Marlowe?"

"Yes."

"I'll see that you have an invitation to our next hop, then. Good morning."

When they were gone Ralph returned to his work, murmuring:

"The one invited me to church; the other, to a dance. But neither invited me to their home. The thing I need most—the refining influence of a good home—neither offered me. I do not wonder, however; they know nothing of my character—my past. Yet why should they be willing to meet me at church or ball, and not within their own doors—at their own fireside? Human ideas and notions are the most puzzling and conflicting things in the universe."

One rainy evening a few days subsequent to the meeting with his employer's daughters, Marlowe sat in the drugstore alone. He had been quite busy all day; and was weary and sleepy. Tilting a straight-backed office chair against the wall, at the end of the bench near the stove, he dropped into it; and crossing his legs, fell into a reverie—as was his habit when alone.

A sense of impending danger or trouble weighed heavily upon him. He felt more depressed, more lonely, than at any time since coming to the village. In vain he called himself a fool and strove to shake off the melancholy that beset him. It clung to him like a veritable nightmare.

"Great heaven!" he muttered at last, irritably springing to his feet and walking up and down the room. "Why am I so tormented? Why must the dead past arise in its grave clothes and haunt me? It is dead—it should remain buried. Pshaw![29] I am morbid. What has come over me tonight? I am safe here; no one connected with the old life knows ought of me or my hiding place. I wish someone would come in. A dog would be welcome company. Listen, how it rains! Where's that Jep with his nonsensical stories? He's like the proverbial small boy—not to be found when one wants him, and under one's feet at all other times."

As if in answer to Ralph's muttered query, the door swung open and Tucker ambled into the store. Turning down the collar of his ragged coat and shaking the water from his dripping cap, he remarked

---
29 pshaw: used to indicate impatience, irritation, disapproval, or disbelief

droningly:

"Black all over an rainin' right straight down in the middle. The ol' doc hain't got back yit, hey? He alluz manages to be out such nights as this. What's the reason that the worse the weather an' the darker the night, the more sickness there is? Seven-levenths o' all the babies that ever come into the world was born on dark, rainy nights—sometime 'twixt midnight an' mornin'. Ever think 'bout it? Didn't? Well, it's a fact. Say!"

"What is it, Jep?" Ralph responded pleasantly.

"W'y, I saw Lon Crider, the drug man, on the street jest a minute ago. He's jest drove down from Malconta—missed the evenin' train. He was askin' 'bout you an' the ol' doc; an' told me to tell you he'd drop in sometime this evenin'."

Ralph nodded affably, but said nothing. He wanted Tucker to ramble on; the eccentric's idle chatter drowned the insistent voices that had been dinning in his ears.

"Do you know what such a night as this alluz reminds me of?" Jep asked after a moment's silence.

"Of what?" Marlowe replied with assumed interest.

"Of the story they used to tell on ol' Bobby Silvey. He was a cooper an' lived in that little frame over back o' the lodge buildin'. By jeeminy! He was the hairiest human bein' I ever set eyes on. Used to wear his shirt bosom open winter an' summer; an' his breast was hairier'n a buffalo robe. An' honest Injin! His face looked like the face o' one o' them white French poodles—like Miss Dolly has. His whiskers growed clean up to his for'ead; an' his eyebrows was so bushy he had to comb 'em. Some people said they was so long he had to curl 'em, to keep 'em out of his eyes. I guess that was stretchin' it a little, though.

"But I was goin' to tell you the story they used to tell on him. He was a great hand to play the fiddle; an' fer sever'l years was the leader o' the Republican Glee Club here. One rainy night—jest such another as this—in the fall o' 'eighty-four, the Glee Club went to a political meetin' out to Foxtown. They got treated to ginger cakes an' cider—ol' Bobby said afterward the cider was so hard he had to break it with a hammer—an' the ol' feller an' his fiddle come home purty well rossumed.

"Well, he didn't git home till late of course; an' he dropped asleep soon as his head hit the piller. But 'long in the after part o' the night, he woke up so dry he thought he'd swallered a good-size-strip o' the Sahary Desert. Out o' bed he tumbled an' made a break fer the kitchen, to git a drink o' water. After he'd drunk 'bout a gallon o' water, he thought he'd jest take a peep out o' doors, to see if the weather had cleared off. But bein' kind o' befuddled with the cider, an' havin' got up in a hurry, he'd got sort o' turned 'round; an' w'en he went to hunt fer the outside door, he got hold o' the one leadin' into the pantry. The next minute his ol' woman heerd him screamin':

"'Git up, mammy! Fer the good Lord's sake git up an' come out here! The end o' the world's come at last! It's blacker 'n a stack o' black cats outside—an' *smells all cheesy!*'

"His ol' woman had a time gittin' him quieted an' back to bed; an' ol' Bobby never heerd the last o' that joke, to his dyin' day."

As Tucker finished he glanced toward the door. Two young men had just entered and were sauntering toward the rear of the room.

"It's Airly Chandler an' Morris McDevitt—ol' Hugh's son," Jep whispered to Ralph.

"Is there something I can do for you, gentlemen?" Marlowe asked as he arose and advanced to meet them.

"No; we just came in to get acquainted," answered the red-headed young man, laughing jerkingly. "Sam Clark sent us. He'll be in himself in a few minutes. You remember me, of course; I was in here the day after you arrived. My name's Chandler."

"I remember you, Mr. Chandler," Ralph replied suavely. "And this is—"

"Morris McDevitt, the junior partner in the McDevitt store—McDevitt and Son, you know. Hello, Jep!"

Marlowe shook hands with both and gave them seats by the fire.

McDevitt was a light-complexioned, thickset young man of twenty-six, with heavy jowls, and light-blue, restless eyes. A drooping blonde mustache half hid his narrow, sensitive mouth, but accentuated his weak, retreating chin. His features were expressive of moodiness and taciturnity.

Barely had a desultory conversation sprung up, ere Clark arrived—followed almost immediately by Lon Crider.

The latter was as well-fed, his cheeks were as rosy, and his black mustache was as symmetrically waxed and twisted, as when Marlowe had met him upon the train. His clothes were carefully brushed, his linen was spotless; and the ever-present carnation was in his buttonhole.

He shook hands all around, greeting each individual with a personal remark, a musical chuckle—and a tender of a cigar. Then as a fitting finale to the whole, he familiarly slapped Ralph upon the shoulder, exclaiming:

"How are you anyhow, old man? I'm beastly glad to find you here—thought maybe I'd hear you'd 'flew de coop.' You've been cleaning up things, too. By grab! You've got everything shining like a silver doorplate. You're a hot number, Marlowe, my boy. But where's the old doc? Don't say he's out in the country, now, and won't be back tonight. You'll break my heart."

"That's just what I must say, if I tell the truth," Ralph answered, resuming his seat and pointing Crider to a vacant chair.

"Then I'd just as well spend an hour gassing to you fellows, before I return to the hotel to write up my orders. You must want some goods this time, don't you, Marlowe? The old man has held me off the last two or three trips. I don't know what's the matter."

"We need some goods," Ralph answered. "But you'll have to see Dr. Barwood."

"All right. I'll catch him for an order this trip, if it takes a week of my three-thousand-a-year time to do it."

The conversation became general. Crider, Clark, and Tucker vied with one another as to who could talk the most and say the least. The weather, the state of the country roads, the trade of the village, and the coming election were all discussed. Marlowe and Chandler occasionally ventured a remark or asked a question, to keep the conversation from flagging. McDevitt listened attentively and nodded or shook his head when appealed to, but said little.

At last the talk drifted to hunting; at which the loquacious Jep brightened visibly—until he completely outshone his younger rivals.

"Talkin' 'bout huntin'," he drawled through his nose, "ther' used to be an ol' feller in these parts, by the name o' Josh Springer, who could spin some o' the whoppin'est huntin' yarns you ever heerd tell of. He was a funny lookin' critter, too. One leg was two 'r three inches shorter'n t'other; an' he sort o' hitched along when he walked. An' his face would 'ave made a pattern for a comic volentine. His chin was double, his nose was blue an' bumpy; an' he chawed his tobacker on his snaggledy front teeth—like a ground squir'l gnawin' a nut.

"But I started out to tell you some o' his whoppin' yarns. One of 'em was 'bout shootin' a squir'l off 'n a tall shellbark hick'ry. Said he treed it, an' tried fer quite a spell to git a shot at it; but it kept movin' 'round an' 'round the tree, fast as he did. Said at last he got mad an' hit the tree a clite with his gun, bendin' the bar'l till it looked like a half a wagon tire.

"The squir'l was on the opposite side o' the tree from him, of course. So he ups an' pokes the muzzle o' the gun 'round the trunk—elevatin' the bar'l at the proper angle—an' blazes away. Well, sir, he said the result was startlin'. Said the bullet went circlin' 'round that tree trunk, zippin' the bark an' climbin' higher an' higher as it went. Said the squir'l got 'xcited at the bang o' the gun; an' it went to circlin' 'round the tree, too. 'Cordin' to his own tale, Josh stood an' watched the p'rformance—an' nearly died a laughin'. 'Round an' 'round went the squir'l—faster'n a streak o' greased lightnin'; an' after it—an' gainin' little by little—whizzed the bullet. Josh said it was 'bout fifteen minutes by the watch, 'fore the bullet ketched up with that squir'l an' killed it."

Jep scored a hit. His auditors laughed heartily—more at the serious manner in which he told the absurd tale than at the tale itself. Encouraged by the applause, he went on:

"That's jest a sample o' the yarns that ol' feller used to spin.

He was chuck full of 'em—fuller'n a pumpkin is o' seeds. But the one that knocked the persimmons was the one he used to tell 'bout shootin' the nineteen pigeons. Ever hear that one?"—With a sweeping glance at his audience.

"I never did," laughed Crider. "Go on—tell it, anyhow."

"Well, the way ol' Josh told it was this: He was out huntin' pigeons one day in the fall o' the year—ther' used to be scads o' pigeons in this part o' the country in the early days—an' he run 'cross a small flock of 'em roostin' in a big ellum tree. They was all settin' in a row on a long, slim limb—jest like clo'es pins on a line. Josh said he had a rifle with him, but only two bullets—one in the gun an' one in his pocket. So he studied how he could git all them pigeons at one shot, knowin' that what he didn't kill the first crack 'ld up an' fly away.

"At last he hit on a plan. He makes a little noise in the leaves, to skeer 'em; an' jest as they was tiptoein' to fly away, he cuts loose with his ol' rifle. The bullet split the limb; an' the toes o' nineteen o' the pigeons was ketched in the crack. He said ther' was twenty of 'em, all together; but one of 'em didn't happen to git ketched.

"Of course folks 'ld ask him how he got 'em down out o' the tree. An' he'd say he loaded up ag'in, shot off the limb they was strung to—an' down they dropped kerslap.

"One time Cy Plumley said to him:

"'Josh, if I was tellin' that story, I'd say I ketched the whole twenty. I wouldn't spile an even number, the way you do.'

"'Well,' says Josh, crustier 'n a burnt corn dodger, 'maybe *you'd* tell a *darn lie* fer one pigeon, Cy Plumley; but *I wouldn't.*'"

Again they laughed—Jep boisterously. It is but fair to state, however, that Clark surreptitiously consulted his watch, and that Marlowe and McDevitt yawned behind their hands.

"Say!" Crider exclaimed abruptly. "I had an experience the other day, worth relating. Want to hear it?"

"Is it another Josh Springer yarn?" McDevitt asked gravely, winking at Ralph.

"Now hear him try to outdo Tucker," remarked Chandler.

"Stop your chaffing, you fellows," Clark cried.

"Let him spread himself. We're tough—we can stand it. Go on, Crider. Your hour's about up."

The drummer deliberately lighted a fresh cigar, puffed away in silence for some seconds, and then began:

"Let's see—today's Friday. Well, it was last Monday; and I was on the *Katrina,* coming from Marietta up to Lowell. There were quite a number of passengers aboard; and among them a tall, scrawny, oldish-like man, who had been over in the West Virginia mountains, hunting deer. That's what he said, at least; and I suppose he told the truth, for he had two deer hounds chained up on the boiler deck, and the cabin was littered with his traps—guns, belts of shells, leggins, and all the paraphernalia of a Nimrod[30].

"Of course we got to talking to him, asking him how many deer he had killed and all manner of questions, and trying our best to draw him out. But it was no go; he was closer than next election day, and to our questions returned answers that were shorter than good pie crust. The rest of the passengers finally got discouraged and gave up trying to smoke him out; but like a fool I persisted. At last he smiled benignly on me—in a way that made me feel bigger than a conquering hero—and said:

"'Young man, such persistency as you have shown should not go unrewarded. I take it you want me to spin you a yarn, to while away the tedium of this short but slow voyage—to tell you an adventurous story of hunting wild animals, in their native haunts.'

"That was exactly what I *did* want; and I was not slow in so expressing myself. He went on smiling that benign smile and looking thoughtful, for some time. Finally he said:

"'I can tell you a good bear story.'

"'All right—tell it,' I answered with alacrity.

"He commenced in an easy, smooth way that attracted and held everybody's attention. His story—as near as I can remember it— was about like this:

"I was born up at Andover, Maine—a little hamlet occupying

---
30 nimrod: a hunter

a green amphitheater among the granite-capped spurs of the White Mountains. Just north of the village lies a string of small lakes, today the Mecca of hundreds of city fishermen. When I was a lad, thirty-five years ago, the woods surrounding the town were full of bear, deer, and smaller game; and, like all the other boys of the neighborhood, I wasted much time hunting and fishing. As you see, the idle habit has clung to me.

"'One day in summer, when I was about fifteen years old, I shouldered my father's old musket and set out across the hills. I tramped mile after mile without discovering any signs of game. But along in the afternoon, when I was about ready to abandon my quest and return home, I came upon a bear track in the soft, wet sand along the side of a brook. I was hunter enough to know the track was a fresh one; and, boy-like, I rashly resolved to follow it, if possible, and have a shot at the animal. I succeeded only too well. For I had not gone a hundred yards along its trail, when—with a great crashing of brush and a roar that made my hair stand on end—the bear sprang out of a clump of bushes and advanced upon me. It was a female; and the cause of her aggressiveness was the fact that she had two small cubs with her.

"'Instantly I threw my gun to my shoulder and pulled the trigger. But I was trembling with excitement and my aim was bad. As a consequence I only succeeded in wounding the mother bear and enraging her the more. Ere I could think about reloading my empty piece, she was upon me. With a blow of her paw she sent the musket spinning from my grasp. Then, rearing upon her hind feet and growling hideously, she stretched forth her arms to give me a fatal hug. I saw her burning eyeballs, her red mouth, and flashing teeth; and felt her hot breath upon my face. I was paralyzed with fear; my limbs were like lead. I tried to scream—but could not.

"'Then of a sudden I recovered my presence of mind. And whirling like a flash, I dashed away as fast as my strong and nimble legs could carry me. The bear dropped from her erect posture and swiftly rolled after me. I had never known until then what powers of speed the lumbering brutes possess; and as I crashed through brush and brambles in my mad flight, I cursed the temerity that had led me to put the question to a test. For in spite of my best endeavors, the bear steadily gained upon me.

"'Just when I was ready to drop from exhaustion, I spied a narrow cleft between two large granite rocks that lay in my path; and I made a final effort to reach the asylum that so providentially offered. I felt if I could reach the rocks and wedge myself between them, the infuriated brute could not reach me. But I was doomed to disappointment. For when within ten feet of the place, my foot caught upon a running vine and I fell headlong to the ground. In a moment the bear had pounced upon me and was tearing at my vitals.'

"Well," Crider continued, "the mighty Nimrod stopped right there, as if he'd got to the end of his story. Of course everybody was on the tiptoe of expectancy—myself included. But the old fellow calmly and deliberately lighted his pipe, took a few long-drawn and delicious pulls, and commenced to turn the pages of a magazine he had been reading. We all looked at one another in wonder; but nobody said anything. At last I couldn't hold in any longer, and I asked as unconcernedly as I could:

"'Well, how did it come out?'

"'Eh?' the old fellow answered, looking up as if greatly surprised.

"'How did your adventure terminate?" I asked.

"Terminate?" he said softly, again smiling that sweet, benign smile. *'Oh, the bear killed me!'*

"And I got up and took a sneak," Crider concluded, "followed by roars and peals of laughter at my expense. Those other passengers had been laying to catch me on that story, ever since I had boarded the boat at Marietta."

The drummer arose; and chuckling until his countenance assumed an apoplectic hue and his watch charm danced a merry jig upon his protuberant abdomen, hurried toward the door.

With the knob in his hand he paused long enough to fling over his shoulder:

"Be in to see you in the morning, Marlowe;" Then he was

gone—a zigzag plume of tobacco smoke marking his wake.

"What do you say to that one for a whopper, Jep?" Chandler laughed, tenderly toying with the mole upon his chin.

"I'll bet ten dollars it never happened," cried Clark; "bet Crider made up the whole thing."

"No; he did not invent the story," Marlowe stated positively, "I have heard it a few hundred times before."

"It's a good one, anyhow," McDevitt remarked dryly. "Perhaps it's like whisky—improves with age."

"A lie's a lie," Tucker said musingly. "Some of 'em's good an' some of 'em's bad; but all of 'em's immortal an' lives fer ever.

"There's somethin' funny 'bout that," he continued philosophically. "Ever think of it? If one o' you fellers 'ld start out through the country tonight an' tell ev'rybody you met that Babylon was burnt to the ground, ninety-nine people out of a hundred 'ld b'lieve it. An' a dozen truthful men might foller in y'r track, sayin' the story was a lie; and ther' wouldn't be one in a hundred but 'ld still have their doubts 'bout the matter. Talk 'bout truth bein' mighty an' bound to prevail! W'y, one lie well told an' properly 'mpressed 'll live longer 'n holy writ. 'Tain't right, p'raps—but it's so."

Then Jep picked up the lighted lantern he had brought in with him, turned up the wick, arose stiffly, and went out mumbling:

"Can't be with you fellers alluz. Got to go and bed down the hosses—an' go to roost myself."

"Now," said Clark briskly, when the sound of Tucker's footsteps had died out, "those two gassers are gone, Marlowe, I'll tell you what we came in for. A crowd of us boys and girls are going up to Malconta, next Tuesday night, to the show. We want you to go along with us. We'll find you a girl—"

"Perhaps he would rather make his own selection," McDevitt suggested.

"That's all right," the agent went on. "He can make his choice; and we'll see that he gets it. No trouble about that. What do you say, Marlowe, will you go with us? We're going to drive up and back—

two or three barouche[31] loads. It'll be an elegant trip. What do you say?"

"I shall be pleased to go with you, if I find I can leave on that particular evening. Dr. Barwood is very busy now; and—"

"You can lock up the old ranch," Clark cried impatiently; "it won't run off. We'll have a jolly good time. We'll start about six o'clock—we can make the drive in two hours, easy. McDevitt's going to take Mame Gridley; I'm going to take his sister, Rose; and Chandler's going to take Gertrude Bentley. There's lots of pretty girls for you to pick from—Jennie Gridley, Bell Akers, Fannie Richards, Dolly Barwood, and so on. You might prefer the other Miss Barwood—Julia; but she don't go to shows."

"What kind of show is this?" Ralph asked.

"A theater—a play," Clark replied. "They've got a dandy new opera-house up there at Malconta; and are getting some good shows. This one's a kind of a farce-comedy, I guess—lots of dancing and singing and fun in it. Let's see—What's the name of it, Morris?"

"The Cider and the Pie," was McDevitt's answer.

At the announcement Marlowe caught his breath sharply and turned pale to the lips. His companions noticed his agitation, and looked wonderingly at him—and at one another. Recovering his equanimity, by a strong effort, he said calmly:

"I turned sick suddenly—a pain in the region of my heart. In regard to the show. I have seen it—and do not care to see it again. It is light—frothy. You will be disappointed in it."

They did not urge him to alter his decision; but after a few moments of embarrassing silence arose and took their departure. Each of the three suspected he had stumbled upon a hidden tragedy; yet hoped he was mistaken—and feared to mention his suspicions to his comrades.

Left alone, Ralph Marlowe sat with bowed head, murmuring softly, sadly, to himself:

"The past dogs me—a merciless Nemesis. I thought I had buried myself alive; but the prying eye of inexorable fate has spied out my

---

31 barouche: a 4-wheeled horse-drawn carriage with a folding top and a driver's seat outside

tomb. The walled city of Babylon even"—And he smiled grimly—"is not a secure hiding place. And yet it may be. I will dissuade Clark from attending the performance at Malconta; he is the moving spirit. Yes, I must do that. For if my name should be spoken in the hearing of certain members of the troupe—and it might be, the agent and his friends noticed my agitation at mention of the title of the play—it would get to *her* ears; and that would mean my undoing, my ruin."

Arising, he agitatedly walked to the front door and peered through the glass at the dark, wet night without. Then mechanically he turned down the lights, passed out, locking the door behind him, and hurried away in the direction of the hotel.

* * * * * *

CHAPTER VII

THE DAY following—Saturday—Marlowe was early at his post of duty. Tucker, as was his custom, built the fire and helped with the sweeping and dusting. Just as they had finished, Dr. Barwood hustled into the store, saying:

"I am going to spend an hour or two in posting my books and writing letters. I do not wish to be disturbed, unless it be a matter of importance."

"The Baldy Drug Company's man called to see you last night," Ralph remarked carelessly.

"Crider?"

"Yes. He said he would be in again this morning."

"He desired to see me, did he?"—With lifted lip and flashing teeth.

"That's what he said, doctor."

"And *I* wish to see *him*," the physician snarled as he started for his private room. "When he comes, call me."

Barely had the doctor's bullet head disappeared through the rear door, ere the drummer's smiling visage appeared at the front entrance.

"Good morning, Marlowe," he cried cheerily.

"The old doc turned up yet?"

"He has just gone into his office," Ralph replied.

"Good!"—Gleefully rubbing his' hands.—"You told him I called last night—and that I was coming in this morning?"

"Yes."

"What did he say?"—In a tone of eager expectancy.

"He said he wished to see you; told me to call him when you came."

"That surely means an order, eh?" whispered Crider, beaming seraphically[32]. "Tell him I'm waiting to see him."

Smiling to himself, Ralph did as requested. A minute later, Dr. Barwood fiercely scowling stood facing his caller.

"Good morning, doctor," the latter cried advancing with outstretched hand, "How's the world using you, anyhow?"

"The world uses me much better than the people in it do," growled the doctor, ignoring the proffered hand and resolutely holding his own behind him. "What do you want?"

"Ther's a jimmycane a brewin'," muttered Jep sidling toward the front door. "An' as I ain't hankerin' to see it, I'll jest tunnel a hole through the atmosphere an' make my escape."

Dr. Barwood's frigid manner and brusque question greatly disconcerted the jolly drummer. Blushing like a schoolmiss, he stammered awkwardly:

"Why, I—I came in to see you, doctor; thought maybe you'd want to—to—"

"Do I owe your house anything?" the physician interrupted coldly.

"No, doc—that is, doctor," Crider hastened to say; "you remember you paid off the last bill a month or two ago. You haven't bought anything of me since."

"And I owe you nothing?"

"Not a red, doc—doctor, I mean."

"Then," Dr. Barwood fairly hissed, "your room is more desirable than your company—and you can go!"

---

32 seraphically: angelic-like

"Why, doctor, I—I don't understand"—Crider began sputteringly.

"Oh, you don't!"—With a sneer.

"No, doctor, I don't," answered the traveling man in a hurt tone. "What have I or the house done to deserve such treatment?"

"You have robbed me—that's what!"

"Robbed you?"

"Yes."

"Have they been stuffing your orders?"

"Worse than that—as you well know. Your house has charged me with things I never ordered and they never sent."

"Doc, I—I can't believe it—"

"Hold!" thundered Dr. Barwood. "Not another word along that line, I warn you. You doubt my word, but you will not doubt your own sense of sight, perhaps. Look here."—Drawing a folded paper from his coat pocket and hastily opening it.—"Here I am charged with articles I never ordered and never received. Look!"—Running his long, white index finger, along the lines.—"One-twelfth dozen leather-covered, screw-capped, pocket flasks; one dozen Mumm's extra dry champagne; one hundred fine, pure Havana cigars; one-sixth dozen enameled playing cards; five hundred rubber poker chips; and so on. *I* never *ordered* those things."

Crider had partially regained his composure. Now he answered blandly:

"That's so, doc. But Snedeker, your last clerk before Marlowe, *did* order them."

"And I never *received* them!" the doctor shouted, slapping his palm with the folded bill and glaring ferociously at the little drummer.

"The house shipped them, doctor; *somebody* received them," Crider replied meekly.

"And *I* paid for them."

"Yes, you paid for them, doc—I mean doctor!"

"Yes!" fairly bellowed the physician. "You and your house knew that scoundrel was robbing me; and you gave me no warning. I'll never buy another cent's worth of goods—"

"Doc," Crider interrupted in a plaintive, wheedling tone, "listen to me just a minute—please do. I tried to tell you more than once what was going on; and you—"

"Go to perdition—and stay there!" Dr. Barwood roared, stamping into the rear room and banging the door.

"Look at that now!" Crider wailed tearfully, dropping into a chair and looking appealingly at Ralph. "How unreasonable a man can be! I tried a dozen different times, to hint to the old doc that his clerks were ordering stuff for themselves and having it charged in his bills. But every time he gave me to understand it was his business; and advised me to attend to my own. What could I do but take the orders; and what could the house do but fill them? And now I've lost his trade; and the firm'll give me a currying. Confound the luck! A drummer sees the toughest time, of anybody on earth. Do you think you could do anything with him, Marlowe?"

"I don't know," Ralph replied, musingly stroking his chin.

"Better not try it," Crider said dejectedly. "He might get mad at you—and fire you."

"I'll make the venture at any rate," answered Ralph with sudden resolution.

"You will?"—Springing joyfully to his feet and grasping the other's hand.—"Marlowe, you're a trump! But no—I'm selfish. You shan't do anything of the kind. It'll do no good—and get you into trouble."

But at the same time he anxiously scanned his companion's face, to see if he still held his resolve.

Without more ado Ralph walked to the rear door, opened it—and bearded the lion in his den, thus:

"Doctor, there are some goods we need. Shall I give the order to Mr. Crider, or send it to a Columbus firm?"

The doctor was writing busily. Without looking up, he answered:

"Order *what* you please, of *whom* you please."

"But what is *your* pleasure, doctor?"

"That you do what you like," the physician muttered irritably.

"I give you license."

"Thank you," Ralph replied, quietly withdrawing.

On returning to the drug room, he gave Crider an order for the goods needed. The latter was delighted, and was profuse in his thanks, saying among other things:

"Marlowe, you have saved the day for me. If I can ever accommodate you, all you'll have to do is to say the word. It appears that you can twist the old doc around your finger; and you're the only person that I ever knew that could do it. I wish you all kinds of good luck; and feel that I'm under everlasting obligations to you. I'll be around again in a few weeks. So long."

When the drummer had taken his departure, Ralph again invaded the privacy of Dr. Barwood's office.

"I have nothing to do at present," he said. "Can I not help you with your work?"

"Do you *desire* to do so?" the doctor asked, a peculiar light dancing in his beady eyes.

"Of course."

"Very well. Leave the door ajar, that you may watch the outer room. Here."—Shoving him a ledger and pointing to pen and ink.—"You may post books while I look after my accumulated correspondence. There's my pocket visiting list at your elbow."

For a while they worked away in silence. At last the older man laid down his pen, sealed the envelope he had addressed, and leaning back in his chair and half closing his eyes, asked tentatively:

"How do you like your place, by this time?"

"With you, doctor?"

"Certainly."

"I am well pleased with it."

"You say that to gratify me."

"And does it gratify you, doctor?"

"If it be the truth, yes."

"Do you doubt my word?"

"N-o. Yet—"

"Well?"

"To hear anyone speak well of me or my employ is a new experience."

And Dr. Barwood laughed a grating laugh—that had in it a ring of sadness.

"I like your employ—and I like you, doctor," Ralph boldly ventured.

"Huh! No doubt *you* believe what you are saying," was the ungracious rejoinder.

"But *you* do *not,*" Marlowe completed.

Dr. Barwood made no reply; but sullenly resumed his work. A half hour later he looked up to inquire:

"Are you comfortably situated at the hotel?"

"The meals are fair, and the bed is clean," Ralph replied, busily scratching away with his pen.

"What of your room?"

"It is small; has no fire in it—and is not gorgeously furnished."

"You are satisfied with the fare?"

"Yes."

"But not with your quarters?"

"Hardly."

For a few moments the doctor contemplatively bit his thin mustache and fingered the long watch guard that encircled his neck. Then he remarked casually:

"I own the large frame dwelling just above here—the one with the broad portico and green shutters. Mrs. Hammond and her two grown sons occupy a part of it; but there are two large, communicating, front rooms on the ground floor, that are vacant. You are welcome to them, if you care to go to the expense of furnishing them."

"I shall be glad of the opportunity, doctor," Ralph answered quietly. "But how much rent will you expect?"

"None," snapped the doctor.

"Then I will not occupy the rooms."

"Why?"

"You know my reason, doctor—the reason you would have."

"You are independent—you do not care to be under

obligations."

Marlowe nodded and went on writing.

"Well, to satisfy you," Dr. Barwood said, his black eyes sparkling, "I will charge you a nominal rent. Make out an order for the furniture and furnishings you want, sign my name to it, and send it to Burn Brothers at Malconta."

"I may not have the money to pay for the things, when they come," Ralph objected.

"I'll pay for them," the physician returned dryly. "If I have to discharge you before you have reimbursed me, I'll have furnished rooms for your successor. Will you send the order?"

"On the conditions you have named."

There the subject was dropped.

The next day being Sunday, Marlowe had more or less leisure. In the afternoon he and Clark took a walk around the village, and back onto the adjacent hills. The sky was cloudless; the sunshine was genial. Upon a rocky point overlooking the broad expanse of valley, the two young men seated themselves and silently contemplated the beauties of the scene.

Through the center of the rolling plain—ramparted by brown hills—flowed the bonny Muskingum, sparkling and dancing in the yellow sunlight. To the right stretched the broad acres of Flat Bottom dotted with cosy farmhouses and checkered with fields of golden corn stubble and tender green wheat. To the left reached the rich alluvium of The Backwater—the site of an ancient lake—corn shocks mingling with clumps of russet willows, and the towering white shafts of giant sycamores punctuating the level page. Up the river, in the far distance, loomed the rock-ribbed sides of Bishop's Ridge, blue and indistinct; and at their feet nestled the peaceful village—somnolent and still.

"Pretty scene, isn't it?" Clark remarked at last, his pale face alight with genuine admiration.

"Yes," Marlowe answered softly.

But he did not look at his companion; and a faraway expression was in his dark eyes.

"What are you thinking of?" the operator asked, laughing. "You're staring out into space, like a dog pointing a covey of quails. Come—wake up."—Playfully shaking his companion's arm.— "What are you thinking about?"

"I? Oh! I hardly know," Ralph stammered, rousing himself and smiling confusedly.

"Guess you're a little homesick," Clark said at a venture.

"No, I am not," Marlowe answered decidedly.

"You wouldn't want to live here all your life, though?"

"Yes. Why not?"

"Well, I'll be blowed!" was all the astounded operator could ejaculate.

Silence reigned for several minutes—Ralph resuming his reverie, Clark narrowly observing him. At last the latter cried:

"Say, Marlowe! You remind me of a story they tell on Joe Staffer, an old stonemason and bricklayer who used to live here—just died last year."

" Indeed?" Ralph returned absent-mindedly.

"Yes, you do. Let me tell you the tale. For by Christmas! you need something to wake you up."

"Go on."

"Well, open your eyes and listen to me."

"I am all attention."

"Yes—so's a dead man. But here goes anyhow. Old Joe was a mighty good workman at his trade, but *would* drink—had been a heavy drinker all his life. And that reminds me of some of the schemes he resorted to, to get liquor.

"A few years ago—while the old man was still living, of course—the people voted for local option here and run out the saloons for a season or two. That made it pretty tough on the habituals, like Joe; for the drugstore sold only on prescription—and for such as him to get a prescription was out of the question. But he was equal to the emergency, you bet.

"He worked it like this: He put in his leisure time making rings and canes for his friends; and he used an alcohol lamp in doing the brazing of ferules and so on. Well, when that local option went into effect—and he couldn't get whisky—he commenced to drink alcohol. He'd go over to the drugstore two or three times a day, carrying his lamp with him; get it filled, and go back home and water and sweeten and drink the contents.

"The old doc tumbled to the racket, and ordered the clerk not to fill the lamp any more. Joe was disappointed but not discouraged. He got an open-mouthed bottle; went over to the drugstore, and asked the clerk to put a few cents' worth of gum shellac in it and fill it up with alcohol. Said he wanted to make shellac varnish to varnish canes with.

"Of course the clerk didn't suspect the old man meant to drink the mixture—nor did he do it. But you know better than I can tell you how long it takes alcohol to cut shellac. And Joe hurried home, poured off the alcohol before it had time to get its work in, and had a square drink.

"Well, the old doc got onto *that* game, too; and put a quietus[33] upon it. But Joe still held a trump card up his sleeve. He next bought a half-pint of spirits of camphor; diluted it with water, to precipitate the gum; and took a snifter of the clear liquid that was left. That pretty near fixed him. Old doc was up working with him all one night.

"About this time, Philetus Palmerson over on Heathen Ridge hired Joe to build a chimney. It was an outside concern of stone and brick—stone up to the taper, and brick the rest of the way. Joe got a gallon jug of whisky from Malconta, and went at it—chimney and whisky, too. He kept so drunk all the time, that when he got the chimney up to the comb of the roof, it looked as if it had been twisted by a bolt of lightning, and was tottering to its fall. The old man felt it quivering and shaking, and knew what was going to happen. So he clambered off onto the roof and bellowed to the helpers below, who were mixing mortar and sorting bricks:

"'Look out down there! I've changed my plan!'

"And over the chimney went. And," Clark concluded, laughing heartily, "that'll be the way with you. One o' these fine days you'll

---
33 quietus: death; a final discharge

wake up—and find the earth slipping from under you. Then you'll suddenly change your plan—and get out of this place on double-quick."

Marlowe smiled; but at the same time he suspiciously eyed his companion, whispering to himself:

"What does he mean? Does he suspect something? Nonsense! What could he suspect—he knows nothing."

So fixed was the druggist's gaze that the agent asked petulantly:

"What the deuce ails you, Marlowe? Are you crazy or drunk, that you gawk at me so wildly?"

To this outburst Ralph laughingly replied:

"Neither, my peppery friend. I was just thinking that you are badly mistaken in your surmises—that you have made a false application of the moral of your story."

"How so? What do you mean?"

"Just this: I have determined that I like Dr. Barwood; that I like to work for him."

Clark. opened his eyes very wide, dropped his jaw and stared hard at his companion as though questioning his sanity. At last he managed to exclaim:

"The—mischief—you—do!"

"Yes," Marlowe went on quietly, "and I have made up my mind to stay with him as long as he will let me. Yesterday he tendered me two nice rooms in the house occupied by Mrs. Hammond, at a merely nominal rent; and offered to advance me the money to furnish them. I shall be deserting my kennel at the hotel soon."

"Say!" cried Clark, slapping his thigh and haw-hawing heartily, "You've hypnotized the old doc, Marlowe—you surely have. I'm glad to hear of your good luck, anyway. The first thing you know he'll give you a share in the business and throw one of his daughters at your head—Dolly, likely."

"That will do," Ralph said sternly.

"What's the matter?" his companion asked with concern.

"Please do not couple the young lady's name with mine. Indeed,

I am not in the matrimonial market. At any rate, I am no fortune-hunter."

Then in as careless a tone as he could assume:

"Is your set going to the show at Malconta, next Tuesday night?"

"No, I suppose not," Clark replied, wrinkling his pale features serio-comically. "You took good care to knock that in the head."

"I?"

"Yes, you. You talked disparagingly of the show—said it was frothy, and frivolous, and all that. The manner in which you spoke of it made Chandler believe it an immoral play; and he's gone around and told all the girls. The result is you couldn't haul one of them within gunshot of it, with a rope around their necks. Then McDevitt's opposed to going, too. I don't think he really wanted to go in the first place."

"He *appeared* anxious to go."

"Oh, yes—he *appeared!* But all the same he *wasn't* anxious. He don't want to do anything any more unless Julia Barwood sanctions it; and she don't believe in shows and dances, and such things. Morris hasn't been to but one dance in the last three months. There's just two things he's in the habit of doing that he knows displeases her. He will attend his own church—he's a Catholic; and he can't resist the fascination of a little game of poker. I don't know whether she knows about *that,* though."

"Do you play poker, Clark?"

"Yes—sometimes. All the boys do, more or less, except Chandler. Maybe he would if he wasn't afraid of losing his certificate as a pedagogue[34]—I don't know."

"Where do you play?"

"Sometimes in the room back of the hotel bar—"

"What!"

Unheeding his companion's exclamation, the little operator went on glibly:

"Sometimes in my room, and sometimes—on Sundays—in

---

34. pedagogue: a schoolteacher

the back room of McDevitt's store. We think of having a game this evening. Won't you join us?"

"No."—Flatly.

"Why?"

" I think it wrong to gamble."

"You can't call the game we play gambling. We just play for amusement. No one's ever out, in any one game, more than a few dollars."

"The principle involved is the same, whether the stake be one dollar or a thousand."

"Then you don't believe in any games of chance?"

"Not if played for a stake. Gambling—the effort to get something for nothing—is wrong, no matter what the device used."

"How about lotteries, betting on elections and other things, dealing in stocks, and so on—are they gambling?"

"Let me repeat. Wherever money is risked or invested, with a hope of winning and a chance of losing—and without the winner giving or the loser receiving adequate compensation in return—it is gambling."

"I see. Then a good many so-called business transactions are merely gambling schemes."

"Yes. And that fact is the paramount reason why our economic system is not a success—why the rich are growing richer and the poor are growing poorer. Everybody thirsts for money; desires wealth, no matter how acquired. So they gamble. And the few win; the many lose."

"That's so," Clark said soberly. Then smiling:

"But what would you call selling prize packages and raffling, like they do at church fairs—gambling?"

"Certainly."

"Say! you're better than some preachers."

"Yes—I am a moralist," Ralph laughed.

"I don't care what you are," his companion said solemnly. "You are talking good sense—and you're giving me something to think about. I like to listen to you. Now I want to ask you a few questions—

for information."

"Go on."

"Isn't insurance gambling—life insurance and fire insurance?"

"I think not," Ralph answered promptly. "A life insurance company does not deal with a single individual only, but with many. What it loses to one it wins from another. In the aggregate it makes—or should make—but a fair profit on its investment. It does not seek to get something for nothing. Nor is there any chance about the business—taking the risks collectively. The company is sure of a profit—that is all it asks. Nor does the party insured strive to get something for nothing. He does not wish to win until late in life. He is perfectly satisfied to live and pay his premiums. Yet he—or his heirs— are bound to win in the end. Do you follow me?"

"Yes. But don't the parties insured gamble against each other, then—like fellows betting on a wheel of fortune? And isn't the company like the owner of the wheel—getting a per cent of the stake at every whirl?"

"You are shrewd and farseeing," Marlowe laughed. "There is a seeming similarity, I admit. It is one of the instances where legitimate business nearly approaches gambling. But here is the marked difference between the two. The man who loses twenty-five dollars on a single turn of the wheel of fortune—or in any game of chance—and has no more money to risk, gets *nothing* in return; the individual who pays twenty-five dollars premium on a thousand dollar policy, and who has no more money—and must drop his insurance at the end of the year—receives a *year's protection* in return for his cash. And he is—or ought to be— satisfied."

"I see," Clark answered, nodding and batting his eyes.

Then after a moody silence of several minutes:

"Honestly now, Marlowe, what harm can there be in my playing a fair and square game of poker, for small stakes? What I lose in one game I win in another. And it's such good sport!"

"You argue just as I used to do," Ralph replied gravely.

"Herein lies the harm—the danger, rather: You are cultivating an appetite that is inherent in most human beings, an appetite that is all too easily developed—the appetite for gambling; the dishonest desire to take without giving ought in return; the taste for high and reckless play. I venture the assertion that you young fellows who have been gambling, play for larger stakes now than you did in the beginning. Am I not right?"

"Y-e-s, you are," Clark reluctantly admitted. "And some of the boys are constantly urging that the limit be raised still higher. You're right in what you say; I can see it. McDevitt and one or two others have been going to Malconta lately, to play in bigger games. But look here. Taking your view of the matter, wouldn't it be better not to play cards at all—for fun even?"

"Would you refuse to speed your horse on the public highway, because gamblers bet on horse-races; or fear to exercise the right of suffrage, because they place wagers on elections?"

"Hardly. But playing cards is different."

"Listen," Marlowe said earnestly. "The sun is sinking; we have not time to discuss the matter further. However, let me say this,—it is my opinion, and you are not bound to accept it as a final solution of the knotty problem—there is no hard and fast line between right and wrong. The one imperceptibly merges into the other. On the one side is temperance, on the other, intemperance. But the point that divides them is illy defined. Some things are essentially right; some things are essentially wrong. Others still are debatable. A course of action may be questionable, not because of inherent evil, but because of some remote or possible temptation or danger connected with it. Some moralists would say avoid it—and thus avoid the danger; others would say follow it—face, defy, and overcome the temptation, thus gaining strength to resist greater ones, and thus developing moral stamina and character. Each individual must decide for himself. To my mind, the final test of any course of action is the effect or result of it. If it invariably—or generally—produces a bad result, it is wrong; if it usually produces a good result, it is right. It is the duty of each person to get all the light he can—from whatever source—make conscientious use of his reasoning faculties, and decide mooted questions for himself."

Slowly Marlowe arose, brushed the dust from his clothing, and with the words—"Let us return to town"—started down the slope. Clark silently walked at his side, pondering deeply what he had heard.

On reaching the level at the foot of the hill, Ralph turned to the agent with the remark:

"You said something about McDevitt shaping his habits to please Miss Barwood. What did you mean?"

"Eh?" Clark returned vacantly, staring like one suddenly wakened. " Oh! You want to know what I meant by saying that McDevitt don't like to do anything that displeases Julia Barwood? Well, just this: they've been keeping company off and on for several years. They like each other, I'm sure; but they'll never get married."

"Why?"

"For two reasons: In the first place, her father opposes the match—not because he has anything against McDevitt, but just because he *is* a McDevitt—though he lets him come to the house and call on his daughter. But I don't *think* the old doc's opposition would cut much figure with Julia, if she once made up her mind to marry McDevitt; and I *know* it wouldn't with Morris. But the second reason—and the main one—is that Julia's a Protestant and Morris is a Catholic; and neither one's willing to give up their belief for the belief of the other. He wants her to come over to the Catholic Church; she wants him to join the Methodists. That's the lay of the land exactly. So I don't think they'll ever get married. And one of these days Morris McDevitt'll get discouraged—he's inclined to fits of the blues, anyhow—and he'll cut loose and go to the devil, like old Number Six on a down grade, with the throttle wide open."

"Does he drink?" Ralph asked carelessly.

"Not much—a little once in a while."

"As you do."

"Yes." And Clark laughed uneasily.—"We don't drink much—any of us fellows—just a few glasses of beer occasionally. Do you think *that* wrong?"

"It is not wrong, perhaps. But you are running an unnecessary risk, it may be. You ought not to drink at the bar of a common groggery, that is certain; and you ought never to drink to excess, nor gamble. Barroom loafing is a most seductive idleness; it winds itself insidiously around its victims until they are bound and helpless in its thralls. When I have fitted up my rooms, I will offer you and your comrades a rendezvous. You may drop in every evening, if you like. We will form a social club: read, chat, and play games. But vulgarity, profanity and kindred bad habits will be tabooed. Temperance—in the sense of self-reliance and self-control—will be our aim and motto. How does the idea strike you?"

"All of a heap!" the operator cried joyfully. "You couldn't suit *me* better. You understand us fellows—you do. I can see what you're after; you want to reform us young heathens. But you don't go after us like Julia Barwood does; you don't preach at all—you reason. She nags—and that don't do any good. You're right, too. As near as I can understand, you mean that it's a fellow's duty to study out what will hurt himself or others, and let it alone; and his privilege to indulge in any pastime that won't injure himself or others. Isn't that it?"

Ralph nodded.

"Well," Clark continued, "you can count on me; and I know the other fellows will fall right into line. Julia Barwood, now—she lectures us on all occasions. She says it's wicked to dance, play cards, and go to theaters. When I asked her why, she said because the discipline of her church forbids it. And when I answered that I could see no harm in such things, that the Bible didn't say anything against them, she got mad and called me an unregenerate wretch. Yes, she did. She says that everybody'll go to perdition that don't believe and do as she does—her father, and Dolly, and everybody. I don't believe any such stuff. Do you?"

Marlowe smilingly shook his head.

The two walked on in silence, through the quiet village streets, each busy with his own thoughts. They passed the drugstore and reached the hotel steps.

"Say!" Clark ejaculated, pausing suddenly.

"Well?"

"What are you going to do tonight?"

"I am going to church."

"What one?"

"The Methodist."

"You don't belong?"

"No."

Then after a moment's hesitation:

"Can I go with you?"

"You can and you may."

"All right," Clark chuckled, "I'll go. It'll break up the poker game, for this evening—and start the ball of reform a rolling. Let's hunt up something to eat; I'm half famished."

Together they attended the Methodist Church that evening. The sermon was stereotyped and dry. Marlowe listened attentively, unmindful of the many eyes fixed upon him. Clark idly gazed about him—and occasionally nodded sleepily.

When leaving the church they met Dr. Barwood's daughters at the door; and went toward home with them.

"I am surprised to see *you* at church," Dolly whispered to Clark, as she walked beside him.

"No more than I am to see *you,*" he answered.

"Oh! I attend here every once in a while—to please mamma and Julia."

"I came to please myself. I like Marlowe's society. I wouldn't give his reasoning philosophy for all the cant of all the preachers I've ever heard."

"Hush! Julia will hear you, and preach another sermon; and I can't stand two in one evening. Do you like Mr. Marlowe?"

"Like him? Well, I should say! You want to get better acquainted with him, Dolly; he's grand. But then I hope you won't."

"Why?"—In an eager whisper.

"Because you'd fall in love with him."

Dolly laughed softly, musically, as she replied:

"I am not so easily smitten. But what difference could it make to you, Sam?"

"What difference? Do you think I'm anxious to lose you?"

Again Dolly laughed.

"You can't very easily lose what you don't possess," she said.

Then she lapsed into silence; and to her companion's vapid prattle answered only in monosyllables.

"Mr. Marlowe, I am glad you came out to church tonight, and that you brought your—your *acquaintance* with you," Julia said as they reached the corner where their ways parted.

"Thank you," he replied simply.

"You can do much good here," she went on hurriedly, "if only you will do what you know to be right. The young men of this town are sunk in the mire of sin; are negligent of their religious duties and heedless of their souls' salvation. Many of the young women are equally irreligious—equally reckless. Even my own dear sister is of the number. Both sexes dance, play cards and other godless games, and attend theatrical performances—when opportunity offers. I have prayed for them, and argued, labored, and plead with them; but without avail. You are a born leader; I see it in your face, I hear it in your voice. You can do so much, if only you will. But to lead them into the path of righteousness, you must first set your own face in that direction. You ought to belong to church, Mr. Marlowe. Don't you think so?"

She uttered the last few sentences wheedlingly.

"What church, Miss Barwood?" Ralph asked quietly.

"Our church, Mr. Marlowe—the Methodist. We need you. Or"—Hesitatingly—"any good, Protestant church."

"Why not the Catholic?"

Clark and Dolly came up just in time to hear Marlowe's question. Both listened breathlessly for Julia's reply.

"Now you are laughing at me," she cried petulantly peering into her companion's face.

"Not at all," he answered gravely. "I asked the question in all seriousness. The Catholics adduce as much evidence in support of their creed as do the Protestants of any denomination. However, I could not honestly subscribe to the tenets of any man-made belief.

I am a moralist—not a church man. But it is too chilly to stand here talking. I bid you good night."

"Good night," she returned in a tone of pique.

"I am disappointed in you, Mr. Marlowe. You are as bad as my father. He—"

"Dear old daddy's all right," Dolly broke in "He's always been good to you and me, sister mine. I think—"

"You don't know *what* you think, Dorothy," Julia interrupted sharply; "and you are talking too much nonsense."

"I was going to say," Dolly resumed placidly, "that *I* think daddy'll go to heaven, if anybody does. He's rough—but he's *so* good."

"Come, Dorothy," her sister said icily. "We must be going."

Then turning to Ralph:

"As I said, Mr. Marlowe, you are capable of doing much good in the world. But you will fail to accomplish anything—should you really desire to do so—because your heart is not right, because you are not an avowed Christian. There is but one way to do good; desert the world and its frivolities, and join those who are striving to lead sinners to the light. Good night."

"Good night, Sam; good night, Mr. Marlowe," Dolly said cheerily, offering her hand to each.

Both murmured a "good night," in return—each feeling he was especially favored. And the memory of the warm, fluttering fingers in his palm accompanied each to his place of rest.

* * * * * *

CHAPTER VIII

ON THE following Tuesday morning, three men clad in rough-and-ready style, and wearing soft hats and thick-soled, high-topped, lace shoes, entered the drugstore; and the leader of the trio asked for Dr. Barwood. Marlowe conducted them to the rear room, where the grumpy physician was poring over the pages of a small, calf-bound memorandum book.

The three disappeared within the private office, carefully closing the door behind them.

But the transom was open; and Ralph could not avoid hearing a part of the animated conversation that followed their entrance into Dr. Barwood's presence. Such cabalistic[35] expressions as—"good for a hundred a day"—"best wildcatter yet"—"pack her off and let her stand"—floated out to him.

The young man glanced at his watch from time to time, and fidgeted. At last he walked to the back door and knocked upon it. In a moment all was still within.

"Come," was the gruff invitation of Dr. Barwood.

Marlowe opened the door a little way and said:

"Doctor, the goods I ordered from the Baldy Drug Company have

---

35 cabalistic: understood by only a small group

not arrived. We are needing them badly. Shall I send a telegram?"

"Yes."—Explosively.

"Will you look after things while I go to the station?"

"Yes— yes!" —With candid impatience. —"Leave the door open—and be off."

Ralph silently withdrew, followed by the scowls of the oil men, whose confab[36] with his employer he had interrupted.

A few minutes later he stood with his head in the ticket window of the station and his arms spread out upon the projecting ledge—like a prisoner in the stocks—and said to the agent:

"Clark, I want to send a dispatch."

The operator silently tossed a pad of blanks upon the shelf, still keeping up his manipulation of the telegraphic instrument. Ralph hastily scribbled away at his telegram. The sharp clicking sound of the key alone broke the stillness. Then of a sudden the shrill, vibratory screech of a locomotive smote upon their ears. Springing to his feet and looking at his watch, Clark cried:

"There's the north-bound passenger, this minute. She's on time, too—right to the tick of the watch. By the way, Marlowe, this is the date of the show at Malconta. They showed at Marietta last night; and they'll be up on this train. We'll get a chance to peep at the pretty girls maybe, anyhow."

And smirkmg and grimacing in a prankish manner, the operator spread himself before the front window and pressed his face to the smoked pane.

At the words of his companion, Ralph started and paled slightly; and the hand that held the telegram trembled.

"Here!" he cried irritably. "Take this. I must get back to the drugstore."

"Eh?" said Clark turning his head. "All right. I'll send it as soon as the train's gone. But you're not going to rush off and miss seeing the pretty girls, are you?"

Marlowe made no reply, but whirling around made for the door. Just as he reached the place of exit, however, he became aware of

---

36 confabulate: to talk informally

the thunderous roar of the approaching train and the brazen clang of the locomotive bell.

"Too late," he muttered angrily; and shrank into a shadowy corner of the waiting room.

There he made a pretense of studying a dusty map upon the wall. Several persons were in the room, waiting to take the train, but they gave no heed to his actions. The breathing, snorting demon of wood and iron rolled up to the station and came to a stop. The waiting passengers hurried from the room and mingled with the surging crowd upon the platform.

Ralph heard the babel of voices, the rumble of trucks, and the bump of heavy baggage. He was alone; but he shivered and glanced apprehensively around. Then some irresistible curiosity drew him toward the doorway. Slowly, reluctantly, he approached the exit. With bated breath he shielded his body behind the swinging door and peeped out. He could see nothing but the engine and baggage car. Farther and farther he extruded his head, until the whole train lay within the plane of his vision. One particular car attracted his attention—and held it. He saw not the bustling throng; heard not the confused murmur of many voices. Ravenously his eyes devoured the gaudy lettering upon the blue-and-gold rolling palace. His dry lips moved, as he read:

THE CIDER AND THE PIE FARCE-COMEDY COMPANY

A WARM NUMBER

PLUMP FORMS   :   :   PRETTY FACES

A CARNIVAL OF MUSIC

DANCING, SINGING, JOL-
LITY AND LAUGHTER. : : : :

SPLENDID COSTUMES : : SPECIAL SCENERY

Of a sudden he started and caught his breath spasmodically, his gaze immovably fixed upon a dark, piquant face that had appeared at one of the windows of the blue-and-gold car.

"It is she!" he panted, drawing back and shuddering.

"Thank God! She did not see me."

Again he peered forth cautiously. The train was starting; the people were deserting the platform; the pretty face was no longer at the window of the blue-and-gold car. He fetched a sigh of relief, and retreating from the door, dropped upon the bench running along the side wall.

He had not observed a lithe, well-dressed young man, who had stood in the rear door of the show car as it rolled by, and stared unblinkingly at the station building.

Marlowe forgot where he was; and wringing his hands moaned softly to himself:

"It was she—Stella. My God! The disgrace—the awfulness of it! I ran a fearful risk in looking out; but she did not see me. I could not help it, though—something impelled me. Why have they come into this part of the country—Why was I at the station? Fate—blind fate! What risk—What danger! But it is past—thank heaven!"

Slowly he arose and started to leave the room. Blindly he groped toward the door, staggering as he went. His face was drawn; his lips were bloodless. Clark's voice aroused him to a sense of his surroundings.

"You here yet, old fellow?" the agent called through the ticket window. "I thought you left long ago."

With a mighty effort Ralph pulled himself together and managed to articulate:

"I am just going; I waited to see the train."

"You did, did you?" Clark laughed. "I thought you'd wait to see the pretty girls. But say! You look like you'd seen a trainload of ghosts. You look like a dead man. What's the matter with you—Are you sick?"

"I am not feeling well," Ralph muttered chokingly as he passed through the door.

The operator craned his neck through the narrow window and gazed after Marlowe's retreating form, muttering:

"Now what's the matter with that fellow? He's all broke up

about something—and that *something's* connected with that *show*. I wonder if the little woman who peeped out of the window of the show car had anything to do with his uncanny looks. Jinks! She was a beauty. I only saw the one. The others kept as close as nuns in a convent. There's a mystery about the thing. Ralph Marlowe knows more about that show than he tells—or means to tell. I don't care, though; he's a royal good fellow. I'd swear by *him*."

And mumbling and shaking his head, he returned to his work.

Marlowe made his way back to the drugstore, his nerves racked and tingling, his self-possession gone. He found Dr. Barwood alone and impatiently pacing up and down the long front room.

"I'm delayed on account of your absence," the physician grumbled. "I ought to have been off to the country a half hour ago. What kept you so long? Did you wait to send a message to some of your capitalist friends in the city, that we are striking oil in paying quantities, down here?"

Dr. Barwood's gruffness was assumed; and he meant his last question for a joke. At any other time Ralph would have recognized it as such, and would have returned a facetious reply. But now he was not himself. He was unstrung; every sensory filament was protruding and vibrating. He became furiously angry at the fancied insult. With flushed face and quavering voice he demanded:

"What do you mean, Dr. Barwood?"

"Mean?" echoed the older man.

"Yes. What do you mean by your insulting question?"

It was the doctor's turn to grow angry—no difficult thing for him to do.

"You understand the English language," he growled. "Interpret my question to suit yourself."

In a moment Marlowe was coldly calm—his features pale and rigid, a baleful light in his brown eyes.

"Am I to understand that you mean what your words imply?" he asked icily.

"I am not in the habit of saying what I do *not* mean," was the perverse reply.

"And you mean to impugn my honor—to insinuate that I am a sneak, who chancing to overhear a private conversation forthwith uses it to his own advantage?"

The doctor grinned maliciously but said nothing.

An unbiased observer would have said the medical man was enjoying the tilt. His sneering expression, his silence, so exasperated Ralph that the young man quivered with suppressed rage.

"Here are your keys," he hissed, jerking the bunch from his pocket and tossing it upon the counter.

Dr. Barwood started. Instantly his manner and attitude underwent a change. The mocking smile left his face; and a look of deep gravity was there in its stead. Drawing himself up dignifiedly, he said:

"I do not want the keys. Keep them; you will need them. I am going to the country."

"There—are—your—keys," Ralph repeated slowly pointing toward the bunch.

"You are going to quit my service?"

"I am."

"When?"

"Now."

"For what cause?"

"Because you have basely insulted me, Dr. Barwood. You have called my honor in question. Were you a younger man, I would demand an apology."

"If you should—and I should refuse?"

"I would administer the personal chastisement you deserve," Ralph cried fiercely.

"Do you think you could?"—With twitching features and the merest semblance of a smile.

"I *know* I could!"

And the young man sprang forward menacingly, his hands clenched.

Dr. Barwood calmly stood his ground and fearlessly faced his enraged employee. Their eyes met—the one pair gleaming savagely, the other pair expressing mute surprise mingled with repentant grief. Marlowe was instantly disarmed; and his hands dropped to his sides. Retreating a step he leaned heavily against the counter, trembling and panting.

Advancing, Dr. Barwood affectionately laid a hand upon his companion's shoulder and said:

"Ralph, my boy, we are much alike—both too prone to outbursts of unrighteous anger. I wish to apologize for hurting your feelings; though I meant my question as a joke. I will not attempt to excuse myself, however; I should not have asked it at all. I sometimes say cutting, brutal things for which I am sorry a moment afterward. It is a bad habit—I wish I could break myself of it. There" —Smiling sadly—"you have the apology you had a right to demand, that I had no right to withhold. But you do not know what an effort it has cost me to offer it. It is a new experience to me. Will you accept my apology and take my hand?"

"Gladly," Marlowe murmured almost inaudibly, his eyes downcast. "I am heartily ashamed of my hot-headedness, doctor. But I was disturbed when I came in; I was not myself. I trust you will pardon me. But I thought you meant to insinuate that I had purposely played eavesdropper—"

"Had I thought so meanly of you," the older man interrupted, "I would have asked you no questions. I would have discharged you without any ado. In all kindness I desire to say one thing, however. Your threat to do me bodily harm was unworthy of you. You are a trained athlete—I am not blind to that fact—while I am an old man whose sinews are stiffened by exposure and hard usage. There was a day—years ago—when your purposed task would not have been an easy one. And even yet—but pshaw!" —Laughing.—"We are not pugilists[37]; we are men—and friends. We understand each other—and I will say this: In the short time I have known you, I have learned to like and admire you very much. Take me as I am—not as I appear at times—and perhaps you may learn to tolerate me, at least."

There was a ring of pitiful pleading—a reaching out after love

---

37 pugilist: boxer

and sympathy—in the physician's voice, that was touching. Ralph was strangely moved by it, so much so that he cried:

"I do not have to learn to tolerate you, Dr. Barwood—to like you even. I have learned the lesson already—and it has not been a hard one."

"Then I need not take back my keys?" His black eyes suffused with moisture, yet twinkling humorously.

"No, doctor."

"All right. Help me to gather up my things, please. I must be going."

As the older man bustled around, getting ready to depart, he whistled softly to himself. At the door he turned and said:

"You sent the telegram to the Baldy Drug Company?"

"I did," Ralph replied.

"Say?"

"Well?"

"Don't you wish to invest some money in the oil business?"

"I have none to invest," was the frank reply.

"Well" —Stroking his thin beard meditatively—"that difficulty's easily overcome. I'll invest five hundred dollars for you."

Ere Marlowe could speak the objection that rose to his lips, the doctor had closed the door and trotted down the steps.

With a sigh Ralph dropped into a chair and buried his face in his hands. There he sat pondering over the exciting events of the morning. At the end of a half hour Tucker came slouching in; and remarking the young man's attitude of dejection, drawled:

"In the dumps ag'in, hey? You're settin' humped over there like a rabbit in a patch o' dead dog fennel. But ther'll be somethin' happen here next Saturday night, that'll stir you up an' put you on y'r nettle. I guess it's next Saturday night. It's the night o' the twenty-fourth, anyhow. Le's see—yes, this is the twentieth; it'll be next Saturday night. If you don't git waked up 'fore *that* time, you'll git waked up *then—an'* no mistake."

Ralph lifted his head and asked with as much interest as he could evince:

"What's going to happen, Jep?"

"Hain't you heerd?"—Incredulously.

"No. Or I would not have asked."

"W'y, ther's goin' to be the riproarin'est big Republican meetin' held here next Saturday night, that's been held in these parts since Adam's off ox was a yearlin'. The bills is up all over town. A feller come down from Malconta an' put 'em up this mornin'. I'll show you one of 'em. The chap give it to me, fer lettin' him paste one on the ol' doc's barn door."

Tucker jabbed his clumsy fingers into the inside pocket of his ragged jeans coat, and spasmodically fumbled about, all the time keeping up a running fire of talk.

"What's become o' that blame thing, anyhow?" he grumbled. "I put it in here—I know *that*. W'y great Josephus's almanac! Here's a hole in here that a shock o' corn fodder could go through. The ol' woman don't somehow seem to keep my duds in order no more. Oh! Here it is—way down in the linin', two 'r three degrees from the south pole. It must be as bashful as I am myself—hidin' from human sight that way. Aha! Now I've got it."

With these words he drew forth a folded paper, shook from it the accumulated lint and crumbs of tobacco, and gingerly spread it upon his knee. It was a flaming[38] poster; and announced the fact that the Honorable Jay B. Tenacre would address the citizens of Babylon and vicinity on the evening of the twenty-fourth of October, upon the momentous issues of the campaign. All this was displayed in bold, full-faced type. More modestly—but just as clearly—it was set forth that the Honorable Jay B. would be accompanied by the Malconta Band and McKinley Guards, three hundred strong; and that the Foxtown Glee Club was expected to be in attendance. In still smaller type—as though the parties who had taken it upon themselves to give forth the information were uncertain of the truth or propriety of their statement—it was asserted that excursion rates would prevail on all trains and boats. From the signatures printed at the bottom, it appeared that General L. T. Green and Major D. C. Waller—chairman and

---

38 flaming: intense or ardent; vehement; passionate

secretary, respectively, of the county executive committee—stood sponsor for this remarkable bundle of information. And last—and least in this case—down in an obscure corner were the words—"Herald Job Print."

"I'll read it to you," Jep volunteered.

And without waiting for his victim to raise a point of order, he began, running his blunt forefinger along the lines in slow succession, and laboriously and dilatorily enunciating one word after another—mispronouncing about three out of five. Several times he stalled and choked down upon some polysyllabic monstrosity; but each time—just as his auditor hoped the difficulty was insurmountable and the end had come—he mumblingly climbed over the obstacle and dragged himself forward.

"There!" he exclaimed triumphantly, when at last the agony was over. "Now you know all about it. An' there'll be a big time—no doubt about that. In the first place, that feller Tenacre is a bully good speaker. He's what some folks calls an orator. Ever hear him? You say you have? Then you know 'bout as much 'bout him as I do—*I* never did. Then in the second place the Foxtown Glee Club's comin' in, and they'll bring a crowd with 'em—horseback an' in wagons. An' word's been sent out to Quakerville; and they won't miss it, you bet. They're *all* Republicans out there. There won't be less 'n eight 'r ten thousan' people in town that night, I'll wager."

"That's more people than there is in the county, isn't it, Jep?" Ralph said, laughing at the fellow's enthusiasm.

"Darned if *I* know," Jep admitted with a grimace.

Then he went on:

"We're goin' to have marchin' an' music, an' speakin' an' cheerin', an' fireworks, an' a big bonfire. Then we've talked it over—I'm a member o' the township committee, you understand—an' we're goin' to git out the ol' brass cannon that's laid down in the ol' coopershop on the river bank, covered over with shavin's, fer the last twenty-five years, an' fire a salute when the boat comes in with the McKinley Guards on."

"You say the cannon has not been fired for twenty-five years?"

Marlowe inquired.

"That's what I said—an' it may be longer'n that. You see that partic'lar piece of artilery has a history." —And Jep expanded with the importance of his communication. —"Ol' Ed O'Neil brought it here from 'way down south some'rs—sometime 'fore the war. He was an Irishman—an' an ol' Jacksonian Democrat. It was him I told you 'bout; said he wouldn't scratch his ticket to save Christ from the cross.

"He used to run a tradin' boat from this river to New Orle'ns; an' on one trip he brought back this cannon. He *said* him an' his crew tackled a pirate ship at the mouth o' the Mississippi an' sunk it; an' that he jest brung the cannon along to prove his story.

"But lawzee! He was such an ol' liar nobody could b'lieve a word he said. W'y that ol' codger 'd rather tell a lie on ninety days credit than the truth fer cash, any time. He was a reg'lar ol' pirate hisself; didn't b'lieve in nothin' but drinkin', an' gamblin', an' such like. Used to say that tobacker was the staff o' life, an' whisky was life itself. An' I've seen him stand up to the bar an' down a half pint o' raw liquor, an' never take a drop o' water 'r bat an eye. When he'd see fellers takin' water with the'r liquor, he'd cuss an' ask 'em what they meant by buildin' a fire an' then drowndin' it out. He said he was an ol' thoroughbred—an' I guess he was.

"His pardner in the tradin' boat business was a man named Mulrain. *He* had folks livin' out 'bout Chapel Ridge—nigh the Perry County line; an' when he died they took him out there to bury him. Ol' Ed went along—an' rode on the hearse with the undertaker; an' w'en the funer'l pr'cession was passin' through Foxtown, one o' the storekeepers come out to see it go 'long. An' knowin' ol' Ed, he ups an' asks:

"Who's dead, Mr. O'Neil?'

"The man in the hearse,' answered Ed. An' on they drove.

"But pshaw! I'm gittin' clean off 'n my subject—as I alluz do. The only reason I wouldn't make a good preacher is, I couldn't stick to the text. Well, w'en O'Neil brought that cannon to Babylon, he give it to the Democrats to use at the'r political meetin's an' jollifications.

It hadn't been here a month till the Republicans up an' stold it from 'em. Then the Democrats raised a crowd an' captured it back; an' purty soon the Republicans stold it ag'in. An' so it went on fer years. Ther' has been more bruised heads an' bloody noses over that ol' gun, than you could shake a stick at.

"Finally the war broke out; an' that put an end to the quar'lin' fer a while. An' w'en Morgan's Raiders come through, the first thing people thought of was that ol' gun. I can remember all 'bout it. First the news come that Morgan's men was goin' to cross the river at this place; an' everybody was skeered to death. Then Jim Rush an' another feller went' out toward Deavertown, an' learnt that the rebels was goin' to cross at Eagleport, above here.

"Say!" —Chuckling explosively. —"You ort to 'ave seen Rush when he brought the news here. He was a tall, ganglin' chap—an' set a hoss like a clo'espin sets a line—an' w'en he come ridin' in that mornin' he was a sight. He had lost his hat—an' his brains under it, fer that matter—an' was skeered plumb into a coniption fit. He said, as soon as he could git breath to talk, that Morgan would try to ford the river jest below the Eagleport dam, that afternoon; an' advised that we send the women an' children to the hills, hide our hosses, raise a company, an' go up an' head the rebels off. Some people—an' they was the sensible ones—thought we'd jest better let 'em cross an' be gone; but others was in favor of Rush's projeck. The upshot o' the matter was that the men gethered up the'r guns an' axes, loaded the ol' cannon on the steam ferryboat, an' set off up the river.

"On the way up they charged the ol' piece with a few pounds o' blastin' powder, an' rammed 'er full to the muzzle with pieces o' logchain, kingbolts, an' other pieces o' scrap iron. Then they stood back an' laughed the'rselves 'most sick, thinkin' how they'd mow down them rebels an' send 'em to kingdom come.

"But when they got up to Eagleport—lo an' behold you! Morgan an' his men had crossed the' river a' ready—an' was gone. So ther' was nothin' to do but turn 'round an' come back. That they done, growlin' an' threat'nin' what they'd 'ave done, if they'd got there in time.

"When they got in sight o' town comin' back, some one says:

"'Le's shoot off the cannon an' let the women folks know we're all safe an' sound.'

"Well, sir, they put a match to the touch hole. An' what do you s'pose that ol' rip of a cannon done?"

Tucker paused for a reply.

"Failed to go off," Ralph ventured.

Jep shook his head.

"It didn't explode, of course," Marlowe said; "or you wouldn't be considering the advisability of using it at your political meeting."

"No, it didn't explode," Jep explained; "an' it went off all right enough—but not hard enough to shake the flies off 'n it, 'r wake up Ben Mason that laid drunk 'long side of it. It jest give a kind of a 'poof,' an' dribbled scrap iron all over the apron o' the ferryboat. They hadn't put in enough powder to load a good-sized popgun."

He stopped and looked quizzically at his auditor, as though expecting him to say something.

"And you are going to use this same cannon to fire a salute, next Saturday night," Marlowe remarked.

"Yes, an' we'll load 'er heavy enough *this* time—you jest bet y'r bottom dollar! We'll wake the ol' town up fer once. By the way, some o' the Democrats is sayin' a'ready—not the smart kind like you, but them that hain't got sense enough to know when they're hungry—that we shan't use the gun. They say they'll be out in a body, an' pr'vent us. If they try that, ther'll be a ruction[39] sure. But I mustn't set here gassin' no longer; I've got work to do out to the barn."

He arose and sauntered forth, humming through his nose:

"Open the winder —do love, do!
 An' listen to the music I'm playin' fer you;
 Whisper'n's o' love so soft an' so low
 Harmonize a voice with the ol' ban-*jo*."

* * * * * *

---

39 ruction: a disturbance or quarrel

CHAPTER IX

THE ENSUING three days passed uneventfully. Saturday, the date of the Republican grand rally, dawned murky and dismal. A pitiless, fitful drizzle followed the fickle wind in its provoking see-saw from one point of the compass to another; and but few persons ventured abroad. Republicans were glum; Democrats were jubilant. The latter winked at one another and smiled broadly—wickedly.

By noon, however, the rain had ceased; the skies had partially cleared. Catching occasional glimpses of the sun through the rifted clouds, the Republican leaders took heart and commenced in earnest, to decorate their houses and places of business, in honor of the occasion. Columns and fronts were soon swathed in yards of bunting; and windows and doorways were decorated with flags—flags by the score and the hundred, and of all shapes and sizes. A speaker's stand was erected in front of the post-office; and, as a crowning glory to the whole, an immense arch of evergreens and bunting spanned the street, near the hotel.

By mid-afternoon the country people began to drift in; and the town took on a holiday appearance. The great pyramid of boxes and barrels, at the intersection of the streets near McDevitt's store, awaited the torch; and the old brass cannon had been removed from its hiding place in the coopershop near the river, and transferred to a vacant lot back of the livery stable. There, securely chained to a pile of heavy timbers, it rested—carefully guarded and ready to do the bidding of its temporary possessors.

A short time after the removal of the old smooth bore to the spot mentioned, Hugh McDevitt and a number of other young Democrats called upon Marlowe, at the drugstore.

"Look here, Marlowe," the leader of the party said. "It's reported that you are a Democrat. How about it?"

"Guilty," Ralph answered smilingly. "Then we want you to help us."

"To help you?" —In feigned surprise. He knew well what was coming.

"Yes, to help us—to be our captain, in fact. It's like this: There's an old brass cannon in town that has been a bone of contention between Republicans and Democrats for years. For the last decade or two—by tacit consent of both parties—it has lain unused, in the old coopershop by the river. But today the Republicans have dragged it out, and mean to use it tonight, to herald the arrival of the boat bringing their speaker and the Malconta Guards. The gun really belongs to our party; Captain O'Neil—as he was called—brought it from the south and gave it to us. To cut a long story short, we intend to keep the Republicans from using it on this occasion, either by spiking it or dragging it to the river and sinking it. And we've come to solicit your advice and help. What do you say?"

"I would say," Marlowe answered mildly but firmly, "that so far as your proposed enterprise is concerned, I am ready to give you advice—but not help."

"You are not in favor of the scheme, then?"

"I am not."

"May I ask why?" —Rather coldly.

"My reason for opposing it is simply this: It would get us into trouble, bring us and our party into disrepute, and accomplish no good. The day for such escapades is gone by. We should come out of the fray with broken heads, perhaps; and with battered reputations. People do not look upon such things as once they did. The Democrats of Babylon would be accused of political intolerance; and the accusation would live to torment us in future campaigns."

"You may be right," McDevitt muttered, meditatively shaking his head. "We counted upon your help; but if you feel that way about the matter, perhaps it would be well to let it drop. What do you say, boys?" —Turning to his associates.

A few expressed their willingness to abandon the project; but the others openly dissented and went out grumbling.

"I don't know yet what we'll do," McDevitt, standing with his hand upon the knob of the door, called back to Ralph. "You'd better have splints and bandages in readiness, though."

And with a careless laugh he sprang down the steps, after his companions.

The short afternoon waned; and night was at hand. A dense white fog arose from the river and tributary streams, filling the valley to the hilltops—a milk-white blanket that saturated everything it touched and muffled all sounds near and far. But the main street of Babylon was a blaze of light. Lamps and lanterns vied with one another in dispelling the enveloping gloom. The pyramid of boxes and barrels at the intersection of the streets, at the touch of a torch turned to a pyramid of fire. The flames crackled, leaped, and swayed; the blue-black smoke eddied and gyrated. Crowds surged along the thoroughfare. A babel of human cries and shouts and laughter mingled with the yelps of scurrying curs and the vibrant, rasping notes of numerous tin horns. The muffled shuffle and tramp of human feet accentuated the pandemonium produced by rattling, rumbling vehicles and neighing horses.

Saloon doors stood wide open; and beer stood in puddles upon the bar-room floors. Squads of drunken men rolled along the streets, talking, arguing, and gesticulating. The fearless small boy and the festive firecracker were in evidence at every corner; and loaded canes in the hands of reckless youngsters abetted the combination, in filling the night with uproar and the hearts of the timid with dread.

Presently the joyful shout arose:

"The Foxtown Glee Club! Out of the way! Here comes the Foxtown Glee Club!"

The cry began in the vicinity of the drugstore; and was repeated and echoed from there to the river. The throng parted to right and left. Shouts and cheers arose on every hand. Drawn by four gray horses resplendent with gay cockades and strings of bells and buckeyes, the great chariot or band wagon rolled swiftly down the main street. Its swan-shaped body of green and gold was festooned with bunting and draped with flags. High in front sat the negro driver, the lines wrapped around his hands, a look of supreme importance upon his black face. High in the rear was perched a chubby cross-eyed man, his fat fingers fondly embracing two pairs of shining ebony bones. And in the hollow between these two prominent individuals, nestled the other members of the club.

The swarm followed pellmell in the train of the gorgeous vehicle. Women and children screamed ecstatically; men and boys tossed their hats in the air and yelled lustily. The black driver majestically drew his team up in front of the hotel, and tightening the lines over the backs of his prancing steeds brought them to a sudden stop. The excited people surged around the wagon and its occupants; the patrons of the bar poured out to swell the multitude.

"A song—give us a song!" someone shouted in a stentorian[40] voice.

"A song!—A song!—Give us a song!" was the thunderous echo on all sides.

The leader of the club slowly arose and dignifiedly waved his baton. A silence—broken only by the low buzz of whispered conversation on the outskirts of the crowd, a rippling, irrepressible girlish giggle, or the spiteful little voice of an exploding firecracker—ensued. The leader whispered a few words to his band. There was the preliminary "plunk-plunk, tum-tum" of tuning banjos and violins, and the impressive clearing of vocal organs. Then came the overture—the indescribable wail and shriek of string and wind instruments—and the song was on.

It was an enlivening, electrifying campaign rattle—a nonsense medley, with a quick and catchy air. The leader of the club threw back his head, and in a clear, mellow baritone voice sang the first stanza, the banjoists and violinists softly accompanying him. Then all the voices and instruments joined in the chorus—until the fog-laden air vibrated

---
40 stentorian: extremely loud

and tingled with the melody.

The words ran:

> "Uncle Sammy had a boy, had a boy, had a boy—
> Uncle Sammy had a boy, and Bryan was his name;
> Bill McKinley blacked his eye, blacked his eye, blacked his eye—
> Bill McKinley blacked his eye, for fighting he was game.
>
> CHORUS:
> Ah-dee! Ah-di! With a bum—ging—ging, etc."

As the chorus proceeded, the chubby player of the "bones" indulged in numerous grimaces and contortions for the amusement and admiration of the delighted populace, finally rising to his feet—upon his lofty perch—and clicking off a clog to the music.

At the conclusion of the first stanza, the audience broke into cheers and roars of laughter. Quickly, however, they checked themselves and breathlessly awaited the second stanza. It followed immediately—the leader of the club indulging in a bit of stage craft, to enhance the effect of words and music. Plucking a large flag from its socket in the driver's seat, he waved it above his head and sang:

> "These are the colors we march under, we march under,
> we march under—
> These are the colors we march under—long summer day!
> Hurrah for McKinley! Give 'em thunder, give 'em thunder,
> give 'em thunder!
> Hurrah for McKinley! Give 'em thunder! Hip! Hip! Hurray!"

The effect produced was magical—wonderful.

His auditors went wild. They cheered, they yelled, they roared. Tipsy men embraced each other, maudlin tears trickling down their cheeks; women laughed hysterically and wrung one another's hands. Staid citizens slapped one another upon the back, and swore it was the best thing they ever heard. Such a hubbub had never been heard in Babylon; such a sight had never been witnessed in the sleepy little town.

Just as the uproar was at its height, a hatless, coatless young man—his suspenders broken, his face smeared with blood—rushed into the jam, elbowed people right and left, and mounting the hotel steps shouted in a voice that rose loud and clear above the tumult:

"The Democrats are trying to spike our cannon! Come, a lot of you fellows, and help us!"

The light from a swinging lantern fell full upon his blood-stained features, as he stood there panting and gesticulating. At the sight women caught their breaths gaspingly; and children screamed.

The young man did not tarry; but springing down the steps, two at a bound, set off for the scene of conflict, closely followed by a score or two of lusty comrades.

The leader of the Foxtown Glee Club began the third stanza of his song. His voice quieted the din—but not for long. For rising above all other sounds, came the rich, resonant notes of a steamboat whistle.

"There she comes! The boat—the boat! To the river!" were the cries that greeted the welcome blast.

And forgetting their erstwhile idols, the natives hurried off to greet the stranger gods that were approaching their shores.

"Let's drive around to the livery stable and put up our team," said the leader of the Glee Club, smiling pessimistically. "They'll have no further use for us till the procession breaks ranks and the speech is ready to begin. In the meantime, we'll see if we can't find something to wet our whistles."

The driver cracked his whip; and the chariot rolled around the corner, into a cross street. "Tramp, tramp!" went the hundreds of feet, down the grade toward the wharf.

"I hear her puffin'!" a youngster yelled lustily. "An' I see 'er lights dancin' in the water," triumphantly announced another, himself dancing up and down on the extreme outer edge of the wooden dock.

"No, you don't," sneered his companion. "Them lights is shinin' from the back winders in Gridley's store. She hain't turned the bend yit."

"Yes, she has. There—there! See that? That light was the fireman openin' an' shuttin' the furnace doors. Here she comes! Hurrah!"

He was right, too.

"Ding! Ding! Ding!" clanged the great bell upon the hurricane deck.

Then the sharp, vicious hiss of a rocket was heard; and an arc of fire cut athwart the blackness overhanging the approaching steamer. Another rocket and another quickly followed the first, penetrating the enveloping fog in all directions and checkering the heavens with their flaming trails. The excited multitude upon the shore howled their delight. Answering cheers came from the boat.

The steady strokes of her engines could be distinctly heard.

"Why don't our fellows shoot off the cannon?" was the question raised by someone.

"That's it—why don't they?" said another.

"Wouldn't wonder the Democrats had—" a third began.

But he stopped suddenly in the middle of the sentence and clapped his palms to his benumbed organs of hearing. The old brass cannon had spoken its welcome to the visiting host; and had done it in a voice that left no doubt of its sincerity. The hoarse, thunderous roar shook earth and air, rattled the glass in the windows, and stirred the placid ocean of fog into tumbling billows.

"There! She's spoke her little piece!" bellowed a bull-necked countryman, as soon as the rumbling echoes had died away. "An' she's spoke in favor o' sound money an' pr'tection, too."

"That's it! You bet!" laughed those in his immediate vicinity.

"'Tisn't so—'tisn't so!" an ardently partisan schoolmiss screamed in reply. "The old cannon's a bimetallist[41]—it's made of tin and copper. It belongs to us Democrats anyhow; you Republicans had to borrow it. Hurrah for Bryan and free silver!"

And frantically waving her plaid cap and tossing her jetty curls, she gave three cheers for her hero.

At that moment the boat, ploughing her way through the dense fog, loomed up suddenly near at hand. The grating of the swinging gangplank came to the ears of all. Then the band on the forecastle struck up the *"Star Spangled Banner."* And amid the clash and blare

---
41 bimetallist: made of two metals

of brazen instruments, the hiss of rockets and the pop and sputter of Roman candles, the flare of torches and the glare of furnace fires, the steamer rounded to and approached the landing.

The Malconta Guards—resplendent in oilcloth caps and capes of gaudy hues, and bearing torches inscribed with the motto: "An Honest Dollar" quickly disembarked and fell into marching order. The band of fifteen pieces took its place at the head of the column; and two barouches containing the speaker, the gentlemen who accompanied him, and the members of the reception committee, brought up the rear. On each side, packing the sidewalks, surged the rabble.

"Attention, company!" bawled the doughty commander of the guards, waving his sword and frowning a military frown. "Forward—march! Left, left, left!"

A mischievous urchin complemented:

"Left foot, right foot; Hay foot, straw foot!"

At which everybody, including the guards themselves, laughed heartily.

To the inspiring strains of "Dixie"—at the recognition of which sundry Democrats nudged their Republican friends and playfully accused them of stealing the tune—the procession ascended the grade, passed under the welcoming arch, and reached the speaker's stand. There, after performing a few evolutions, the guards broke ranks.

The speaker and his escorts ascended the canopied platform; while the band huddled at its base, continued to render a number of national airs. Then the Glee Club again put in an appearance, and treated the willing populace to several campaign songs. When the latter organization had run short of wind and music, the speaker of the occasion was introduced by a member of the local committee; and the serious business of the evening began.

Let us leave the ardent adherents of the cause of sound money and protection, standing in the muck of the street and listening patiently and stoically to the words of eloquence—while shivering at the touch of clinging fog—and look in upon Ralph Marlowe at the drugstore.

Few customers had been in that evening; and the young clerk had spent much time standing upon the damp steps, viewing the animated scene. At the close of the band concert he had retired to the interior of the building; and now he sat alone, drying his shoes by the fire and moodily dreaming.

A one-gallows urchin tiptoed into the room and said breathlessly:

"Morris McDevitt wants you to send him a roll o' stickin'—stickin' plaster, an'—an' some anarky. He'll pay you for 'em some other time."

Ralph made no reply; but smiling grimly, went behind the counter, procured a two ounce bottle of tincture of arnica and a roll of court-plaster, and gave them to the lad—who hurriedly made his exit.

Left alone the druggist muttered to himself:

"McDevitt wants 'anarchy,' eh? He and his gang of young swashbucklers have attempted to carry out their design of recovering that cannon; and have ignominiously failed. Well, it will prove a lesson, I hope. I wonder that he sends for 'anarchy,' however"—Again smiling. —"One would suppose he had had enough."

A few minutes later Jep Tucker popped his head in at the door; and kept it there long enough to say:

"Didn't I tell you we was goin' to have the riproarin'est time on record? An' we're havin' it. Ev'rything's gone off lovely so far—even to the cannon. But jeeminy! We had a tussle over that gun. Morris McDevitt an' some o' the other Democrat boys come over to the lot an' said the gun belonged to them; an' they was goin' to have it. Of course us fellers didn't b'lieve them statements. So we all got into a little argyment—an' argied with tongues and claws both. Some on both sides is kind o' chawed and scratched up; but nobody is bad hurt. Morris an' his fellers, w'en they found we was too many fer 'em, took it all good-natured and went away laughin'. We've loaded the ol' gun up ag'in—clean to the muzzle; an' we're goin' to fire a s'lute w'en the boat leaves, that'll kill the fish in the river an' jar the paint all off the buildin's. Well, good-bye. I must be goin'; I don't want to miss no more o' that speech 'n I can help. I tell you he's wakin' up the snakes an' callin' 'em to judgment—you better bet he is!"

Hardly had the delighted Jep withdrawn his head, when Sam Clark entered the store, followed by Dr. Barwood.

"Good evening, Marlowe," the little operator said chirpingly— not aware that the owner of the store had entered.

"Where've you been keeping yourself? I haven't run across you since Tuesday. Don't you eat or sleep nowadays—or have you found a new boarding place?"

"It happened that we did not meet at meals, that is all," Ralph explained. "I have my rooms partially furnished, and am occupying them. I do not get my meals until you have eaten and gone to the station, usually."

Then to his employer, who stood scowling at the agent and uneasily shifting from one foot to the other:

"Is there something you wish me to do, doctor?" At the question Clark suddenly became cognizant of Dr. Barwood's presence, and mumbled confusedly:

"Good evening, doctor."

"Good evening," the physician grunted in reply. Then he went on in answer to Marlowe's interrogatory:

"Yes, Ralph, there *is* something I want you to do. I want you to go out upon the street, hunt up my daughters, and look after them. I am feeling some twinges of rheumatism; and do not care to be out in the damp air. But I am concerned about the girls; the town is full of reckless; drunken rowdies tonight. I will stay here. Will you go?"

"Certainly, doctor."

"Very well. Please go at once."

And with a grimace, indicative of the pain he was suffering, Dr. Barwood dropped into a chair near the stove.

Marlowe donned overcoat and hat, and accompanied by his friend left the store. When they were outside and the door had closed behind them, Clark laughed:

"Surely you do stand in with the old doc. To hear him calling you 'Ralph'— as if you were his beloved son-in-law, already—and telling you to go out and hunt up and protect the apples of his eye, almost knocked me off my pins. Then, he even condescended to speak to me—a thing he hasn't done since we had a little difference of opinion over a freight bill, some months ago. The old fellow's improving under your—Great Snakes! Marlowe, look at that pair coming up the sidewalk, there. It's Crawford and his crony—Brady, the bridge-tender; and they're drunker than old Bacchus[42] ever was. Listen at 'em singing! Ha, ha, ha!"

The two young men stepped aside to give the reeling bacchanals[43] room to pass. Brady was swinging his hat and vociferously hurrahing at frequent intervals. Crawford was singing and hiccoughing. The two walked with arms locked and shoulders braced, swaying from side to side and leaving a devious and tortuous trail of tracks and rum-laden atmosphere behind them.

As the inebriates passed, Marlowe and Clark caught the words of the song Crawford was singing. It ran:

> "Once I was a pussy ol'landlord's pet,
> An' I had money to spend;
> But I spent it in drink,
> An' did fairly think
> It never would come to an end .
> But now I have nothin' but rags to my back,
> An' my boots won't hide my toes;
> While the rim o' my hat
> Goes flippity-flap,
> To keep the flies off o' my nose."

The two young men looked at one another in silent disgust, for several seconds. Then Clark muttered:

"Well, now, aren't they a pair of peaches! They're enough to make a man ashamed of his kind!"

Marlowe made no answer; but taking his companion's arm moved on down the street.

---
42 Bacchus: the god of wine
43 bacchanals: participants in a drunken or riotous celebration

As they neared the post-office they caught sight of the speaker's stand lighted with lanterns and torches, and the black mass of humanity in front of it. The orator's clear, ringing utterances and the approving cheers of his audience fell upon their ears. Down a cross street, a squad of boys had started a bonfire and were shooting firecrackers.

On reaching the outskirts of the crowd, Ralph remarked:

"It will be a difficult task to find the young women in this multitude. I want your assistance, Clark. You go to the right; I will go to the left. If you run across them, tell them I am looking for them, and conduct them to the strip of pavement in front of the hardware store."

"All right," Clark answered. And the two parted.

Marlowe followed the left semicircular border of the dense pack of people, edging in and out as opportunity offered and peering into the face of every female figure he encountered. But he did not find those he sought. At last he completed the detour and reached a point near the foot of the stand, where the band was stationed. There he stopped and leaned against one of the supports of the platform, undecided what to do next.

The Honorable J. B. Tenacre had closed his argument, and was treating his audience to a peroration[44] consisting of flights of fancy and oratory, of which he alone was capable. The members of the band were working the keys of their wind instruments, and sorting out their parts, from a stack of sheet music that lay upon the head of the bass drum—all the while softly whispering among themselves.

Of a sudden the squad of boys down the cross street set off a giant cracker. The startling report was followed by the snorts of frightened horses and the rattle of chains. Then came a crash and the rumble of a heavy vehicle. A farmer's team tied at the blacksmith's shop had pulled down the rack, and was galloping pell-mell toward the crowded thoroughfare.

"Here comes a runaway team! Out of the way! Look out!" were the warning cries that rent the damp night air.

Men turned pale and gasped for breath; women and children

---

44 peroration: to speak at great length

screamed frantically. Panic seized upon the huddled multitude. The instinct of self preservation gained ascendency over every chivalrous sentiment or desire. The concourse of peaceful citizens became a frenzied mob—a mob that surged this way and that and emitted hoarse cries of rage and fear. Men forgot they were civilized human beings—and were selfish devils. They howled like wild beasts and struggled and fought to disentangle themselves from their fellows—to escape the impending danger.

Barely had the team started ere it had been stopped. But only those on the edge of the crowd learned the fact, at the time. In vain the speaker raised his voice, shouted that there was no danger and begged the people to consider what they were doing. His words fell upon deaf ears.

Ralph Marlowe took in the situation at once.

He realized that something must be done to allay the mad fears of those irresponsible human beings, to bring them to their senses, or dozens of them would be trampled under foot and killed or injured. With him, to think was to act. He was out of the way of danger himself—he thought only of others. Springing to the side of the leader of the band, he cried in an agitated voice:

"Play something at once! Anything—anything!"

"Play 'Yankee Doodle,' boys!" the bandmaster bellowed. "And play it like hell!"

And they did play it—played it like all the imps of the inferno had broken loose at once, and were wailing and screeching their miseries and torments, to an unregenerate world. But it had the desired effect. Crazed men and frenzied women, who felt themselves as good as dead, checked their mad impulses and wondered if the danger were past—or if the band were trying to render a dirge suitable to the catastrophe.

A few of the throng, however, were not so easily controlled. Marlowe saw a wedge-shaped body of men still fighting to extricate themselves from the general mass. To right and left they shoved and knocked all who barred their way. A young woman attempted to get out of their path; but tripped and fell. In a moment they would have been upon her; but the young druggist leaped forward and caught her up in his arms.

"Back!" he commanded sternly—fiercely, supporting his limp burden upon his left arm and essaying to retreat from his perilous position. "Back, men! There is no danger! Would you crush the life out of a helpless woman? Back, I say!"

They gave no heed to his words. Swiftly they pressed upon him and around him, giving him no chance to turn and escape. A number of times he was almost thrown from his feet, as he retreated backward. The young woman had recovered sufficiently to stand; but she clung tremulously yet tenaciously to his arm. Her trusting touch—he knew not why—aroused him to instant fury and action. Once, twice, thrice his right fist shot out from the shoulder; and as many of the ruthless, wild-eyed maniacs went reeling back among their fellows. For a moment the human avalanche was checked. In the brief interval Marlowe threw his arm around the young woman's waist and hurried her to a place of safety, upon the pavement in front of the hardware store.

The flying wedge, reaching open ground, broke and scattered harmlessly.

Ralph bent and peered into the face of the woman he had rescued. By the aid of the mellow lamplight streaming from the store window, he discerned a fair young face framed by a mass of tousled golden hair, and a pair of heavenly violet-blue eyes looking into his own.

"Dolly!" he exclaimed involuntarily.

"Yes," her pale lips whispered falteringly. "And you have saved my life, Mr. Marlowe. How can I ever repay you?"

She was still clinging to him, trustingly—tremblingly. His heart beat rapturously, as he kept his arm around her lissome[45] form and steadied her. But he answered brusquely:

"It was nothing. Probably you would have escaped without my aid."

"You know better," she returned earnestly, her mouth quivering

---
45 lissome: limber, lithe

like that of a grieved child.

There they stood, each silently gazing into the other's face. Unconsciously he pressed her to his breast; and she did not resist. The band had ceased to play. The people had regained their senses; the speaker was closing his address.

"Oh, Dorothy! I have been searching everywhere for you."

It was Julia's voice; and she stood before them. "In the rush of the crowd," Ralph explained calmly, "your sister was thrown down. I was near; and aided her to this place. But she is nervous and weak. I think we would better take her to the drugstore. Your father is there; and anxious about both of you. He sent me to look for you."

"Are you hurt, Dorothy?" Julia inquired, genuine concern in her voice.

"No; I am upset, that is all," Dolly murmured faintly.

Marlowe released his hold upon his fair charge. But she tottered; and again he placed his arm around her.

"Let us go," he said simply.

Up the sidewalk they went, Julia on the one side of her sister and Ralph on the other.

The great political event was over; and the crowd was dispersing. The Malconta Band, playing a lively national air, was leading the way toward the boat landing. Farmers were untying their teams and tumbling into their lumbering vehicles. Dogs were barking; horns were tooting. The fierce, defiant staccato[46]—"Hurrah for Bryan!" was answered by the sepulchral groan—"Mc—Kin—ley! Mc—Kin—ly!" Lights were disappearing in stores and shops; empty torches were winking—fading and dying. The damp air was foul with the smell of burning oil and gunpowder.

Clark came upon Marlowe and the young women, halfway between the post-office and the drugstore.

"You found them, I see," he remarked to Ralph. The latter nodded a reply.

"Well, you don't need any more of my help, I guess. Good night. I've got to get down to the station—telegrams to send."

---
46 staccato: composed of abrupt, distinct parts or sounds

And he was gone.

Dr. Barwood painfully arose and came forward to meet the young people, as they entered the drugstore.

"What's the matter?" he demanded, sharply eying Marlowe, who was still half supporting Dolly.

Ralph explained briefly, saying in conclusion:

"I think you would better give her a glass of wine, doctor. She is suffering from nervous shock—nothing more."

"No!" Julia cried in a tone of mild horror. "Don't give her *that stuff!*"

But her father went behind the counter, poured out a glass of wine, and handed it to Dolly, saying:

"Drink this—all of it. Then get home and to bed. You are completely upset; you are shaking like a leaf."

"Isn't there something else that will do as well as an intoxicant?" Julia protested.

"Don't be silly, child," the father said sternly. "I have a little sense left; I still know what a patient needs—even if that patient is my own daughter."

Dolly's hand shook so she could not hold the glass; and Ralph placed it to her lips. When she had swallowed the contents—with a wry face and an involuntary shiver—her father said:

"Now, Dolly, Mr. Marlowe will take you home. I would accompany you myself, but I am suffering the torments of the damned, with the cursed rheumatism. Put her to bed, Julia—and see that she is warm."

The three young people went out as they had come in—Ralph half leading, half supporting the younger sister, the older walking in dignified silence beside them.

The street in the vicinity of the drugstore was deserted; but the subdued sound of many voices came from the direction of the boat landing, and the rattle of farmers' vehicles crossing the bridge sounded like the roll of distant thunder. Occasionally arose the prolonged whoops and cheers of half-drunken partisans. Then the light breeze that bore the sounds died down; and all was silent as the grave.

A walk of a few minutes brought the sisters and their escort, to the family residence—a big two-story brick house standing back from the main street, in the center of a large yard filled with trees, shrubs, and flower beds. An iron fence surrounded the premises. A broad flag walk ran from the gate to the stone steps leading up to the recessed front door.

On reaching the gate, Julia remarked:

"Mr. Marlowe, we will put you to no further trouble. I can get Dorothy into the house."

"I will go with you to the door," Ralph answered quietly but firmly.

Julia said no more; but sighing resignedly went on ahead, quickly ascended the steps, and flung open the door. The lamplight streaming out fell full upon Dolly's face and showed that the color was returning to her cheeks and lips.

"You are feeling better," Ralph remarked smilingly.

"Very much better," she replied, attempting to smile in turn—at which her mouth quivered and the moisture glistened in her eyes. "Oh, yes! I am better. The wine has quite restored me. It was babyish in me to be so easily upset."

"I will bid you good night," he answered releasing her.

"Will you not—not come in?" she faltered, glancing beseechingly at her sister—Ralph thought.

"Not tonight," he made answer. "You heard your father's orders. To bed with you."

He turned and started down the steps.

"But you will call some evening, will you not?" she called after him. "I desire an opportunity to thank you for your kindness."

"You are taking a good plan to keep me away," he laughed, pausing momentarily.

"You do not wish me to thank you for what you have done?"

"I do not."

"Then," —And he could see her cheeks dimple and her eyes glint mischievously, in the lamplight, —"I will promise not to thank you, much as I feel under obligations to you. Will you come?"

"Dorothy!" he heard Julia say in a horrified undertone.

"Yes, I will call some evening," he answered as he sprang down the steps and ran toward the gate.

He heard the door close; and he was alone upon the street. Breathlessly he hurried along, his heart beating wildly and his mind in a tumult of sweet unrest. Just as he was drawing near the drugstore, the mellow clang of the steamboat's bell broke the stillness. She was pulling out into the stream, upon her homeward voyage. Then suddenly, like the crack of doom, came a deep thunderous roar that staggered him and almost lifted the hat from his head. It shook the town like an earthquake shock, jingling the glass in the windows and causing bricks to tumble from time-shattered chimneys. The hoarse-voiced echoes boomed and reverberated up and down the valley—and gradually died out.

Ralph took a step forward; and paused to listen.

From the direction of the river came the faint sound of hurrying footsteps and sharp cries and exclamations.

"What was that?" Dr. Barwood inquired, appearing upon the steps of the drugstore.

A bent, limber-jointed figure emerged from the shadow of the wall; and Tomp Nutt's stuttering voice answered:

"G-Guess it was ol' Gabri'l s-soundin the f-final trump. M-Must 'ave b-b-bu'sted his h-horn."

" Nonsense!" the doctor snorted angrily.

"T-Then the b-boat's b-bu'sted 'er b-b-b'ilers."

"It was the cannon they were using to fire a parting salute," Ralph explained, stepping forward. "They have overcharged it; and it has exploded, probably."

"And somebody's hurt or killed," the physician completed fault-findingly. "Of course it must be so right at a time I am really unable to perform a difficult surgical operation. Why won't people exercise common sense? Hark!"

The three men listened intently. They heard the faint puffs of the retreating steamer and the soft patter of approaching footsteps.

"I hear someone running," Marlowe declared.

"An' a p-pantin' like a l-lizard on a h-hot f-f-fence r-rail;" Nutt added.

The hurrying footsteps drew nearer. The trio upon the steps strained their eyes in an effort to pierce the gloom. Presently out of the fog emerged a man's lumbering figure. He was moving as fast as his ungainly legs could carry him, his long arms swinging like pendulums and his head thrust forward. His heavy breathing could be distinctly heard. A moment more, and he stood beside them—his chest heaving, his eyes protruding.

"Who's hurt or killed, Jep Tucker?" Dr. Barwood demanded angrily. "Out with it. Somebody's had to pay the fiddler for your infernal nonsense. Who's hurt?"

Tucker tried to speak; but only a husky rattle came from his parched throat. He gasped and rolled his eyes, and appeared to be on the verge of collapse.

"You dumb fool!" the doctor cried roughly. *"You're* not hurt. Speak out. Someone may die while you are standing here chewing your tongue."

"H-He's p-pale as a r-rabbit's b-belly," Tomp remarked. "M-Maybe he *is* h-hurt."

"No, I ain't," Jep spasmodically jerked out. "But Jim Crawford is. The cannon bu'sted; an' he was drunk an' wouldn't git out o' the way w'en we touched 'er off. He's—he's got his arm tore off nearly; an' his head's all cut up. An' he's bleedin' like a stuck pig. It made me sick to see him. Fer God's sake, doc, come as quick as you can!"

"It's a pity it didn't kill the sot—and the rest of you fools, too," Dr. Barwood snarled savagely. "Where did you take him—home?"

"Yes, doc. But do hurry!"

"I'll be in more haste to serve him, than he'll be in to remunerate me," the doctor muttered, turning and walking into the drugstore.

Tucker and Nutt—two picturesque old ruins—took themselves down the dark street. Ralph followed his employer through the door.

"Help me to gather up what I need, Ralph," the physician

requested mildly. "I want you to go down with me and lend me what aid you can. I am not fit to undertake an operation tonight. You will have to administer the anesthetic for me, at least!'

"Perhaps you would better go down to the house at once, doctor," Marlowe suggested. "I will bring the instruments and other things. Crawford's wounds were bleeding freely—so Tucker said. May not the hemorrhage prove dangerous?"

"No," the physician snapped, thrusting a bottle of chloroform into his pocket. "Lacerated wounds—such as an explosion makes—do not bleed dangerously, as a rule."

"But flying missiles with cutting edges make incised wounds sometimes, and they bleed severely," Ralph replied as he set a jar of aseptic gauze upon the counter.

"Y-e-s," the doctor said with lifted brows and wide-open eyes, looking his clerk full in the face.

Then briskly: "I will go at once. You know what I will be likely to need—and where Crawford lives?"

"I do," was the quiet reply.

Without another word, Dr. Barwood crushed his hat over his eyes and hurried forth. As he went down the black street, he knowingly nodded his head and talked to himself.

Marlowe quickly collected the necessary articles; made them into a package; and five minutes after his employer's departure, passed out, locking the door behind him.

Jim Crawford's humble abode was on a cross street, near the vacant lot back of the livery stable, where he had been injured. The house was a story and a half frame with sagging roof, small windows, and gray weather boarding. His diminutive shop stood on one corner of the lot.

As Marlowe reached the obscure place, he saw a number of men standing around the doorway, conversing in low, awe-struck tones. Pushing his way through the crowd, he knocked upon the door. It was opened from within; and he entered.

The small, low-ceilinged room was full of people; the air was close and foul-smelling. A small hand lamp upon the mantel over the grate faintly lighted the interior. The floor was bare, the windows curtainless; the furniture, mean and scanty.

The young man took in all this at a glance and a sniff. From a bedroom adjacent came the groans of the injured man; and down the rickety stairway leading to the loft, floated the wails and sobs of weeping children.

"Is Dr. Barwood in the next room?" Ralph inquired of Brady, the bridge-tender, who stood leaning against the mantel—sobered by the accident to his boon companion.

"Yes," that worthy replied sullenly. "Go right on in."

Marlowe did as directed. Upon a poorly furnished bed in one corner, lay the injured man, his head and left arm swathed in bloody cloths; and by his side sat his wife, dry-eyed and calm, patting and stroking his uninjured hand and speaking encouragingly to him. He was moaning and sniveling pitifully. Neither paid any attention to the newcomer.

Walking up to Dr. Barwood, who stood at a high, old-fashioned bureau, filling a hypodermic syringe, Ralph asked in a low, distinct tone:

"How badly is he hurt?"

"Not so badly as reported," answered the doctor, coolly testing the point of the hypodermic needle, by thrusting it into a piece of chamois skin. "His arm is considerably lacerated and contused; but it will not be necessary to amputate it, I think. Then he has two or three cuts upon the head and neck. We will have to take a lot of stitches."

"You can't dress his wounds in this room?"

"No."

"Then I would better clear the other of people, and get things ready."

"Yes," the doctor replied in a matter-of-course tone and manner.

Marlowe quickly rid the small sitting room of curious cumber[47]; threw up a window and left open the outer door, to admit fresh air; and proceeded to get things in readiness.

---

47 cumber: encumber by being in the way

From the crowd outside, he called in Sam Clark and Airly Chandler to aid him; and said to them:

"Unload the kitchen table and bring it in here. Then stir up the fire in the stove and boil some water in a clean vessel—two or three gallons at least."

Mrs. Crawford came out to ask him what he needed. She was stoop-shouldered and sallow; and had a heartbroken expression of countenance. With her help he soon transformed the bare kitchen table into a firm and comfortable couch. Then—the water having boiled—he immersed in it the instruments he had brought, and prepared antiseptic solutions. Next he cut a lot of ligatures and threaded a number of needles; made a funnel of a folded napkin, upon which to administer the anesthetic; and last of all arranged everything he thought would be needed, upon a stand, in orderly array.

"Everything is ready, doctor," he announced, thrusting his head in at the bedroom door.

Dr. Barwood was sitting at his patient's bedside, his fingers upon the pulse.

Arising he answered:

"Then call help, and carry him out and administer the anestheic. He was suffering from shock and the effects of hemorrhage when I came. But his flagging pulse has rallied; he is all right now."

Soon the moaning sufferer was upon the table and under the influence of the anesthetic. The cleansing and dressing of the wounds proceeded swiftly and systematically. Marlowe, with the tacit consent of the physician, did much of the stitching and bandaging. With deft fingers, he ligated arteries and tied surgeon's knots. Clark and Chandler looked on in silent admiration and astonishment; but Dr. Barwood manifested no surprise.

When all was finished and the patient had been returned to his bed, the doctor placed a package of powders upon the bureau, and pointing to them remarked to Mrs. Crawford:

"Give him one of those every hour or two, when he does not rest well."

"All right, doc," she answered meekly.

"And you'd better have some one or two of your friends stay with you tonight."

She nodded humbly.

"That's all then—except this." And the physician looked around to see that no one overheard him. —"Have you any money to pay me for this?"

"No, I hain't, doc," the poor woman replied, dropping her eyes before his fierce gaze.

For a full minute the stillness of the room was broken only by the stertorous breathing of the unconscious husband upon the bed. Then Mrs. Crawford looked up—the tears trickling down her sunken cheeks—and said between sobs:

"It's a sin an' a shame, Doc Barwood—I know it is. You've been awful good to us. But I hain't got a cent to give you, fer what you've done tonight. Jim's drunk up everything he's made this week. An' you're 'bout sick y'rself—I can see that. Oh, I'm jest heart broke!"

"And you have no money to give me?" Dr. Barwood mumbled crustily.

She silently, chokingly shook her head.

"Then *I'll* have to give *you* some," he growled, thrusting a ten dollar bill into her hand and hurrying from her presence.

The miserable wife and mother stood crumpling the bill in her toil-hardened hand and staring wildly after his retreating form. When the door had closed behind him, she threw herself upon the floor and sobbed convulsively.

Marlowe was alone in the sitting room, awaiting his employer's coming.

"Are you ready to go?" asked the latter.

In answer Ralph arose with alacrity; and together they left the house. Silently they trudged up the deserted street. At the drugstore steps the older man remarked:

"You may put things away; I am going home."

"Very well," was the reply.

"Say!" said the doctor with startling suddenness.
"Well, doctor?"
"Where's your diploma?"
"My diploma?"
"Yes—your medical diploma."
Marlowe was silent for a moment. Then he answered coolly:
"In my trunk at my rooms."
"You would better have it framed, and hang it up in the store."
"I will consider your suggestion."
" Good night, Dr. Marlowe."
"Mr. Marlowe—or better, Ralph—if you please, Dr. Barwood."
"At any rate, good night," the older man chuckled.
"Good night."

The one limped painfully toward his home; the other entered the drugstore—and sat by the fireless stove till almost morning.

* * * * * *

CHAPTER X

ELECTION DAY came and went quietly, with but one incident of note. Dr. Barwood—as ardent a Republican as ever placed a cross under the eagle—whose rheumatism had steadily grown worse, in spite of his own prescribing and dosing, hobbled down to the polls and voted among the first. Then he dragged his pain-racked body back home and settled down among his cushions, liniments, and potions.

Hardly had he regained a degree of comfort, when an enthusiastic Republican—a local politician of ignoble instincts—dropped in to inform him that Ralph Marlowe's vote had been challenged.

"He did vote, though, didn't he?" the doctor said, fixing his black orbs upon his caller.

"No," the man answered.

"Why?'—In surprise and anger.

"Well, you see, the judges wasn't satisfied that he's a resident of this state, doc; and—"

"Wasn't he willing to swear that he is?"

"It may be—I don't know. Anyhow—"

"And he left the polls without casting a ballot?"

"Yes, he did, doc. He's a Democrat, I understand; and it's a gain o' one vote fer us. So of course I didn't say nothin'."

"You?" snarled Dr. Barwood, his features contorted with pain and anger. "Of course not! You wouldn't say anything; but I will. Democrat or Republican, he's got a right to vote here; and what's more, he's going to vote here. You go down street, find Jep, and send him up here with the phaëton.[48] I'll go down to the polls; and I'll raise the fuzz on somebody's back, if that young man doesn't get to vote."

Knowing that remonstrance would be worse than useless, the politician withdrew—figuratively kicking himself that he had not kept all knowledge of the affair from the honest and honorable old partisan.

The result was that Marlowe was allowed to vote—and that his employer was privileged to suffer torture all the afternoon and evening, owing to the excitement and exertion of his second trip to the polls.

Ralph and Clark met at supper, and the latter remarked:

"Say! Why can't you lock up and come down to the office tonight? I'll have to stay there till after midnight, perhaps, receiving the returns; and I want company."

"I can't do it," Ralph replied. "Dr. Barwood is ill; I must stay at the store."

"I'm sorry—but say! You want to hear the returns as they come in, don't you?"

"I should like to, of course."

"And if you can't come to the office, you can't go to the townhall, where the two parties have arranged to have their headquarters together?"

"No."

"I'll tell you what. I can make you duplicates of the dispatches and send them to the drugstore. It won't cost you but a few dollars. Get McDevitt and Chandler and some of the other fellows to go in with you. You'll have a warm and comfortable place; and won't have to stand up and mix with all the drunken riffraff in the township."

"It is a good idea," Marlowe answered. And so it was arranged.

The polls closed at six o'clock. An hour later the crowd began to gather at the townhall; and one by one, those to whom Ralph had spoken dropped into the drugstore.

---

48 phaëton: any of various light four-wheeled horse-drawn vehicles

The day had been fine and warm; and the night was clear and starlit. Down at the polling place—a small room in one end of the town building—the election officers were monotonously droning over the ballots, one by one. Semicircles of anxious partisans pressed their faces to the outside of the dusty window panes and their ears to the keyhole of the bolted door, and listened and peered breathlessly to catch the names as they were read off—thereby gaining a vague idea of how the vote was running. Upstairs, in the big barn-like hall, members of both political parties were surging to and fro, discussing the events and probabilities of the local election, merrily chaffing one another, and impatiently awaiting outside returns. Tobacco smoke hung like a heavy pall over the picturesque scene, further dimming the light of the dim lamps; and the close atmosphere reeked with the pestilential[49] effluvia[50] of many pairs of lungs.

The streets were deserted save for the presence of the ubiquitous[51] small boy and an occasional pedestrian hurrying to or from the polling place. A prolonged whoop or a blast from a tin horn now and then disturbed the wonted silence of night.

By seven o'clock a small crowd of Democrats and Republicans had gathered in Dr. Barwood's drugstore and grouped themselves around the stove. They were young men, for the most part; and thought themselves vitally interested in the result of the election. For their blood was hot—as young blood always is—and their passions and prejudices were strong; and each felt that the salvation or ruination of the country depended upon the election or defeat of his particular candidate. But like their elders at the townhall, they hid their anxiety under masks of smiling indifference; chaffed, chatted, and told stories; and indulged in forced merriment and horseplay, to pass the time.

"It's after seven o'clock," Morris McDevitt remarked at last, impatiently consulting his watch. "We ought to be getting some

---

49 pestilential: tending to cause death
50 effluvia: foul or harmful emanation
51 ubiquitous: being or seeming to be everywhere at the same time

dispatches by this time."

"It's a little too early yet," replied Airly Chandler, pensively rubbing the mole upon his chin.

"The first returns 'll come from the east," McDevitt insisted; "and it's time they were beginning to get in. There's quite a difference in longitude and time between here and the Atlantic seaboard. They've counted out two hours or more ago, in New York—"

"Surely you Democrats are not itching to hear from New York?" interrupted a young Republican, laughing.

His party allies joined in boisterously. McDevitt was a little nettled.

"I'll bet the cigars for the crowd we carry New York," he said defiantly. "There!"

His adherents clapped their hands and cheered; his opponents hooted derisively.

"Shut up or shove up," Morris cried boldly.

"I'll take the bet," was the cool reply of the challenged party. "Set up the cigars, Marlowe. The loser pays for them. I'm anxious to smoke a good cigar on Morris."

Marlowe smilingly took a box of cigars from the case and passed them around; and soon the smoke from a dozen or more rolled hazily toward the ceiling.

"I wonder how they're getting along down at the polls," someone suggested.

"I just came from there," answered a new arrival. "They've counted out a little over a hundred votes; and the Republicans have about ten the best of it."

"How do you like that ginger—McDevitt, and Marlowe, and Carston, and the rest of you?" yelled an enthusiastic Republican.

"We like the brand first-rate," McDevitt answered promptly and decidedly. "There's about four hundred votes polled. If your rate of loss holds out, you'll carry the township by about forty—the lowest majority you've had in twenty years.

You usually carry the county by from four to six hundred. If our rate of gain keeps up, we'll carry it this time, by two hundred. How do you fellows like the ginger?"

The Democrats laughed and cheered; the Republicans looked glum. Carston—the miller's stalwart son—threw his arm around McDevitt and gave him a bear-like squeeze.

"Stop!" the latter cried chokingly. "Look at my suit, now—flour all over. You hurt my head, too."

And the young merchant feelingly rubbed his temple, where a strip of court-plaster hid an abrasion.

"Carston didn't hurt that," chuckled George Hammond—a son of the widow who occupied the house in which Marlowe had rooms. "Some Republican hurt that the night of the Tenacre speech."

"You have no room to say anything," grinned Morris. "Look at your eye. It's still decorated with all the colors of the rainbow. Besides, we're both Democrats. You keep still."

At that moment the door opened. All turned their heads, expecting to see the messenger boy with dispatches. Instead Jep Tucker ambled in, smoking a long Wheeling stogie and smiling complacently.

"It's Tucker! —Hello, Jep! —Where've you been, Tucker? —What's the news, Jep?" were the cries that greeted his advent.

Sidling into his accustomed corner and seating himself with a sigh of content, the eccentric answered:

"I've jest come up from the polls. They've counted out 'bout a hundred an' fifty votes; an' us Republicans is 'bout twelve 'r fifteen ahead. I'm a feelin' purty good—"

"Over the prospect of our losing the township?" Airly Chandler sneered, agitatedly thrusting his freckled hand through his red hair—until it fairly bristled.

"No, not 'xackly over that," Tucker explained coolly. "I ain't worryin' much 'bout it, though. The Republicans o' this township alluz did know how to make 'tarnal fools o' the'rselves. But the news I'm feelin' good over is what I heerd as I was comin' up street."

"What is it? —Out with it!" —From several at once.

"Well, dispatches has jest come in from a whole batch o' the eastern states; an' they're all showin' strong Republican gains."

"That's the stuff! Hurrah for McKinley! Mc—Kin—ley, Mc—

Kin—ley! Whoopee!" shouted those of Tucker's political faith.

The others maintained a grim silence.

"Did you hear the dispatches read, Jep?" Marlowe ventured to ask.

"No; but—"

"You came direct from the townhall?"

"Yes. I jest stopped a minute to talk to two fellers on the street, John Davis an' Cad Burbank. An'—"

"And they told you the glorious news, eh?"

"Yes."

"Oh, stuff!" ejaculated Airly Chandler disgustedly, his countenance falling.

"There's not a word of truth in the report," McDevitt asserted positively. "It's a grapevine dispatch. You bet if there was such good Republican news as that, Clark would fire it up here *too* quick. He'd want to clip *my* tail feathers—and he knows I'm here."

Again the door swung upon its hinges; and Lon Crider entered. He shook hands all around, bowing and smiling to each in turn. Then turning to Ralph, he said in his quick voluble way:

"I told you I'd be around in a few weeks; and I've made my promise good. I've put in a faithful day to get here. Well, I reckon! I voted in Zanesville this morning—one more ballot to swell McKinley's majority, you know; took the morning train for Malconta; worked that place this forenoon; drove out to Foxtown and back in the afternoon; took the evening train for this place; got my supper with jolly Charley Williams; and come up here. How's the old doc—and where is he?"

Marlowe vouchsafed[52] the desired information.

"Sorry to hear the old man's under the weather," the drummer replied, toying with his watch charm and smiling as though Dr. Barwood's indisposition was a royal joke. "But you can give me an order just as well as he can—you did on my other trip, you remember. Goods came all O. K., didn't they? Of course—I knew they would. You say you had to telegraph to hurry them up? That so! I'm sorry about the delay. But it won't happen again. I'll blow the shipping clerk up—or who-

---

52 vouchsafe: to grant or give

ever's to blame—when I get in. How's the election going here, Marlowe?"

"Democratic."

"What!"

"Yes."

"Sure?"

Ralph nodded; and the congregated villagers smiled at the traveling man's tone and manner.

"Well, don't that beat—! Why, I'm surprised! This township's usually Republican. It'll be the only precinct in the state that'll show Democratic gains."

"I'll bet you five dollars it won't be the only one," cried Morris McDevitt, rising to his feet and flashing a roll of bills.

"Put your money into your pocket, McDevitt," Marlowe said quietly. "I won't allow any betting in here—except the stakes be candy or cigars, or some equally inexpensive trifle."

McDevitt grumblingly obeyed the behest.

"I don't want to bet anyhow," Crider laughed good-humoredly, "I always lose. But I *am* surprised at the result here. Are they through counting out?"

Ralph shook his head.

"But you know how the vote's running, eh? Well, boys, have a smoke on me, anyhow. Here's some fine ones. I like to see people enjoy themselves. Pass them around, McDevitt." —Handing the latter a bunch of cigars.

Then he continued:

"I'm interested in the election here, Marlowe. How do you explain the fact that this precinct shows such strong Democratic gains?"

"It's due to the big Tenacre blow-out you Republicans had here," George Hammond interjected.

"I don't understand," Crider said perplexedly. "Wasn't the Tenacre meeting a success?"

"The Democratic gain," Ralph said solemnly—but with a roguish wink and a nod of his head toward Tucker, who was wheezingly puffing at a fat cigar, "is due indirectly to the Tenacre mass meeting. You see, Crider, there was an old brass cannon in the town—I say was, advisedly, for it is here no longer—and one Jep Tucker conceived the idea of disinterring it from its resting place beneath the moldy shavings of the coopershop, where it had reposed in peace for many years, and using it to welcome the visiting hosts and speed their departure. He did not know—or he had forgotten—that the old gun was a Democratic mascot. So he carried out his intent, in spite of the advice of friends and the opposition of foes. The hoodoo piece exploded at the second and parting shot; and the result is as I have stated."

The crowd laughed at Jep and guyed him unmercifully. At last he pulled himself up from his lounging attitude, and chuckled phthisically[53]:

"I guess that statement's 'bout right. It's part right, anyhow—an' a feller'd jest as well be killed fer a sheep as a lamb. 'Tain't no more sin to eat the devil 'n it is to sup his broth. That ol' cannon lost us one Republican vote that I know of—Jim Crawford's. I've had enough o' cannon shootin' to last me a lifetime. I'm like Tomp Nutt was 'bout his fight with Alf Sanders. I'm no hog; an' I know w'en I've got enough."

"Tell the story, Jep," they chorused.

"Not tonight," he said, shaking his head undecidedly.

It was evident he was itching to spin the yarn. "Yes, now—while we are waiting for the dispatches," they insisted.

"Well, if I *must, I must,*" he answered with assumed reluctance, discarding his cigar stub and taking a chew of tobacco.

"The thing happened 'way back 'fore the war—an' durin' it. I've heerd Hen Olcott tell the story a hundred times. Some o' you fellers ought to know ol' Hen. He lives down on Flat Bottom; 'an' has a crippled arm he carries in a leather sling—got shot in the war. He's a kind o' curious critter, too. His business is loggin', movin' buildin's, sawmillin', an' so on. Says his game arm keeps him from doin' *heavy* work.

---

53 pthisically: illness of the lungs or throat, such as asthma or a cough

"But to hurry 'long with the story—'cause them telegraphs 'll be comin' in purty soon, I feel it in my bones—in them days jest 'fore the war, ol' Tomp Nutt—he was young Tomp, then—was the best man in Stonebury township. He could out-run, out-jump, throw down, drag out, an' whip any man o' his inches—no matter what his politics 'r religion might be. An' it got so nobody 'ld toe the mark to meet him, 'r knock the chip from his shoulder.

"Ev'ry neighborhood, in them days, had its boss fighter. Out on the head-waters o' Monday Creek—'bout thirty miles from here—the cock o' the walk was a big red-headed, raw-boned, lantern jawed feller named Alf Sanders. He heerd o' Tomp, an' Tomp heerd o' him; an' each one was anxious to have a try at the other. Well, finally they come together—an' this was the way of it:

"Sanders rode into Malconta, one day in the spring o' 'sixty, to 'tend to some business 'r other; an' he fooled 'round so long he had to put up an' stay all night in the town. The next mornin' he bought a pint o' whisky, straddled his hoss, an' rode down the river—lookin' fer cattle to buy, he said; but most people thought he was lookin' fer Tomp Nutt. If he *was,* he got accommodated—but didn't know it till it was all over.

"He crossed on the ferryboat at this place an' set off out through Red Brush, toward the Ellis schoolhouse—close to which Tomp's folks lived.

"That very mornin', as it happened, Tomp an' Hen Olcott an' Elick Miles—all of 'em young men at that time—was settin' on a rail fence close to the schoolhouse, chawin' the'r tobacker an' swappin' yarns 'bout coon huntin'. By-an'-by they saw a feller ridin' a big gray hoss, up the hill, toward 'em.

"'That's a purty nice nag,' Elick Miles remarks.

"'An' th-that's a mighty g-g-good man astraddle o' h-him;' says Tomp takin' in the stranger's p'ints.

"It was Sanders. An' he rides up even with the three fellers on the fence; throws one foot out o' the stirrup; an' kind o' lollin' over in the saddle, says—as sassy as a chipmunk:

"'I hain't got no money to throw at the birds; but I'll bet three dollars I can whip any feller on that fence—an' not half try.'

"Tomp an' Hen an' Elick was knocked all in a heap. They wasn't expectin' nothin' o' the kind; an' they couldn't do nothin' but hold the'r breaths an' look at one another.

"'I mean what I say,' Sanders goes on. 'I'll bet three dollars I can whip any man in the crowd. Now! Chip in—'r don't cheep out.'

"Tomp studied a minute, an' then he says: "'I've a n-notion n-not to b-b-b'lieve it.'

"'Put up y'r stuff an' shed y'r wamus, then,' says Sanders. 'I'll 'light an' hitch; an' we'll have it out right here.'

"'I hain't g-got n-no three d-dollars,' Tomp 'xplains; 'b-but I'll p-put up this w-watch 'g-gginst y'r m-money.'

"An he drawed out a big silver timepiece worth three 'r four times three dollars.

"'It's a bargain,' says Sanders, his eyes sparklin' at sight o' the watch.

"So he got down an' hitched his hoss, skinned off his coat, an' tied his gallowses[54] in a knot. Tomp done the same. Then they put up the stakes in Hen Olcott's hands, an' went at it. It was nip an' tuck, I tell *you*. It was knock down an' drag out, rough an' tumble, claw an' tooth. The fight lasted jest an hour—by Tomp's own watch; an' most o' the time they was down on the ground, fightin' like a couple o' bulldogs.

"At last Tomp got his thumb in Sanders's eye, an' gouged it out onto his cheek. Then the bully from Monday Creek come to a sudden c'nclusion he was a whipped man; an' he sung out:

"'Cavy! I've got enough—I ain't no hog!'

"'B-B'gosh, I'm g-glad of it!' Tomp panted staggerin' to his feet.

"Tomp pocketed his watch an' money. Then they shook hands, went out to the schoolhouse well, an' begun to wash the'rselves.

"'Is ther' many more fellers in this strip o' timber, that's as good men as you?' Sanders asked, feelin' of his gouged eye.

---

54 gallowses: a pair of suspenders or braces

"'P-Plenty of 'em,' says Tomp. 'The w-woods is f-full of 'em. H-Here's H-Hen Olcott an' Elick M-Miles—they're b-both b-b-better men 'n I am. F-Fact is I'm the limberest s-saplin' in the c-c-clearin."

"'If I wasn't 'fraid you'd jump onto me ag'in', answers Sanders, 'I'd call that a lie.'

"'Want to bet th-three dod-dollars on it?'

"'No,' says Sanders, shakin' his head till the water flew from his long red hair. 'But what might be y'r name?'

"'It m-might be J-Julius Ceasar—b-but it ain't,' answers Tomp, with a grin that made his swelled face look awful.

"'What is it, then?' asks Sanders.

"'Tomp N-Nutt.'

"'The devil!' says Sanders.

"'P-Purty n-near it, I g-g-guess,' says Tomp.

"'My name's Alf Sanders.'

"'Th-That's what I thought,' stutters Tomp, 'An' y-you ain't m-much of a fi-fighter, after all.'

"Well," Jep continued, "that was the end o' the fight. Sanders bid 'em good-bye, got on his hoss, an' rode away. Him an' Tomp didn't meet no more till after the war broke out. But it happened that all four of 'em, that was together that Sunday, 'nlisted in the same regiment; an' down in front of Atlanta they was all in camp together.

"One day Sanders got on a spree an' come a prancin' up through camp, crackin' his fists an' a swearin' he could lick any man on top o' ground. Tomp an' Hen Olcott was settin' on a log in front o' the'r tent, whittlin'. Sanders come right up to 'em, danced 'round, bragged an' threatened, an' finally rubbed his fist under Tomp's nose an' told him to smell of his master.

"But Tomp jest set there—smilin' an' whittlin'—an' never said a word back. At last Sanders got tired o' the one-sided game an' went away.

"'I don't see how you could stand it, Tomp Nutt,' Hen Olcott says. 'Surely you wasn't 'feared of him. I don't see how you could stand his blowin' an' braggin', an' rubbin' his fist under y'r nose an' tellin' you to smell o' y'r master. I don't see how you could stand it, at all.'

"'I c-could s-stand it,' Tomp grins.

"'But you whipped him once'—Hen begins.

"'Y-Yes,' Tomp answers. 'An' I can wh-whip him ag'in. B-But it t-takes an hour to d-d-do it—an' I ain't h-hankerin' f-fer the j-j-job.'

"An' that's the way with me," Jep concluded hastily, as the door opened and a messenger boy from the station put in an appearance; "I ain't hankerin' fer no more cannon shootin'. Sing out, youngster! How's the 'lection goin'?"

"Here! Give me those dispatches," Morris McDevitt cried excitedly.

"Let Marlowe read them," Airly Chandler suggested.

"Yes, let Marlowe read them," a number of others seconded.

The messenger boy handed the roll to Ralph and hurried away. The latter proceeded to read the telegrams, in order. There were a dozen or more of them—all from the east—announcing great Republican gains in that section of the country.

Perfect silence reigned during the reading; but at the conclusion, the Republicans sprang to their feet and cheered.

"Hurrah for McKinley!" shouted Lon Crider. And then he laughed apologetically.

"Mc—Kin—ley! Mc—Kin—ley!" chorused his *confrères*[55].

"Just wait until you hear from the west and south," McDevitt cried.

But his countenance was downcast.

"No matter how the election goes," Crider whispered to Marlowe, "you'll still want some drugs. Can't you give me your order tonight?"

"We are not needing anything," was the reply.

"Nothing at all?"

"Nothing."

---

55 confrères: colleagues

"Then I'll go down to Charley's and turn in. I'm tired out. See you next trip—in a few weeks. Hold an order for me. Good night."

Quickly and quietly he withdrew.

"Let's go down to headquarters and see how things are going," Airly Chandler suggested.

"Come on," said George Hammond, rising.

"Agreed," cried several more.

And out the door they trooped, leaving Ralph and Jep alone.

"Did you notice that somebody'd been drinkin'?" the latter asked, leaning back against the wall and peeping through his half-closed lids.

"Who?" Ralph inquired, searching his companion's face.

"Well—anybody?"

"You speak in the impersonal. Please be more definite."

"Morris McDevitt, fer instance."

Marlowe walked about the room and made no reply for some seconds. Then he said:

"Keep your observation to yourself, Jep. Perhaps you are mistaken."

"P'r'aps I am—an' then ag'in, p'r'aps I *ain't,*" Tucker muttered. "But I'll mind what you say—I won't say a word to nobody. An' I guess I'll go home an' go to bed. Whichever way the 'lection goes, it won't make no differ'nce to me. I'll have flapjacks fer breakfast, tomorrer mornin', jest the same anyhow."

With the words he arose and sauntered out, yawning, stretching, and glancing into the showcases as he went.

Marlowe followed him to the door and stood upon the step, his hot forehead bared to the cool night air.

Far down the street he heard the buzz of voices.

All else was silence. "Mc—Kin—ley! Mc—Kin—ley!" floated faintly to his ears. Then out of the blackness emerged a figure; and Morris McDevitt ascended the steps.

"Any more news?" Ralph queried.

"Yes," McDevitt growled. "Everything's gone Republican, I-I guess. Dispatches 're coming in from all over the—the—country."

His breath was redolent with liquor; his tongue was thick.

"Come in here," Marlowe said, taking him by the arm and drawing him within doors. "McDevitt, you have been drinking too much,"

"Me?" —With tipsy surprise and gravity.

"Yes, you," Ralph answered, looking squarely into the flushed face and bloodshot eyes before him.

"Well, whose—whose business is it?" was the sullen rejoinder.

"Your friends."

"*They* needn't worry, if *I* don't. And I don't care—"

"You don't care!" Ralph interrupted in a tone of mild amazement.

"No, I don't. Why should I care? Nobody cares—cares for me; and the girl I love won't marry me. So there!"

"You are discouraged, broken-hearted, and ready to throw yourself away, eh?" Marlowe said sneeringly.

"Yes, I am," answered McDevitt with maudlin solemnity.

"You wouldn't talk such stuff, if you were sober, McDevitt."

"Maybe I wouldn't *talk* it," grinned the befuddled young man, staggering slightly as he shifted his position; "but I'd *think* it."

"Did you come here to make a confidant of me?"

Marlowe asked, shrewdly guessing the truth.

"That's—that's it; that's what I did."

"Well, you are in no condition to make confession or receive advice. I'll take you for a walk. Sit down on the steps out there till I close up; you'll get sick in this warm room. First, however, take a whiff of this."

Ralph took a bottle from the shelf, removed the stopper, and shoved the open mouth under his companion's nose. The latter obediently took a deep inspiration—and clutched at the empty air with both hands, in an effort to recover his breath, the tears starting from his eyes.

"Hartshorn!" he gasped at last.

Marlowe smilingly replaced the bottle upon the shelf and motioned toward the door. McDevitt silently withdrew to the outer air. A few minutes later the lights were out and the two were walking briskly up the street, arm in arm.

To the far end of the town they went, beyond the last twinkling light, neither speaking. Then they turned and started back at the same smart pace—Ralph hurrying his lagging companion, McDevitt's leaden feet grew lighter; his brain began to clear. At last he said in a cautious undertone:

"I'm coming around all right."

"Glad to hear it," muttered Ralph without slacking his speed.

"And I'm heartily ashamed of myself, Marlowe."

"Of course. Come on—step lively."

"Say?"

"Well?"

"Let's stop. I want to talk to you."

"Wait until we are again within the drugstore. Someone might overhear us."

"I'm not going back to the drugstore."—Stopping suddenly and irritably jerking loose from his companion.—"I'm going to dodge down this alley and take the back street, for home. I'm afraid of meeting somebody I know, if I go down Main Street."

"You had no such fear an hour ago."

"I am sober now—or nearly so."—Forcing a low laugh.

"And you were drunk then—or nearly so." McDevitt made no reply; and Ralph continued:

"I think your resolve to get home as quickly and as secretly as possible, a good one. Good night."

"Wait," the other whispered. "I want to say a word or two before we part. You have proven yourself my friend tonight. I'll be ashamed to meet you again—in daylight. And here and now I promise you I will not again—"

"Don't!" Marlowe interrupted. "The best way to keep a promise is to keep it to one's self; the easiest way not to break a resolve is not to make it. Simply do not do again that for which you are sorry or ashamed."

"Let me shake your hand, at least."

Silently they clasped hands in the damp darkness. The liquor had died in McDevitt's arteries; and he was shivering with cold and nervousness. His teeth chattered as he said:

"Ralph Marlowe, I have known you but a few short weeks; and I do not know why I should make a confidant of you. But I am going to do so, if you will let me."

"Wait until another time. It is late; and you are cold and ought to be abed."

"No, now!" Morris insisted obstinately, still retaining his companion's hand. "I am going to the devil as fast as I can—and I want your help. For several months I have been drinking considerably and gambling heavily. I am fast losing money and morals; and it's all on account of Julia Barwood—"

"Another case of Adam and Eve—the old, old story," Marlowe said sarcastically.

"How?"

"'The woman gave me of the tree and I did eat.'"

"Oh! No; you understand what I mean. And I want your advice and assistance."

"Do you love Julia Barwood?"

"With all the ardor of my being."

"And to prove your love you sneakingly do the things no good woman can approve—and can hardly tolerate or forgive. For of course she is not aware of your drinking and gambling?"

"No."—In a weak and humble whisper, the single syllable quavering.

"Does she love you?"

"Yes—she says she does. But she won't marry me."

"What is her reason for refusing—if she loves you?"

"I am a Catholic."

"And she is a Protestant."

"Yes."

"She will not marry a Catholic."

"That's it."

"And you will not marry a Protestant."

McDevitt hesitated before replying. Then he said:

"I would if I could; but I can't."

"Why?"

"It would mean my ruin. My father would disown me, disinherit me, and cast me adrift without a penny."

"With you, then, it is not so much a matter of filial piety or religious principle, as it is a matter of financial policy."

"You—you don't understand me, Marlowe"—McDevitt began falteringly.

"Yes," Ralph hastened to say, speaking rapidly and coldly, "I understand perfectly. With Julia Barwood it is a matter of religious belief—bigoted though that belief may be. With you, as I have intimated, it is a matter of dollars and cents. You have no religious convictions nor scruples. You would renounce your faith, espouse hers, and marry her—if you were not loth[56] to lose your father's money-bags. You do not care for your church or for your father's approval; all you desire is his tacit consent to your marriage with a Protestant. I despise such a spirit. It is mean, despicable. I have no advice to offer you; and I would give you no assistance, if I could."

"You're pretty severe on a poor devil," McDevitt said in a whining tone. "You've never been in such a fix, Marlowe."

"True," Ralph replied in a softened tone. "Were I in your place, I might look at the matter differently. But you will catch cold standing here; you are shivering. Go home—be a man. I will think over what you have told me. If I discover an honorable way to disentangle your love snarl, I will not fail to communicate the secret to you. Good night."

McDevitt dodged into a black alley and disappeared. Marlowe turned up his overcoat collar, thrust his gloved hands deep into the pockets, and hurried down the street. As he went he muttered under his breath: "Bah! A miserable weakling—without moral stamina or manly courage. I doubt if he knows what love is; he is too utterly weak and selfish. How *can* such a woman as Julia Barwood love such a man? She is strong, virile, self-reliant. Yet her strength

---
56 loth: variant of loath

is her weakness. For it is but narrow-minded egoism and self-righteousness. She might save him from himself by marrying him. But will she—when she learns the truth? And is he worth the sacrifice? And a sacrifice it would be—to her mind, at least. What a tangle—what a snarl! Yet I would cut the gordian knot at one stroke. If I loved her as I love—well, somebody else, I would win her love and her consent to marriage, no matter what barriers—religious or otherwise—stood between us. I would not be balked and discouraged by a little opposition. I would have her—have her in spite of all considerations of worldly gain or heavenly security!"

As he entered the front hall leading to his rooms, the tall clock in the corner struck the hour of eleven.

Down at the station, Sam Clark—his green visored cap pulled low over his eyes—was still receiving telegraphic returns.

But the townhall was almost empty, a few only of the most tenacious of both parties still figuratively clinging to the wires and hoping against hope that the vague and conflicting dispatches would soon bring the certainty of victory or defeat. They talked in drowsy monotones; and figured and disputed in a half-hearted way. The lights burned low and dim. All was silence without. The great presidential election was over; but the result was still in doubt.

* * * * * *

CHAPTER XI

THE MORNING following—just as Marlowe had finished the dusting and sweeping, of course—Tucker drifted into the store, and anchoring himself upon a chair near the stove remarked:

"Well, ther's more dispute 'bout the 'lection this mornin' than ther' was when I went home last night. Then ev'rything was Republican; an' I went to bed calkylatin' on a place in McKinley's cabinet. But this mornin' ev'rything's whopper-jawed an' topsy-turvy. No tellin' what the outcome's goin' to be, I guess; both sides is claimin' the victory. Wouldn't wonder my cabinet p'sition had gone glimmer'n, would you?"

"McKinley is elected," Marlowe asserted positively.

"You think so? Hain't had no vision have you—like ol' Phar'oh used to have? Well, I don't know 'bout my friend McKinley bein' 'lected. This 'lection business is a good deal like snipe huntin'; the feller that holds the bag don't alluz git the snipes."

Then after taking an enormous chew of tobacco and finding for it a comfortable resting place in his cheek:

"But I come in to tell you that I've been up to see the ol' doc this mornin'."

"How is he feeling?" Ralph inquired, rearranging the cigar boxes in the case.

"Too sick to git well an' not sick enough to die," Jep drawled nonchalantly. "I found him settin' propped up in a big rockin' chair, an' a lookin' like one o' the before-takin' pictures in an almanac.

He's got one ankle swelled up bigger 'n a nigger maul; an' he's grumpier 'n a hoot owl with a crippled wing. He told me—after a good 'eal o' talk 'bout rheumatiz an' its beauties an' advantages—that I was to stay here an' send you up to the house. Said he wanted to give you 'nstructions 'bout some work that must be done—"

"Why didn't you tell me?" Ralph interrupted testily.

"Why didn't I tell you?" Jep went on placidly. "'Cause I hain't had time yit. An' ain't I tellin' you now? Say! you put me in mind o' ol' Cale Wiseman that used to live out on the Quakerville road. He was the funniest ol' codger; an' was alluz gittin' ev'rything back'ards that he went to say. One time Chalkley Hanson drove down to town—come right past ol' Cale's place—an' got his load o' millin' an' started back. Ol' Cale was out at the gate watchin' fer him. He says:

"'Where was you goin' this mornin', Chalkley, when I saw you goin' down to town?'

"'I was goin' down to *town,* of course,' answers Chalk; 'goin' down to mill.'

"'Well, I wish I'd seen you,' says Cale; 'I wanted to send a letter down to the post-office.'

"'Thought you said you *did* see me,' says Chalk, coverin' his mouth with his hand, to hide a grin.

"'Oh! Well, I did *see* you,' answers Cale; 'but it was after you got out o' *sight.*'

"Course the ol' man meant all right; but he sort o' got things mixed. He meant to say that he saw Chalk after he got out o' hearin'. But—"

Jep broke off abruptly and looked around the room. He was alone. His words had been addressed to empty air; Marlowe had taken his hat and slipped out. With a sigh of disappointment and resignation, the eccentric lounged behind the counter and betook[57] himself to the large black bottle for consolation.

Ralph rang Dr. Barwood's door bell, unconsciously rearranged his tie and smoothed his hair—and awaited an answer

---

57 betook: to cause oneself to go

to his summons. A moment later the door opened; and Dolly stood before him. She wore a short frock of gray flannel, the entire front of which was concealed by a big gingham apron—a checkered monstrosity that hung two or three inches below her dress. Her wealth of golden hair was drawn tightly back from her white forehead and twisted into an immense knot upon the back of her coquettish head; but in spite of the hard usage to which it had been subjected, little ringlets and tresses had escaped confinement and were dallying about her ears and temples. One dress sleeve was pushed above her dimpled elbow; and with nervous fingers she was tugging at it, striving to pull it down.

Ralph's face mirrored the admiration he felt.

She appeared more childish than ever; but he thought he had never seen her look so beautiful. He was a man, you know.

"Oh!" she said with a little scream. "I did not know it was you. I should not have come to the door at all, but mother and Julia are both out. I was at work in the kitchen."

Then she stopped speaking, blushed—yes, actually blushed, and pulled frantically at her refractory[58] sleeve, succeeding at last in restoring it to its proper place.

"Good morning," he said, smiling and extending his hand.

"Good morning," she returned with a confused but merry laugh, placing her soft, taper fingers in his palm. "Come in. Of course you've come to see father. Dear old daddy!"—Her voice softening tenderly. —"He's been suffering awfully for a few days. Come this way. He's hobbled down to the sitting room again this morning. We can't keep him in bed. This hall is *so* dark. Don't fall over that old eight-day clock. It takes up as much room as a bedstead—almost; and it doesn't run eight days out of the year. But father will have it here; it's a family relic, you know."

At the second door on the right she stopped; and pointing to the knob said:

"You'll find him in there. Dear grumbling, grumpy old daddy! Don't mind his growls—he won't bite."

---

58 refractory: obstinate; unmanageable

Then laying her hand on his sleeve and smiling archly up at him:

"You failed to come at my request; but you came promptly at my father's bidding. Explain, sir."

"I mean to keep my promise"—he began.

"When?" she broke in impatiently.

"Some evening in the near future."

"When?" Insistently.

"As soon as your father is better. Do you think it will prove agreeable for me to call formally?"

"Agreeable?"

"To the other members of the family. You alone have extended me an invitation."

"Oh!"—And she laughed softly, yet uneasily glanced toward the rear of the dark, wide hall, as though fearing or expecting the advent of someone. —"You are over-sensitive, Mr. Marlowe; I will not say over-egoistical. Father likes you—you are aware of that; mamma wishes to make your acquaintance—she has so expressed herself; Julia desires to argue with you; and I—I am anxious to enjoy your company. Through me the others extend you a most cordial invitation to call early and often. Now, most exacting of mortals, are you satisfied?"

In the dusky light of the hall, he could not see her features distinctly; but he knew she was noiselessly laughing at him. The wild impulse came to him to catch her in his arms and kiss her saucy mouth. As though divining his mad desire, she drew away from him, saying:

"But I may not stand here—idling away time with you, Mr. Dignity. I must go to my pots and kettles. Julia will return soon and accuse me of dilatoriness[59]. We keep no servant. Just think of it! Mamma is old-fashioned; and won't have one around. But listen to this awful threat, young sir and take warning. If you do not call soon, I'll get sick and send for you—as daddy has done."

Ere he could make reply she had disappeared through the rear

---

59 dilatoriness: tending to delay

door of the hall, closing it behind her.

For a moment he stood staring blankly at the wall through which she had gone, puzzling over her words. Did she know he was a physician? If so, how had she ascertained the fact? Had her father informed her? Did her words imply anything; or had she simply uttered them to relieve her own embarrassment? But she did not seem to be embarrassed. He gave up the enigma and turned the knob of the door handle before him.

"Is that you, Marlowe?" growled a voice from the depths of a cushioned and padded armchair.

"It is Marlowe," the young man replied, closing the door and moving toward the center of the room.

"Come around here where I can see you. I can scarcely stir hand or foot this morning. Take that chair. Where the mischief have you been so long. I sent that good-for-nothing Tucker after you, an hour or more ago."

"I came as soon as he told me I was wanted," Ralph replied, taking a seat before the fire.

"You did, eh?"—In a crusty, ungracious tone.—"And when you got here you stood out there in the hall for five minutes, talking to that chit of a girl, instead of coming in to see if I was dead or alive. I don't blame you so much for that, though."—His black eyes twinkling, his features drawn into a scowl.—"Dolly would make any donkey stop and talk. How are you getting along at the store?"

"Smoothly, doctor," Ralph answered, looking around the room. "How are you feeling this morning?"

"As if I had slept on a bed of sickles. There's no definite news from the election yet? No. I wish you'd move that foot a little; it's gone to aching again. Be careful—be careful!"—With a grimace and a half groan. —"The devil never invented worse torment than articular rheumatism. There—that feels better. You *do* know how to handle an inflamed joint. Now, sit down. I want to talk with you."

Marlowe resumed his seat, again looked around him, and waited for his employer to go on. The room was big and comfortable. A bright fire blazed in the grate; the floor was thickly carpeted. The windows were high, narrow, and small-paned. The walls were hung with rich, dark paper; and upon them were a few prints, engravings, and etchings.

"Well, what do you think of my prison?" the older man demanded. "I see you are taking an inventory."

"I would pronounce it a comfortable place in which to be ill," Ralph answered.

"Oh, you would! That shows you've never *been* ill. I'll let you know there is no such thing as a comfortable place for the poor unfortunate with rheumatism. Ouch! Hand me that bottle on the mantel."

"What are you taking?" Marlowe asked, shaking the bottle and holding it up to the light.

"What am I taking?"—Fiercely.

"Yes." —Coolly.

"It's none of your business!"

"Possibly. You need not go to the trouble of informing me. I know what it is."

"You do?"

"Yes. It's a mixture of colchicum and guaiac—a nasty mess."

"No matter. It's indicated in my case."

"Is it?"

"Is it! Isn't it?"

"I think not."

"You think not?"

Marlowe nodded—and replaced the bottle upon the mantel. For several seconds silence reigned. Then Dr. Barwood said:

"You object to *my* treatment. What would *you* advise?"

"Do you wish me to prescribe for you?"

"No." —Flatly.—"I wish your opinion—that's all."

"I would suggest the Alkaline treatment—the salicylates, lithia salts, or lithia water in abundance."

"Humph!"

"You have my opinion."

"I have no faith in the Alkaline treatment."

"It is not a faith cure; it is legitimate therapy."

"Well said!" cried Dr. Barwood with a wholesome laugh—that was cut short by a spasm of pain.

"Take my case and treat me. I have made a miserable failure of it thus far. No physician can treat himself intelligently; he allows his feelings to influence his judgment. Prepare what you think I need and bring it up with you this evening. I'll take it, if it kill me."

"Very well, doctor," Ralph replied, repressing a desire to laugh. "What external treatment are you using?"

"Oh, a stinking, disagreeable mess! An old woman remedy—hops and salt and vinegar."

"It's good enough—in its way. Has it given you any relief?"

"Very little—none in fact. Do you know of anything better?"

"I'll make you an embrocation."[60]

"Embrocation!" the doctor snorted angrily.

Then, instantly controlling himself and smiling whimsically:

"Bring it along, though. I'll try it. It'll be like everything else I've used; it won't do any good. But I can put in the dreary time rubbing it on. It will help to amuse me. And you seem to understand that it's necessary to amuse the patient, while nature works the cure. I know what *would* make an excellent soothing application—if only I had it."

"What?"

"A plant that grows out on the headwaters of Monday Creek, thirty miles from here. I've forgotten its name even. But when I was a boy the natives used to make poultices of it; and it relieved pain like magic."

"Can't you get it?"

"Get what?"—Irritably.

"The plant, the drug—whatever you please to call it."

"Get it? How?"

"By sending after it."

A sharp twinge of pain contorted the sufferer's features; and he snapped angrily:

---

60 embrocation: liniment

"I could get fire in hell, on the same conditions—by sending after it. And one trip would be about as hard as the other. Are you anxious to undertake the mission?"

"To hell or Monday Creek, doctor?" Marlowe inquired with assumed innocence.

Then both laughed heartily.

"Enough of myself and my ailments," the older man remarked presently. "Fix up your *armamentarium*,[61] and fire it into me. Now I wish to talk about yourself. I want you to do some work for me. Will you?"

"What is the character of it?"

"You seem to suspect."

"I do."

"That I desire you to look after some of my patients?"

"Yes."

"Well, will you do what I want? *Somebody* must wait upon them."

"I would rather not."

"You have taken *my* case."

"*You* know that I am a physician; your *patients* are not aware of the fact."

"They'll soon learn it—if you treat them."

"That is just what I fear."

"Stuff!" snorted Dr. Barwood. "Why do you wish to hide your light under a bushel? Some of the villagers, who know of the assistance you rendered me in the Crawford case, already suspect that you have a sheepskin. I laid a trap for you there; and caught you. The whole town is talking about that operation—your part in it. People have called here on purpose to question me. Your sins are bound to find you out. You may as well throw off the mask. Hang your diploma in the drugstore and go to work. I have more than I can do when I am able to be about. What do you say—you shall share in

---

61 armamentarium: a collection of resources available or utilized for an undertaking or field of activity; especially the equipment, methods, and pharmaceuticals used in medicine

the receipts?"

"Your offer is flattering, doctor—and I appreciate the motive that prompts it; but I must decline."

"Why?"

"My reasons are private, doctor."

"I see. Then you will see my patients and my practice suffer?"

"No."

"No? What will you do?"

"I will wait upon all you indicate; but I will not proclaim myself a physician."

"Oh! Very well. Have your will and your way—for the present. Time will do what you refuse to do. Until I am able to get out, you must dress Crawford's wounds once a day, make regular visits to this list of patients,"—Handing his companion a folded paper,—"and attend to all emergency cases."

"And should I decline to do what you indicate?" Ralph interrogated, receiving the proffered paper and thrusting it into the inside pocket of his coat.

"You will not decline," Dr. Barwood replied composedly. "Have Jep stay in the store when you are out. He can keep the fire going and inform people of your whereabouts. Report to me once a day, at least, how things are coming on. Another thing—if any oil men call to see me, bring them up here. Don't *send* them; *come* with them. I might need your assistance in dealing with them. I think that's all. Now, Dr. Marlowe, you may go to work as soon as you like."

And his keen, black eyes—shadowed deeply by his corrugated, beetling[62] brows—sparkled with a peculiar light, half humorous, half ironical.

Ralph took up his hat, bade the human oddity good morning, and passed out.

When the front door had banged and the young man's retreating footsteps had died away, Dr. Barwood picked up a small hand bell that stood upon the stand near his chair, and jangled it vigorously.

In answer, Dolly came into the room, wiping her hands upon

---
62 beetling: protruding

her checkered apron.

"What is it, daddy?" she asked, advancing to his side, and caressingly smoothing his short iron-gray hair.

"Don't stand behind me, daughter," he cried crossly. "You know I can't turn around; and you *ought* to know I like to face the person I address."

Obediently, smilingly, she moved in front of him and dropped upon a low stool near his knee.

"Where's your mother and Julia?" he asked brusquely.

"Don't you remember, daddy? They went down to see Mrs. Carston, the miller's wife. She's quite ill this morning. They had a physician from Malconta to see her yesterday."

"And does that account for her increased illness this morning?"

"Oh, daddy!"—Softly patting his hand that lay upon the arm of the chair, and laughing merrily.

A benign smile for a moment smoothed the harsh lines from his countenance. Stretching forth his hand and smoothing her golden hair, he asked:

"What have you been doing for the last hour, that you have not been in to see me?"

"Doing the morning's work in the kitchen. Mamma and sister wanted to make their call early in order to get back to their sewing."

A shaft of pain, at that moment, shot through the doctor's swollen ankle, causing him to catch his breath and groan sharply.

"Poor daddy!" Dolly murmured sympathetically, the tears starting in her violet eyes. "I wish I could do something more for you."

"Confound it!" he growled savagely. "It hurts like the—the devil, Dolly! And our mother and Julia have not returned?"

"No, daddy."

"Humph! I could have made six calls in the length of time; and done six times as much good—and not one-sixth as much harm. If Mrs. Carston isn't dangerously ill, she *will* be. For every busybody in the town will push into her sick room to hear what the *savant* from Malconta had to say about her case. It matters not that they may be her friends and interested in her welfare; the result will be the same. They will wear her nerves threadbare with their chatterings and clamorings; and then wonder why she doesn't improve. And when she dies—as die she will, if *they* have *their* way—they'll lift their hands in holy awe and prate about a mysterious dispensation of Providence."

Dolly simply smiled. His hand still rested affectionately upon her head—and she was content.

"Dolly," he said so suddenly and sharply that she started.

"What, daddy?"

"What were you and that young clerk of mine talking about?"

"When—where?"

"When! Where ! You sly minx! In the hall as he came in. I heard you buzz—buzzing out there."

"Oh!"—With mock innocence.—"I had asked Mr. Marlowe to call upon us; and was taking him to task because he had not done so."

"You had asked him to call!"

"Yes, daddy."

"You! A mere child—a baby!"

"I am seventeen, daddy."—poutingly.

"Seventeen! A ripe old age! Why did you ask him to call?"

"Why?"

Her father nodded, his eyes sparkling.

"Because—because I thought I ought to ask him to call—because I *wished* him to call—because I—I like him."

"Like him? You hardly know his face, Dolly."

"I know him well enough to like him—to enjoy his company."

"Look here, Dolly. We are comrades. Let's be honest with each other. You entertain no silly notions in regard to Ralph—Mr. Marlowe?"

"Silly notions?"—Blushing hotly.

"Yes. You do not fancy you love him, do you? Speak out."

She remained silent—toying with her apron, her eyes

downcast.

"Answer my question—speak out," he insisted in a firm but kind voice.

"I—I do—not know," she faltered.

"Has he mentioned love or marriage to you; or—or tried to caress you?"

"No—never!" she answered stoutly, looking her parent straight in the eyes. "As you say, father, I have barely made his acquaintance. But I like him. There!"

"And he has not expressed or intimated a liking for you?"

"No."

"Well," he went on meditatively, earnestly, "keep a tight grip on your affections, Dolly. Once misplaced they are not easily reclaimed. He may care nothing for you—probably he does not; and he may be wholly unworthy of you. I know as little of him as you do. Besides you are but a child—entirely too young to think of such things. He may call to see you—all of us—in a social way. Enjoy his company as much as you please; but continue to make a confidant of me. Will you, daughter?"

"I will, daddy."

"Very well. Kiss me now—and go back to your work."

Silently she obeyed him—placing her plump arms around his neck, fondly kissing him several times, and leaving the room, a tear sparkling upon her cheek.

For some time Dr. Barwood sat shaking his head and pondering deeply. He frowned—and anon[63] he smiled. At last he muttered huskily:

"I love the child dearly—and she loves me. I understand her better than I understand her mother and sister; and she understands me better than they do. It has been so since she was a little thing—since she could barely toddle after me. A child—yet a woman I can hardly realize it. She trusts in me; I must watch over her. He has won her affection—I can see it—as he has won mine; and without apparent effort. Who is he—what is he? I wish I knew. I *must*

---

63 anon: after a while

know—soon. The idea of my permitting him to prescribe for me! I believe I am growing childish."

Frowning and smiling by turns, he sat gazing into the depths of the fire. Occasionally his lips moved; and he nodded his head approvingly or shook it decidedly.

"You are to remain here," Marlowe, on his return to the drugstore, remarked to Tucker. "I am going out to make some calls for the doctor."

The imperturbable Jep was for the once rudely lifted out of his normal state of chronic placidity. He was surprised—thoroughly surprised. His dropped jaw and lifted brows showed it, as he smoothed his stubby mustache with his knotty forefinger and ejaculated:

"Huh?"

"You heard what I said," Marlowe answered coolly, filling his pockets with sundry articles he had placed upon the counter.

"Goin' out to make calls fer the ol' doc!" Jep murmured gaspingly.

Ralph merely nodded as he went on with his preparations for departure.

"Well, I'll—be— everlastin'ly—doggoned!" Tucker muttered—and lapsed into silence.

The latter state was abnormal, however, and therefore of brief duration.

"Say!" he exclaimed.

"What is it?" Marlowe inquired, starting for the door.

"W'y, you ain't no doctor."

"No?"

"No, you ain't—are you?"

"*You* say I am not."

"Well, what do *you* say?"

"I say for you to maintain your opinion, no matter what you may hear to the contrary."

Then the door closed behind the younger man; and the older was left alone with his thoughts.

Jep pinched himself to discover if he were asleep or awake.

Having satisfied himself upon that important point, he arose; and dragging his feet up and down the long room, whispered to the four walls:

"Goin' out to make calls fer the ol' doc! Well, don't that beat anything you ever heerd of? Of course he must be a doctor, then. But he wouldn't say so. An' why? I tried to ketch him; but he was too slick for me—slicker 'n a greased pig at a county fair. Ther's some mystery 'bout that young man. But he's a mighty nice feller; an' I like him. He makes friends with ev'rybody, without tryin'. The way he does it puts me in mind o' that ol' buckwheat straw story. I mustn't fergit to tell that one to him sometime. Ev'rybody's talkin' 'bout the way he managed things down to Jim Crawford's that night—an' callin' him a doctor. Wher' ther's so much smoke ther' must be a little fire. Ther's nothin' fer me to do, though, but wait an' see. No matter what comes of it all, I'll stick to him like clay mud to a cowhide boot. I like the young feller."

Marlowe's first visit was at Jim Crawford's. When he entered the humble domicile and announced his intention of re-dressing the cobbler's wounds, the latter eyed him askance[64] and grumblingly gave his consent to the procedure. But Mrs. Crawford greeted him effusively, got him the hot water he requested, and appeared to place full reliance upon his skill and knowledge.

Two or three whining, weakly-looking children clung to the mother's skirts, as she went about the room, and impeded her movements.

With deftness and celerity Marlowe performed his surgical duties. The patient proved himself an *im*patient, by complaining and swearing throughout the operation; but his spouse openly expressed her admiration at the quick and skillful way in which the young man rerolled and reapplied the bandages.

"What ought I to eat? "Crawford condescended to inquire as Ralph was preparing to leave the house.

With the dignity and aplomb[65] of a veteran practitioner, the

---
64 askance: with a sidelong glance or with disapproval or distrust
65 aplomb: self-confidence; poise

young doctor imparted the desired information.

"What's a feller goin' to do when he hain't got *nothin'* to eat?" was the cobbler's next question—put in a surly, fault-finding tone.

"Are you in want?" Marlowe asked bluntly.

"Are we in want!" the cobbler echoed sneeringly.

"Do you see any signs o' wealth an' opulence 'round here? Course we're in want; an' we'll alluz *be* in want—so far as *I* can see. This arm ain't goin' to be of no account. If ol' Doc Barwood had knowed his business, he'd 'ave cut it off at the start. But the ol' ignoramus don't know nothin', an'—"

"Hush, Jim," his wife interrupted. "The ol' doc's been mighty good to us."

"Good to us?" the husband snarled. "I'd like to know how."

"You *do* know how," Mrs. Crawford went on calmly—sadly. "What would me an' you an' the children 'ave done, if the ol' doc hadn't left us that ten dollars, on the night o' the accident, I'd like to know?"

"Oh, shut up!" he snapped—and himself was silent.

"It's not too late to amputate the limb," Ralph said coolly. "I can take it off at any time."

"You?" questioned Crawford.

"Yes."

"You ain't no doctor."

"Possibly. But I can take off your arm—with an axe, for instance."

And the young athlete looked so savage, so in earnest, that the little cobbler could only gasp and stare.

Marlowe next visited Mrs. Crumbaker, a consumptive. He percussed[66] and ausculated[67] her thorax, took her temperature, and ascertained her subjective and objective symptoms—and all so quietly and scientifically that he won the admiration and confidence of the emaciated patient and her female friends assembled. After he had finished his examination, he ordered her—as one having

---

66 percuss: to tap sharply
67 ausculate: diagnostic monitoring of the sounds made by internal organs

authority—to continue her medicine; and bowing and smiling, softly withdrew from the house, leaving a buzz of wonder and favorable comment behind him.

His next call was to see a child with tonsilitis, in a cottage a few hundred yards down the Stonebury road. How he immediately gained the little one's favor, and sprayed its throat and otherwise ministered to it, was a subject for conversation among the gossips of that suburb, for many a day.

Thus he made the rounds, returning to the drugstore at eleven o'clock—to find Tucker asleep upon the bench by the stove and the fire almost out.

That afternoon he saddled a horse and made a wearisome trip of fifteen miles—including three or four calls—over the rough and muddy country roads. At five o'clock he was again behind the counter—tired, sore, and hungry—with enough work piled up before him, to keep him busy until late bedtime. Yet he was happier than he had been in weeks; he felt that he had been doing something worth the while.

"Jep," he said, "I am going to supper. I will be back in a half hour. If anyone calls for Dr. Barwood, or to leave a message for him, have the party await my return."

On his way back to his place of employment, he stopped at the post-office. Amongst the papers, packages, and pamphlets for his employer, he found a letter for himself. He started as he made the discovery; and hastily studied the postmark and superscription. The former was—"South Bend, Indiana"; the latter—"Dr. Ralph Marlowe, Babylon, Ohio," written in a fine feminine hand.

He turned pale as he read; and slyly glanced around to note if his agitation was observed. Then he hurriedly shot out of the post-office and made his way to the drugstore.

"Gosh!" Tucker exclaimed as he clapped his eyes upon Marlowe's white face. "You don't look as if playin' the doctor agreed with you over an' above well. You wouldn't stand it year in an' year out—as the ol' doc has—if one day knocks you out like that. What's the matter of you, anyhow?"

Without attempting to make reply, Ralph passed into the private office and turned the key in the lock. There he tore open the envelope, and read:

"*Dear Ralph:*

"*I dropped onto your hiding place by the merest accident. Harry Davenport is positive he saw you standing in the door of the little station of the village to which I send this letter. I was on the car with the troupe and looked out of the window, at that place—that I remember distinctly—but I saw nothing of you. Yet Harry is certain he saw you. Of course he may have been mistaken; and this letter may never reach you. How funny it seems—writing to a person of whose existence even one is not sure!*"

"*But supposing that Harry is right, I have written you. On my return to Cleveland, from our summer tour of the watering places and resorts, I found you had left the city; and none of your old friends and associates knew of your whereabouts. I understand all; you deliberately ran away and left me. Do you think that was right?—I presume you thought I was a disgrace to you. And I have been—I admit it. But I love you, Ralph—so there! And I am going to hunt you up as soon as the season is over. Of course it is foolish in me to tell you this; it will give you a chance to skip again. But then—as you know—I am always doing foolish things.*

"*Now, Ralph, listen to me. I am making good money with the company this season. 'The Cider and the Pie' is playing to crowded houses; and the manager has twice advanced my salary. I am saving it, too. Won't you come back and live with me and Freddie when the season is over? I'll be good—and we'll go to a new place, if you don't wish to live in Cleveland. See—I don't scold you nor blame you. You have put up with a great deal. But I won't make you ashamed of me any more; I have turned over a new leaf. Let me hear from you. Address me in care of the company, New York. The letter will be forwarded.*

"*Lovingly yours—as ever,*
"*Stella.*

"*P. S.—Freddie is well; and contented with Mrs. Bush, in Cleve-*

land. He looks more and more like you as he grows older—I think. And why shouldn't he? I am glad that he does. Do not expect to escape me by not answering this. I will hunt you up.

"STELLA."

Ralph Marlowe was pale as death as he finished the perusal of the brief and rambling epistle. But with steady fingers he refolded it, replaced it in the envelope, and thrust it into his pocket. Then he dropped into a chair, buried his face in his hands, and groaned in agony of spirit:

"Just as I feared—expected! She is my Nemesis; I cannot escape her. Oh, Stella—Stella! I will not answer her letter—of course. But I shall live in constant dread of her coming and come she will, I feel—I know. Shall I again flee? What is the use? If I am not buried in this obscure village, where could I find concealment. It is hard—hard! Poor little Fred! I love and pity him! Poor little lad! What can I do? Nothing but stay here—and face the inevitable. When it comes it will mean ruin. And I thought to find a hidden haven here! It is a shock—an awful shock! Just when my prospects were brightening, too!"

He arose, smoothed his rumpled hair, and composed his features as well, as he could. Then he resolutely opened the door and returned to the drug room. It was deserted; Jep had gone.

At eight o'clock Ralph closed the store and went to report the day's doings, to his employer, taking with him the medicine he had prepared. On reaching the house he found the front door standing open and the hall brilliantly lighted. The tinkling notes of piano music came to his ears, He entered and knocked upon the sitting room door.

"Come," was the gruff response from within.

The young man accepted the invitation—or obeyed the summons, as you please—and found himself in the presence of the master of the house. The latter still sat huddled in the big armchair in front of the grate, a look of intense suffering resting upon his countenance. The spicy smell of boiled hops and vinegar pervaded the apartment.

"How are you this evening, doctor?" Ralph inquired pleasantly.

"Getting no better fast," Dr. Barwood jerked out. "You've been a long time in putting in an appearance, young man. Why didn't you keep me waiting all night?"

"Apparently you forget, doctor, that I have had something to do today."—Wearily seating himself and thrusting his feet toward the fire.

"Huh! Perhaps so—perhaps you have. How did you get on?"

"So-so. All of your patients I visited accepted my services gratefully, except one."

"Jim Crawford?"

"Yes."—And Marlowe smilingly related what the cobbler had said.

"The infernal drunken scoundrel and—Ouch!" The sufferer gritted his teeth and grasped the arms of his chair, as a paroxysm of pain shot through his swollen ankle, warning him that he must not get excited.

"Let me give you a dose of this medicine and rub your foot with this embrocation," Marlowe suggested, taking the articles from his pocket.

Then, without waiting for the other's consent or refusal, the younger man threw off his overcoat and went to work. In a remarkably short time he had removed the manifold cloths that enveloped the inflamed joint and was rubbing and kneading it gently but firmly. The pungent, aromatic smelt of the liniment mingled with the spicy odor of the discarded poultice.

"Whew!" sniffed Dr. Barwood. "That stuff smells enough to do good, at any rate. It'll drive the company out of the parlor, maybe." —With a suppressed chuckle. —"If it does, I'll bless the day you compounded it; for they've been gabbling and thumping the piano, till my teeth are on edge. Say! Go gently there. Remember that ankle's fearfully tender. What are you going to do now—wrap it up in flannel?"

Ralph nodded; and went on with his work. The foot and leg rebandaged, he arose from his kneeling posture and asked:

"How does it feel now?"

"Better," the doctor admitted. "Give me a dose of your prescription."

When—with a wry face and a shudder—he had swallowed a teaspoonful of the mixture and wiped his lips upon the back of his hand, he said briskly:

"Now let's get down to business. Is there anything that needs my attention at the store—or elsewhere?"

"Yes."

"What?"

"Crawford can't get well unless he has something to eat. I can't keep him alive on medicine alone."

"Let him die—the miserable ingrate!" Dr. Barwood barked angrily. "I've done the last in that respect that ever I'll do for him. There!"

"But his wife and children, doctor," Ralph interposed in a pitying tone .

"Let the township trustees look after them."

"But will they?"

"I don't know—and I don't care. I'm done."—Sullenly.

"Then, there is Mrs. Crumbaker, the consumptive," Marlowe suggested.

"See that she gets what she needs."—Snappishly.—"You seem to think I ought to treat these people free of charge, keep them in food, clothing, and shelter, and pay them a bonus for the privilege. You'll find out you can't make money that way. Is there anything else?"

"Yes, doctor."

"Out with it."

"I would like to have the drug room repainted and repapered."

"It doesn't need it."

"But it does, doctor."

Dr. Barwood frowned darkly at his companion, who sat calmly facing him. The older man was thoroughly angry. He gurgled and panted for breath. At last he succeeded in gasping:

"You dare to flatly contradict me?"

"The drug room needs renovating, doctor," Ralph answered smoothly.

Again Dr. Barwood was knocked speechless.

He could only sit and stare. But little by little the tense lines of his visage relaxed; and a moment later a smile elevated the drawn corners of his mouth.

"You are the most positive, the most obstinate man I ever met," he said.

"One cannot meet one's self," Marlowe laughed.

"Well said," the doctor chuckled dryly.

Then he went on:

"Now, Ralph—my boy, I'll tell you what I'll do. I'll grant you permission to fix up the drug room, to your own taste—on one condition."

"Name it."

"That you throw aside your foolish, squeamish notions—no matter what may be their origin—hang your medical diploma at the side of your certificate of registration as a pharmacist, in the drug-store, and thus let the public know you are a physician."

For a moment Ralph Marlowe nervously hesitated. Instinctively his hand flew to the letter in the inner pocket of his coat. Then compressing his lips and wrinkling his brows, he turned suddenly, strode to one of the side windows, and stood silently looking out at the night.

The older man closely watched his companion's every movement and expression of countenance; but said nothing. A full minute the younger stood still as a statue. Then wheeling about he said with startling abruptness:

"Dr. Barwood, I accept your proposition."

A smile of gratification lighted the older man's face; and he held out his hand saying:

"I'm glad to hear you say that, my boy. You will never regret your decision—my word for it. From this day you do not work upon a salary; but for one half of the net proceeds of the drug business and the practice. There—there! None of that,"—As Ralph started and shook his head.—"I mean to have my way with you this once. Now, go ahead and run things to suit yourself—until I can get out. Then I will assist you."

He uttered the last sentence with a humorous expression of countenance and a jerky chuckle.

Marlowe was dumfounded. He tried to thank his benefactor; but his voice was husky with emotion, and the words would not come. Seeing which, Dr. Barwood—his own eyes gleaming with moisture—again held out his hand, crying cheerily:

"Never mind. I don't want to be pestered with your thanks. Here! Shake hands and be off. I'm feeling better—and I want to go to bed."

Marlowe—his features working, his chest heaving—grasped the outstretched hand and gave it a hearty squeeze. Then he hurriedly donned his hat and overcoat and made for the door. While blindly groping for the knob, he managed to say in tremulous accents:

"Good night, doctor. I'll see you tomorrow evening."

"Say!" the older man cried.

"Well?"—Without turning around.

"In regard to Jim Crawford. How long will it be before he is able to work?"

"Four or five weeks."

"Well,"—Slowly and reluctantly—"look after the family until I get out. You understand?"

"Yes."

"Good night."

"Good night."

As Marlowe was passing through the door, Dr. Barwood again called after him:

"Step across to the parlor door and tell Dolly I want her."

In answer to Ralph's knock, the younger daughter herself came to the door; and stepping out closed it behind her.

"Your father desires your presence," he murmured gutturally, attempting to brush past her and escape her keen observation.

"I should have been with him," she replied in an apologetic, explanatory tone, "but I was helping to entertain some stupid callers. Mamma and Julia desired me to play. Then"—Brightly—"I heard you come in, and felt daddy was in good hands."

As she finished she looked him full in the face; and observing his agitation she started back, exclaiming:

"Father is not worse?"

"No, he is feeling better," he answered reassuringly, again essaying[68] to pass her.

But she planted her small self resolutely in his path and demanded:

"Then have you and daddy been quarreling?"

"No—no!" he hastened to say. "Everything is right. Go to him."

Grasping his arm with both her hands, she pushed her face up close to his—he involuntarily bending toward her—and said pleadingly, plaintively:

"You never will get angry at dear old daddy's growls and snarls, will you, Mr. Marlowe?"

"No, never," he answered decidedly, fervently. "What is the matter, then?" she coaxed. "You are excited—worried. I read it in your face."

"Nothing—nothing!" he whispered hoarsely. "Good night."

And gently but firmly pushing her aside, he almost leaped through the door and down the steps. She stood and watched his swiftly flying figure until it passed through the iron gate at the foot of the flag walk, and was swallowed up in the darkness. Then she quickly turned and sought the sitting room door.

Marlowe crushed his hat over his eyes and ran hurriedly toward his apartments—on the opposite side of the street and halfway between the Barwood residence and the drugstore—muttering under his breath:

"It is done—for weal[69] or woe, it is done! Right or wrong, the die is cast! I will stay here now and face whatever may come. I will flee no more—no farther. I can but be disgraced—ruined; and as well here as elsewhere. I have tried to reform her; I have stood by her. All in vain! Twice have I tried to escape her thraldom;[70] twice

---

68 essay: to make an attempt at
69 weal: a sound, healthy, or prosperous state
70 thraldom: a state of complete absorption

have I returned to it. This is the third effort—and the final one. Let her come on—let her plead and promise as she will, I will not listen to her—will not own nor countenance her. I have done my duty by her; I have tried to save her—to redeem her. Each time it was black and bitter failure. I will fail no more—for I will try no more!"

On reaching his rooms he threw himself upon the bed, without disrobing, and pillowing his head, upon his crossed arms moaned:

"God knows I have loved her—her and her child! And my heart bleeds for the little lad! I wish I had him away from her—had him here with me. But she would come and take him from me; I have no legal right to him. And she will come for me—I know it. What then? A scandal—a dish for carrion crows!"

Awhile he lay silent and motionless. Then impatiently he arose, and flinging himself into an easy chair thus communed with himself:

"And my present prospects are bright—the brightest I have ever known. If only I were rid of the incubus[71] that hangs like a millstone about my neck! Dr. Barwood likes me; I like him. Fortune lies within my grasp; but fate says—'nay.' Does it? It shall not! And Dolly—Dolly! I love her already—fondly, passionately. And she shall be mine; I vow it—I swear it!"

At last he staggered to his feet, wearily and mechanically disrobed, and crept into bed. After hours of wakefulness, and acute mental agony, he fell into a troubled sleep—in the after watches of the long night.

* * * * * *

---

71 incubus: something nightmarishly burdonsome

CHAPTER XII

RALPH MARLOWE came out of his nocturnal struggle, looking a little pale and worn but with an expression of fixed determination upon his handsome face.

During the week following he completed the furnishing of his own apartments, had the drug room altered to his satisfaction and his diploma framed and displayed to the view of the curious—all this in addition to his multifarious[72] duties as physician and druggist. He would have appealed to Dolly for potted plants to place in the front windows of the store, but he realized that—with the system of heating the building boasted—the tender things would perish as soon as the weather grew severe.

He worked early and late; and many nights was so tired that he could hardly sleep. Yet the unremitting toil was a mental relief.

His medical diploma, thus flaunted in the face of the public, created a nine days' wonder—that died in forty-eight hours. For everyone wished to be able to say to his neighbor—"I told you so." Therefore, each individual who saw it concealed the surprise he felt and treated the unexpected revelation as a matter of course. Within a few days after its resurrection and appearance the villagers had forgotten its existence,

---

72 multifarious: having great variety

apparently, and had begun to speak familiarly—and affectionately, even—of its possessor, as "the young doc."

Sam Clark heard of the diploma being hung up, the first day it shook off the dust of obscurity and braved the censorious eye of the public; and that evening when he met Marlowe at supper, he followed him out upon the veranda and said:

"Hung out your sheepskin, have you?" Ralph nodded and smiled.

"I knowed it was coming," Clark laughed, dancing about and gleefully clapping his hands. "You couldn't fool *me*—not muchy! I told Airly Chandler, that night after we left Jim Crawford's, you was a doctor. He 'lowed you wasn't—said druggists got all such training in drug schools, nowadays. But I give him the laugh; and he shut up. No, sir! I wasn't a particle surprised when I heard your diploma was hanging up in the drug store."

Then in a lower tone—and with mock gravity:

"But you're more and better than a doctor, Marlowe."

"Indeed? —Explain."

"You're a wonder-worker—an eastern fakir. You're a *hoodoo* doctor, that's it."

"I fail to catch your meaning."

"Oh! You can be awfully dense when it suits you. You can't understand the multiplication table, even. What's the use of letting on? You understand well enough what I mean. You've mesmerized the old doc and got everything coming your own way—drugstore all fixed up, a nice suite of rooms for yourself, doing his practice, and so on. And all in a month or so. I wouldn't be afraid to bet a week's salary you'll be in partners with him, in less 'n six months, and—"

Ralph smiled complacently—but sadly.

"Married to Dolly before next fourth of July," Clark completed.

"That will do," Marlowe said, lowering his brows and speaking sternly.

"What?"

"Please leave the young lady out of your prophecy."

"I'm not going to publish my predictions," replied Clark in an aggrieved tone. "You might let me tell *you* what I think and predict."

"What more do you desire to tell me?"

"That Dolly Barwood loves you already," Clark answered quickly.

"Nonsense!" Ralph muttered—but a pleased expression for a moment rested upon his countenance. "Why do you say that?"

"Because I think it—that's why."

"Why do you think it, then?"

"Do you take me for a blind fool, Marlowe?" Clark grinned. "I can read women, as well as the next fellow. And I've read Dolly Barwood—and she loves you."

Ralph carelessly snapped the toothpick he held in his fingers, but made no reply. Clark went on:

"I've got over my infatuation for Dolly; you're welcome to her. I've got the prettiest, smartest little girl there is in the valley—*I* have."

"Off with the old love and on with the new," Ralph remarked absent-mindedly.

"You bet!"—Hilariously capering about the floor.—"Black eyes and hair, rosy cheeks, white teeth, and red lips. But you've met her?"

"I do not know."

"Yes, you have—Mame Gridley."

"I have seen her."

"Well, isn't she a beauty—say?"

"She is a very pretty girl. How long have you been—been—"

"How long have I been going with her—keeping her company?"

"Yes."

"Oh! A week or two. And we're engaged."

Ralph laughed outright. Then he said—the corners of his mouth still twitching:

"You railroad men are swift fellows—in your courting as well as in other matters."

"Swift?" Clark grinned good-naturedly. "Well, I reckon! And

I'm going to run this thing through on schedule time, or blowout a cylinder head. I've got her parents' consent; and the day's set—thirtieth of next May."

"You have made progress."

"Well, you see, I always *did* have a hankering for Mame—ever since I come here. But somehow she always shied away from me till just lately. For a time I *thought* I was in love with Dolly Barwood; but I *wasn't*. A fellow can't get very deep in love where he knows he hasn't a ghost of a show. I can't, at least. And Dolly always laughed at me when I got spoony. It sent the shivers up my spine and cooled me off *wonderfully*. Yes, I'm going to get married and settle down here."

"I thought you didn't like the place," Ralph said.

"I thought so, too."—And the pale young operator grinned a silly grin.—"But that was before I was in love. It's different *now*. This is a bully old town—all sunshine and roses. But I must tote the mail. See you later."

Whistling merrily he set off toward his place of employment.

Marlowe sauntered up the street, musing:

"What a magic thing is reciprocated love—coupled with a successful wooing! Here is Clark in the seventh heaven of delight, all because he is engaged to the maiden he loves—or fancies he loves. On the contrary, McDevitt—poor devil!—is in the fourteenth hell of misery, because he can not marry the woman of his choice. The success or failure of the wooing makes the difference."

He had left Jep in the drugstore; and found him there on his return. That voluble bumpkin was standing with legs far apart, looking unblinkingly at the newly displayed diploma and vainly trying to decipher it. He turned, as Ralph stepped into the room, and said grumblingly:

"Of all the darned unsatisfyin' things to try to make out, one o' these diplomers is the darnedest! I seen that thing"—Pointing with his forefinger—"hangin' on the wall there, at noon, but I didn't take no p'rtickler notice of it. But while you was at supper, in comes Sol Washburn, an' settin' his specs astraddle of his pr'boscis[73] says:

---
73 proboscis: a long, flexible snout, as the trunk of an elephant

"'So that's the young doc's diplomer.'

"Then I took a squint at it; an' I've been squintin' at it ever sence. It's worse 'n a railroad map o' purgatory—it is, by gosh! The ol' doc's hangs in the back room; an' one day w'en I was helpin' him to red up some, I spent the biggest part o' the forenoon tryin' to read it. Read it! I couldn't even read the p'rfessor's hen-track scribblin' at the bottom. Why the nation don't they print 'em in United States lingo? Of course I've knowed for some time you was a doctor; but I might live to be older'n my great gran' daddy's gran' mammy's spinnin' wheel, an' I never could prove it from that thing. I don't know this minute whether it says you're a hoss doctor 'r a Mormon preacher."

Marlowe did not think it necessary to make reply; but passing behind the counter busied himself with the compounding of a prescription. After a brief silence—and a final squint at the offending diploma—Tucker seated himself and said:

"Young feller, you're gittin' to be some punkins, ain't you?"

"I fail to catch the import of your remark, Jep," Ralph answered, as he skillfully balanced a five-pint jar in his palm and poured a part of its contents into a small bottle. "It is obscured by the metaphor in which you clothed it."

"Yes, an' *I* fail to ketch the meanin' o' *your'n* when you use them 'tarnal, big, jaw-breakin' words. But I mean that you're feelin' y'r oats—gittin' to be some punkins—rollin' in clover. I can't make it no plainer."

"I think I understand you. You mean that I am in good health—"

"I don't mean nothin' o' the kind," Tucker interrupted in a tone of disgust. "If I'd meant that, I'd 'ave said so. I'd 'ave said you was friskier'n a yearlin' colt an' pearter 'n a pet coon. What I *do* mean is this: You're a wearin' mighty good clo'es, an' you've got money in y'r pocket. You've ketched holt o' the coat tails o' prosper'ty, an' 're hangin' on fer dear life. There!"

"You think I am prospering, eh?"—As he shook the ink to the point of his fountain pen and pulled a label toward him.

"Yes, you are. Been here a month 'r so, an' in cahoots with the ol' doc a'ready."

"In cahoots?"—With lifted brows and a blank stare.

"Yes, sir. In cahoots with him—goin' it on the sheers with him."

"Who told you anything of the kind, Jep?" Ralph cried in an irritated tone, ceasing to write—pen in air.

"The ol' doc hisself."—Grinning triumphantly.—"Told me this mornin', when I was up to the house; an' mentioned that I was to do whatever you said jest the same's if it was him givin' the order. Said you was in cahoots with him now."

Marlowe frowned and went on with his work. Jep continued:

"Yes, you're doin' purty well, fer a young buck—I thank you. An' it's all on account o' y'r understandin' human natur'. Other folks, all the'r lives, has been knucklin' to the ol' doc an' doin' the'r best licks to please him. That didn't suit him—it made him mad an' cranky; an' he despised 'em fer weaklin's an' hadn't no use fer 'em. You come along—holdin' y'r head high, an' champin' the bit an' ready to kick over the traces at any minute—an, the ol' doc thinks you're all ther' is. He pitches in to bring you to time—jest as he's done with ev'rybody else—but hopin' all the time he won't be able to do it. An' he wasn't"—Jep concluded—"an' in cons'quence he thinks the world an' all o' you; an' means to do a good part by you. It's all as plain as the nose on y'r face, to me."

Still Marlowe pursued his task and made no answer. Shifting his position and recrossing his legs, Tucker took a fresh start :

"The way you've handled the ol' doc puts me in mind o' ol' Bob Huff an' the buckwheat straw. Never told you that one, did I?"

Ralph was counting a number of pills into a box; and abstractedly shook his head.

"Ol' Bob Huff—," Jep began.

But at that moment a customer entered and engaged Marlowe's attention. Nowise[74] discouraged, Tucker bided his time, determined to unburden himself of the yarn. When the man was gone, the

---

74 nowise: not at all

eccentric again commenced:

"*Now* I'm goin' to tell that story 'r bu'st a button. Ol' Bob Huff an' ol' Bill Leggett was neighbors, twenty years ago, out on the road 'tween here an' Onionville—on the other side o' the river. Both of 'em had good farms an' was well-to-do; an' both of 'em had a fam'ly o' purty, peachy-cheeked gals.

"Ol' Bob was a short, dumpy man with a double chin that hung down like a rooster's wattle; an' w'en he talked he wheezed an' panted like a cornfed shoat[75] at butcherin' time. He was so c'ntrary an' bull-headed he used to quar'l with hisself, w'en he went to go to bed, 'bout which side o' the bed he'd lay on. Used to say the climate here was the choicest in the world; 'cause if you didn't git the kind o' weather that suited you one day you was purty sure to git it the next. It was him that made the remark 'bout the rest o' the jurymen in the Hance line fence case. He was on the jury; an' they disagreed. After it was over somebody asked him how the jury stood.

"'Oh!' says ol' Bob, 'I was fer the plaintiff; the other 'leven, fer the defense. 'Leven o' the c'ntrariest men I *ever* saw.'

"Ol' Bill was as tall an' lanky as ol' Bob was short an' thick. People used to say he was so tall he couldn't walk under his own umberell. An' when he set down in a chair, his knees stuck up so high he couldn't see over 'em. That's what folks used to say, anyhow.

"But I started in to tell you the buckwheat straw story. As I said, both ol' codgers had a number o' purty gals. Bob's was jest as good-lookin' as Bill's; an' Bill's was jest as smart an' jest as good housekeepers as Bob's. But somehow'r other, ol' Bob's gals all got married off young; while ol' Bill's growed up an' staid at home. So not understandin' the reason o' the matter, Bill says to Bob one day—w'en they was workin' in 'joinin' fields:

"'Bob,' says he, 'how does it come your gals is all married off an' mine's left on my hands?'

"Bob squints one eye an' looks kind o' wise an' says:

"'When a young feller comes 'round courtin' one o' y'r gals, how do you use him?'

---

75 shoat: a young hog and especially one that has been weaned

"'First-rate,' answers Bill. 'I put his hoss in the barn, let him stay with the gal all night, an' give him his breakfast 'fore he leaves in the mornin'. Sometimes I even coax him to stay over Sunday an' go to church with us.'

"'Huh!' snorts Bob. 'Ther's wher' you make y'r mistake. You ort to set the dog on him an' chase him off the place.'

"'That so?' says Bill, kind o' surprised like. 'Why?'

"''Cause you had' answers Bob. 'That's the way *I* done; an' *my* gals is all off my hands—all married an' doin' well. An' they wasn't no purtier n'r smarter 'n your'n. You try my plan an' you won't have a gal left to pester you in a year's time. W'y, I used to git the shot-gun out an' jest rip an' tear ev'ry time a young feller I *liked* come 'round the house. That made him think I didn't want him to have the gal; an' he was jest crazy to git her from that on. I had six gals; an' five of 'em 'loped—an' me a chucklin' in my sleeve when they done it. Now all my son-in-laws is on good terms with me—pattin' the'rselves on the back, you know, an' feelin' good to think they outdone me—an' ev'rything's lovely an' the goose hangs high. You jest try my plan, Bill, an' see how nice it works.'

"'Durned if I don't do it!' says ol' Bill. 'Ther's a young school-teacher comin' to see Melissy this very night. I've been good as pie to him—been boardin' him an' his hoss over Sunday fer six months. An' I've noticed of late he's gittin' kind o' cold on the trail—don't come once wher' he used to come two 'r three times. When he shows up tonight, I'll let his hoss stand out in the weather, kick the dog an' cuss 'round, an' wind up by tellin' that young feller his room is better 'n his company. Durned if I don't do it!'

"'That's it—that's the way to do it,' says ol' Bob, wheezin' an' chucklin'—an' finally chokin' on his tobacker.

"Then," Tucker continued, "each of 'em started to make another furrer 'round the lands they was ploughin'. But jest as they got well started, ol' Bill drops his lines, an' runnin' back to the fence hollers an' motions to ol' Bob.

"Bob toddles back to the fence an' asks: "What d' you want, Bill?'

"'Want to know what ever made you think o' such a plan o' gittin' y'r gals married off?' answers Bill.

"'Oh!' laughs Bob. 'I'll tell you. Remember that year back in the 'sixties, w'en we all raised so much buckwheat?'

"'You bet I do,' answers Bill.

"'An' I s'pose you remember ther' wasn't a hoof o' stock that would eat the straw, don't you?'

"'Well, I reckon I remember that,' says ol' Bill, makin' a face.

"'Well,' ol' Bob goes on, 'I tried an' tried to git my stock to eat that straw. But the hosses sniffed up the'r noses at it, an' the cattle bawled ev'ry time they come in sight of it. At last I got a c'ntrary spell an' I vows to myself: If they won't eat it, they shan't tramp it into the ground. I'll pile it out in the middle o' the field, put a stake-an'-rider fence 'round it, an' let it rot fer manure. Well, I fenced it in. An' what do you s'pose happened, Bill?'

"'I hain't got no idee,' says Bill.

"'Well, dang me,' says ol' Bob, laughin' fit to kill, 'if when I got up the next mornin' them hosses an' cattle hadn't broke down that fence' durin' the night, an' wasn't in there eatin' that straw, like they'd never tasted nothin' as good in the'r lives! I set the dog on 'em, drove 'em out, an' fixed up the fence. The next night they got in ag'in. An' so it went—me a fixin' up the fence an' them a breakin' it down. An' the end of it was they didn't leave a straw o' that stuff—an' stood 'round an' whinnied an' bawled fer more. From that, Bill, I learnt a lesson; an' w'en my gals got big enough to think o' havin' beaux, I follered the same plan with them. Try it, Bill—try it!'

"'Durned if I don't!' muttered ol' Bill, goin' back to his plough.

"Well," Jep wound up as Ralph was turning down the lights, preparatory to leaving, "ol' Bill give the scheme a go; an' it worked like a charm. Melissy 'loped with the young schoolteacher 'fore the moon changed; an' in less 'n a year ther' wasn't a caliker dress on the place—'ceptin' the ol' woman's. An' you've played the buckwheat straw racket on the ol' doc, young feller—that's what you've done; an you've done it in good shape, too. Made him think you didn't keer fer nothin' but to have y'r own way, an' didn't want to please him n'r be friendly with him; an' 'mediately he got dead set on makin' friends with you an' givin' you a good show. Say! you're closin' up rather early, it 'pears to me. Must be goin' up to the ol' doc's, ain't you?" — his last with a sly grin.

At last Ralph saw fit to make reply. He said: "I have some medicine to deliver. After I have done that I may call to see how Dr. Barwood is resting. Good night."

"Good night to you," yawned Tucker sidling through the door.

Then he shuffled down the steps and around the corner, humming through his nose:

> "Come, love, come—the boat lies low;
> She lies high an' dry on the O-hi-o,
> Come, love, come—an' go along with me;
> I'll take you down to Ten-nes-see."

That evening—and many subsequent evenings—Marlowe called at the Barwood residence. He met Mrs. Barwood—a soft-voiced, matronly woman of forty-eight, still showing distinct traces of youthful beauty—and won her favor. She always accorded him a smiling welcome to the family circle and treated him affably. Dolly did not attempt to conceal her liking for his company. At times the master of the house was frankly friendly; at other times, markedly morose. But Ralph understood him; and did not worry. Julia was the only thorn in the young man's flesh. Otherwise he would have felt quite at home at Dr. Barwood's fireside. But the older daughter—always coldly courteous—held him at a distance and resisted his magnetic power, to the utmost.

Dr. Barwood slowly improved. Soon he was able—with the aid of crutch and cane—to hobble about the house; and on fine days he rode down to his place of business. But he remained anæmic[76] and weak; and it was patent to the keen observer that "the old doc" was permanently broken in health—that never again would he be able to do the hard work he had been in the habit of doing.

---

76 anæmic: chiefly British variant of anemia, anemic

Almost daily, drilling and pumping machinery for the oil fields back in the hills was unloaded from train or boat, and was hauled out through the town. Of evenings oil men swarmed at the hotel, saloons, and other places of business. Excitement ran high; for a number of lucky strikes had been made in the wildcat territory a few miles away. Every one was mad with the oil fever. Fabulous prices were paid for leases—leases that in most cases proved utterly worthless. All talk was oil talk. Capitalists, prospectors, and adventurers and gamblers flocked to the village. Many needy families reached easy circumstances by keeping boarders. Money was plentiful; and business became brisk.

Still the oil men whom Dr. Barwood had been expecting, and for whom he had been inquiring, did not put in an appearance until near the end of the month—November.

One bright morning he hobbled down to the drugstore; with great difficulty climbed the steps; and gritting his teeth and panting hard, limped back to the stove and sank into a chair.

Marlowe was getting ready for a trip to the country. Pausing in his preparations, he remarked casually—carelessly:

"Why didn't you have Jep drive you down, doctor?"

"Because I wanted to see if I could *walk* down," muttered the irascible physician, nursing his painful ankle and grimacing. "And I *did* it. You needn't waste any pity on me; I don't desire it. I don't like to be babied and coddled."

"I was not offering you pity, doctor," Ralph answered, turning his head to hide a smile. "I was asking for information, merely."

"Well, you got it," growled the doctor, picking up the poker and viciously prodding the fire.

Ralph shrugged his shoulders and said no more.

Presently Dr. Barwood asked pleasantly:

"Where do you have to go this morning, Ralph?"—Adding quickly and apologetically—"I ought to call you doctor—but I can't."

"I prefer that you address me as you have been in the habit of doing," Marlowe returned. "In answer to your inquiry, I am going to make two visits on Heathen Ridge, recross the river at Hawksburgh ferry, call at George Hummill's, and return by the way of Norton Ridge and Bald Eagle Creek."

"A long and hard trip—the condition the roads must be in," the older man remarked musingly. "Yet I have made hundreds as long and as hard; and may make many hundreds more, when I get over this infernal rheumatism. But no—I never will. When I get well I mean to take things easier. You are young and strong; I'll let you do the country riding. I'll stay in town and play the gentleman. I have done my share of hard work, and have earned a rest."

As he finished he flung up his head, his nostrils dilating like those of a wild beast that scents danger, the lines of his face stiffening perceptibly. Entering the door were the oil men he had been so long expecting.

"Good morning," said the leader of the trio, nodding toward Marlowe and advancing to where the doctor sat. "Heard you was sick, since I got into town this morning, doc. Glad to see you're out. How are you this morning, doc, anyhow?"

Utterly ignoring the oil man's friendly tone and gesture, and pointing to the bench running along the wall, Dr. Barwood countered:

"Where have you been in hiding so long?"

A little disconcerted by the physician's brusque behavior, the oil man dropped upon the seat indicated—where he was joined by his two silent companions—and embarrassedly rasping his calloused palms together, replied:

"We haven't been hiding anywhere, doc. But things was going all O. K.; and we thought it was well enough to let well enough alone. But we've come in now to talk business."

"Well, go on—talk it," Dr. Barwood said curtly, placing his lame foot upon the rung of a stool, and leaning back in his chair, with an explosive exhalation of breath.

"Hadn't we best go into the back room, doc," the oil man suggested timidly.

"No."—Tartly—"There's no fire in there this morning."

"You don't want to talk out here, do you, doc?"—With a meaning glance at Ralph who was buckling on a pair of canvas leggings.

"Go on—say what you've got to say," the doctor commanded sharply. "It's nothing to you who hears our conversation. It's *my* business, not *yours.*"

"Of course it's *your* business and not ours, doc," the man said humbly; "but you've always been so careful and bound us to such secrecy, I thought—"

"No matter what you thought.—Bringing his fist down upon the arm of his chair.—"If you have a report to make, make it here and now."

"I am going, doctor," Marlowe called as he was passing through the door, saddlebags and overcoat upon his arm.

"No!" roared Dr. Barwood, "Not yet. Come back here."

"But I ought to be off," Ralph objected. "It is now ten o'clock; it will be dark before I get back."

"The devil!" shouted the angry physician, his face purple. "You drive me crazy with your pigheadedness, Ralph. Come back here. I want you to hear what these fellows have to say—to witness the settlement I make with them. It won't injure your complexion to be out a little after dark. I'll stay in the store today; the business shan't suffer by your absence. There —that's reasonable."—As the young man returned, threw down his things, and resignedly seated himself.—"Now"—To the oil man—" make your report; and cut it short."

"Well," the man began hurriedly, "of course you've been getting your returns, through the Standard, from the wells on the Worden lease, doc?"

Dr. Barwood nodded, his brows contracted.

"And the same with the Gaddus tract?" the fellow pursued.

"Yes."—With a scarcely perceptible movement of the compressed lips.

"Well, as near as I could find out by a deal of spying 'round, doc, the rest of the company is playing fair with you in them two fields. Last month's output was in the neighborhood of six thousand barrels. Does that correspond with your checks from the Standard and your report from the company."

Dr. Barwood made a swift mental calculation, batting his eyelids and biting his nether lip. Then he replied:

"Nearly so. Go on."

"I think they're doing a square business with you, doc—"

"Never mind what you think," the doctor cried irritably. "Proceed with your report."

"To come down to our own work in the wildcat district, then, after we was in here the last time, we went back and packed off the well and plugged her. Then I set about taking leases, as you suggested. I've succeeded in getting everything within a mile or two of the well. I didn't have no particular trouble in getting them, for everybody thought the well was a greaser—just that and no more. I've had the leases all recorded; and here they are—nine of them."

He took from the pocket of his greasy coat a packet of folded papers and placed them in Dr. Barwood's outstretched hand. The latter untied the knotted cord that bound them, and unfolded and minutely inspected each in turn. Then having rearranged and retied them, he slapped his thigh with the bundle and tittered a sharp—"Well?"

The spokesman for the oleaginous[77] trio resumed:

"After I'd got all the leases I thought you'd care to have, doc, I moved a couple of tanks over from the Worden place—it took us two days to do it, the roads was cut up so—and set the pumps to going. I filled the two five-hundred-barrel tanks in nine days. Then we had to stop, of course. Then I got some extra help, laid a pipe line to connect with the Standard's, and commenced to punch down another hole, a quarter of a mile further up the run. People come 'round and laughed—said it was wildcat territory and we was wastin' time and money. But"—With a self-satisfied smile—" they was mistaken badly; fer last evening we drilled in, and the grease commenced to flow as soon as we pulled the tools. She's a better well than the other, by all odds. The word's got out; and everybody's crazy. The woods is full of prospectors already. They're leasing all the land

---

77 oleaginous: resembling or having the properties of oil; oily; also containing or producing oil

they can get within three miles of your strip; and cursing me and you black and blue, doc, fer stealing a march on them and getting all the 'joining land. That's the shape things is in at the present time—and I guess that's 'bout all I've got to tell."

With a quizzical expression of countenance, Dr. Barwood turned to Marlowe and asked:

"How much will you take for your interest in the new field?"

"*My* interest?" Ralph returned, greatly puzzled.

"Yes," answered the doctor, dryly chuckling.

"You have a half interest in the new well and these nine leases." —Tapping them with his long, white forefinger.

"I cannot understand you, doctor," the young man replied gravely. "I did not invest a cent—had nothing to invest—"

"True," his benefactor interrupted. "But *I* invested—or set aside, rather—one thousand dollars, five hundred for myself and five hundred for you. We've got a good well, leases on all the adjoining land and the thousand dollars isn't all gone yet. Eh, my friend?"— The question to the oil man.

The latter smilingly shook his head, and answered:

"No; enough left to put down another hole, anyhow."

"But, doctor, I cannot—I must not accept your kind—," Ralph blundered.

Dr. Barwood silenced him with a frown and a wave of the hand; and turning to the oil man said briskly:

"Have you made out an account of time and expenditures?"

Silently the man produced a greasy memorandum book containing a folded paper and handed it to the doctor. After carefully inspecting both book and paper, and comparing the figures in the one with the figures upon the other, the latter said:

"Ralph please bring me my receipt book from the other room. You will find it in the top drawer of the table. Here is the key."

While the young man was gone upon his errand, the physician drew forth a check book and began to fill out a check.

"I've forgotten your name," he said suddenly, looking up from his writing.

"J. F. Rose," prompted the oil man.

Ralph returned with the receipt book. Dr. Barwood handed the check to Rose, and requested him to sign a receipt for the amount. This transaction over, the physician said:

"Now go back to the field and sink another well, farther up the ravine. Select your own site. We may as well have a string of wells; we can pump a dozen as easily as we can pump two or three—it will take no more power. Well—what is it?"—As Rose stirred uneasily and opened his mouth to speak.

"I was going to say, doc—if you won't take it out of place—that the tanks at the first well being full, we'll have to turn into the pipe line before we can pump any more. And oil being a fair price, I thought we'd better keep the grease flowing. What do you say?"

"Yes, you're right. Attend to that, of course. Now, that's all. You can go."

The three oleaginous individuals arose and took their departure. Once outside the door one of them remarked to his companions:

"The ol' cuss's crosser 'n the braces on a derrick, an' harder to git at 'n a string o' lost drillin' tools; but he's good pay—an' he don't make no kick on wages."

"I like to work for him," replied Rose, nodding assent to the other's expressed opinion. "Everything's always understood beforehand—no chance for disputes."

And they sauntered down the street—their destination the hotel bar.

When the door had closed behind the trio, Dr. Barwood carelessly remarked:

"You are free to start upon your trip now, Ralph."

"Doctor," returned Marlowe.

"Huh?"—Without looking up.

"I cannot accept—"

"Hush!"

"You have done too much for me already."

"What have I done?"

"You have given me an opportunity to earn two or three times as much money—"

"Yes. And I have given you a chance to do two or three times as much work, too."

"Dr. Barwood," Ralph said decidedly. "I will not draw a cent of the profits of your venture—"

"Good!" the older man laughed softly. "I'll save it for you—place it to your credit in the bank."

Realizing that he could not move him from his purpose, Marlowe took up his traps and hastily left the store.

* * * * * *

CHAPTER XIII

CHRISTMAS WAS drawing near. The earth was covered with snow and the weather was severe. At the Methodist Church a great revival was in progress. Nightly the resident minister and a sensational evangelist held forth to immense congregations. Many professed conversion and united with the church.

But the cold weather had driven the workers in the oil fields to the village; and that rough element held high carnival. Feasting and fighting, guzzling and gaming, was the order of the day—and night—with them.

Marlowe saw little of Morris McDevitt. When he did meet the young merchant, he noted that the latter bore upon his countenance the unmistakable stamp of dissipation and profligacy.[78] Ralph shrewdly guessed that the advent of the roistering oil men had been no advantage to the vacillating young Irish-American, and that he was drinking and gambling heavily. To a certainty, the young physician knew that Morris did not now call at the Barwood residence and that he and Julia were seldom seen together.

Ralph's waking hours were well occupied. La Grippe[79] was prevalent; and the demands upon his time were many. For Dr. Barwood—although able to limp down to the drugstore and help in looking after the trade during the hours of daylight—was not able to do outside work or to be out after nightfall. Nevertheless the junior

---
78 profligacy: completely given over to self-indulgence and vice
79 La Grippe: Influenza

member of the verbal[80] firm managed to find time to accompany Julia and Dolly to church, occasionally, or to go to a private hop, with the younger sister. What other leisure hours he could steal from sleep or his pressing duties, he spent in his rooms; reading, or chatting with Clark, Chandler, and other acquaintances. Morris McDevitt seldom joined them; and when he did, he appeared ill at ease and did not long remain in their company.

On several occasions Ralph sought a private talk with the young Catholic, meaning to caution and advise him anew, against the course he was pursuing; but McDevitt adroitly avoided the interview.

One morning, a week before the holidays, Dr. Barwood bustled into the drugstore—he was fast recovering from his lameness—frowning angrily and thumping the floor with his heavy cane.

"Good morning, doctor," Ralph said pleasantly.

"Good morning," returned the doctor, in a tone 'twixt a grunt and a growl.

Then suddenly:

"Ralph, Jep informs me you have been treating members of the Gridley and Bentley families for the grip. Is it true?"

"Quite true, doctor." —Looking his companion squarely in the face.

"Well,"—With an angry snort,—"I am greatly displeased."

"I am sorry to displease you," Marlowe replied in a tone of sincerity.

"Then will you give up the cases?"

"I will not," Ralph answered sturdily. "They applied to me for aid; I took charge of them. I will not relinquish them to satisfy your whim."

"Whim?" gurgled Dr. Barwood almost choking with rage.

Marlowe nodded, his eyes flashing warningly.

"You are impudent!" shouted the older man, bringing his cane down upon the floor, with a resounding thump.

"I am right, at any rate," Ralph said, unmoved. The older physician stood and glared at the younger in speechless rage. At last he said gutturally:

"I cautioned you against becoming intimate with those people.

---

80 verbal: expressed in speech; unwritten

You have unheeded my injunction. Perhaps I ought not to ask you to give up cases you have taken; but you ought not to have taken those cases. However, it is done now. Have your hard-headed way—go on and treat them to recovery. But I exact one thing."

"What is it; doctor?"

"That you place their accounts in a separate book, and collect and keep all the money yourself. I will not have a penny of it. There!"

"I shall deposit it to your credit in one of the Malconta banks, doctor," Ralph laughed; "as you have done my half of the proceeds of the new oil field."

"I'll never draw it out," muttered the irate man.

"Then you will have money in bank, always. Be reasonable, doctor. You have been accepting and using money from those families—the McDevitts included—for two months or more. They have been trading here ever since I came, almost."

Dr. Barwood stared at his partner in helpless amazement. He moistened his dry lips with his tongue and tried to speak; but could not articulate a word. He had been trapped—beaten; and he was consuming with impotent rage. At length he uttered a contemptuous, explosive "Huh!" Then turned upon his heel, strode into the rear room, and slammed the door.

After a lapse of fifteen minutes, he emerged from his den, his demeanor completely altered. His countenance was unruffled; the storm had spent itself. Seating himself, he said cheerily:

"Ralph, my rheumatism is better this morning than it has been in weeks."

"I am pleased to hear it, doctor."

"And I see Jep—for a wonder—has built a fire in my office, and swept and dusted the room."

"Jep?" laughed Marlowe. "Not he. I did it myself. I have been here since five o'clock."

"And did you fill the coal hod,[81] too?"

"I did."

"Confound that lout!" Dr. Barwood grumbled. "He's becoming

---

81 hod: a coal scuttle

lazier and more nearly worthless every day he lives. He doesn't desire to do anything but sit by the fire, toast his shins, and tell silly stories. Yes—he does. He wants to eat and sleep. I shall have to haul him over the coals."

"Why don't you discharge him, doctor?" Ralph asked, stooping to recover a cork he had dropped—and thus concealing the smile upon his face.

"Discharge him?"—Whirling around in his chair and looking at his companion in open-mouthed astonishment.

"Yes."

"Discharge Jep?"

Marlowe pursed his lips and nodded, his eyes fixed upon the bottle he was wrapping.

"Why, man!" Dr. Barwood ejaculated. "Do you want the poor devil to starve? His wife and I have to keep him—have kept him for twenty years. She can't do it alone. He'd starve, sure as the sun rises, and sets, should I discharge him. For he's too shiftless to get another position; and too lazy to hold one, if he had it. No, I can't discharge him. It would be a cruelty of which I am not capable. But I'll warm his jacket, figuratively speaking, for his negligence. But say, Ralph."

"Well, doctor?"

"You'd better get out and make your morning calls. I'll attend to things here for a few hours."

"I am just ready to start," was the reply.

And the younger partner donned hat and coat and hurried forth, leaving the older sitting by the fire and smiling inscrutably to himself.

The twenty-fourth of December dawned cold and clear. A sleighing snow was upon the ground. All the forenoon the still air was filled with sifting particles of hoar frost; but by one o'clock the temperature had risen, the skies were clouded, and snow was falling.

There was a hurly-burly[82] in Babylon that afternoon. Sleigh bells jingled incessantly. Sleds and sleighs glided into the village; and

---
82 hurly-burly: uproar, tumult

glided out, laden with packages and bundles. The stores, groceries, and other places of business were crowded with eager buyers, from noon till dark. Dozens of Kris Kringles were abroad; hundreds of little hearts were throbbing expectantly. The evening trains brought large numbers of travelers—come to spend the holiday week with friends or relatives in the village or adjoining country.

By nightfall it was again still, and clear and cold. At the Methodist Church was a Christmas tree, resplendent with wax tapers and laden with strings of popcorn, bags of candy, and presents innumerable. At the saloons were light and warmth, free and easy comradeship, hot soup and free lunch. Many an aching heart left the house of worship that night—for some holiday gifts are not as costly and fine as others; and not a few aching heads emerged from the haunts of good fellowship in the small hours of the morning.

Christmas eve! What joys it brought—what different joys for different individuals! A Christmas tree for the children and their piously inclined elders; a country dance and oyster supper at Hawksburgh for the young people—to which two sled loads went, laughing and rollicking as they left the village; and bacchanalian merriment and the feverish delights of the card table for those that were of the earth, earthy.

And everyone was glad or happy or thankful—or should have been. For each one had something for which to be glad or happy or thankful. Julia Barwood was *serenely glad,* her father had given her money to spend upon her Sabbath School proteges, and had contributed fifty pounds of candy for the Christmas tree. Dolly was *exuberantly happy,* she had the promise of a gold watch and a sealskin jacket. Dr. Barwood himself was *thankful*—though he would not have confessed it—that his rheumatism was fast leaving him, that he was financially able to give good gifts to his children, and that Christmas comes but once a year. Marlowe was thankful—how thankful he himself only knew—that hard and incessant labor brings with it the balm of forgetfulness. And last, but by no means least, Sam Clark was supremely and ecstatically glad, happy, and thankful; he was a lover—an accepted suitor.

At eight o'clock that evening, Marlowe closed the drugstore and went over to the church. It was packed to the doors. The minister, the Sunday School superintendent, and other notables had had their say; and the distribution of the gifts was in progress. With many pranks and antics, a pursy[83], bearded Santa Claus was reading the names upon the packages taken from the tree by his nimble young assistants, and was passing the articles back through the crowd. Their rightful owners, with hands upheld and madly waving, were clamoring for them. Little lassies were hugging huge dollies to their hearts and softly crooning to them;—sturdy laddies were critically examining new skates and sleds, and loudly detailing their many points of excellence to admiring comrades.

All was bustle, chatter, confusion, and good nature. Yet a few of the little people looked sad and disappointed. Some childish lips trembled and some baby eyes were moist with unshed tears. Poor little tots! They were learning the bitter lesson that Santa Claus is a truckling[84] respecter of persons and worldly conditions.

Marlowe walked home with Mrs. Barwood and her daughters, carrying their manifold[85] bundles and parcels. At the door he stopped and bade them good night.

"Are you not coming in?" Dolly asked plaintively.

"Not tonight. It is late; and all of you are tired and sleepy."

"Yes, come in, Dr. Marlowe," Mrs. Barwood said shiveringly. "It is only half past nine."

Ralph yielded, and entered the big sitting room with them. But he held his hat in his hand, while he warmed at the fire, and did not remove his overcoat—though Dolly urged him to do so.

Dr. Barwood was already abed. Mrs. Barwood went to look after some household duties that had been deferred. Presently she called Dolly to her assistance; and Ralph found himself alone with Julia.

It was the opportunity he had been seeking; and he hastened to improve it.

---

83 pursy: short of breath; asthmatic; fat
84 truckling: to act in a subservient manner
85 manifold: of many and diverse kinds

"Miss Barwood," he said, "ere your mother and sister return, I desire to have a few words of private conversation with you."

Interlocking her white fingers in her lap and looking him full in the eyes, she replied calmly:

"I am listening, Dr. Marlowe."

"Do you love Morris McDevitt?" Ralph asked bluntly.

"Sir!"—Her thin lips compressed, her black eyes flashing.

"Perhaps you think I am taking an unwarranted privilege, but—" he started to explain.

"I certainly do," she interrupted icily.

"But," he went on unheeding, "I come as Morris McDevitt's friend—at his request. I insist that you answer my question."

For a moment her eyes blazed and her chest heaved. She half arose from her chair; then frigidly reseated herself. Ralph kept his eyes fixed upon her. At last her lids drooped and her lips trembled.

"Do you love Morris McDevitt, Julia?" he repeated softly.

She flung up her head, her black eyes swimming with tears, and cried impulsively—a catch in her voice:

"Yes, Ralph Marlowe, I love Morris McDevitt—love him more than you think me capable of doing!"

"Pardon me," he said kindly, "if I have been abrupt or rude. But I fear the return of your mother or sister—I had to come to the point at once, and insist upon your answering my question before I could proceed. Julia, if you love Morris McDevitt, why do you not save him?"

"Save him?"—With wide eyes and in a voice barely above a whisper.

"Yes. Do you not know that your refusal to marry him has discouraged him—unmanned him; that he is drinking and gambling heavily, is on the highway to ruin?"

Paling visibly, she gasped:

"I—I did not know. I have—have noticed that he has not been himself of late; but I thought—" She stopped abruptly. The blood surged to her face; she drew herself proudly erect and said scornfully:

"Dr. Marlowe, what kind of man are you—to come to me and

speak disparagingly of him to whom you claim you are a friend?"

Again she was her hard cold self.

"And I *am* his friend," Ralph answered earnestly; "and will be yours, Julia—if you will accept my friendship."

"Which I will not do," she said in a decided tone. "I do not need your friendship; I do not desire it. I despise you for a meddler."

Marlowe's dark face flushed; but he answered calmly:

"Miss Barwood, you are cruelly unjust. I came to you at the solicitation of Morris McDevitt—came as his sincere friend and well-wisher. But I will not pursue the matter further."

"Thank you," she replied sneeringly.

For a few seconds a painful silence reigned.

Then Ralph said chokingly:

"Just one word more, Miss Barwood. What answer shall I carry to Morris McDevitt?"

"None,"

"He is expecting one."

"He has his answer from me."

"You will not marry him—although you confess you love him?"

For one brief moment she appeared on the point of breaking down—of yielding. Her lips trembled; her eyes glistened with moisture. But she clenched her white hands, set her teeth, and fairly hissed:

"No! I will not marry him."

"Because of his religion?"

"Because of his *lack* of religion."

"He is a Catholic."

"Catholicism is not true religion—true christianity. I will not marry him—and I have told him so, over and over—until he renounces his false faith and embraces Protestantism."

"Not to save him, even?"

"Save him!" she laughed scornfully, harshly. Then rapidly—the fire of fanaticism in her voice and eyes;

"No one can be saved unless he is willing to put himself in the way of salvation. When Morris McDevitt feels the need of salvation

I will aid him all I can. But I will not risk my soul in a vain effort to save his. He is need of heavenly salvation—not earthly salvation; and must first help himself."

"Then you do not give credence to what I have told you—in regard to his habits?"

"I do not."—Flatly.

Ralph smiled sadly but attempted no reply. At the moment Dolly bounced into the room, crying:

"Let me have that morocco case I told you to put in your pocket, Ralph—Dr. Marlowe." And she blushed confusedly, prettily.—"It contains my finest present, a new watch from daddy. I want to show it to you. And I thank you ever so much for the books you gave me. How do you like your tie? It's the prettiest one I could find. Julia helped me to select it."

All the time she was rattling on, Marlowe was searching his pockets for the tiny gold timepiece.

"Ah!" he said at last, "here it is. I had forgotten which pocket I put it in."

He drew it forth and placed it in her palm. As he did so, an envelope came out with it and dropped to the floor. There it lay unobserved.

A few minutes later Ralph took his departure, Dolly accompanying him to the outer door.

When the two had passed into the hall, Julia discovered the envelope and picked it up. It bore—in a woman's fine chirography[86]—"Dr. Ralph Marlowe, Babylon, Ohio."

Julia made a movement toward the door, intending to restore the letter to its owner. But at that moment she heard him descending the steps and Dolly returning along the hall, to the sitting room. So, hastily thrusting it into her bosom, the older sister made her exit by the rear door and went to her room.

Several days elapsed ere Ralph became aware of the loss of the letter. Then, of course, he made diligent search for it; and, of course, did not find it—and was greatly worried in consequence.

---

86 chirography: handwriting, penmanship

Christmas day was cold and clear. Most of the business places were closed; and a Sabbath-like stillness prevailed in the village. There was skating upon the backwater north of the town; and many of the children and young people were enjoying the exhilarating pastime. Sportsmen were abroad in the fields and woods. The middle-aged and old gathered around their own hearths and softly, sadly talked of the past. So the streets were practically deserted. The black smoke rolling heavenward, from time-racked, crumbling chimneys, a gliding sleigh, or a solitary pedestrian, were the only signs of life. The silence was broken only by the reverberating roar of a shotgun in the distance; the musical jingle of sleigh bells, or the faint, far-away shouts and laughter of the skaters upon the glassy pond.

At nine o'clock in the forenoon, Dolly Barwood was at work in the upper chambers of the big brick house she called home, caroling like a bird. Suddenly she threw down the dust cloth she was using, passed from the room she was putting to rights, and tiptoed softly to the front end of the hall. There, with her warm breath, she melted a space upon the frost-incrusted pane of the window, wiped it dry with her apron, and peeped out. She saw no one abroad. A brief time she stood gazing down the wide street—in the direction of the drug-store, which she could not see. Then, with a little fluttering sigh, she returned to her work; and a minute later her clear young voice was again ringing through the old house.

Down in the warm, spotless kitchen, Mrs. Barwood and Julia were preparing the dinner. Savory odors pervaded the place. The table was laden with pie dough, jars of mince-meat, and open cans of fruit. A turkey was roasting in the oven of the big steel range; and upon its top, a number of vessels simmered and danced. Dolly's merry voice floated down the back stairway.

"Mother," Julia said suddenly, brushing a spot of flour from her apron and laying down the spoon with which she had been stirring the contents of a vessel upon the range, "will Dr. Marlowe be here to dinner?"

"Of course," Mrs. Barwood replied, arising from a kneeling position in front of the oven and looking inquiringly at her daughter.

"Your father has invited him."

Julia walked to a window and silently gazed out upon the snowy scene.

"Why did you ask?" queried Mrs. Barwood.

Turning quickly and facing her mother, Julia replied:

"I asked, mother, simply to introduce a subject upon which I wish to speak to you. It is very well for father to take in Dr. Marlowe as a partner; no doubt the young man is capable, industrious, and honest. But it is an entirely different matter for us to receive him into our home—to make an associate, an intimate, of him. Don't you think so?"

"Why, I—I don't know," Mrs. Barwood stammered.

She had fallen into the habit of trusting largely to her older daughter's opinions and yielding to her desires.

"We know nothing of him," Julia suggested.

"He seems like a genteel, moral young man," the mother replied waveringly.

"Seems—yes," answered the daughter. "But, as I said, we know nothing of him—his antecedents, his past. And appearances are deceptive. If father knows more of him than we do, he has never told us."

Mrs. Barwood grasped at the straw.

She said meditatively:

"Undoubtedly your father knows Dr. Marlowe is a moral gentleman or he would not invite him here to dine—would not permit him to call at all, in fact. Do you know anything against his character, Julia?"

"No," the daughter replied deliberately, slowly shaking her head. "But I have an opinion, mother, that he is not what he would have us believe—that he is sailing under false colors."

"Have you a reason for your unfavorable opinion of Dr. Marlowe, Julia?"

"I have," the daughter replied, turning her back upon her mother and stooping to baste the turkey in the oven.

"What is it?" Mrs. Barwood inquired quickly—keen curiosity in voice and manner.

Arising from her stooping posture and dropping upon a chair, Julia wiped her flushed face upon a corner of her apron as she answered:

"I cannot tell you my reason, at present, mother; that is, I *may* not—I *will* not. But it is a good and sufficient one, I assure you."

"You worry me—you vex me, Julia," Mrs. Barwood cried irritably. "And one ought not to be worried or vexed on Christmas day—of all others. Let us drop the subject. You do not like Dr. Marlowe, at any rate—"

"I—do—not!" Julia interrupted in a low sibilant[87] tone, her features hardening. "But that is not the reason of my opinion of him, nor why I desired to discuss his social relations with us."

"Your father is very fond of him."

"And you, mother?"—Fixing her black eyes upon her parent's face, where rested a troubled expression.

"Why, I—I like him, I think," Mrs. Barwood answered in halting, undecided accents. "He appears to be a moral young man, intelligent and genteel—"

"He is not a Christian."

"No," Mrs. Barwood admitted, "nor is your father—nor Dolly."

"But we *know* father and Dorothy," Julia persisted. "We know their past. They have done nothing criminal, and little that is immoral—though they are irreligious."

Then she proceeded earnestly, almost fiercely:

"Mother, do you think it proper and right to let a young man come into your home and associate with your daughters, who is avowedly irreligious, of whose past life you know nothing—for Dr. Marlowe has given no one a glimpse of its record—simply because he makes a good appearance and speaks you fair? If you care nothing for me, you should think of Dorothy."

"Why of Dolly?" Mrs. Barwood inquired calmly—but with a shade of anxiety in her voice.

"Why of Dolly?" Julia cried excitedly. "Are you blind, mother? Can you not see that Dorothy is growing very fond of Dr. Marlowe's company?"

"Do—Do you think she is growing fond of—of *him,* Julia?"

---
87 sibilant: to hiss.

Mrs. Barwood asked faintly, falteringly.

"Not *growing* fond of him," Julia answered, with a covert sneer; "she *is* fond of him already. The mischief is done."

"I cannot believe it," cried the mother wringing her hands in great distress. "You must be mistaken, Julia; Dolly is but a child."

"She is nearly eighteen," Julia returned coolly. "Quite old enough to fall in love with a handsome, fascinating man like Dr. Marlowe; and she has done so."

"Oh, what is to be done!" groaned Mrs. Barwood. "Why do you worry me with this, Julia? I can do nothing. Why do you not go to your father? He is responsible for the state of affairs—for Dr. Marlowe ever calling here, for Dolly ever being in the young man's company. And your father has not seemed to care; and I have felt perfectly at ease. Why do you not go to him?"

"You know I cannot talk to father—on any subject," Julia answered. "He is so opinionative, so obstinate—"

"You are so much alike," the mother whimpered.

"I cannot go to him with this," Julia pursued. "He would rebuff me—would command me to attend to my own business. But you can talk to him, mother; and you ought."

"Oh! I wish you and your father got along better, Julia," Mrs. Barwood moaned.

"As you say, I suppose we are too much alike," the daughter returned, with a toss of her head.

"Dolly and your father get along together—are comrades, indeed," Mrs. Barwood said, drying her tears and taking up the rolling pin.

"I am not Dorothy," Julia replied coldly. "But will you talk to father on this subject, mother?"

"I suppose I must," murmured Mrs. Barwood shuddering involuntarily; "but I fear it will do no good. Your father is so set in his opinions; and he is so fond of Dr. Marlowe. However, I must bring this matter to his notice—"

A short while she stood at the table, in an attitude of indecision. Then she laid down the rolling pin and said with sudden resolution:

"He is in the sitting room; I will go to him at once. I may as well have done with the disagreeable duty; I shall know neither peace nor sleep until the interview is over. When Dolly comes down keep her here to help you."

Dr. Barwood was reading the morning paper and did not look up as his wife entered the room.

"Ephraim," she said timidly.

"Huh?" the doctor grunted, reading industriously.

"Ephraim, I want to talk to you."

"Well, aren't you talking to me, Hannah?"—Chuckling dryly, and noisily turning the pages of his paper.

"Do stop your reading," Mrs. Barwood requested pleadingly.

"I'm listening," the husband replied, running his finger down the oil market column. "Go on—go on!"

"But I want your undivided attention," the wife insisted.

Dr. Barwood continued reading for a few seconds, silently moving his lips and occasionally nodding his head. At last, with a sigh of resignation, he removed his nose glasses and held them aloft, threw down his paper, and said:

"Now, Hannah, out with it."

"Ephraim, what do you know about Dr. Marlowe?"

"What do I know about Dr. Marlowe—Ralph?"

"Yes."

"I know *all* about him."

An expression of relief and gratification rested upon Mrs. Barwood's countenance as she said:

"You don't know how glad I am to hear you say that, Ephraim. I feared you might know no more of him than the rest of us. Tell me."

"Tell you what?"—Taking out his watch and yawningly consulting it.

"How provoking you can be!" grumbled the wife. "You know what I desire. Tell me what you know about Dr. Marlowe."

Dr. Barwood pocketed his watch, deliberately produced his knife, opened it, and commenced to pare and file his nails.

"Hurry—hurry!" Mrs. Barwood exclaimed, playfully placing

her hands upon his shoulders and gently shaking him. "I must get back to the kitchen."

"Well, *go* back to the kitchen," he replied placidly. "The door isn't locked."

"Ephraim, you would provoke a saint."

"Don't you think that remark smacks of egotism, Hannah?"

"What do you mean?"

"Calling yourself a saint."

"Pshaw!" she laughed. Then earnestly:

"Please tell me what I want to know."

"But I do not know what you want to know."

"You said you did."

"No; I said I knew all about Ralph Marlowe. You may not want to know all I know—"

"But I *do*."

"Very well. I know that he has a diploma from a reputable medical school and that he is a graduate in pharmacy."

"What else?"

"That he is a capable physician and a painstaking and careful druggist."

"Hurry—go on!"

"That he is intelligent, industrious, and honest; that he is as proud as Lucifer and as independent as the devil."

"Ephraim!" she exclaimed in a tone of mild horror and reproof.

"What?"—With an expression of serene surprise.

"Don't use such language. You do it just to tease me. Now, go on."

"There's no more to say."—Stooping and recovering his paper.

"What do you know of his past life, his antecedents?"

Dr. Barwood squinted shrewdly—almost closing his eyes—and said drawlingly:

"Julia sent you to ask that question, Hannah. I know her hobby;—her language."

"Yes, she did;" Mrs. Barwood admitted, blushing.

The husband's face flushed also—but with anger, not embarrassment—as he returned hotly, shaking his finger at his wife:

"Go back to that girl and tell her I said for her to attend strictly to her own business. She will have all she can do to look after Morris McDevitt—who is not half the man Ralph Marlowe is. There!"

Mrs. Barwood drew down the corners of her mobile mouth and said in as reproachful a tone as she could command:

"Ephraim Barwood—"

"M. D.," he interjected.

Unheeding she went on:

"Is it possible you have taken this young man into partnership with you, brought him into your own home and permitted him to associate with your wife and daughters, when you know nothing about him?"

"I tell you I know all about him," the doctor replied smoothly, as he again unfolded his paper and replaced his glasses astride his nose.

"You know nothing of his past life.—"

"Nor do I care to know anything of it," he interrupted shortly. "I know his present behavior—that is better."

"But, Ephraim, I fear that Dolly may—may—" She hesitated and came to a stop.

"May what?"—Scanning the column of editorials.

"May grow too—too fond of Dr. Marlowe," Mrs. Barwood resumed quaveringly. "It is so easy for susceptible young girls to fall in love with handsome, fascinating men."

"Some more of Julia's talk," grunted the doctor.

"Do put down that detestable paper and listen to me!" Mrs. Barwood cried tearfully.

"What is it, Hannah—what is it?" he answered crustily.

"Don't you fear that Dolly may fall in love with Dr. Marlowe?"

Looking his wife squarely in the face, Dr. Barwood replied calmly:

"She has already fallen in love with him—as you express it."

Mrs. Barwood burst into tears; and covering her face with her apron and rocking herself to and fro, sobbed convulsively.

Quickly arising, her husband put his arm around her, smoothed her hair, and said kindly—tenderly:

"There—there, Hannah! There is no need of taking on. Leave Ralph's and Dolly's affairs to me. You were not at all concerned nor alarmed until Julia put in her oar—and began her splashing. Dry your tears now. No harm shall come to Dolly, I promise you; and you know how much I think of her."—A quaver in his voice.—"Let Julia look after her own love affair. She will have enough to do. And my word for it, Hannah, she will be sorry some day that she has not made a confidant of her father, as her sister has done. That's all now. To please *you*—*not* because *I* have any doubts or fears—I will ascertain what you so much desire to know. Here—give me a kiss. I am going down to the store."

Mrs. Barwood uncovered her face, wiped away her tears, and complied with her husband's request. But when he had put on his hat and overcoat and had reached the door, on his way out, she ventured:

"Ephraim?"

"Well?"—Curtly.

"Julia has reason to think Dr. Marlowe is not what he would have us believe, that he is sailing under false colors—"

"Stuff!" he snorted angrily. "Julia has reason to think the moon is made of green cheese, too; and that heaven is a place for holding close communion—doors barred to all but Methodists. Nonsense! Go back to your work. I'll have Ralph up here to dinner, about half past eleven."

The door closed behind him. Mrs. Barwood removed all traces of her recent outburst of vexation and grief, and smiling—half contentedly, half sadly—returned to the kitchen.

* * * * * *

CHAPTER XIV

RALPH MARLOWE was astir and abroad early that bright Christmas morning. Barely had he entered the drugstore and begun to stir the dying coals in the stove, when Tucker came in, slapping his palms together and shuffling along briskly.

"Cold enough to freeze the horns off 'm a muley cow," he remarked shiveringly.

Ralph looked the surprise he felt at Jep's early appearance and abnormal alacrity.

"What's the matter?" grinned that worthy.

"I can do no better than fling your question back at you," laughed Marlowe shoveling a quantity of coal into the stove and closing the door. "What's the matter with *you?*"

"Well, you see, it's like this," Jep explained, shoving his hands deep into his trousers' pockets and stamping his benumbed feet. "The ol' doc give me a goin' over the other day— said I wasn't half quick enough on trigger an'—"

"Not quick enough on trigger?" Ralph echoed questioningly.

"Yes. Not peart[88] enough—not fast enough, you understand. Said I was affected with laziness, an' dilatoriness, an' idleness;

---

88 peart: being in good spirits; lively

an' shiftlessness, an' sleepiness, an' hungriness—an' a few other complaints; an' said if I didn't turn over a new leaf an' do better, he was goin' to give me my walkin' papers. So I made up my mind that the beginnin' o' the new year I'd commence an' do better."

"This is not the beginning of the new year," Marlowe suggested, seizing a broom and sweeping vigorously.

"'Tain't?"—In open-eyed astonishment.

"No. It's the twenty-fifth of December. The year begins with the first of January."

"Well, I'll—be—durned!" Jep exclaimed, his jaw dropping.

Then bursting into a hearty laugh, he bawled.

"Ain't I a precious dunce, anyhow! Here I've crawled out in the cold this mornin'—thinkin' all the time it was the beginnin' o' the new year—when I might 'ave been snoozin' the snoozes o' the righteous, fer two hours yit. Well, drat my fool head! What's the matter of it? Leavin' Christmas clear out—and jumpin' to New Year's. Huh! Wouldn't the ol' woman laugh at me, if she knowed!"

Then suddenly:

"You won't never tell her, will you—Say? I wouldn't never hear the last of it."

"I shall not inform her."

"All right, then. An' maybe it's jest as well I made a mistake an' started in to turn over a new leaf five 'r six days ahead o' time. I can kind o' come at the thing gradual-like—won't be so much chance o' strainin' myself. But I mustn't stand here gabblin', though. I've made up my mind I won't tell a yarn this comin' year. I don't mean a lie; I mean a big story—antidotes, I guess you call 'em. Now I'll go an' build a fire in the ol' doc's room, an' fill up the coal boxes. I'm goin' to git a move on. You jest watch me."

To Ralph's unbounded astonishment, Tucker did get a move on. The angular and awkward fellow bustled from drug room to basement, and from basement to private office; and soon had finished what he had set about to do. Then he helped Marlowe with the dusting, all the while whistling softly but cheerily.

"'Bout breakfast time, ain't it?" he remarked when they had

finished.

Looking at his watch, Ralph answered:

"It is six-thirty. I do not breakfast until seven."

"An' I eat mine whenever the ol' woman comes to the door an' flirts her apron an' hollers— 'hoo-hoo!' Then I know the buckwheat flapjacks 'r corn dodgers is done an' the coffee b'iled; an' I don't lose no time in reportin' fer duty. Say young feller?"

"Well?"

"If you hain't no radical objections an' such like, I b'lieve I'll take a snifter out o' that big black bottle—seein' it's Christmas, an' Christmas don't come but once a year."

"I have no objections. But you will be better off without it."

"Don't you think nothin' o' the kind. It'll give me an appetite fer ham an' eggs. You won't tell the ol' doc."

"No. But you would better leave the black bottle alone."

"Why?"

"Because it contains spirits of camphor. The whisky is in that large jar having the gilt label. I made the change several days ago."

"Jeeminy crickets!" gasped Jep. "Lucky I wasn't here alone. I'd 'ave—"

Then he stopped in confusion.

Ralph smiled but said nothing. His companion quickly recovered his composure; and going behind the counter poured out a small quantity of the raw liquor and tossed it off. Then, smacking his lips and wiping his mouth upon the corner of his coattail, he came around and said:

"If I hadn't made up my mind not to tell any more yarns, I could tell you a good one this mornin'—one jest suited to the 'casion."

"A rash resolution is better broken than kept," Marlowe remarked.

"'Twon't do," Jep replied, lugubriously[89] shaking his head. "Still I'd like mighty well to tell it to you."

"It's not the first of the year yet," Ralph suggested temptingly.

"That's so," Tucker answered brightening.

---

89 lugubriously: exaggeratedly or affectedly mournful

"You won't say nothin' to the ol' doc 'bout it—if I tell you jest this one?"

"Not a word," Marlowe said gravely—but inwardly convulsed with laughter.

Thus assured, Tucker began:

"Years an' years ago—when I was jest a little shaver—ther' used to be a saloon stood down on Water Street, right wher' the depot now is. The buildin' was a shackledy[90] ol' frame, with up-an'-down weather boardin' an' an outside chimbly.[91] The man that kept the saloon was a one-legged feller named Ike Beech—a hard drinker hisself an' a tough customer. He stumped 'round on a wooden peg—an' could walk straight when he was so drunk he couldn't knock a fly off 'm his nose. Used to say the reason was he couldn't git that wooden leg drunk; an' used to pat it an' say one member of his fam'ly was a teetotaler. Fer ol' Ike was a bach'lor—and hadn't no fam'ly but hisself.

"Well, 'way back in the early 'sixties—while the war was goin' on—there was a half-witted loafer here in town, by the name o' Shem Frowser. He had a freckled face, a short upper lip, an' great big butter teeth—an' wasn't nothin' but a bundle o' rags an' bones. He used to spend his days an' evenin's hangin' 'round Beech's saloon, waitin' fer some one to treat him; an' he lived on cheese an' crackers an' done his sleepin' in the ol' mill shed.

"One Christmas mornin' he come shiverin' into the saloon, an' squatted down on the hearth an' huddled up to the fire in the big fireplace, his teeth fairly chatterin'. Ol' Ike went on a waitin' on customers an' didn't pay no 'tention to him. People come in, got the'r hot toddy, an' went out; an' never offered to treat Shem—an' him nearly dyin', fer a drink.

"At last ev'rybody had got the'r nip an' gone home to breakfast. Shem couldn't stand it no longer. Straightenin' up an' sidlin' over to the bar, he stood there smackin' his lips an' hintin' his best licks fer a drink. But Beech still didn't pay no 'tention. Finally Shem says:

---

90 shackledy: shaky; rickety
91 chimbly: dialectal variant of chimney

"'Ike, I'm purty dry this mornin'.'

"'Then go an' jump in the river an' git wet,' growls ol' Ike.

"'Oh! Now, Ike, you know what I mean,' the poor feller says coaxin'-like. Bein' half simple, he didn't know the meanin' of a joke, an' took ev'rything in dead earnest. 'I want a drink,' he says.

"'Ther's a pump right 'cross the street,' grins Beech, puffin' away at his pipe.

"'I don't want water,' Shem answers mighty solemn. 'I'm cold.'

"'Well, you're welcome to warm at the fire,' laughs ol' Ike, enjoyin' teasin' the poor wretch.

"'I want whisky—an' I must have it!' yells Shem.

"'How you goin' to git it?' sneers Beech—layin' down his pipe an' takin' a nip hisself, jest to ta'nt the feller.

"'Goin' to git it from you,' says Frowser. 'This is Christmas mornin'; an' you ort to treat me, Ike. I spend ev'ry cent I git with you. Christmas gift!'

That made Beech mad; an' he bellers out:

"'Now, Shem Frowser, you git right out o' here! I won't have you loafin' an' spongin' 'round here no more. You ain't worth the powder to blow you up. Git out—an' stay out!'

"Shem looks up at Beech—the tears in his red eyes, an' a look on his face like a whipped dog has when he licks his master's hand an' tries to make friends with him—an' whines:

"'Ike, you won't be so hard on me as all that, will you? Give me jest one drink, an' I'll go out an' not come in ag'in today.'

"Ol' Ike frowned an' chawed his mustache fer a little while. Then he says:

"'I'll tell you what I'll do, Shem.

"'What?' says Shem.

"'I'll give you a drink, if you'll take *all* I want you to, an' in the *way* I want you to.'

"'I'll do it,' answers Shem.

"'Come on, then,' says ol' Ike.

"An' motionin' Shem to foller him, he went into the back room.

In there was three 'r four bar'ls o' liquor, restin' on a rack, 'bout a foot from the floor. Beech p'inted to one of 'em an' says:

"'I guess 'bout the hottest stuff is in that 'n. Lay down on the floor with y'r mouth under the faucet.'

"'What're you goin' to do?' Shem asks, kind o' startin' back an' lookin' toward the door.

"'Goin' to fill you up fer once,' answers ol' Ike, with a string o' cuss words longer 'n a rake handle. 'I'll learn you how to come 'round, whinin' an' snivelin' fer a Christmas gift. I'll bet a peck o' shin plasters you won't want no more, when I git through treatin' you this time. Git down there an' take y'r medicine. An' you're to drink the stuff right down, fast as I turn it on; an' not stop swallerin' till I turn it off. Git down under that spigot an' turn y'r mouth up.'

"Shem knowed ol' Ike well enough to know he was in earnest this time an' meant jest what he said—no more an' no less. The poor simple critter turned pale clean to the end of his nose—which mostly was as red as a goose's foot on a frosty mornin'—an' sort o' hung back.

"'Git down there,' says Ike.

"Shem was famishin' fer liquor. So down he flops on his back, gits his head under the faucet an' opens his mouth. Beech—a chucklin' to hisself— stoops an' turns the spigot. Shem shuts his eyes, to keep the fumes o' the liquor out of 'em, an' gulps an' swallers like this."

And Jep gave a pantomimic illustration of the picture he had in his mind.

"Well," he continued, "ol' Ike finally got skeered—thought maybe he'd strangle the feller 'r give him so much it 'ld kill him; so he stooped and shut the whisky off. An' what do you s'pose was the first words Frowser said—when he could git his breath an' say anything?"

"I have no idea," Marlowe said, shaking his head.

"W'y, sir," Jep cried, slapping his thigh and laughing uproariously, "that simple critter jest winked at ol' Ike an' hollered—'*New Year's gift!*'"

Marlowe laughed softly, indulgently—albeit a little wearily. Jep finally controlled his own merriment; and drawing down the corners of his mouth said with mock gravity:

"Ev'ry story ort to have a moral to it, ortn't it, young feller?"

"Y—e—s," Ralph admitted, wondering what was coming.

"Well, this one ain't no 'xception to the rule," Jep said, grinning broadly. "The moral of it is—when you hain't got enough of a good thing don't be afeared to ask fer more. An' like Shem Frowser, I'm a sayin'—'New Year's gift.'"

"Help yourself," Ralph laughed—this time really amused.

Tucker promptly complied with the invitation.

Then smacking his lips—and with his battered cap rakishly cocked over one eye—he sauntered out, bent on getting his morning meal. A few minutes later Marlowe went to his own breakfast, still smiling over the eccentric's ruse to obtain an extra drink.

A little after ten o'clock Dr. Barwood put in an appearance at the drugstore.

"Good morning," he said pleasantly. "Are you all alone, Ralph?"

"All alone," was the cheery response. "It's a nice Christmas morning, doctor. How are you feeling?"

"Better—getting better every day. I'll be able to take to the saddle in a few days. Then you can take things easier."

He seated himself; and idly drummed a tattoo upon the arm of his chair, while vacantly gazing out at the side window. Presently he heaved a sigh, and turning to his companion inquired:

"Have you had much to do this morning?

"Very little."

"Did Jep build a fire in my room?"

Ralph nodded.

"I administered a course of sprouts to him, figuratively speaking," the doctor chuckled. "He promised to curb his story-telling propensity and attend more faithfully to his duties."

Again both men were silent. The older resumed his abstracted drumming upon the arm of his chair; the younger went on with his work behind the counter. Several minutes passed. Marlowe felt that some fateful event was impending—though why he felt so he could not make plain to himself. Suddenly Dr. Barwood arose and sauntering up to the counter asked with assumed interest:

"What are you doing?"

"Sorting these corks," was the answer. "They have become badly mixed."

"Well, let them remain mixed until another time," the older man said airily. "This is a holiday—a holy day—and you ought not to do work that you can postpone. Besides, you are to go up to dinner with me; and before we start I desire to have a talk with you. Come into the office."

Marlowe gave his companion one searching, inquiring glance; then silently followed him into the back room.

When they were seated, Dr. Barwood toyed with his long black watch-guard and bit his nether lip for some moments. At last he asked abruptly:

"Ralph, is there any reason why I should not invite you to my house—should not permit you to associate with my wife and daughters?"

Marlowe felt the hot blood mounting to his face.

His lips moved; and he was on the point of making an angry reply. But with rare mastery he controlled himself. The hot tide receded from his countenance, leaving him a little pale as he answered in cold sarcasm:

"I know of no reason, doctor. It is odd that you should ask the question. You ought to know your own family better than I. So far as my knowledge and experience goes, your wife and daughters are estimable ladies. If there be a reason why I should not associate with them, you should have informed—"

Dr. Barwood sprang to his feet, his features working.

"Hold!" he shouted. "You may be joking; but you will find that Ephraim Barwood permits no man to call his wife's and daughters' good names in question—even jokingly."

Ralph retained his composure and his seat.

"I have not called your family's reputation in question, doctor," he replied quietly.

"You have!" cried the other, bringing his fist down upon the table. "And I demand an apology."

"For what?"—Coolly.

"For the question you have raised."

"You raised the question, doctor."

"I?"—Glaring savagely at his companion.

"Yes, doctor. You asked me if I knew of any reason why I should not associate—"

"You understood what I meant."

"Of course. And I returned the answer such a question merited."

Dr. Barwood took a few turns around the room, muttering angrily to himself and breathing heavily. At last his features relaxed and his brow cleared. Resuming his seat, he said tremulously:

"I don't blame you, Ralph, for resenting such a question. I should have done the same. It was an insult. Forget that I ever asked it; and come to my house whenever it pleases you."

"I will never again enter the portal of your home, Dr. Barwood," Marlowe said softly but firmly, "until I have answered your question—until I have entirely satisfied you that I am a gentleman."

"But I had no right to ask the question," the older man said, laying his hand upon his companion's knee and looking at him pleadingly.

"And *I* had no *reason* to refuse to *answer* it," returned Ralph smiling.

"I am already satisfied," Dr. Barwood pursued. "I should not have thought of asking you such a question, had it not been to keep peace in the family. My older daughter suggested to her mother that there might be something in your past—"

"Listen, doctor," Ralph hurriedly interrupted. "Let us settle the matter once for all. There is no reason, so far as I know, why I should not be the intimate friend and associate of you and your family. But I do not purpose to reveal my past, to convince you of the truth of my statement. You must take my unsupported word. Is my answer satisfactory?"

"Eminently. Now, let us drop the subject—and forget it."

Smilingly the two men arose. Silently the older extended his hand, which the younger grasped and shook warmly. Then the latter said, his face flushing slightly:

"Doctor, I have a question to ask you—a question I have wished for some weeks to ask."

"Well, ask it," was the crisp reply.

Ralph cleared his throat, dropped his eyelids, and nervously shifted his position. Evidently he was embarrassed. Dr. Barwood smilingly awaited his companion's pleasure. After a half minute of painful silence, Marlowe flung up his head and blurted out:

"Dr. Barwood, I love Dolly. Have I your permission to try to win her love?"

The smile suddenly left the older man's face. Puckering his brows and tightening his thin lips, he said sneeringly:

"Well, you are a modest young man! You—of whom I know little or nothing—presume to ask me for my favorite daughter's hand in marriage. Do you think because I have given you an opportunity to earn a living, have taken you into a business partnership, that I am bound to go farther—take you in as a member of my family and give you a share of my property?"

"I shall not answer your question, doctor. You do not mean what you intimate."

"I don't?"—Fiercely.

"No, you don't. You have not so poor an opinion of me, I know. I love Dolly; I do not care a whit for your wealth—and you know it. Give me your answer—do not keep me in suspense."

"And if I refuse to grant you permission to court my daughter?"—With a curl of his short upper lip.

"It will not deter me from trying to win her."

"No?"

"No."

"And you would marry her against my wishes?"

"I would."

"I might disinherit her."

"I should not care—except for her sake. But you will grant my request, doctor."

"Oh, I will!"

"Yes."

"Well, I will *not.*"—In a tone of irrevocable decision.

"Why?"

"Because it would be useless for you to try to win Dolly's heart."

"She—she loves another?" Ralph asked falteringly—his heart throbbing sickeningly.

"No."

"Then I—I can't understand—"

"You can't win her heart, my boy, because she already loves *you.*"—Affectionately slapping him upon the shoulder. "You are a proverbial lover—blind as a bat. Now, let's have no more love-sick nonsense. You fancy Dolly; she fancies you. You have my consent to keep her company—to have an understanding with her at any time you choose. But you must not think of marrying until I give you permission. Do you agree to the arrangement?"

"I do—certainly," Marlowe replied, rapture beaming in his countenance. "And now let me thank you, doctor, for the most precious Christmas gift—"

"Stuff and nonsense!" snorted Dr. Barwood striding toward the door. "Come on. Let's go up to the house; dinner will be waiting."

As they were leaving the drugstore, Morris McDevitt springing up the steps almost bumped into them.

"Good morning," he muttered in confusion.

"Marlowe are you leaving?"

"Yes."

"I would like to see you a moment."

"Come into the store then."

Dr. Barwood remained standing upon the steps; his countenance set and stern. The two young men retired to the interior.

"Now what is it, McDevitt?" Ralph inquired briskly.

"Have you a Christmas gift for me?" the young merchant asked in return.

"A Christmas gift?"—And Marlowe glanced toward the cigar case.

"Oh! You know what I want," McDevitt muttered snappishly.

Ralph gave his companion a searching look of inquiry. He saw that the latter's eyes were burning with the fire of a feverish unrest, that his hands and lips were tremulous. His whole appearance betokened[92] nights of sleeplessness and dissipation.

"Do you want liquor?" the young physician asked coldly—though pity was in his heart.

"Hell—no!" McDevitt hissed, shaking his head and gritting his teeth. "I can get that at the saloons—too much of it. This is Christmas—the day of peace on earth and good will toward men—and I want a share in it. Have you had an opportunity to talk to Julia?"

"I have."

"When?"

"Yesterday evening."

"What did you say to her?"

"That you were disheartened over her refusal to marry you and were going to the bad. Did I do right?"

"Of course. What did she say to that?"—Eagerly.

"She said she would gladly save you, if you would put yourself in the way of salvation; but that she would never marry you until you had renounced Catholicism and embraced Protestantism."

McDevitt's countenance fell.

"She said that?" he murmured in a smothered tone.

"She did, McDevitt," Marlowe answered pityingly. "But you should be a man; you should not let her decision ruin you. Desert your haunts and your companions; reform yourself. You can do it, if you will. So one day she may change her mind."

"She never will," he answered gloomily. "No, she doesn't care for me. I know it now. And if she doesn't care for me, I don't care for myself. I am on the toboggan slide that leads to hell."—Laughing gratingly.—"It's a mad and merry ride I'm taking; but I am fully aware of what awaits me at the bottom. I thank you for what you have tried to do for me. You have proven yourself a— true—friend."

---

92 betoken: give evidence of

His voice broke a little. Recovering himself, he went on:

"If only I had your will power—but I have not. Well, I'll keep you and the old doc waiting no longer. I wish you better luck in your wooing than I have had."

With assumed recklessness, he jauntily cocked his hat over one eye and crying—"Ta-ta! I must get to my dinner; there's a big poker game this afternoon," sprang through the door and down the steps.

When Marlowe had relocked the door and rejoined Dr. Barwood, he saw the young Irish-American swaggering down the street, whistling merrily as be went.

The Christmas dinner at Barwood's passed pleasantly, in spite of the fact that Mrs. Barwood was rather silent and thoughtful, and Julia, distantly, coldly polite to the single guest. Dolly, however, was all smiles and dimples; and Dr. Barwood beamed benignly upon all around the board. Ralph ate heartily of the savory viands[93] and toothsome dainties; and feasted his eyes upon Dolly.

He prolonged his stay at the Barwood residence until three o'clock. Much of the time he spent in the parlor, alone with Dolly. She played and sang to him, while he lolled upon the sofa and drowsily listened. At last she arose, gave the piano stool a dizzy whirl, and seating herself beside him cried with playful petulance:

"Talk to me."

"Of what or whom?" he asked, smiling.

"Of yourself."

"A most uninteresting subject," he laughed.

"Not to me," she smiled, showing her white and perfect teeth.

"You are interested in me, Dolly?"—His voice growing tender.

"Yes."—A faint murmur.

"How much?"

"Oh! ever so much," she replied in the same low tone.

"And you wish me to talk of myself—to you?"

"Yes."

And she coquettishly[94] dropped her lids and averted her face.

---

93 viands: an item of food; especially a choice or tasty dish
94 coquettishly: flirting

"Dolly, look at me."

But she did not. Instead, she trembled slightly and made a move to arise. Quickly he slipped his arm around her waist and whispered something in her ear—something that caused her to settle back upon the sofa and nestle close to him. Her cheeks flushed to the roots of her golden hair, her breast heaved; and she looked apprehensively toward the door.

But what is the use? It is the old, old story so sweet to the children of men. Yet there is no need of repeating it here.

When he took his departure, she accompanied him into the hall and assisted him in donning his top coat. As a reward for her thoughtfulness he bent and kissed her.

One by one—what a favor it is they do not depart in pairs!—the short winter days flitted away. The nights plumed their black wings and flew after them. Life in the humdrum little village of Babylon pursued its usual course—kept in its shining, well-worn grooves.

Dr. Barwood so far recovered his health as to relieve Ralph of a little of the outside practice and more of the drudgery and confinement of the store and office. Jim Crawford was back at his bench—"as good as new," Tucker expressed it. But the ungrateful cobbler devoted his leisure time to the unstinted criticism and abuse of his benefactors. Lon Crider made his regular bimonthly visits to the town—always smiling, and with a carnation in his buttonhole.

Sam Clark continued to worship at the shrine of his lady love—and incidentally, to attend to his duties at the station. And Jep Tucker, Tomp Nutt, and other eccentrics still persisted in making life a dreary farce-comedy to Ralph Marlowe.

All through January and the early part of February, the weather was so wet, cold, and disagreeable, and the roads were so nearly impassable, that the oil men could do little or no work. In consequence, they remained in town, drinking and gambling as was their habit—Morris McDevitt taking part in their nightly carousals.

On the morning of St. Valentine's day, Marlowe went to the post-office for the mail. In the lot passed through the wicket to him, he discovered an envelope bearing Dolly's name and the local postmark.

"A comic valentine," the young man smiled as he hastily glanced at the scrawled address. "Whoever sent it has tried hard to disguise his handwriting. I shall take it to the house myself. I desire to see my young lady open it."

Fifteen minutes later he stood in the dimly lighted hall of the Barwood residence. Mrs. Barwood had admitted him and, at his request, had gone to call Dolly. Presently that young woman came tripping down the stairs, a muslin cap atop her fluffy curls.

"Mamma says you have a valentine for me, Ralph," she exclaimed gleefully. "Let me have it."

"Will you open it in my presence?" he asked, holding the envelope beyond her reach.

"Is it a comic?"

"Yes—at any rate it bears a one-cent stamp and the village postmark."

"And you sent it yourself, you scamp," she cried archly, shaking her finger at him.

"I did not."

"No?"—With an incredulous shake of the head.

"No."

"Well, give it to me."

"Will you let me see it?"

"Maybe."

"Promise!"

Incautiously he had lowered his arm. With a sudden movement she snatched the envelope from his hand; and laughing merrily danced halfway up the stairs. There, stopping and peeping over the banisters at him, she cried teasingly:

"Do you want to see my valentine, Ralph?"

"I see mine," he replied, looking up at her admiringly.

"Answer my question, sir," she cried, imperiously stamping her little foot and frowning. "This is no time for idle compliments. Answer the question put to you by your queen. Do you wish to see my valentine?"

"Yes," he laughed; "but there is no mirror at hand."

"Egotist!" she smiled.

Then she calmly inspected the address upon the envelope, turning it toward the transom to catch the light.

"A woman sent it," she announced. "Probably she is envious and jealous because I am leading you captive, sir—"

Abruptly she broke off, and crinkled the envelope between her fingers.

"This is no comic valentine," she resumed; "it is a letter. And posted in the village—who can have sent it?"

Marlowe silently shook his head.

"Well," she said, "I will not let you see it till I know what it is, at any rate. Come up this evening. There—that's your valentine."

She had descended a few steps, leaned over the banisters, and kissed him.

As Ralph passed through the doorway, he saw her waving her hand to him, from the landing.

Dolly went direct to her room. There she tore open the envelope. It contained another bearing the address—"Dr. Ralph Marlowe, Babylon, Ohio." It was the letter Ralph had dropped in the sitting room and Julia had picked up.

With trembling fingers—a nameless dread tugging at her heart strings—Dolly drew forth the crumpled sheet. As she unfolded it she murmured under her breath:

"Of course Ralph posted it himself. But why did he send it? If he wanted me to have it, why did he not give it to me, simply?"

She began a perusal of the brief enclosure. As she proceeded the blood deserted her face—and she shivered. When she had finished she sat for some time, staring wildly, vacantly at the opposite wall. At length she moistened her dry lips, with the tip of her tongue, and whispered shudderingly:

"What does it mean—what can it mean? Who is Stella—his wife? Oh, my God! My God! It is his letter—addressed to him in a woman's hand. Yes, there is no doubt about that. But why did he send it to me? He? He did not! I see it all—I see it all now! He lost it; somebody found it and sent it to me. My valentine! False—a deceiver—a married man! Oh, Ralph—Ralph! And I love you so fondly—so dearly!"

The hot tears started from her eyes and slowly trickled down her pale cheeks. Resolutely she dashed them aside; and again closely examined the envelope bearing her own name.

"Some *woman* sent it to me," she concluded. "Who was it? Oh, cruel—cruel! I was so happy —and now my life is marred—ruined! What shall I do? Shall I show the letter to daddy—dear old daddy? Shall I make a confidant of him, as I have always done? No—no! I cannot—I must not! He would drive Ralph away—expose and ruin him."

Again she sat panting and staring at the blank wall for some minutes. Then she sprang to her feet, and lifting her hands toward heaven groaned in a voice of wild intensity:

"Oh, God! How can I bear it? Ralph—Ralph! You are false and deceitful!—But I love—you still—I love you still!"

Overcome by her conflicting emotions, she threw herself upon the bed and wept and moaned.

At length, however, her native resolution reasserted itself. Calmly arising, she bathed her face and rearranged her disheveled tresses. When she had done this—and closely scrutinized her features in the mirror—she mechanically resumed her morning duties, whispering sobbingly to herself as she moved about the upper floor:

"It is all over—only a beautiful dream! Shall I return him his letter? No, I will never let him know that I am aware of his—his— Oh! I cannot utter the harsh word. For I love him; and—God help me I—I still believe in him, in spite of this revelation. But I will refuse to see him. No, that will not do. I will meet him and break off our engagement. Engagement! Oh, the mockery! I will tell him I have found I do not love him. No—no! I can't do that—I can't. He would read the lie in my eyes. I must not meet him at all—until I am stronger. For I love him; and I am weak—so weak!"

All day she went about the house, quietly—apathetically. Except for her unwonted silence and paleness, she showed no outward sign of the emotional storm she had experienced.

Mrs. Barwood noticed her daughter's unusual lack of vivacity and questioned her concerning the cause; but received only monosyllabic, unsatisfactory replies. The father became cognizant of her pallor and listlessness—and forthwith resolved to prepare her an iron tonic. Julia was not blind; but she kept her own counsel.

That evening Marlowe called. Mrs. Barwood came into the sitting room and informed him that Dolly was indisposed and would not be able to see him. After expressing his concern, he took his departure, greatly worried.

The evening following, the young man again called; and again he was informed that his sweetheart was confined to her room and was not able to see him.

Dr. Barwood being present supplemented his wife's information, by saying:

"It's nothing alarming, Ralph. A little anaemic neurasthenia,[95] I think. She'll be all right in a short time. She complains of headache, has no appetite, and wishes to remain undisturbed in her room. Come up tomorrow evening. Perhaps she will be able to be down stairs by that time."

Marlowe slept little that night. By nine o'clock the next forenoon, he was wild with anxiety. For Dr. Barwood had gone to the country some time during the hours of darkness, and the lover had had no opportunity to hear from the object of his adoration. At last he could stand the suspense no longer; and he went to the house to inquire about her.

"I am going up to see her," he said positively, when Mrs. Barwood had once more told him her daughter was no better and was still confined to her room.

"No," the mother replied, shaking her head, "You must not."

"May I ask why?"

"She is nervous and—and—" Then the good lady hesitated and ceased speaking.

---

95 neurasthenia: a psychological disorder marked especially by easy fatigability and often by lack of motivation, feelings of inadequacy, and psychosomatic symptoms

"Is she dangerously ill?" Ralph inquired in a voice tremulous with emotion.

"Oh, no!" Mrs. Barwood hastened to say, wrapping an end of her apron string around her index finger, in a nervous, embarrassed way. "But she told me to say to you that—that—"

"What?" Marlowe interrupted impatiently.

"That she does not desire to see you," Mrs. Barwood completed. "She breaks down and cries whenever your name is mentioned in her presence; and says she will never meet you again. Still she will give no reason for her strange behavior."

A moment the two looked at each other in grave silence. Then Ralph muttered hoarsely:

"I cannot understand her humor, Mrs. Barwood. She must be more seriously ill than you suspect. Has she fever—is she delirious, do you think?" Mrs. Barwood shook her head. Then, her eyes glistening with moisture and her voice quavering, she asked abruptly:

"Dr. Marlowe, do you love Dolly?"

"Yes, Mrs. Barwood—with all my heart," Ralph answered in a tone of deep sincerity.

"And you and she are engaged?"

"Yes, Mrs. Barwood. I supposed you knew."

"No. Dolly has not told me; but I suspected. She has never made a confidant of me; she has always gone to her father for advice and counsel. I presume she obtained his consent to the engagement—or you did. But now she will not confide to her father, even, the cause of her trouble. You and she have not quarreled, Dr. Marlowe?"

"Indeed, no," Ralph answered in a tone of surprise and perplexity. Then with sudden decision:

"Mrs. Barwood, I can stand this uncertainty, this suspense, no longer. I am going up to see Dolly."

With the words he began to ascend the stairs.

"But she does not desire to see you," the mother objected, closely following him.

"The more reason I should see her and have an explanation," was the resolute response.

Mrs. Barwood raised no further objections.

On reaching the upper hall, she stepped in front of Dolly's door and said:

"Let me go in first."

Ralph nodded assent; and leaning against the wall impatiently awaited a summons to enter. Through the partly open door he caught the petulant, tearful query:

"Oh, mother! Why did you permit him to come up here?"

This was followed by Mrs. Barwood's mumbled reply. A moment later she threw wide the door and signed for him to enter. Stepping into the room, he observed Dolly occupying a reclining chair near the window. His professional eye and intelligence made note of the fact that she appeared a little pale and worn—but not at all ill.

At sight of her visitor the young woman trembled visibly and turned away her face. Without a word Ralph drew a chair to her side and gently but firmly took her hand. At this juncture, Mrs. Barwood discreetly withdrew, closing the door behind her.

"They tell me you have been ill, Dolly," he remarked, with forced cheerfulness.

"Do they?" she replied in cold inflexible tones.

"Then they misinform you."

"Have you not been ill?"—In great surprise.

"No, I have not."—Still keeping her face averted and attempting to withdraw her hand from his restraining clasp.

Marlowe was nonplused. But he resolutely persisted:

"Then why have you thus secluded yourself, Dolly—why have you refused to see me?"

"To both your questions," she replied icily, "I answer—because it pleased me to do so. But you are so little a gentleman you invade my privacy—force your unwelcome presence upon me."

Stung to the quick, Marlowe dropped her hand and sprang to his feet.

"Dolly," he cried, "I demand an explanation."

"Oh, you do!"—Suddenly facing him, her cheeks and eyes ablaze.

"I do."

"And if I refuse?"—With a faint sneer.

"Then, indeed, I will never again force my unwelcome presence upon you," he answered solemnly, decidedly.

For the first time during the interview, she wavered. The thought of losing him was torture. But her inherited will power came to her rescue; and setting her teeth she thrust one hand into her bosom and drew forth the fateful letter.

"There is the explanation you so much desire" she cried shrilly, dramatically thrusting the missive toward him. "Also, it is the valentine you were so anxious to see."

Marlowe did not recoil or turn pale, as she expected, Instead he quietly took the proffered letter, and unflinchingly fixing his eye upon her face said in a tone of deep sadness:

"And this is the valentine you received, Dolly—and the cause of your strange behavior, your cruel treatment of me?"

"Yes," she replied in an almost inaudible whisper, a sweet hope springing in her breast, in spite of her fixed resolve not to believe a word he said.

"Poor little girl!" he said huskily, the tears shining in his eyes. "You have doubted me; you have struggled and suffered. Yes, this is my letter. I lost it. Some unprincipled person found it and sent it to you—some one that desired you to lose faith in me, that wished to see you suffer. Have you any idea who is guilty of the base act, Dolly?"

"No," she answered faintly.

"Will you believe me, Dolly, if I tell you I am guiltless of the crime of which this letter seems to accuse me? Will you accept my word unsupported by any proof or explanation?"

She looked at him helplessly, pleadingly—but was silent.

Smiling sadly he thrust the letter into his pocket; and holding out his arms to her said:

"Come to me, then. I will tell you all. I should have done so sooner. Come."

Totteringly she rose to her feet and made a step, toward him.

Then she halted and drew back, panting:

"I must not listen to you. Do not tempt me—go away—"

Springing forward he caught her in his arms, whispered a few words in her ear, and smilingly released her. The next moment her arms were around his neck and she was sobbing upon his shoulder.

As he left the house, a half hour later, she playfully threw him a kiss from her window; and that afternoon she went about her household duties as usual, singing blithely.

* * * * * *

CHAPTER XV

ON A DARK and stormy evening in the early part of March, Ralph Marlowe sat alone in the drugstore, hugging the hot stove and glancing over the evening paper. All day he had ridden in the wind and rain; and now he was stiff, chilly, and drowsy.

Outside, the wind whistled around the gables and chimneys and screamed and chuckled as it sped away among the leafless tree tops. The rain fell fitfully, alternated with showers of snow pellets that rattled like handfuls of birdshot against the window panes.

The door opened, and Tucker dragged his water-soaked boots into the room, leaving a trail of wet footprints upon the floor. Tumbling into his accustomed seat behind the stove, and relaxing into a limp and lazy heap, he produced a long cigar and lighted it. Then placing his wet footwear upon the projecting hearth of the upright stove, he puffed away meditatively for some time.

Ralph went on with the perusal of his paper. The horsy smell arising from Jep's steaming boots and garments filled the room. Presently he knocked the ashes from his cigar and remarked drawlingly:

"Mighty bad night out, ain't it?"

Marlowe nodded slightly.

"Yes, *sir,*" Jep continued; "it's a mighty bad night. Guess the groundhog must 'ave seen his shadder an' gone back into his den. That means six weeks more o' winter. It's turning cold fast, too; an' blowin' stiff enough to untie a hard knot in a shoestring. By mornin' the ground 'll be froze harder 'n ol' Phar'oh's heart; an' ther'll be ten inches o' snow on."

"So much?" Ralph smiled, turning his paper. "Well, maybe not quite that much," Jep grinned. "But a few inches more 'r less don't make much differ'nce in anything—'cept on the end of a feller's nose. One inch there makes a heap o' differ'nce. Ever notice that, young feller?"

"Frequently," Marlowe replied abstractedly, without taking his eyes from the printed sheet.

Again Jep was silent for a few moments, puffing vigorously at his cigar which threatened to go out. When the lighted end of the roll of cheap tobacco was once more aglow, he resumed musingly.

"This sort of a night is bad for all kinds o' business 'cept drinkin' an' gamblin'. That business goes on in all kinds o' weather—an' week days an' Sundays. Them oil men is keepin' things a goin', I tell *you;* an' Morris McDevitt's tryin' to keep up with 'em. He'll bu'st hisself an' his ol' daddy, too, 'fore he quits, if somethin' 'r somebody don't head him off. He gambles ev'ry night; an' ev'ry night he gambles he loses money. Well, let him go it. I never did like him very well, anyhow. He was alluz too stuck up fer me. Thinks he's made of a little better clay 'n anybody else; when the fact is he's nothin' but common crock'ry-ware—an' a cracked vessel at that. Him an' the ol' doc's oldest gal is a good deal alike. She's stuck up, too—not much like Miss Dolly. Yes, sir, Morris an' Miss Julia ort to git married; it's a 'tarnal shame to spile two houses with 'em. She wants to reform the universe; an' if she'd marry him, she'd 'ave a piece o' timber to begin on—an' one that 'ld try her little hatchet—"

"Jep," Ralph broke in, "you should not talk so about your employer's daughter."

"You're 'bout right," Tucker admitted. "An' I won't say no more 'bout *her*. But I can't keep from thinkin' 'bout 'er. An' as fer him—I'll say what I please. I don't like a bone in his body."

Marlowe refolded his paper, and leaning far over tossed it upon the end of the counter. Then, settling back in his chair, he said mischievously:

"If Morris McDevitt should hear of your remarks, Jep, he might chastise you."

"You mean he might whip me?"

"Yes."

"He'd better hire the job out," Tucker replied, scowling. "W'y,"—His features immediately relaxing into a grin—"I could take the little whiffet 'cross my knee an' break him in two—like I would a stick o' kindlin'."

"But you should not seek to injure his reputation, Jep."

"It's purty toler'ble hard to spile an addled egg," Tucker retorted. "The truth is he's got his tail in a crack; an' he's goin' to git it pinched.—He's hatchin' a chicken that'll come home to roost at last, no matter what other people may do 'r say. W'y; ev'rybody knows what he's doin'; an' ev'rybody's talkin' 'bout it, too. His poor ol' daddy an' mammy looks ten years older 'n they did twelve months ago."

"That is one very good reason," Ralph answered soberly, "why people should be more careful what they say. They should have regard for the feelings of Morris's relatives and friends, if they have no respect for him. They should be more charitable."

Jep silently pondered his companion's words. At length he roused himself and said slowly—and with evident reluctance:

"Y-e-s, I guess that's so. But ther's somethin' funny 'bout that word charity. The Bible says—I guess it's in the good book—that charity covers a multitude o' sins. That must mean that it's stretchier 'n a lawyer's conscience. An' w'en it gits drawed out so everlastin' thin, it can't be o' much account, it 'pears to me. Then some folks says charity begins at home. That's as *true* as gospel, whether it *is* gospel 'r not. Charity begins at home; an' with most people it never goes abroad. An' w'en it does happen to take a trip, it travels in a circle an' comes right straight back to its place o' beginnin'."

Then cocking his head and casting an eye toward the door:

"There's that Lon Crider. He comes round as reg'lar as tax-payin' time."

The drug drummer bustled into the store, bringing the chill, moist breath of the storm with him. "How are you, Marlowe, anyhow?" he cried effusively, slapping the young physician upon the shoulder.

"Beastly night out, isn't it? Hello, Jep!"—With a nod and a smile. "You bet—a beastly bad night! And the day wasn't any better; either. You're a lucky dog, Marlowe—sit by the fire and toast your shins. I've been out in this weather ever since seven o'clock this morning—"

"I have ridden all day myself," Ralph interjected.

"That so!"—Pulling up the lapel of his coat and sniffing at the flower in his buttonhole.—"Well, I hope you've made more out of it than I have. I haven't taken an order today. But *you've* got an order for me, haven't you?"

"A small one."

"Small favors are gratefully received—and big ones in proportion," laughed Crider, growing red in the face and producing his order book and pencil. "By the way, how's the old doc?"

"He is in fair health and humor," Ralph replied. "Good!" cried the traveling man. "Glad to bear it."

Seating himself and nervously tapping the back of his book with his pencil, he continued:

"Now, I'm ready for that order. Business first and pleasure afterward is my motto. Get your list; I don't want you to miss anything. You are a lucky dog, Marlowe—and no mistake. They say a good man can't be kept down; and I'm beginning to believe it. You came to this town a few months ago, a poor drug clerk. Now you've blossomed out as a full-blown physician; and are in partnership with the old doc and running things to suit yourself. Then I hear since getting in tonight that you've got a good thing in oil, and that you're going to marry the old doc's youngest girl and become one of the family."

"Crider, I am ready to give you the order," Ralph said frigidly.

"And I'm ready to take it," hastily replied the jolly commercial man, suddenly growing grave and blushing like an embarrassed urchin. "I meant no offense, Marlowe."

"And I have taken none." Ralph answered. "Please say no more.

You may send me ten pounds of borax."

Thus they went on for some time, the one naming the things he wanted, the other industriously writing. Tucker arose, yawned, stretched himself, and wandered around the room, softly whistling.

"That is all," Ralph said at last.

"Much obliged," answered Crider slapping together the lids of his order book and returning it to his pocket. "Now have a smoke with me. You won't. Then I'll have to burn incense all by my lonesome. Oh! Here's Tucker. Have a smoke, Tucker?"

"Don't care if I do," grinned that human oddity receiving and fondling the pursy cigar.

"You'd better have a care, Jep," Marlowe remarked roguishly; "that cigar may be loaded."

Jep did not deign to make reply, until he had lighted his cigar and started it going to his satisfaction. Then he drawled between puffs:

"Maybe 'tis; but I'm goin' to smoke it, anyhow. If a feller crawfished from ev'rything that *might* be loaded, he wouldn't git no pleasure out o' life. Fer most things is loaded more 'r less, is my 'xperience. Ther' ain't no rose without its thorn; an' ther' ain't no spree without its headache. Speakin' o' loaded things, though, puts me in mind o' the story 'bout ol' Ezry Barnhouse an' the sleigh bells."

"Let's have it," laughed Crider, winking at Marlowe.

"No," Jep replied, soberly shaking his head, "I ain't tellin' no stories these days. Am I, young feller?"

"You haven't told many of late," Ralph answered.

"*Many?*" Jep gasped. I hain't told *none*—not a single one fer months an' months. An' it's beginnin' to wear on me, too. I'm a little off on my feed an' can't sleep more 'n twelve hours at a stretch. Don't know how long I'll be able to hold out."

He cast an appealing look at Marlowe, as though expecting the latter to say something in reply—something that he, Jep, desired very much to hear.

He was not disappointed.

"Considering your suffering condition," Ralph laughed, "I think you would better break your rash resolve—this once, at any rate—and tell us the story, Jep."

"Of course neither one of you'll ever say anything to the ol' doc 'bout it," Tucker said with a dubious shake of his frowsy head.

"Certainly not—go ahead," cried Crider.

Thus assured, and having reseated himself and disposed of his clumsy nether limbs, Tucker yawned sleepily once or twice and began punctuating his sentences with sundry puffs at his vanishing cigar.

"'Tain't a very long yarn; but I alluz thought it was a purty good one. 'Spect neither one o' you fellers ever knowed ol' Ezry Barnhouse, did you?" His auditors shook their heads.

"He was a Quaker an' lived out at Foxtown," Jep proceeded. "Outside he had all the symptoms of a dyed-in-the-wool Broad'rim—the hat, the shad-belly coat, an' the thee-an'-thou lingo; but inside he was a worldly ol' ripscallion—drunk whisky, played cards, an' swore like a deck hand.

"One time he moved down here to Babylon, an' lived in the town sev'r'l years. Bought a little dinky of a steamboat named the *Lindy;* an' run 'er in the trade from here to Zanesville an' back. He acted as captain; an' carried a crew that was as drunken an' worthless as hisself. The end o' the matter was that they all got boozy one day, run the *Lindy* over the dam at Eagleport, an' bu'sted 'er all to flinders. Wasn't enough left of 'er to build a decent-sized johnboat. Whole caboodle come purty near drowndin'.

"Ol' Ezry finally j'ined the Murphies, moved back to Foxtown, an' went to makin' temper'nce speeches over the country. Used to tell 'bout his steamboatin' 'xperience; an' 'ld alluz wind up by sayin':

"'Yes, ladies an' gentlemen, the reason the *Lindy* was wrecked, thee knows, was because o' strong drink. Fer she drawed fourteen inches o' water an' sixteen inches o' whisky; there was more steam in the officers than there was in the b'iler; an' they blowed off twice to the b'iler's once. It was drink wrecked the *Lindy* thee knows—it was drink.'

"But I've sort o' got out o' the main channel. I started to tell you 'bout ol' Ezry an' the sleigh bells. One winter day—years 'fore he moved down here to Babylon—the ol' scalawag went down to Malconta an' got on a rousin' spree. A lot o' the young dudes o' the town got a hold of him an' was havin' a heap o' fun—fer he was a comic ol' scamp when he was rosumed up a little. Finally them young bloods got him up to the hardware store an' strung strings o' sleigh bells all over him an' had him prancin' an' dancin' up an' down street, while they laid back an' nearly died a laughin'.

"Well, the'r little game was loaded—though of course they didn't know it. Ol' Ezry—trigged out worse 'n Santy Claus ever was—went a prancin' up to the corner o' the street 'bove the hardware store, jest a pawin' the ground an' a neighin' like an army hoss on parade day. An' them young fellers seen him turn the corner, an' heerd the people talkin' an' titterin' on the next street, an' they slapped one another on the back an' whooped an' hollered like a pack o' Injins, thinkin' what a picnic they was havin'.

"But purty soon they didn't hear the jingle o' the sleigh bells no more; an' they looked at one another kind o' questionin' like.

"'Guess we'd better go up there an' see what's become o' our ol' hoss,' says one. 'Maybe he's fell down an' can't git up. He was purty full o' barley juice.'

"'Oh!' says another, 'he's stopped to gab to somebody. He'll be back in a minute.'

"But they all stopped the'r laughin' an' stood grinnin' sickly grins at each other an' a listenin' fer the sound o' sleigh bells. Then all of a sudden all of 'em started an' run up to the corner, tight as they could go. Ol' Ezry wasn't nowhere to be seen; an' his hoss was gone from the hitchin' rack. The joke was he was on his way to Foxtown fast as hoss flesh could carry him, takin' twenty dollars' worth o' sleigh bells with him. An' he never brung 'em back; an' them young dudes had to foot the bill at the hardware store an'—"

Jep stopped suddenly. Then exclaimed:

"W'y, there comes Tomp Nutt. What's brung that Ol' codger out such a night as this?"

Tomp entered—a dripping bundle of loose and ragged clothing—and, as if in answer to Tucker's exclamation, stuttered:

"The ol' w-woman's g-g-got the n-newrology, I w-want s-somethin' f-f-fer it."

While Marlowe was preparing the desired anodyne, Nutt stood leaning against the counter, idly shaking the wet from his saturated headpiece.—Crider and Tucker smoked on in silence.

Presently Tomp remarked:

"I c-come up p-p-past T-Torbert's s-s'loon. They m-must be br-breakin' up h-housekeepin' in there; fer I n-never heard s-such a r-rumpus in my life—"

"Think they was havin' a free-fer-all fight, Tomp?" Tucker asked, craning his neck to peep around the stove.

"D-Don't know," Nutt answered with a shake of the head.

Then receiving his package of medicine he shuffled toward the door.

As he passed out Sam Clark and Airly Chandler came in. Both looked pale and agitated.

"Come here a minute, Marlowe," Clark requested, beckoning with his finger.

"They're having a regular Indian war dance down to Torbert's place," he went on breathlessly when Ralph had reached his side. "McDevitt's down there pretty tipsy. We want you to go down with us, and see if we can't get him out—and up home. There's going to be hell there before morning."

"Have you been down there?" Marlowe inquired in tones too low for Tucker's and Crider's ears.

Airly Chandler nodded; and Clark made cautious reply:

"Yes. We was passing the place—me and Airly—and we heard a rumpus in there, as though there was a fight going on. We thought Morris might be mixed up in it, so we went in. Three or four fellows were fighting over a game of seven-up—dollar a corner. McDevitt was among them. Torbert finally got them quieted down; and then we tried to get McDevitt to come away with us. But it was no go—he's drunk, you know. Two or three oil men have him in tow; and they'll fleece him good. Besides there's a young cattle dealer there from Foxtown. He's got three hundred dollars in his pocket, and is drinking and gambling. Somebody'll swipe his roll before daylight. Then there'll be a trial, likely, and exposure for everybody concerned—Morris included. Maybe you can get him to come away. Won't you go down with us and try?

Ralph answered with an almost imperceptible nod of the head; and turning to the two by the stove, said briefly:

"I'm going to close up."

"All right," replied Crider, with alacrity rising and making for the door, closely followed by Tucker.

A few seconds later, Marlowe and his two companions were on their way to Torbert's saloon. That den of iniquity was on the ground floor of a barnlike building of two stories, standing just south of the village hotel, at the intersection of a cross street and side street. Its front door looked toward the river and was reached by a flight of crazy wooden stairs. Its rear entrance was upon the cross street.

The three young men entered at the rear door, and found themselves in a large bare-floored room containing a bar, a lopsided pool table, a number of card tables, and sundry chairs and stools. The walls were adorned with unframed chromos[96] and lithographs—pictures of pugilists, jockeys, and actors and actresses. A stove occupied one corner of the room; and three or four big oil lamps hung from the ceiling.

Everything presented a quiet and orderly appearance. Two oil men stood at the bar, leisurely sipping at schooners of foaming beer and talking in low, confidential tones. They scowled as the trio of newcomers put in an appearance. Near the stove, Crawford and his comrade, the bridge-tender; sat with their chairs tilted against the wall. The cobbler was tipsily humming a few bars of his favorite drinking song and batting at the lamp over his head. Brady had fallen into a drunken sleep, and was breathing stertorously.[97] At one of the small tables a number of men were playing seven-up, for the drinks; and at another a game of poker was in progress. At the latter table sat Morris McDevitt.—Several onlookers were watching the two games.

---

96 chromos: chromolithograph
97 stertorously: characterized by a harsh snoring or gasping sound

"Good evening," Torbert grunted gruffly, as Marlowe and his companions passed the end of the bar on their way to where McDevitt sat.

None of the three returned an answer to the surly greeting. They reached the poker table, Ralph in the lead. The green baize was piled with chips and coin. Evidently the play was for high stakes.

For a short time McDevitt remained unaware of the presence of his friends. Ralph noted that the young merchant's face was flushed and that his hands shook as he scanned his cards. Then the young physician's attention was drawn to a player on the opposite side of the table—a mere boy, he appeared, with wavy chestnut hair and regular features.

"It's up to you, Edgerton," one of the players cried. "Rader's bet three dollars—an' crowded ev'rybody out but you an' McDevitt. Stay with him—if you think you've got the best ones."

"I see that, and raise it five dollars," said Edgerton—the youthful stranger Ralph had noticed—shoving a stack of chips and coin to the center of the table.

"I'm out," muttered McDevitt with an oath, angrily throwing down his cards. "Everybody skins me."

"The young rooster from Foxtown can't knock me off the roost," leered Rader, an oil driller of forty. "I'll just learn him to stay out till he's got something. My cattle dealing friend, I raise you ten dollars more."

"And I call you," replied the youthful gambler, tossing a ten dollar bill upon the pile of chips and money. "What have you?"

"Four little ones," laughed Rader.

"That beats an ace-full," Edgerton returned quietly.—But his mouth quivered and he swallowed a lump in his throat.—"Take the money."

Marlowe had seen all he cared to see—and more. Stepping behind McDevitt's chair, he laid a hand upon the latter's shoulder and whispered:

"Morris, I desire to speak with you a moment. Come outside."

McDevitt wheeled at the sound of the familiar voice in his ear and stared stupidly at the speaker. Then, recognizing Ralph, he staggered to his feet and said:

"Hello, Marlowe! What the devil are you doing here?"

"I came to see you."

"Did, eh? Won't you take a hand in the game? There's room for another good player."

Shaking his head, Ralph answered:

"No. Come outside. I have something to say to you."

"Can't you talk here? I don't want to leave the game, and—"

Suddenly he became aware of the presence of Clark and Chandler. The sight of them threw him into an instant rage.

"Sam Clark," he cried hoarsely, "you brought Marlowe down here—you sneak! Well, you've had your trouble for nothing. I'm going to stay here until I get ready to leave. There!"

"That's the stuff!" shouted Rader. "Sit down and let's go ahead with the game. If your missionary friends don't like the company you keep, let them take a walk—let them chase themselves."

"Will you not come with me, Morris?" Marlowe asked in persuasive tones.

"No, I won't," McDevitt answered sneeringly.

"Who appointed you my guardian, Mr. Ralph Marlowe—hey?"

The gamblers around the tables laughed heartily.

Torbert winked and grinned at the two oil men who stood at the bar; and Jim Crawford began to sing lustily—"Once I was a pussy ol' landlord's pet."

Of all the players, Edgerton was the only one who did not join in the laugh. He sat with drooped eyelids and set features, nervously drumming upon the table.

Rader arose, softly approached McDevitt, and taking him by the arm whispered wheedlingly:

"Sit down, and let's go ahead with the game. Pay no attention to the old grannies."

Ralph Marlowe saw the driller's sly movements and heard the whispered words. Instantly the young physician's mobile features froze to stony hardness.

"Loose his arm and stand aside," he said in low, intense accents, looking Rader squarely in the eyes.

"You mean that for me?" the latter asked blusteringly.

"I do."

"Take that for your smartness, then!" shouted Rader, springing forward and shoving his fist full at Ralph's face.

The latter easily parried the blow; and the next instant the surprised driller measured his length upon the dusty floor. In a moment there was a wild scramble and uproar. Clark and Chandler turned deathly pale, but drew near to Marlowe's side—the agent shoving up his sleeves and clenching his blue-veined hands. The other oil men sprang to their feet and assisted their prostrate comrade to rise. Then, with muttered threats and maledictions, they surrounded the young doctor. The latter calmly stood his ground, his arms folded, his brown eyes alert. Torbert, the saloon keeper, made no move to quell the disturbance. Plainly his sympathy was with his customers. He wished to see Ralph receive chastisement at the hands of Rader and his friends.

But the driller had no intention of again putting himself within reach of Marlowe's fist. Feelingly rubbing his bruised jaw and shaking his head in a dazed way, he sullenly drew away from his excited and angry companions.

"Come on, Rader!" cried one of them. "You don't have to take that."

"Oh, don't I!" growled the driller. "Well, I'd have to take more if I got in his reach again. I've had plenty. If you fellows want to fight him, you can. I know a prize fighter when I run up against his fist!"

But those who had not tested Marlowe's prowess were not so easily satisfied. With scowling faces and threatening gestures—two or three of them had caught up chairs and were holding them aloft—they gradually drew nearer to the object of their wrath.

Marlowe's face was a trifle pale; but he made no move to retreat.

"Back!"

Like a flashing blade leaping from its sheath, the single word sprang from the young physician's lips. His eyes were flashing; his nostrils quivering. His assailants looked upon him and instinctively recoiled. Taking instant advantage of their hesitation, Ralph proceeded:

"I did not come in here to participate in a saloon brawl, but to rescue my friend from your clutches. I was attacked; I retaliated. I am unarmed. Throw aside your weapons, and I will fight any or all of you, single-handed."

Partially sobered by the turn affairs had taken, Morris McDevitt placed himself at Marlowe's side, saying:

"Yes! And by all that's right and just, Ralph Marlowe, I'll stand by you and see fair play!"

The oil men had counted upon McDevitt's sympathy and support, and were completely taken aback by his sudden change of sentiment—his resolute avowal. Slowly they lowered the chairs they held aloft, and silently looked at one another. Still they were very angry; and it is problematical how the affair might have terminated had not a diversion occurred.

The rear door flew open and a short, heavy-set man dashed into the room. His hat was in his hand and his long, iron-gray hair was streaming about his round, rubicund face. It was Hugh McDevitt, Morris's father.

Going straight up to his son—totally oblivious of those present—the old man cried wildly:

"Morris, my boy, come home, for God's sake! Your mother and sister are up there, crying their eyes out over your doings. They wouldn't let me have a minute's peace till I promised to come for you. Come home with me. Do—please, do!"

At the sight of his father young McDevitt started.

His countenance underwent a change of expression. The light of noble resolve faded from it; and dogged obstinacy was there in its stead. In answer to his parent's pleading words, the son said sullenly:

"I'm only doing what you did when you were young. I've heard how you sowed your wild oats." —Mr. McDevitt dropped his eyes and sadly nodded.

"And I'm not going to be drug around like a five-year-old boy. I'll come home when I get ready—and not a minute sooner. I'll send Airly Chandler up to console Rose—he'll do much better than I"— The last sentence with a sneer.

"But your mother, Morris!" the father plead tearfully.

"Tell her to go to bed. I'll be up home in an hour or two. That's all now. I won't go with you or anybody else."

Knowing that further persuasion would be idle, the father put on his hat and left the place, sobbing as he went. Marlowe and his two companions followed.

During the whole disturbance, Edgerton had sat at the poker table, his elbows upon it, his chin resting upon his hands—a picture of apathetic despair. Five minutes after the departure of Marlowe and his friends, the game was again going on—as if nothing unusual had happened.

On leaving the saloon, the four men, who had interested themselves in Morris McDevitt's welfare, made their way from the muddy cross street into the main thoroughfare. There they divided, Clark and the young school-teacher crossing to the hotel and Marlowe and Mr. McDevitt continuing up the dark avenue. Until his residence was reached, the heart-stricken father did not utter a word nor did Ralph intrude upon his grief.

At his gate the old man gave his hand to his companion, saying in a moved voice:

"Dr. Marlowe, you were down there trying to get my boy out of that hell of vice. Accept my thanks—and an old man's blessing. As we sow, so shall we reap. In my youth I sowed to the wind; tonight I am reaping the whirlwind."

Then, without waiting for a reply, he turned and groped his way toward the house, his head bowed in sorrow.

Marlowe went direct to his rooms, and to bed. But for hours he could not sleep. His last conscious thought was:

"Yes, Hugh McDevitt is reaping the whirlwind of his own

appetites and passions. What will the harvest be? There are but three things that shape our destinies—heredity, environment, and ourselves."

* * * * * *

CHAPTER XVI

AS RALPH was unlocking the drugstore the following morning, Brady, the bridge-tender—who, also, was the town marshal—came hurrying up to him. It was just gray daylight.

"Have you seen Frank Edgerton this mornin', doc?" the officer asked.

"Frank Edgerton?" Ralph echoed, throwing open the door and making a move to step within.

"Yes," Brady replied in a low tone. "You was down at Torbert's place last night, I was told. I didn't see you;"—With a shameless grin.—"I was too far gone. But you saw the feller there—that young cattle dealer from Foxtown. You hain't seen anything of him this mornin'?"

"No," Ralph answered quickly. "What of him?"

"I don't know what of him," Brady laughed uneasily; "that's jest the trouble. You see when the boys quit playin'—'bout three o'clock this mornin'—the cattle dealer was consider'ble behind the game, an' purty much put out. He was purty drunk, too; but he wouldn't go to the hotel an' go to bed, as the other fellers wanted him to—jest moseyed off down toward the river by hisself. An' nobody's seen him sence.

"I went into Charley Williams's bar, to git a nip, a little while ago; an' some o' the oil men was in there an' wanted me to hunt

Edgerton up. They was worried 'bout him. Well, I started out an' found his horse tied to the rack in the alley by McDevitt's store. The beast had been out in the storm all night; an' was shakin' with cold. I took it to the liv'ry stable an' had it rubbed down an' fed. But I'd like right smart to know where its master is."

Marlowe looked up and down the hoof-trampled street. The scene was wintry and drear. The earth was half frozen; a light fall of snow accentuated the inequalities in the ground. The sky was still overcast with scudding clouds, and the wind was keen.

The young doctor shivered involuntarily as he replied to Brady's question:

"You will find Frank Edgerton in the bottom of the river, is my opinion."

"Don't say that!" gasped the bridge-tender turning pale. "That's just what I'm 'fraid of myself—an' it scares me to think of it. If he's gone an' can't be found, it's goin' to make no end o' trouble fer the boys that played with him. Fer he had lots o' money with him; an' lost the most of it. I wonder—"

"What time did Morris McDevitt leave the place?" Ralph asked.

"Same time the rest did—three o'clock."

At that moment a ragged boy of twelve years came whistling up the street, swinging a limp object in his hand. As he drew near, the two men saw that the thing the lad carried was a water-soaked corduroy cap.

"Where'd you git this, Tom Sandy?" Brady demanded sharply, snatching the wet headgear from the youngster's hand.

"Give it here; 'tain't yours," whined the boy. "No, 'tain't mine," Brady answered deliberately; "but I know whose it is. It's Frank Edgerton's."—To Marlowe who gravely nodded. —"Where'd you git it, Tom?"

"Down on the 'proach o' the bridge," the lad answered sullenly. "I was goin' over to Downing's after milk; an' I found the cap an' a whisky bottle right together."

"Where's the bottle?" asked Brady.

"Here 'tis."—Pulling a flask containing a small quantity of liquor from the pocket of his ragged coat.

"Give me that, too," commanded the bridge-tender.

Tom reluctantly obeyed.

"You say you was goin' over to Downing's after milk?" Brady queried.

"Yes, I was."—Sullenly.

"Where's y'r milk?"

"They didn't have none to spare. I left my bucket; an' am goin' back this evenin'."

"You found these things as you went over?"

"Yes, I did."

"When was that?"

"Jest a little while ago—maybe a quarter 'r a half an hour ago. Give 'em back to me. They're mine; I found 'em."

"That may be," growled the bridge-tender. But as they was found on the bridge, an' I'm the marshal, I guess I'd better take charge of 'em. Now"—Gruffly, as the boy began to whine—"trot 'long home, 'fore I put you in the lockup fer havin' stolen goods in y'r possession."

Tom Sandy did not hesitate to obey the order. Like all the other boys in the village, he had a wholesome dread of the law—and its unworthy representative, the drunken marshal.

When the lad was out of hearing, Brady turned to Marlowe and said in a stage whisper: "Frank Edgerton's drowned hisself!"

The young doctor silently inclined his head. "He's gone out onto the 'proach o' the bridge," Brady continued in awe-stricken voice, "an' jumped off—leavin' his cap an' whisky bottle behind, so's folks would know what he'd done."

Again Ralph nodded—frigidly; and passing into the drugstore closed the door behind him.

The bridge-tender hurried off down the street.

An hour later news of the youthful cattle dealer's disappearance—of his probable suicide—had spread to the outermost limits of the village. His name was upon the tongues of all; and more or less distorted reports of the night's doings at Torbert's were current.

Sullen murmurings arose—the first breath of the storm that was to clear Babylon of its undesirable element; and open threats against Torbert and those who frequented his den were heard.

Brady and a gang of volunteer helpers began an effort to recover the body from the cold, silent depths of the river. They anchored the hulk of the old ferryboat just below the bridge; and armed with grappling irons and gaff hooks, proceeded to drag the bottom of the stream. About nine o'clock the body was found and brought ashore.

The recovery of the remains of the young suicide increased the excitement—the intensity of feeling against those who had been instrumental in driving him to his death. The oil men—who during the search for the body had stood upon the bank and interestedly, anxiously watched the proceedings—now perceiving the scowls and threats directed toward themselves, sought the security of the hotel and remained there.

A messenger was dispatched to Foxtown to apprise Edgerton's relatives of his death; and another to Malconta to bring the coroner. Upon the arrival of the latter, warrants were sworn out for the arrest and detention of Torbert and all who had participated in the poker game of the night before, pending an investigation.

The oil men were easily secured; but Morris McDevitt had disappeared from home and could not be found.

A coroner's jury was quickly impaneled and an investigation begun. Within the pockets of the dead youth was found nothing of value but a silver watch and three dollars in coin. No marks of violence were upon the body.

Shortly after noon stern-faced men came riding in from Foxtown, by dozens and scores, until more than a hundred had arrived. The opinion of one and all was that Edgerton had been murdered for his money and his body cast into the river. No amount of reasoning or argument could convince them to the contrary; and they demanded that swift and stern justice be dealt out to the guilty, threatening to take the law into their own hands, otherwise. Many of the Babylonians believed as did Edgerton's friends, and openly lent them support. Excitement was at fever heat. The surging crowd upon the village street became a mad mob. A reckless leader alone was needed to precipitate another tragedy—a tragedy compared with which the initial one would have paled into insignificance. It was all that cooler heads could do to avert the threatened act of vengeance. And Torbert, the saloonist, and his companions under arrest sat in the dark, damp rooms of the village caladoose[98] and trembled as they heard the blood-curdling threats and imprecations[99] without.

Marlowe spent the forenoon in the country; Dr. Barwood, in the drugstore. When the latter went to dinner his older daughter did not appear at the table. Dolly was mute and evidently greatly depressed in spirits. Mrs. Barwood's face showed traces of recent grief.

"Where's Julia?" the father inquired with assumed carelessness.

"In her room," the mother made reply, surreptitiously wiping away a trickling tear.

"Is she not coming to dinner?"

"No, she is lying down; she has a headache."

"She has heard the reports of that young man's death, then; and what people are saying about the men who gambled with him?" Dr. Barwood ventured lamely.

"Of course she has," his wife replied tartly. "How could she help but hear when so many kind friends have taken it upon themselves to come in and tell her? She knows all."

No more was said on the subject. Dr. Barwood finished his meal in silence and returned to the drugstore.

Julia rejected the proffered sympathies of her mother and sister, who sought to console with her. Cold and white she lay upon her bed, her face turned to the wall. No moan escaped her; no tear wet her lashes. Yet it was patent she was suffering as few have the capacity to suffer.

The afternoon passed, and night fell, bleak and black.

Excitement still ran high; and squads of vociferous[100] men were upon the streets until almost midnight.

---

98 caladoose: jail, especially a local jail
99 imprecations: prayers calling down God's wrath upon the wicked
100 vociferous: making an outcry; clamorous

Ralph Marlowe went to his rooms at nine o'clock. He did not go to bed; but sinking into the depths of an easy chair and stretching his feet toward the grate, he lay back and gave himself up to thought. The hours passed. The fire burned low, leaving the room in semi-darkness—for he had not lighted a lamp; and the wind whimpered and wailed about the gables. At last his lids drooped; and he slept.

Suddenly he awoke with the impression he had heard some one calling his name. The fire had almost expired; and the room was cold and dark. Yawning and shivering, the young physician arose and stared vacantly into the black corners, listening intently. But he saw nothing but the dim outlines of the furniture; heard nothing but the voice of the gale.

"I must have been dreaming," he muttered.— "I thought I heard Morris McDevitt calling me."

At that moment his quick ear caught the sound of a gentle tapping against the pane of an end window. Striding quickly to the spot, he cautiously lifted the blind. Pressed closely against the glass was a human face; but the light was so faint he could not distinguish the features.

"Marlowe—Ralph, let me in."

The occupant of the room caught the faint but distinct words.

"All right," he whispered in reply—his mouth to the crack beneath the sash. "Go around to the door."

The face immediately disappeared. Marlowe went into the hall and undid the outer door. A moment later Morris McDevitt stood within the double apartment.

"Don't strike a light," he cautioned. "They are still on the outlook for me."

"Have a chair," Ralph said.

McDevitt accepted the invitation; sighing wearily.

"Where have you been?" Marlowe asked carelessly.

"I've been hiding in the attic of the store building since nine o'clock yesterday."

"Yesterday?" Ralph exclaimed.

"Yes. Talk low. It's now one o'clock in the morning."

"Oh!"

"You're still dressed; you haven't been to bed, Marlowe."

"No. Did your parents or your sister know of your hiding place?"

"No. I didn't tell them; I didn't want them to have to lie for me—a worthless cur! An hour ago—when things had got quiet upon the street—I slipped out of the store and into the house. As soon as my sister could prepare it, I got something to eat. Then I bid them goodbye, pocketed the money my father gave me, and came directly here. 1 am going to leave the town tonight, never to return."

"It is best," Marlowe returned quietly. "But I could not do it. I would stay and face—"

He broke off abruptly, muttering under his breath:

"But would I—did I?"

"You would stay and face the storm," McDevitt completed. "I know *you* would; but *I* can't. I haven't the moral courage; I never have had the moral courage to do right. But what would be the use in my staying? I am guilty of no crime. No crime has been committed, except the crime of winning Edgerton's money. I got none of it; I lost fifty dollars myself. The oil men fleeced us both. Edgerton had the grit and sense to commit suicide. I wish I had as much. No, there is nothing left for me to do but to leave here. I have brought disgrace upon myself, and sorrow to my parents and sister. I am going away tonight—never to look upon their faces again."

He said all this in hard, hopeless tones. Marlowe made no reply. He did not know what to say.

"I came to say good-bye," McDevitt went on, rising to his feet. "But before I go I want you to do me one more favor. I want you to carry this note to Julia and bring me her reply. Will you?"

Marlowe hesitated a moment. Then he said:

"Do you mind telling me what you have written, McDevitt?"

"No. I have simply assured her of my innocence—so far as the death of Edgerton is concerned—and have asked her if she will come to me when I have made a man of myself. Of course I am a fool to ask the question; I know pretty well what her answer will be. I cannot go to her myself; I fear her father might hand me over to the authorities. Will you carry this note to her?"

"Yes. Give it to me; and stay here until I return."

A few minutes later Marlowe stood within the hall of the Barwood residence, facing the master of the house, who in gown and slippers—had shuffled down the stairs to answer the alarm at the door. In answer to the older man's wondering look, the younger said:

"Here's a note for your daughter, doctor."

"For Julia?"

"Yes."

"Morris McDevitt sent it."

"He did."

Marlowe expected his admission to be greeted by a storm of rage. On the contrary, Dr. Barwood's voice and demeanor expressed naught but pity and sadness as he made reply:

"I'll take it to her at once. It may bring her comfort. Ever since nightfall she has been almost delirious from anxiety and grief. She has done nothing but walk the floor, wringing her hands and accusing herself of absurd things. She says she has driven Morris McDevitt to ruin; and that she will have to suffer for the loss of his soul. Musty nonsense! Also, she keeps saying, over and over, she is being punished for a sin she has committed; but she won't tell what it is. I fear for her sanity—I do, indeed. She has lost her self-reliance, and has turned to me in her great trouble—a thing unprecedented. But she will not allow her sister to enter the room; and hardly can bear the sight of her mother. Yes, I'll take the note to her at once. Go into the sitting room, you will find light and fire there."

Marlowe entered the apartment named and seated himself. A shaded lamp turned low burned upon a stand in the middle of the room; a few dying embers shone between the bars of the grate. In front of the hearth was Dr. Barwood's easy chair; and his daily paper lay beside it.

Ralph heard the tramp of feet overhead and the opening and closing of doors. Occasionally he caught the muffled murmur of conversation. Several minutes passed. Impatiently he drew forth his watch—and stretched his limbs and yawned. At length Dr. Barwood entered and asked agitatedly:

"Ralph, where is this—this young scal—young man?"

"Why do you inquire?" Marlowe asked in return.

With a sly grin the older man replied:

"Oh! I don't intend to betray him into the hands of the officers of the law. Where is he?"

"At my rooms."

"Well, bring him here at once. Julia desires to see him. For the first time in years—the first time in her life, almost—she has appealed to me for advice and help. Hitherto she has looked upon me as an old bear, a hard-hearted tyrant, a wicked unregenerate monster. Her mother has been her companion and confidant. She has held me aloof. But tonight she became desperate; she needed a stronger arm to lean upon—a cooler, clearer head to advise. In her extremity she turned to the old father she has ignored—condemned."—His voice quavered slightly.—"And that father pities her, loves her—has always loved her, in spite of the usage he has received from her—and means to stand by her. For I have not been blameless. Both of us have been proud—and foolish. Go, Ralph, and bring Morris McDevitt here. He is a McDevitt—one of my enemies—but he may come here and talk with Julia; and whatever they decide on doing, they shall do. He is a weakling—I despise him. Julia with all her faults is worth a dozen such specimens of humanity. But she says she loves him; and if she decides to marry him, I will do all I can for them—not in this town, however, but elsewhere. Bring him here."

Without making reply, Marlowe put on his hat and left the house. When he returned with McDevitt, Dr. Barwood met them at the door, saying coldly:

"Julia is in her room, Morris McDevitt. I will conduct you to her."

The two silently ascended the stairs; and Ralph again entered the sitting room. There he found Dolly and her mother, clad in loose robes—and in tearful dejection. They looked up at his entrance. Dolly attempted to speak; but choked, swallowed —and was silent. Mrs.

Barwood rocked herself to and fro and moaned heart-brokenly.

Presently Dr. Barwood came in. Mechanically he threw a few shovelfuls of coal upon the grate and dropped into his chair. There he sat staring into the fire, his brows contracted, his jaws set.

A half hour passed. Outside the wind sobbed and wailed; inside the silence was unbroken by human speech. At last footsteps descended the stairs. Dr. Barwood did not change his attitude nor expression. Dolly and her mother looked at each other and heaved sighs of relief and expectancy. Ralph glanced toward the door. It opened; and Morris and Julia came in, hand in hand. The young Irish-American held his head defiantly erect, as though challenging anyone to take her from him; and upon his countenance rested an expression of stern resolve—real or assumed that was unusual with him. Julia was ghastly pale; but her eyes were shining and she walked with firm and elastic step. Stopping just inside the door and fixing her gaze upon her father's bowed form, she said in low, measured tones:

"Father, I am going to marry Morris and go away with him."

Dolly gave a fluttering little gasp. The mother burst into tears and pillowed her head upon the arm of her chair. Dr. Barwood stiffly arose, and turning toward his older daughter uttered the one word:

"When?"

"Tonight," Julia answered.

"No—no!" sobbed Mrs. Barwood. "Not tonight—not tonight!"

"Hush, Hannah," the father commanded gently but firmly. "She shall have her way. What are your plans, Julia?"

"We will drive to Malconta tonight, father. There be married; and tomorrow morning—this morning—take the train for Texas. Morris has an uncle in business in Austin, who will give him employment."

"Very good," her father answered quietly.

"Hannah, rouse yourself. You and Dolly must help Julia to pack her things. Ralph, will you go to the livery stable and engage a team and driver. Have them at the gate in a half hour."

Marlowe started toward the door; but Julia stopped him.

"Wait a moment," she said in a semi-whisper, her white lips twitching.

Then recovering herself and taking his hand, she looked him full in the face and began:

"Dr. Marlowe, I have a confession to make. It was I who found your letter and sent it to Dorothy. I didn't like you—I envied her her happiness. It was a mean, low act. Can you forgive me?"

Dr. Barwood and his wife looked at Julia and at each other, in mute surprise, neither understanding what the penitent meant. Dolly sprang to her feet, her eyes flashing fire; but as quickly sank back into her seat, pale and trembling. McDevitt paid little heed to what was passing. He was thinking of his own affairs—was impatient to be gone.

"It was a despicable act, Julia," Ralph replied with great emotion; "but I freely forgive you."

At her lover's words Dolly again arose; and throwing her arms around her sister, wept silently. For a few moments their sobs mingled.

"Come—come!" Dr. Barwood cried briskly.

"Tears mend nothing. We are wasting precious time. Ralph, be off upon your errand. Julia, here is money for your trip. When you are settled, I will send you more. Hurry with your preparations for departure, now. Take only what you must have; we will send you the rest. Daylight should find you in Malconta."

Three quarters of an hour later a closed carriage was at the door. Julia calmly took leave of her weeping mother and sister. Then throwing her arms around her father's neck, she kissed him again and again, the tears raining down her wan cheeks.

He gently put her from him, saying huskily:

"Good-bye, my daughter. Sometimes trouble is a blessing. At last we understand each other."

Then he shook hands with McDevitt, muttering hoarsely:

"Good-bye. Try to be a man—try to be worthy of the great love she bears you."

The door closed behind the young couple. They entered the waiting carriage and rolled away into the night, leaving two homes in mourning.

* * * * *

CHAPTER XVII

JUNE HAD come—June with its sunshine and roses, its moonlight and dew. The clattering rattle of mowing machines in the meadows adjacent to Babylon mingled with the incessant twitter of birds in the branches of the trees bordering the village streets. One perfect crystal day succeeded another; and to the town loafer, life was a lazy dream of physical delight.

One afternoon, about the middle of the jocund[101] month, Ralph Marlowe occupied a chair upon the broad top step in front of the drugstore, alternately perusing the pages of a medical journal and listlessly gazing up and down the main thoroughfare. The sun's rays were fierce; the shade of the awning was welcome. The vagrant breeze, drowsily sweet with the smell of timothy and clover blooms idled by and toyed with the young man's brown locks. He was well dressed, well fed, healthy, and prosperous; and, in consequence, was contented and happy. To add to his tranquil happiness—raising it to the sublimity of absolute bliss, almost—he was in love with Dolly Barwood and was to marry her in the early autumn.

---

101 jocund: marked by or suggestive of high spirits and lively mirthfulness

At the young physician's feet, lazily lolling upon the flight of stone steps, rested Jep Tucker his cotton trousers rolled up, his feet and legs bare; and, squatting upon the brick pavement, his back supported by an upright of the awning frame, was Tomp Nutt. Both eccentrics were idly smoking; and the fishy smell exhaling from their garments and persons—but ill-masked and not at all improved by the rank tobacco smoke eddying about them—proclaimed them disciples of Izaak Walton.

Marlowe continued to read; Tomp and Jep smoked away in silence. At length Tucker removed the corncob pipe from his lips and drawled dreamily:

"Mighty purty day, I tell you. Clear sky, an' water jest a little r'ily—good time fer fishin'. We ort to ketch a wagonload today, Tomp Nutt."

"Y-Yes," Tomp stuttered, without lifting his half-closed eyelids.

"Better go down an' run the line purty soon, hadn't we?"

"I g-guess s-so."

Tucker lapsed into silence, puffing feebly—sleepily. Presently, however, he roused himself and turning to Ralph said with a yawn:

"Say, young feller?"

"What is it, Jep?"—Turning a leaf and reading industriously.

"Me an' Tomp's goin' down to run the trot-line purty soon. Want to hear a mighty good yarn, 'fore we go?"

"A good one—yes."

"Well, I'm the feller can tell it to you. Shut up that almanac. I never could talk to a feller with his nose stuck fast 'tween the pages of a book."

"I am all attention," Ralph replied, closing the medical journal—but keeping his place with his forefinger.

Without further preface Tucker proceeded:

"You know Ol' Abe Kackly an' his wife that lives in that little shack on the river bank, down at the foot o' Silverheels riffle? I know you do; 'cause you was down there once last winter to see Mary Ann—that's the ol' woman—w'en she had the grip.

"Well, they've lived there fer years an' years. Abe fishes in summer an' traps in winter; an' Mary Ann picks berries in summer an' knits stockin's an' mittens in winter. That's the way they make the'r livin'. Mighty honest, good ol' people—but kind o' foolish an' superstitious like. Abe's a powwow doctor—cures by layin' on of hands; an' Mary Ann's a fortune teller. She reads people's fortunes in the coffee grounds o' the'r cups. Read mine once—I give her a dime fer doin' it. She told me I was very 'ndustrious an' savin', an' said I'd be rich some day. But that day hain't come 'round yit—still I keep lookin' fer it.

"Abe used to make some remarkable cures, when he was younger an' could tramp 'round a good 'eal. They sent fer him to come up Turkey Run, once, to see a woman that had the high strikes. Guess that's the name o' the complaint. It's a cross 'twixt the popsylals an' the fantods; an' it's that trouble where there ain't nothin' the matter, re'ly, but the patient makes b'lieve ther' is. It's a disease pecooliar to women; men don't know *how* to have it.

"As I was sayin', ol' Abe went to see that woman on Turkey Run. She'd had about a dozen doctors; an' none of 'em couldn't do 'er no good. Abe powwowed 'er to beat all git out; but she jest howled an' screeched right along, an' didn't git no better—not a mite. So he got disgusted an' took up his hat an' left, sayin' as he went out the door:

"'That woman'll never git well till Christ comes ag'in. He's the only doctor that has the pow'r to cast out devils.'

"But pshaw! Here I am dribblin' 'long, like a grain cradle with two 'r three fingers knocked out, I was goin' to tell you 'bout the time the alligator got after Abe. It was this way: Miles Orton's show wintered up at Malconta sever'l years ago; an' late in the spring when they went to pack up an' leave, they took the stuffed alligator—it was kind o' frayed 'round the edges an' a little moth-eaten, I guess—an' throwed it in the river. It floated over the dam an' lodged 'mong some willers; an' some weeks later it drifted on down to this place.

"One warm day Abe was a fishin' down at the head o' Silverheels riffle—jest at the place the water makes an eddy after comin' over the dam. He was in his skiff an' floatin' 'round an 'round that eddy—fishin' over the stern of his boat.

"All to once that doggoned stuffed alligator popped out o' the water, right at the side o' the skiff, an' shoved its nose into Abe's face. Its mouth was wide open an' its glass eyes was a starin' like a dead man's. Abe dropped his pole an' line, jumped to his feet, an' let off a howl that roused the whole lower end o' town. Then the alligator—jest like a live one would do—sunk out o' sight, passed under the skiff, an' popped up on t'other side, purty near jumpin' into the boat. The thing was so light, an' the water was swirlin' it so, it bobbed 'round like a cork doddler.

"In his young days Abe used to run flatboats down to New Orle'ns; an' he knowed in a minute what the critter was. So he grabbed up an oar an' givin' another yell struck a ton at it. But by jeeminy! He lost his equil'brium an' lummoxed over the gunwale into the river. Abe thought he was a goner; an' he hung onto the side o' the skiff an' screamed an' kicked fer dear life.

"His ol' woman heerd him an' went out to him, in the johnboat. She towed him, an' the skiff an' the fish pole ashore. An' w'en they landed there was that stuffed alligator tangled in the fish line—floatin' belly up.

"Well, sir, do you know what that ol' rip up an' done to keep people from knowin' what a fool he'd made of hisself. He took an' buried that alligator, an' blowed 'round fer a month how he'd killed a live one with an oar. Yes, he did. But the whole thing leaked out at last an'—"

Jep stopped abruptly and flung up his head.

"W'y, the down train's in!" he exclaimed.

"An' here comes Lon Crider up street. I didn't think it was more 'n the middle o' the afternoon. Come on, Tomp. Le's go down an' run over the line."

Crider sprang up the steps, and grasping Marlowe's extended hand said breezily:

"Hello, Ralph, old boy! How are you, anyway?" Then removing his straw hat and vigorously mopping his brow:

"Beastly hot day, isn't it?"

"It's very warm," Ralph replied, smiling at his companion's flustered manner.

"Makes a fellow sweat like a Trojan," Crider rattled on breathlessly. "You look as cool as a cucumber, though. How would you like to be the ice-man? Ha! ha! ha! But"—With a quick change of countenance—"let's go inside. I've got something to tell you."

Marlow led the way into the cool, dusky interior, wondering carelessly what news Crider had to impart. The latter stepped about uneasily, nervously plucked at his mustache, and kept his eyes bent upon the flower in his buttonhole. At last he began—blushing and stammering:

"It's always business before pleasure with me, Ralph—that is, Dr. Marlowe. You—you know that. And—and it's duty before business, too. I've got something to tell you, 1 feel it's my duty to tell you at once. It may amount to nothing at all—I—I don't know; and it may amount to a great deal. I—"

He stumbled and stopped.

"Go on," Ralph said encouragingly.

"Are—are you expecting a call—a visit—from any one—a young lady, for instance?" Crider asked with great effort.

A wave of sickening dread swept over Ralph Marlowe, making him conscious of his heart beats and causing him to heave a deep inspiration. But he answered with outward calmness:

"No—not—at present."

"Well, I must tell you," Crider went on, "that a young woman came down on the train just now, that told me she was coming here to see you. She sat across the aisle from me; and happened to drop her handkerchief. I picked it up and restored it to her; and we struck up a conversation. She got off here—and is down at the hotel now—a dark-complexioned, dark-eyed, stylishly dressed young woman. Do you know her, Marlowe?"

A hunted look had crept into Ralph Marlowe's eyes; an expression of unutterable misery rested upon his handsome face.

"I know her," he answered in hard, even tones.

'Is—is there anything wrong?" Crider inquired in accents of commiseration. "Is she likely to give you trouble, Marlowe? If so, depend upon me to do anything I can to help you out."

"You say she is at the hotel?" Ralph asked.

"Yes."

"No one was with her—a child, no one?"

Crider shook his head.

"Did you notice—that is did she appear to be—be herself—to have full command of her faculties?"

"Since you mention it—no. To be blunt, Marlowe, I thought she was just a little tipsy. She talked somewhat at random; and when she got off the car I noticed she staggered a little."

The young physician shuddered and groaned aloud, clenching his hands until his knuckles showed white through the bronzed skin.

After a moment's embarrassing silence, Crider laid his hand upon his companion's shoulder and said:

"You've been a friend to me, Marlowe; now I want to be a friend to you—and help you out of this tangle, if it can be done. Who is she?"

Ralph's pale face flamed instantly. He appeared about to resent Crider's inquisitiveness and reject his proffered sympathy and aid. But checking himself he answered hoarsely:

"She is my sister."

"Your sister!" Crider exclaimed.

Then, after a moment's consideration, he continued:

"That isn't so bad as I expected. I expected to hear you say—'my wife.' Now what can I do to help you out of the embarrassing situation?"

Ralph replied promptly—though despondently:

"Go up and send Dr. Barwood down here at once. You will find him at work among the shrubbery in the yard."

Crider did not wait to make answer but hurried away upon his mission. Hardly was he gone, ere the doorway was again darkened and Marlowe's unwelcome visitor stepped into the room. Just within the door she stopped and blinkingly surveyed the place and its occupant. Then she staggered a pace or two forward and sank upon a stool, remarking with a tipsy smile—and in a tone of keenest sarcasm:

"Brother mine, I am delighted to find you alive and well. I did not herald my coming, for fear you might put yourself out to meet me—and send me back."

At the conclusion of her introductory words, she lay back against the counter and laughed shrilly, immoderately. Ralph looked at her steadfastly; but his features were working, his chest heaving.

"Oh, Stella—sister!" he moaned. "Why have you come here—and in such a condition?"

Unsteadily she rose to her feet. Her face was flushed; her eyes, preternaturally[102] bright. Her hat was a little askew; her hair, tousled; her clothing, slightly disarranged.

"Oh, Stella!" she mimicked scornfully. "Why have you come here—and in such a condition! That's a fine welcome to receive from a long lost brother! It seems to me I have heard you remark that on more than one occasion. Why have I come here, Ralph?" —Her voice rising higher and higher.—"I'll tell you. I've come to take you back to Cleveland with me. I want you—and Freddie wants you. You never answered my letter; but it was not returned to me, and I knew you had received it. You're going back to live with me, too; you are—you shall."

She was screaming excitedly and stamping the floor.

"Hush—hush!" he cried, springing forward and seizing her arm. "For shame, Stella!"

"I won't hush," she shrieked, striving to disengage herself. "Not until you promise to go back with me. I'll turn this town topsy-turvy. I'll—"

Placing a hand over her mouth, he caught her up in his arms and bore her struggling into the rear room. There he placed her in a chair; and closing doors and windows, said with forced calmness:

"Stella, we must have a full and final understanding. But first you shall sleep off the effects of the liquor you have taken. I do not care to talk to you, in your present condition—and I will not."

"I'm not intoxicated," she panted. "I just took a little wine—"

---

102 preternaturally: transcending the normal course of nature; supernatural

"Stop!" he commanded sternly. "Do not attempt to deceive me. It is useless. Recall the fact that I have seen you in this state many times before. This is not the first time you have grieved me—have disgraced me."

"That's a pretty way in which to talk to your only sister," she whined, squeezing a few tears from her dark, beautiful eyes. "And I'm weak and sick, too. I've been in the hospital two months—just got out a week ago. You don't love me, Ralph."

Unheeding her wild words, he proceeded to spread a large fur rug at her feet; and rolling another into a pillow, said decidedly:

"Stella, lie down here. I will bring you a dose of medicine to quiet your nerves. You must sleep. Remove your hat and lie down."

Apparently she knew it would be useless to demur. Whimpering like a conquered child, she obeyed the command.

"Now," he said, "if you will remain quiet, I will raise the rear windows to admit air."

She made no reply; but covering her face with her perfumed handkerchief, lay sobbing. Her brother opened the windows. Then he brought her the medicine he had mentioned and forced her to take it.

"I must leave you for a short time," he remarked gently. "When you have had a nap, I will take you to my rooms."

On returning to the drug room he found Dr. Barwood and Crider there.

"What do you want, Ralph?" was the older physician's grumpy inquiry.

"Come this way, doctor," answered the younger. "I desire to speak with you."

When they stood together in the entrance leading to the basement, Ralph proceeded to reveal to his partner—and prospective father-in-law—all he had hidden so carefully, hitherto. In conclusion he said:

"I have told you all, Dr. Barwood. Now, I want your advice. Stella is a wreck—a slave to drink; but she is my sister. What am I to do with her—for her? What can I do more than I have done? We were left orphans at a tender age. Against my wish, she went upon the stage: against my will, she married a scoundrel who led her into vice and then deserted her and her child. In sheer desperation at last, I left Cleveland—where I might have done well, but for her escapades—and came here. She was upon the road, with a theatrical company, at the time. But she spied out my hiding place and wrote to me. Her letter to me was the one Julia found and sent to Dolly on Valentine's day. Here it is. You may read it.

The older physician took the proffered sheet of paper and glanced it over. Then he said with a hard and bitter smile:

"Ralph, my boy, every household has its own family skeleton. You have seen mine; I now get a glimpse of yours. I knew all along you had one in hiding—at times I could hear the rattle of dry bones. I see but one thing that you can do with your sister. Keep her at your rooms tonight. Tomorrow take her away to some sanitarium; and leave her there until she has been cured of her appetite for drink. Then bring her and her child here and make a home for them."

"That I have done more than once, doctor," was the hopeless reply.

"Make a virtue of necessity and do it once more. There is no other way open. You say she has just got out of a hospital?"

"That is what she tells me." Ralph answered cautiously.

"Well," Dr. Barwood continued, "I presume the people at the hotel noticed her condition when she stopped there. Something must be done to close their mouths. I will cause the report to be circulated that your sister has been sick and is but just convalescent—that she is still weak, mentally and physically. Crider is a good talker; I'll send him to spread the report. Make your arrangements to take her away on the morning train. I'll get along all right in your absence; there isn't much to do right now."

Then smiling whimsically:

"If you don't want to draw any of your oil money and haven't enough by you, I can let you have what you need."

"I have all I want," Ralph replied soberly. "But I do feel sincerely grateful to you, doctor, for your words of encouragement and your offer of substantial aid."

"Stuff!" snorted Dr. Barwood, wheeling and leaving.

Stella slept until dusk. When she awoke her brother took her to supper at the hotel. From there they went to his apartments.

Ralph lighted the lamps, turned them low, arranged the blinds to exclude the gaze of passersby, and taking a chair by his sister's side, said:

"Stella, I have resolved to make a final effort for your redemption. Tomorrow I will take you to a private asylum for people of your class, in Columbus. I shall take you there because it is near to Babylon, and I can see you frequently while you are compelled to remain an inmate of the retreat."

She was very quiet now—but her white, shapely hands were fluttering nervously. Since her nap she had scarcely spoken. Her face appeared haggard and gray in the subdued light.

"It will do no good," she murmured apathetically.

"To take you to a private sanitarium?"

She nodded.

"Why?"

"I can't be cured."

"But you can—you shall." —Very earnestly.

"You have tried before, Ralph—and failed."

"I shall try once more."

"And if you meet with another failure?"

"Hush! I will entertain no such thought."

"You will be disappointed," she said sadly. "And you have endured enough—too much." Her voice trembled; her beautiful dark eyes were wet with tears. Laying a hand caressingly upon his, she continued:

"I should not have come here. I was mad or I would not have done so. Let me go away by myself. And never more will I trouble you; never more will I cross your path."

"No," he said firmly, placing his hand upon her's. "I was a poltroon[103] to desert you, Stella; for whatever you have done—what-

---

103 poltroon: a spiritless coward

ever you are—you are my sister. But as you just said of yourself; I was mad—mad with the sorrow and disgrace of it all. There—there!" she was quivering in every fiber.—"I do not mean to upbraid you. Let us turn from the past to the future. Let us—"

"Ralph," she interrupted in a shivering whisper, when—when I am cured, what then? Will—will you go back to Cleveland with me?"

"No, Stella," he answered kindly. "But I will bring you and little Fred here."

"To live in this miserable little town?" she gasped. "I could not stand it, Ralph—I don't understand how you do!"

"You will like the place after you are here awhile," he replied with assurance. "The life here—quiet and peaceful—will prove a blessed boon to you after the feverish existence you have known."

"Oh, no—no!" she moaned, wringing her hands and swaying from side to side. "I could not endure it—I could not! Say you will go back to Cleveland with me—please do!"

"No, Stella," he said decidedly, "I will promise you nothing of the kind. There is nothing but heartaches in Cleveland for either of us. You must leave the old life behind—as I have done—and turn toward the new, a quieter and better. My interests are all here. I have a share in a good practice, a half interest in a paying business, and an investment in oil lands. I cannot—I will not leave. If you wish to be with me—you and Freddie—you must come here. I will rent you a neat little cottage and provide for you. It will not take a large house for you and the child."

"And you?" she asked with wide-open eyes. "Do you not intend to live with us? Surely you do not think of keeping your rooms and letting us live alone, do you?"

Ralph hesitated a moment. Then he replied: "Stella, I am to marry my partner's younger daughter this fall."

The sister lay back limp and white and wearily closed her eyes. For several minutes she did not speak. At length she answered vacantly:

"Then you will have no place in your heart for me—and Freddie."

"Do not say that, Stella," he cried in an irritated tone. "It is cruelly untrue. You do me an injustice. I have looked after you in the past; and am proposing still to do so."

She did not look up nor speak.

"Now you must go to bed and get a good night's rest," he said in softened tones. "We will take the early train."

"I shall take the early train for—for no one knows where," she whispered. "But I shall go alone."

"We will talk no more tonight," he answered, "I insist that you go to bed now. I will occupy the reclining chair. I have slept in it many times before."

Silently, mechanically, she arose and went into the adjoining room. He heard her disrobe and retire to rest. Going to the door, he inquired:

"Are you comfortable, Stella? Do you feel as though you could sleep?"

"'Yes," she answered from the farther side of the bed, "I shall sleep soundly—have no fear. Good night."

"Good night," he said in reply; and went back to his chair.

Presently he heard her rhythmic breathing. Reassured, he composed himself to sleep. A few minutes later—completely worn out with the day's exciting events—he was in the land of dreams.

He awoke with a start and sprang to his feet; half awake. A choking sensation, like the clutch of a sinewy hand, was griping at his throat. His mouth was dry; a penetrating odor—the odor of peach kernels—was in his nostrils.

"Hydrocyanic acid!" he muttered, confusedly, pushing his hair back from his forehead.

Then in an instant a full realization of the situation intuitively flashed upon his mind. With two bounds he reached the inner room. Hastily turning up the light, he bent over the still form of his sister, his heart throbbing wildly. One glance was sufficient to reveal the truth. She was dead. A tiny silver-stoppered vial of cut glass, upon the white counterpane, told the tale of suicide. . . .

Ralph Marlowe had his erring sister laid to rest in one of the suburban cemeteries of Cleveland—a cemetery in which they loved to stroll hand in hand when children. On his return to Babylon he brought with him a sturdy lad of five years—a pocket edition of himself—who clung trustingly to his hand and called him, "Uncle Walph."

In the early autumn Ralph and Dolly were married. Her parents insisted on the young couple living with them; and there, also, little Fred found a pleasant home. The old house rang with his childish shouts and laughter. And—strange to relate—he and gruff old Dr. Barwood became inseparable companions.

Four years have passed, bringing marked changes to the sleepy little town. It has taken on a steady growth. Large factories are springing up; and the commercial spirit is rampant. New churches, and public buildings mark the site of the old ones. The streets are paved. The town is sewered, well lighted, and has a telephone system. The saloons are still there—more of them than ever; but law and order prevails. King Oil has worked wonders during his brief reign. Swiftly and surely a new Babylon is rising upon the ruins of the old.

THE END

AFTERWORD

Blessed with a zest and appreciation for life—and an incredible memory—James Ball Naylor began at an early age to absorb his surroundings. As a child he spent many happy hours outside learning the names of every flower, plant, and animal in the area. His interactions with the people around him were equally imprinted in memory. He drew inspiration from everything and everyone with whom he came into contact. His thirst for knowledge was insatiable. He discovered an inner passion and a drive to express himself by writing and, despite a lack of a formal education in writing and literature, he captivated his readers. Poetry was his most passionate endeavor, but that soon expanded into writing short stories and ultimately into novels and children's books.

In the slow-paced environment at the turn of the twentieth century and before, Naylor was the ultimate multi-tasker. Active in politics his entire life, he was a candidate several times as a young man and, in later years, he was an outspoken political columnist. A gifted speaker and entertainer, he was active on the Lyceum and Chautauqua circuits along with such notables as Mark Twain, Amos Branson Alcott, Henry Ward Beecher, William Jennings Bryan, Warren Harding, and others, including his children who often performed on stage with him. In the midst of all these activities he wrote poetry and short stories for magazines, and he published one book after another. Although he viewed all of these endeavors as wonderful distractions, it was his profession as a medical doctor that most influenced decisions about his life—as did his family, to whom he was devoted.

Although he loved the recognition that his writing brought to him, he did not pursue it at the expense of his practice and his family. As a result, his popularity faded over time, and he became a forgotten man, despite a lifetime of literary work that included eight novels, three children's books, numerous short stories, and six volumes of collected verse. Hopefully, my biography of him sheds new light on his importance in the literary history of Ohio and beyond. Today all but one or two of his books are in the public domain, and they are being reprinted by various publishers. My goal is to bring his works back to life with my Tribute Series to James Ball Naylor by reformatting them and adding material, such as notes and analyses, and photographs.

Vintage Verse was selected as the first book in this Tribute Series because poetry was his first love. Naylor's own first two books were volumes of poetry, *Current Coins Collected at a Country Railway Station* in 1893, followed by *Golden Rod and Thistle Down* in 1896, both using his nom de plume, S. Q. Lapius, a play on the name of the Roman god of healing, Esculapius. To Naylor, poetry was the most important part of his literary life. "I wrote for the joy of writing. The most satisfaction and the greatest treat I ever had was the creation of a poem." "I write poetry for the same reason that I read so much of it; because it seems a part of me, and I cannot help doing it." *Vintage Verse* is a one-of-a-kind collection of verse that Lucile Naylor, one of his daughters, culled from old family scrapbooks in an effort to preserve some of the poems that were not included in any of his six published volumes.

Ralph Marlowe was selected as the second book in this Tribute Series because as a best seller it brought worldwide acclaim for Naylor. It was on the *Bookman's* list of top best sellers for six months. Released in early March, 1901, the first edition of *Ralph Marlowe* consisted of a printing of 5,000 books, followed in rapid succession by four more editions totalling 50,000 books. *Ralph Marlowe* could be found in virtually every book store throughout the United States within a short period. Well received in Great Britain and Scotland, his books could be found throughout Europe and even in the public library in Moscow, Russia.

Before the appearance of *Ralph Marlowe,* Naylor wrote numerous short stories and three book-length historical stories that all appeared serially in the *Ohio State Journal*. "In the Days of St. Clair" appeared from December 5, 1897, to February 27,

1898. "Under Mad Anthony's Banner" appeared from November 27, 1898, to March 5, 1899. The *Ohio State Journal* published it in hardback following its completion in the paper in 1899. On the cover appeared "by J.B. Naylor (S. Q. Lapius) Author of 'In the Days of St. Clair' Etc." This edition is now quite rare.

The last of this trilogy, "The Sign of the Prophet," appeared serially in the *Ohio State Journal* from October 28, 1900 to February 10, 1901. It was running in the *Journal* when *Ralph Marlowe* was first published. Saalfield Publishing Company, the firm that published *Ralph Marlowe*, was quick to acquire the rights to it. They published *The Sign of the Prophet,* the last one written, in 1901, followed in 1902 by *In the Days of St. Clair,* the first one written. *Under Mad Anthony's Banner*, the second one written, was the last to be published by Saalfield in 1903 without acknowledgment of its prior printing in in hardback by the *Ohio State Journal* in 1899.

Like many authors, Naylor subscribed to newspaper cutting bureaus in Boston and New York, and his family maintained a scrapbook of them. This collection of reviews and articles preserves contemporary appreciation for his writing. A number of the reviews that Naylor received from throughout the United States, Great Britain, and Scotland after the release of *Ralph Marlowe* are included in this Tribute. Despite what one critic from England called "a superabundance of Yankee humour which does not appeal to the Britisher," the book sold well in Europe and beyond.

The reviews compare *Ralph Marlowe* to other novels of that time and Naylor to the top authors of that period. While the stories and some of the eccentric characters may be similar, it was Naylor's style and ability to bring the story to life that made the difference. His fictional story, based on real life situations and circumstances, captivated the reader. In his own words, he said, "I wrote it because I believe that one writes best of the things he knows best."

The foundation for the overwhelming success of *Ralph Marlowe* was Naylor's ability to paint word pictures that brought his tiny village and its characters to life. Without question, James Ball Naylor was one of the top authors of his time. Like many of his other writings,

Ralph Marlowe will continue to please the final critic, the reading public.

A number of period photographs of Stockport, the Babylon of *Ralph Marlowe*, are also included that provide a genuine sense of the time and place that Ralph Marlowe chose to start his new life.

Theresa Marie Flaherty

ADDENDUM

Book Reviews

Ohio State Journal - Columbus, Ohio

(January 13, 1901)
RALPH MARLOWE, LATEST OHIO NOVEL
DR. NAYLOR HAS FOUND CHARACTERS IN BUCKEYE STATE
Similar to David Harum and Eben Holden—
A Romantic Story Just Published

Ohio, Indiana and Kentucky have been vieing with each other in the production of popular writers of fiction. Indiana boasts of Charles Major and Maurice Thompson; Kentucky of James Lane Allen, and Ohio of Dr. C. F. Goss, John Uri Lloyd and James Ball Naylor. All have stood very prominently before the public eye for the past few years. The State Journal has repeatedly claimed that the Central West has as excellent literary talent as any other section of the country, and it has steadfastly encouraged all literary effort in Ohio which has shown genuine merit. Among the many writers who have contributed to the columns of The State Journal, no one has taken higher rank in the scale of literary endeavor than Dr. James Ball Naylor (S. Q. Lapius), whose novels, "In the Days of St. Clair," and "Under Mad Anthony's Banner," have appeared serially in The State Journal, and whose "The Sign of the Prophet," is now running serially in this newspaper.

Dr. Naylor's latest novel, which the Saalfield Publishing company of Akron has just brought out, bears the title, "Ralph Marlowe," an Ohio story.

The story is laid in the hill country of southeastern Ohio. The plot is romantic, complicated and intensely interesting; and best of all, out of the ordinary. The characters are drawn from life; and so well drawn that on finishing the book, one looks upon them as actualities—acquaintenances. The author's style is vigorous, crisp and clear; no pictures of persons or places are needed to help out the reader's imagination. "Ralph Marlowe" is like—and yet totally unlike—"David Harum," "Eben Holden," and other books of that class.

Most books of that kind depend upon the eccentricities and individuality of one character to make them popular. Dr. Naylor, has been prodigal in this respect. No less than five or six eccentries, all distinct, all worthy of consideration, figure on the pages of his novel: Dr. Barwood, a raw-edged, gruff old village physician—an honest, honorable, lovable old chap: Jep Tucker, a loquacious and incorrigible yarnspinner; Tom Nutt, a stuttering oddity; Lon Crider, a volatile drummer, and his ever-present buttonhole bouquet; Sam Clark, the telegrapher. The story should be dramatized; it would be irresistible.

But the work is not all froth by any means. There is a deep undercurrent of moral philosophy. Questions are raised and left open, that set the reader to thinking. But the author does no preaching.

It is an even, well-balanced work. Dr. Naylor had a story to tell, and has told it well. The book appears in the best dress of the book-maker's art.

RALPH MARLOWE, by Dr. James Ball Naylor, 12mo. Cloth, $1.50. Akron: The Saalfield Publishing Co.

* * * *

ROMEIKE AND CURTICE,
PRESS CUTTING AND INFORMATION AGENCY,
359, STRAND, LONDON, W.C.

American - Baltimore, Maryland

NEW PUBLICATIONS
Ralph Marlowe

(March 11, 1901)

Dr. James Ball Naylor, better known to readers of newspapers as "S. Q. Lapius," over which signature a number of decidedly clever sketches and poems have appeared in print, has written a story which will command widespread interest and achieve much deserved popularity, unless the public taste for good literature has deteriorated to an alarming extent. "Ralph Marlowe" marks the ebbing of the tide which forced the historical novel to the front, and gives us one of the best real, human, modern stories that have been written in a long time. The plot of the story is not intricate, but at the same time it is involved sufficiently to hold the interest of the reader from cover to cover. It is simply a tale of a college-bred young physician who takes a position in a drug store in a little country town in Ohio, falls in love, as all properly described heroes do, and gets married in the last chapter, as is right and happy for all concerned. But the great point of excellence in the story is the marvelous way in which the author has given us the true atmosphere of a country town—not the gawky, burlesqueing, horseplay of the dialectic writers, but the real, homely, honest small-town air, with its lazy scent of apple blossoms in summer and the crisp frostiness of the winter days. Dr. Naylor has given literary immortality to all of his characters, for there can be no doubt that he has drawn them from life. He has not, like the historical romancer, gone far afield and delved into the musty past for his men and women. He has not twisted and distorted history to fit his tale, but he has taken the flesh and blood men and women of these days, told the story of their hopes and fears, their loves and sorrows, their plans and purposes, in a simple, convincing style that wins from the first chapter. There is a certain quaint humor which pervades the story and makes it worth while for anyone who wishes to secure restful entertainment in his reading. The character of Jep Tucker is as real and true to life as if the man himself drawled his anecdotes and passed his odd opinions to the reader's face, instead of through the medium of ink and type. The story has its faults, if you want to be hypercritical, but they are not the glaring anachronisms which detract from the human interest of the historical romance nor are they the prurient suggestions which are supposed to add realism to the problem novel. "Ralph Marlowe" is as homely and pleasing as "David Harum," and has the sweetness and richness of "Eben Holden." It will endure as a story of people who live, and of places that are and of times that we all know. The book is from the press of the Saalfield Publishing Company, New York and Chicago. Price $1.50.

* * * *

The Spy – Worcester, Mass.

(March 20, 1901)

"Ralph Marlowe," by James Ball Naylor, The Saalfield Pub. Co.

"Laugh and the World Laughs with You" has evidently been one of Dr. Naylor's mottoes while writing this book, and he has a happy faculty of making his readers see a goodly share of the ridiculous side of human life. The book is full of laughable incidents, told in a most winning way, and, with its fascinating love story, cannot fail to please all classes of readers. The plot is laid in the picturesque hill country of southeastern Ohio, and the adventures and trials of the hero, Ralph Marlowe, will be followed with the keenest relish until the climax is reached—perhaps a climax not expected by all—but one which will in no wise detract from the attractiveness of the first pages.

Dr. James Ball Naylor ("S. Q. Lapius") has been known to the newspaper world for a number of years as a writer of acceptable verse and fiction, although this is his first real venture between covers. The personnel of his novel are recognized immediately as distinct eccentrics, yet the pictures are made so life like that we forget that they are not real acquaintances. The diction throughout the entire book is pure and simple, and the book, with its lack of profane expressions, slang phrases, etc., is one which will be greatly enjoyed when read aloud in the family circle.

* * * *

Bookworm – Birmingham, Alabama

(April, 1901)

Ralph Marlowe

By Dr. J.B. Naylor: Published by Saalfield & Co.

Redolent with quaint humor and simple pathos of country life is the new novel entitled "Ralph Marlowe."

The vivid rural scenes depicted in this narrative—the realistic village railway station, the excitement due to the drilling of numerous oil wells in proximity to the little town of Bablyon, the squalor of the rickety hotel with its miserable service, the bewitching Dolly with her nicely laid plans, which, owing to the over-burdened conscience of the staid Julia, "oft gang aglee"—are all set forth in the catchy and informing way with which Dr. Naylor unfailingly pleases the public. The book is strewn with anecdotes told by the garrulous Jep, ever ready with his mirth-provoking remarks or "fishy" reminiscences; or by the stammering Thomp with his ridiculous attempts at versifying; or by the jovial drummer, a veritable "bob-up-and-bob-down" agent, appearing at opportune moments. But the book is not all laugher, for many a lesson is unconsciously taught by the true devotion to duty in the face of hard circumstances manifested by the hero, Ralph Marlowe, or through the sound advice of the eccentric Dr. Barwood, or the frank, innocent affection of his winsome daughter.

Dr. Naylor is no mystic painter of life, but one who has had a wide and varied experience in the newspaper field, which gave him unlimited opportunities to study oddities of character and mannerisms of just such people as he has placed on the pages of "Ralph Marlowe." He is by no means a novice, but a keen observer, and has aptly interpreted human nature as he found it in the remote village. He has made his book a bright mirror in which character traits are clearly defined, reflecting without the exaggeration which so often mars works of this sort, all the simplicity and the loveliness of the true country gentleman's life, as well as the base deceits, snares and strategem by which the unsuspecting lads of the rural districts are tempted to ruin and disgrace.

"Ralph Marlowe" embraces all the commendable features of the popular "David Harum," and with the entrancing story connected therewith will undoubtedly meet with a warm reception.

* * * *

Boston Home Journal - Boston

(May 18, 1901)

The Printed Editon

William Hilton

Sometimes the most interesting thing about a book is the way it came to be written. Sometimes the interest comes round by the other way. Once in a while everything connected with a book is of interest. Likewise the book. "Ralph Marlowe" is of these. James Ball Naylor, the author, tells something of himself in telling something of his book. "I was born in a log cabin. My parents were desperately poor. My father was killed at Missionary Ridge. I counted that day lost on which I did not get a trouncing for some misdemeanor. When I was ten we moved to Babylon." (Babylon is the scene of "Ralph Marlowe.") He goes on: "I looked upon a black eye as a badge of courage. I attended school when I could not get out of it. I was without aim or ambition. I was looked upon as a lazy incorrigible. At sixteen a change came over me. A tall lank school teacher aroused my desire to learn. I set out on a quest for books to read." He is now Dr. Naylor. He has been a drug clerk (like "Ralph Marlowe"). He is a doctor (like "Ralph Marlowe"). He lives in Babylon (as does "Ralph Marlowe"). Being afflicted with "the ink fever" he wrote "Ralph Marlowe." And a splendid book it is. He wrote it with the hope big in his heart that it would make him famous and wealthy. The Saalfield Publishing Company announce the seventh edition. And it only came out March 1. Really, Dr. Naylor seems nearing his desired goal. So much for the author. What of his book? I like every bit of it. I was immensely interested in the opening chapter, when Ralph Marlowe arrives at Babylon. I like Dr. Naylor's style of description. He has just enough to give you an idea of the hour and day. And he does not have too much. I liked the breezy "travelling man for the Baldy Drug Company." A better "drummer" seldom gets between covers. I wanted to know about Babylon "first off." Who wouldn't want to know about a town that "covers half a township and has about six hundred population"? I have known some old codgers like Jep Tucker. So he seems a friend. His similes ought to be in literature. "Slicker'n a peeled sapling," is good. So is "hangs onto a bargain like a burr to a cowds tail." Better yet is "slower than thick molasses," in describing the town. In New England we would say "cold molasses." Who hasn't been like Jep, and "felt like a rooster in a millpon', neither ridin' n'r a-walkin'"? And Jep is not the only "character" in Dr. Naylor's book. He himself says "ol' Tomp's funnier'n a funeral." Old Tomp appears ever and anon. Readers learn that he kept a store. When a customer asked for bull tongues Jep said, "Hain't got none, b-but I've g-g-got some in m-mighty good b-b-bolony sausage." The unagricultural need to learn that bull-tongues are part of a cultivator. Ralph Marlowe is supposedly a drug clerk in Babylon. He meets these quaint characters. They tell him stories. He also meets with a peculiar man known as "old doc." Incidentally he falls in love. The course does not run smooth. There's another love story in the volume. Its "come-out" is problematical. Its preliminary course is interesting. A capital feature of Dr. Naylor's book is that he never lets his characters get away from Babylon. The annals of towns arc what genre word painters should produce. "The scene changes"—seldom to advantage. Oh, "Ralph Marlowe" is unique. A last quotation—again from the immortal Jep. It's anent "the high strikes. It's a cross between the popsylals an' the fantods; an' it's that trouble where there ain't nothin' the matter, rel'y, but the patient makes b'lieve ther' is. It's a disease pecooliar to women; men don't know how to have it." Lots more just as quaint in Dr. Naylor's most readable novel. And with the quaintness a capital story, capitally told.

* * * *

Tarboro's Book Review, Tarboro, NC

(June 1901)

Biographical Sketch of Dr. James Ball Naylor, Author of Ralph Marlowe

Dr. James Ball Naylor, the author of Ralph Marlowe was born in Penn Township, Morgan County, Ohio, October 4th, 1860. The log cabin in which he first saw the light of day consisted of one room and was a crude mud-daubed domicile,—with clapboard roof and puncheon floor. His parents were poor, desperate poor. The father enlisted in Co. H 17th Regn., O. V. L. in 1861 and was killed on Missionary Ridge. The mother took up a struggle for existence and hard indeed was the battle.

Dr. Naylor spent his boyhood in the rural districts and attended the district school. According to his own statement an energetic, mischief-loving urchin, and counted that day lost on which he did not get a trouncing for some flagrant breach of school discipline. He earned his first money working for a neighboring farmer at twenty-five cents a day, from sun to sun.

His mother married again and when he was ten years old the family moved to Babylon—the village of which he has so vividly and entertainingly written. There, he indulged in all sorts of boyish escapades and fought his way to the favor of his fellows, looking upon a black eye as a badge of courage, to be valued above all riches. After a year or two, the family tired of village life and removed to the country, a few miles from Babylon. There the subject of this sketch grew from boyhood to young manhood. Of these years he says: I attended school winter and summer—when I could not get out of doing so—about six months each year. I was an idle dreamer, without aid or ambition, caring more for the fields and woods than for the lessons between the covers of a text-book. During vacations, I worked upon the farm my stepfather had rented, but under protest. I toiled simply to obtain immunity from sharp rebukes and was looked upon as a lazy incorrigible. At sixteen, I was deemed a gawky country lad, but a past-master in the lore of wood, field, and stream. I knew the nesting place of every bird, the haunt of every timid beastie and modest wild-flowers sheltered nooks. I was an uncivilized bohemian, a law unto myself.

About this time a change came over me. I flew off at a tangent, and kept on, I fear, in erratic courses. A tall, lank man of culture, one who had a keen insight into boyish nature, came to teach our district school. He took an interest in me and even roused me, to some extent, out of my dreaminess. He showed me the usefulness of exact knowledge; he taught me the beauties of literature, he fired me with ambition; he brought me books to read—Ivanhoe, Robinson Crusoe, Dickens novels, and I eagerly devoured them. My taste aroused, became an unquenchable thirst. Our library at home consisted of a Bible, a Methodist hymnal, and an Ayer's Almanac. I set out on a quest for books to read, I scoured the countryside, all was fish that came to my net. My teacher and mentor had closed the school and gone. I had no one to advise or direct me. I read anything—everything. I resolved to have an education, and I sought it feverishly. One term at the High School at Babylon—and I was a full-fledged pedagogue.

Dr. Naylor taught in the district schools of his native county five years, spending what he earned each winter in attending the Spring and Fall Terms at Marietta Academy. His aim was to acquire a classic education, but the strain was too great—his health gave way. After a few month's rest, he took up the study of medicine. Three years he spent in the drugstore at Babylon, and graduated at the Starling Medical College, Columbus, Ohio, in 1886. He returned to Babylon and entered upon the duties of his profession, and except for one year spent on the road for an eastern drug firm, he has been actively in practice in his native country.

He began to write for the press about ten or twelve years ago to satisfy an inward longing, as he expresses it, and not with any hope of wealth or fame. At first he wrote verse exclusively and not until 1896 did he essay the task of a long story. He has contributed mainly to the western dailies and news syndicates. Ralph Marlowe is his first genuine effort between the covers. Dr. Naylor's methods of literary composition are unique; he has no fixed hours for labor, but writes as time and inspiration permit. He cannot dictate. The clicking of a typewriter is the death knell of inspiration, he says. He never writes upon desk or table, but with a pad of soft paper upon his knees and pencil in left hand, he scribbles industriously. He laboriously copies and corrects with pen and ink. He considers a thousand words a fair day's work.

Dr. Naylor is happily married and had five bright and healthy children,--four girls and a boy. His home is his greatest delight, and he cares little for society. He is an enthusiastic, amateur photographer, and wastes his substance in the riotous exposure of dry plates. With his camera and the companionship of his dog, he loves to wander up and down the green valley, drinking in the beauties of the rural scenery. Many of his poems and shorter sketches have been composed while riding or driving about the country, making professional calls.

Dr. Naylor loves music, nature, and art. He whimsically writes, I wreck my credit upon pictures, bankrupt myself buying books. Mrs. Naylor threatens to move out and leave me, in full and lone possession of my treasured trash. He admires horses and dogs, and loves children. Dr. Naylor's paternal ancestors were Pennsylvania Quakers; his maternal ancestors Virginia English.

* * * *

Book World - New York City

(June, 1901)

"Ralph Marlowe"

A new writer has entered the field of fiction, and has produced a book which compares favorably with many of those stories dealing with rural life which have been immensely popular.

The scene of "Ralph Marlowe" is laid in the little village of Babylon, in the State of Ohio, and the author, Dr. James Ball Naylor, assures us that the plot is founded on fact, and that the characters are "living, breathing entities."

There is no need of an intricate plot to make the story full of interest; it is just a natural narrative of real life, depicting the manners and customs, the peculiar views, passions and prejudices of the villagers. The scenes are laid about the time of the last presidential election, and a Republican mass meeting forms an interesting; feature in the story. The description of the torch-light parade, the brass band and glee club is inimitable; one can almost hear the cheers for McKinley, and the weak counter-cheers for Bryan. There is a riot over an old brass cannon, and the determination of some of the politicians can be understood by the advice to the doctor to have "splints and bandages in readiness."

Ralph Marlowe, a young man, answers an advertisement, and after a brief correspondence, accepts a position as drug clerk in the office of Doctor Barwood, an eccentric, misunderstood but philanthropic citizen of the village of Babylon. Marlowe is warned that he has acted unwisely, for no man has been able to stay long with the doctor. He, however, has, no fear; he maintains his independence and dignity under the most trying circumstances, and refuses to allow himself to be insulted by "Doc Barwood." The doctor is plain spoken. Of one of his enemies, and he has many, he says: "Had he lived in the days of Christ, he would not have cast lots for the Saviour's raiment; he would have taken the whole by force....He would steal the tear from an orphan's cheek, if he thought it had a cash value."

The doctor has a man-of-all-work—hostler, drug-clerk and loafer combined, a man who is always telling stories full of interest, stories which will live and be retold thousands of times by all sorts of people, at all times and in all places. Jep Tucker is one of the most interesting characters in the book, and while his idleness and bad habits must be condemned, the reader will thank the author for creating, or introducing, such a personage. On one occasion Jep's wife makes him work and he rebels. Sidling up to Marlowe—"an expression of injured innocence on his wrinkled visage, he whispered: 'My stomach's emptier'n the bottomless pit. We didn't have nothin' fer breakfast, warmed it over fer dinner, an' used what was left fer supper. Darn it! That woman ol' mine's all right—a mighty good helpmate; but she ain't c'ntent to do a decent day's work. It's go the whole hog'r none with her. Her an' the gal's jest alike—six o' one an' half dozen o' t'other. Not but what I think a whole heap of 'em, you understand; but they hain't got no c'nsideration for my feelin's. I'm igittin' thinner'n a katydid—nothin' left but the runnin' gears. One o' these days I'll jest natcherly dry up an' blow away."

The doctor has two daughters, one a religious enthusiast, the other an "agnorstic," as Jep says, "like the old doc." Of course Marlowe falls in love with the "agnorstic" and—but it would be unfair to spoil a well-told love story, which is nearly interrupted by a tragedy. Ralph is suspected of concealing his past, and a letter, which he loses, is easily misconstrued into a proof of perfidy and guilt. Marlowe clears up the mystery, and the "skeleton in his closet" ceases to be the curse of his life. The other characters in the book are as well drawn as any in the most popular novels of the day. "Doc" Barwood is one of nature's gentlemen, a philosopher and philanthropist combined; the lazy, good-for-nothing Crawford can find his counterpart in every country village; McDevitt, ruined at the gaming table, and saved at last by the doctor's eldest daughter; Lon Crider, the drummer; Clark, the ticket agent, and in fact all the characters introduced, have a charm about them which wins the attention of the reader. "Ralph Marlowe" is intensely interesting, and must become one of the most-talked-of books of the season. It is as good as "David Harum," and as fascinating as "Eben Holden."

"Ralph Marlowe," a novel, by James Ball Naylor. Saalfield Publishing Company, Akron, Ohio, and New York and, Chicago. Price, $1.50.

* * * *

Boston Globe - Boston, Mass

(June 15, 1901)

A realistic, fascinating tale of village life in the Buckeye state is James B. Naylor's "Ralph Marlowe" (Saalfield publishing company, Akron, O). This is a tale really portraying the atmosphere of the country town, the real flavor of the land of the dusty summer roads, the village store and the homely small talk and braggadocio of natural people. The author's long residence in the beautiful Muskingum valley, his keen appreciation of the ridiculous and his droll way of making his characters introduce themselves contribute greatly to make this book well up in the list of these likely to last far beyond present remarkable popularity. Old "Jep" Tucker and his yarns; his employer, "Doc" Barwood; Sam Clark, telegraph operator, and peppery-tempered cobbler Crawford positively decline to leave memory, so true to life and such delicious types are they.

* * * *

Public Library Bulletin - Boston, Mass.

(July 1, 1901)
Ralph Marlowe

Ralph Marlowe, a young pharmacist, comes to the little town of Babylon to accept a position in the drug store of Dr. Barwood, an eccentric man who, owing to his gruff, peculiar, unsociable ways, has scarcely a friend in the village, but who eventually proves to be possessed of a kind heart, and the unknown donor of many a gift to the poor and unfortunate. Ralph Marlowe meets the garrulous Jep Tucker, "the ol' doc's hostler and hired man," on his first visit to the store, and Jep, with his ever-ready yarns, makes himself conspicuous throughout the entire book. The author has so deftly handled this character, however, that his stories never tire, but brighten wonderfully what might otherwise have been a somber tale.

Ralph Marlowe is not an ordinary novel, but is singularly free from exaggeration. Dr. Naylor's pen-pictures are true to life, in no instance are his characters over-drawn, for today we may find in southeastern Ohio, where the plot of the story is laid, just such people as the loquacious Jep Tucker, the stammering Tomp, the jovial Lon Crider, or the old country doctor.

Ralph Marlowe. By Dr. James Ball Naylor. Akron: Saalfield Publishing Co. $1.50

* * * *

The Courier – Dundee, Scotland

(January 12, 1901)

Ralph Marlowe. By James Ball Naylor.—A book well worth reading is this, despite its faults. It does not need the author's preface to tell us that "Ralph Marlowe" is drawn from life, and not the shadowy realm of imagination. It is too original to be anything but real. The scene of the story is laid in an obsure Amerian village, whither comes Ralph Marlowe to fill the post of clerk in the drugstore of Dr. Barwood. About his experiences there is nothing very exciting or uncommon, but we follow them with an interest that never wanes. Ralph himself one admires and likes, not without a lurking wish that he had owned one "redeeming vice," but the "old doc." is thoroughly delightful and we would not lose a single flash of his eye nor lessen his crustiness by a fraction. Jep Tucker, the doctor's man, is good, too, and would be better if he had not quite so many "yarns" to spin. Very good yarns most of them are, but they spoil the thread of the story and become tiresome. The only other adverse criticism which one can make is in regard to the language, which is frequently stiff, stilted, and unnatural. "Your father desires your presence," says Ralph to Dr. Barwood's daughter Dolly when any ordinary young man would simply have said, "Your father wants you." But compared with the good points of the book its bad ones are few, and "Ralph Marlowe" should have little difficulty in fulfilling its author's hope that it will please the "great final critic"—the reading public.

The Werner Company, Ludgate Hill, London.

* * * *

A YANKEE YARN

(From England - February 4, 1901)

RALPH MARLOW is of the peculiar Yankee school in which "David Harum" stands head and shoulders above the rest. The author—Dr. James Ball Naylor—obligingly furnishes us with particulars of his birth and life, from which we gather that the book is partially autobiographical. He certainly writes knowingly of place and people, the plot being merely a very small peg, whereon to hang the tale of daily life in the little town of Babylon. There are good things to be found in its pages, but there is also a superabundauce of Yankee humour, which does not appeal to the Britisher. We have met Jep Tucker, "the ol' doc's hos'ler an' hired hand," the funny man of the book, so often before. We know what to expect, and involuntarily prepare to "skip" when he starts in a drawling voice, "That puts me in mind o' the time Sweety Simson took the smell o' hartshorn. Ever hear 'bout that?" There is, moreover a "bear story," which it was rank sacrilege to exhume from the dust of ages which has gathered over it. On the other hand, we have a fine, welldrawn character in Dr. Barwood, "the ol' doc';" together with Ralph Marlow he saves the book. There is a real human touch about the whimsical old doctor, and he lingers in the memory when Jep Tucker's sayings, which are far better than his interminable stories, have faded away.

"Ralph Marlow." By Dr. James Ball Naylor. (New York: The Werner Company).

* * * *

Glasgow Herald - Scotland

(June 6, 1901)

"Ralph Marlowe." By James Ball Naylor (London: The Werner Company.)

This is apparently the first work of a new American novelist, who confesses to have sketched in its pages the society of his native township in one of the Western States. These sketches, undoubtedly have freshness and vigour, and although one gets rather too much of Jep Tucker and his yarns, he and his fellow-townsmen are none the less vividly and amusingly drawn. The hero of the tale is a favourite American type—a young man of great moral and intellectual grit, hardworking, independent, resourceful, with no weakness or vices, and with a certain inflexible quality not inconsistent with essential kindness of heart. He appears on the first page on his way to the little out-of-the-world town of Babylon, where he has taken a post as clerk to the local doctor. The doctor is a man of rough and forbidding manners, but with an inward tenderness that would do no discredit to Drumtochty; and much to the surprise of everybody, the independent young assistant and he got on well together, and became fast friends. The hero, of course, develops all kinds of excellences—shows himself an accomplished physician, as well as a finished athlete, and without any offensive Puritanism, does a good deal for the moral regeneration of a rather drunken place. Equally, of course, he marries the master's (or as they say in America, his employer's) daughter; but not till the necessary mystery which had hung over his antecedents has been satisfactorily cleared up. The tale is not very artistically constructed; there is for one thing a little too much preaching, and the by-play of the local worthies, as we have hinted, is sometimes allowed to run to excessive length. But the picture drawn is vivid and interesting in the main. The author evidently knows his Babylon thoroughly, and has painted it with liveliness and gusto.

* * * *

The Sunday Special – Strand, W.C.

(June 16, 1901)

"Ralph Marlowe," by Dr. James Ball Naylor (London: The Werner Company), is an American story, racy of the soil, the brightest and most amusing study of life in a small community that we have read in recent years. We have the author's word for it that it is the legitimate child of actual experiences, and that all the characters are actualities. Jep Tucker, if half as original in the flesh as he is in this volume, must be a character worth going far to cultivate. Like old "Eben Holden," in the book of that name, he is an inveterate spinner of yarns; but he is more than that—he is a lazy, good-tempered, ready-witted factotum of the irascible doctor, and his conversation is a joy and an inspiration. We anticipate for "Ralph Marlowe" an instantaneous success.

* * * *

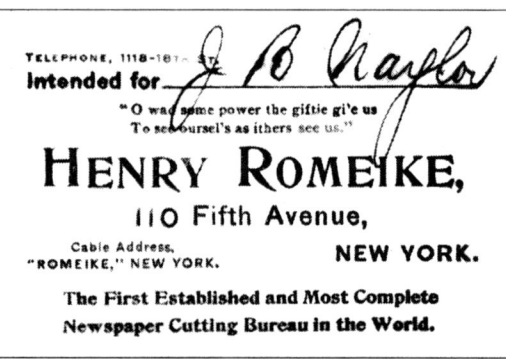

The Birmingham Gazette - Birmingham, England

(June 19, 1901)

BOOK OF THE DAY

Quaint and Queer

Ralph Marlowe. A Novel. By James Ball Naylor. (London: The Werner Company.)

A sort of Dutch art, but art for all that. The writer claims that his story is practically real. Much of the story is actual experience, a part of it he has lived. There is much humour, and for this alone the book is worth reading. A few of Jep Tucker's stories and sayings may be interesting:—"Good morning," was Marlowe's greeting. "That's once you've told the truth, young feller, if you never do ag'in," the man replied in a drawling nasal tone, squinting one twinkling gray eye and narrowly scanning his visitor. "Yes, sir, this is a good mornin'." "You are not Dr. Barwood?" Ralph remarked tentatively. "You seem to be in the habit o' tellin' the truth," the other answered whimsically. "I am not Doc Barwood. I'm Jep Tucker, the ol' doc's hos'ler an' hired hand." "Is the doctor in?" was Ralph's next question. "Yes, he's in, in more ways 'n one," Jep drawled, crossing one leg over its fellow and tenderly caressing his sore foot. "He's in business; an' he's in good health. Do you want to know anything more 'bout him?" . . . "Do you think Dr. Barwood will be in soon?" "Some time 'fore the resur'ection day." Tucker mumbled, nonchalantly biting off a piece of tobacco and rolling it about his cheek. "You in much of a hurry?" "I should like to see the doctor as soon as possible." "I's a going to say it wasn't no use o' y'r gittin' in a hurry in this town. I've lived here all my life; an' I've never saw but one feller in a hurry, in all that time. He was hangin' onto a pair o' runaway hosses, an' couldn't help hisself. He wasn't to blame—he didn't mean no harm. No, Sir, the people o' this place is slower 'n thick molasses on a cold mornin'. I'm 'bout the only hus'ler 'round here; an' I ain't what I was once. I'll tell you what's a fact. I hain't never seen but one feller run, in the forty-five years I've lived here; an' that was a boy that ketched a cold an' run at the nose. I b'lieve one feller did start to run fer justice o' the peace once. But s'ciety got so down on him he had to settle down to a walk. You hain't much a'quainted 'round here, are you?" . . . "He's been away from home some, too; went to school in Zanesvlle a year 'r so ago. Hadn't ever been out o' the country before. An' I guess he learnt a think 'r two—I guess he did. Anyhow he wrote home to his mother an' said:—'Dear Mother—If the world's as big down the other way as she is up this way, she's a whopper." . . . "You're a wearin' mighty good clo'es, an' you've got money in y'r pocket. You've ketched holt o' the coat tails o' prosper'ty, an' 're hangin' on fer dear life. There!" . . . "He was on the jury; an' they disagreed. After it was over somebody asked him how the jury stood. 'Oh!' says ol' Bob. I was fer the plaintiff; the other 'leven, fer the defense. 'Leven o' the c'ntrariest men I ever saw.'"

* * * *

Chronicle - Newcastle, England

(July 4, 1901)

"Ralph Marlowe," by James Ball Naylor. The Werner Company, 3 Broadway, Ludgate Hill, E.C.

We are told that the Americans, in addition to owning what used to be our steamships and controlling our railways and tramways, are going to provide us with all the literature we need. However this may be, more American books than ever are finding their way to this side of the Atlantic, and many of them are being widely read. We think it will be the fate of Dr. Naylor to arrest the ear of the British public with this story, which has already obtained a wide popularity in the United States. There are not wanting signs of the prentice hand, but there is more than sufficient merit on every page to atone for any crudity of style that may be found. The author has quite a Dickens-like eye for quaint character, and it is his two or three delightfully original types which make the book so interesting and amusing. The author need hardly have told us that these are people in real life, for we know them at once as real men. Jep Tucker and Thompson Nutt are characters that will not soon fade from the memory.

* * *

New York Journal - New York

(April 20, 1901)

Dr. James Ball Naylor was asked by Book News to tell how he came to write "Ralph Marlowe," which quickly became one of the best selling books of the week. Here is his story:

"How came I to write 'Ralph Marlowe?' 'Tis a straightforward question and deserves a straightforward answer, yet I hardly know what to say and tell the truth. Let me see. I wrote it because I was afflicted with 'ink fever'—and must write something; I wrote it to get rid of an incubus that had been weighing me down for years—a feeling that I must write it; I wrote it because I believe that one writes best of the things he knows best; and—incidentally, of course—I wrote it with the hope big in my heart that the story might make me famous and wealthy. There! 'Honest confession is good for the soul.'

"I played hooky with Airly Chandler; laughed at Tomp Nutt's stuttering delivery, fearlessly invaded the privacy and sanctity of Hen Olcott's melon patch at night; and boldly raided Philetus Palmerson's orchard in broad daylight. I was a boy in those days.

"I know Babylon and vicinity as I know my own dooryard. I spent three years behind the counter of the village drug store. I went to the country dances at Flat Bottom. A peachy-cheeked village damsel gave me mumps—and 'the mitten,' and Dr. Barwood treated me.

"When I was a clerk in the drug store—long before Ralph Marlowe's advent—Jep Tucker used to come and spin his yarns to me. If there is much of him in the book, it is because there is much of him in my memory.

"One day last summer I strolled into Babylon. Upon the street I met Jep, and said to him:

"'Jep, I think of making you a character in a story.'

" 'Do, eh?' he drawled.

"'Yes.'

"'You'll have an uphill job of it, in my 'pinion.' He said, his eyes sparkling humorously, 'fer I've been tryin' that very thing all my life—to make myself a character. An' I ain't no nearer to havin' one 'n I was w'en I first started. Just go trav'lin' 'round in a circle, I guess—like a dog after his own tail.'

"After graduation, I hung out my shingle in Babylon, and practiced there one fleeting year—spending most of my working hours in a wet saddle. The good people of the community bore with me—and charitably excused by woeful inexperience. Tomp Nutt one time said to me:

" 'Y-you can't d-do no better'n you know, d-doc; y-you've g-got a heap t-to l-l-learn, but y-you'll l-learn it.'

"I took it as it was meant—as a compliment.

"As an afterthought, I would say that I wrote 'Ralph Marlowe' for the reason that it was, and is—a part of me."

* * * *

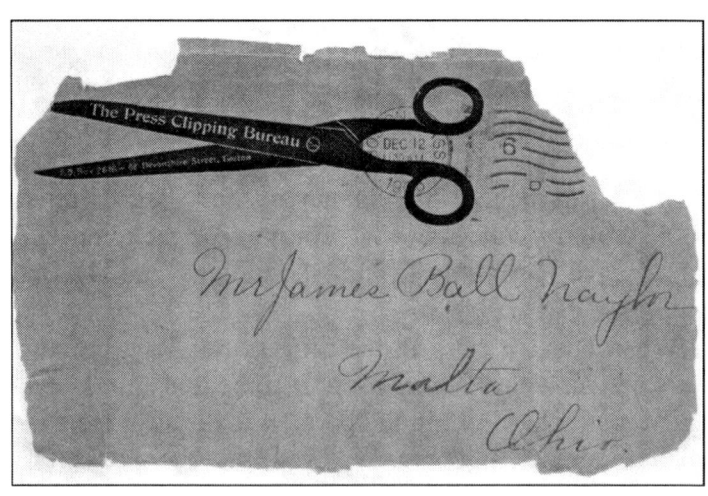

Characters Based on Real People

Besides admitting that he was **Ralph Marlowe**, the author identified three other characters as real individuals: **Dr. Ephraim Barwood** was Dr. Wesley Emmet Gatewood; **Leonidas Walingford Crider,** the breezy drummer, was Ernest B. Schneider of Zanesville, and ***Jep Tucker***, Dr. Barwood's hired man, was John Brooks of Stockport.

When John Brooks died in 1930, he was identified in an article in the *McConnelsville Herald* as the Jep Tucker of *Ralph Marlowe*.

Likewise, after Naylor's death in 1945, Norris Schneider of the *Zanesville Times Signal*, wrote about Earnest B. Schneider's role in Ralph Marlowe as Leonidas Walingford Crider. Like his counterpart in real life, Crider wore a red carnation every day and both were well known throughout the area because of it.

According to local sources, **Jim Crawford** was Popsie Justice, a shoemaker in Stockport, who sued Dr. Naylor for defamation of character for protraying him in *Ralph Marlowe* as a drunken Irish cobbler. The man lost the suit.

Although Naylor did not marry the doctor's daughter, he did marry Mytra Gibson, the daughter of a prominent Stockport merchant. His young bride contracted tuberculosis and died a year and a half later.

In a review in *New York Journal*, Naylor said, "I played hooky with Airly Chandler; laughed at Tomp Nutt's stuttering delivery, fearlessly invaded the privacy and sanctity of Hen Olcott's melon patch at night; and boldly raided Philetus Palmerson's orchard in broad daylight. I was a boy in those days." The person that **Hen Olcott** was based on was Henry Outcalt, a neighbor who hired out at threshing time when Naylor was a boy.

The **bridge-tender** has been identified as Brady Kean; **Sweety Jimson** was Sweetcake Johnson; the **McDevitts** were the McDermotts; the **Gridley's** were the Gormley's. **Baldy Drug Company** was Bailey Drug Company. Old timers no doubt knew the identities of additional characters, but today that knowledge has been lost.

Locales Based on Actual Locations

Quite a number of the locales used in *Ralph Marlowe* were actual locations. Ralph Marlowe's **Babylon** was Stockport, located in southeastern Ohio. It was mistakenly identified as Malta in a number of newspaper articles. Naylor lived in Stockport for a time when he was a boy. He apprenticed with Dr. Gatewood and opened his first practice there after receiving his medical degree in 1886.

Malconta was the name that Naylor coined for the two villages of Malta/McConnelsville. He first used the name in his early short stories.

Flat Bottom referred to Big Bottom, just below Stockport on the opposite side of the river, the site of an early Indian massacre that Naylor wrote about in *In the Days of St. Clair*.

Foxtown is the community of Pennsville where Naylor started a practice after he married Lena Ervilla Naylor, his second wife.

Quakerville was Chesterhill, a Quaker village southwest of Stockport. The Quaker Church there is still active today.

Stonebury Township and Road is Roxbury Township and Road. Roxbury Road is the county road from Stockport down the river on the west side three miles to the hamlet of Roxbury.

Onionville is thought to be Neelysville or perhaps Uniontown.

Norton Ridge was Newton Ridge, where Naylor spent his early years.

Bentlys was Bent Lane.

Haggarts is Taggart's large farm across the river, now known as Silverheels Farm.

Black's Mill on Bear Run is thought to be Sauter Mill on Wolf Creek, a favorite place of Naylor.

Hawksburgh ferry is likely Hooksburg ferry north of Stockport.

The names **Deavertown, Eagleport, Heathen Ridge, Bethel, Red Brush,** and **Bald Eagle Creek** were not disguised.

Period Photographs

Figure. 1 - Original Dustjacket for *Ralph Marlowe* - Courtesy D. W. Garber.

Figure 2 - Overview of Stockport. Courtesy of Rick Shriver.

Figure 3 - Boat on the Muskingum River. Courtesy of Rick Shriver.

Figure 4 - Boat in the Stockport Locks. Courtesy of Richard Walker, Ph.D.

Figure 5 - Boat docked at the wharf in Stockport. Courtesy of Richard Walker, Ph D.

Figure 6 - Stockport Railway Station. Courtesy of James W. Mason.

Figure 7 - Roxbury Railroad Station. Courtesy of Rick Shriver.

Figure 8 - A Street in Stockport. Courtesy of James W. Mason.

ADDENDUM 323

Figure 9 - Another Street in Stockport. Courtesy of Rick Shriver.

Figure 10 - Boarding House in Stockport. Courtesy of Richard Walker, Ph. D.

Figure 11- Church in Stockport. Courtesy of Jeff Carskadden Collection.

Figure 12 - Main Street in Stockport. Courtesy of Jeff Carskadden Collection.

ADDENDUM

Figure 13 - Stockport Mill. Courtesy Rick Shriver.

Figure 14 - Big Bottom School (far right). Courtesy of Richard Walker, Ph. D.

Figure 15 - Winter Street Scene in Stockport. Courtesy of Richard Walker, Ph. D.

Figure 16 - Gatewood Drugstore on Main Street. Courtesy D.W. Garber.

Figure 17 - Gatewood Drug Store in Stockport. Courtesy D.W. Garber.

Figure 18 - Dr. Wesley Emmet Gatewood and Earnest B. Schneider.

Figure 19 - American Legion Malconta Post in McConnelsville. (Naylor coined the name Malconta in short stories in the 1890s.)

Figure 20 - Bridge between Malta and McConnelsville. Courtesy of Rick Shriver.

Writings of James Ball Naylor

Collected Verse

1893	*Current Coins Picked Up at a Country Railway Station*, S. Q. Lapius, Columbus, Ohio, Hann & Adair, Printers and Bookmakers.
1896	*Golden Rod and Thistle Down*, S. Q. Lapius, Columbus, Ohio., Hann & Adair, Printers and Bookmakers.
1906	*Old Home Week*, C. M. Clark Publishing Co., Boston, Mass.
1906-1907	*Old Home Week*, C. M. Clark Publishing Co., Boston, Mass. Governor Rollins Version, (double copyright).
1906-1907	*Old Home Week*, C. M. Clark Publishing Co., Boston, Mass. Mayor Fitzgerald Version, (double copyright).
1907	*Songs From the Heart of Things*, New Franklin Printing Company, Columbus, Ohio.
1927	*A Book of Buckeye Verse*, Tucker-Kenworthy Co. Press, Chicago, Ill.
1935	*Vagrant Verse, Morgan County Herald*, McConnelsville, Ohio.
1968	A *Second Book of Vagrant Verse*, Preface by Lucile Naylor, D. W. Garber. (One copy only).
2011	*Vintage Verse*, Edited and Annotated by Theresa Marie Flaherty, Turas Publishing.

Serialized Writings

1896-1897	"Beggars Awheel," *Ohio Farmer*, December 3, 1896 to January 21, 1897.
1897-1898	"In the Days of St. Clair," *Ohio State Journal*, December 5, 1897, to February 27, 1898.
1898-1899	"Under Mad Anthony's Banner," *Ohio State Journal*, November 27, 1898, to March 5, 1899.
1900-1901	"The Sign of the Prophet," *Ohio State Journal*, October 28, 1900, to February 10, 1901.
1904	"The Witch Crow and Barney Bylow," *National Magazine*, V. 21, No. 3, December, 1904 through V. 22, No. 1, April, 1905.
1905	"The Little Green Goblin of Goblinville," *National Magazine*, V. 22 and 23, September and October, 1905.
1906	"From Jim to Jack; Letters to an Old Time Schoolmate," *Ohio Magazine*, V. l, 1906.
1907-1908	"A Counterfeit Coin," *Ohio Magazine*, Columbus, Ohio, Vol. 3 and 4.

330 ADDENDUM

1926	"Physicians of Morgan County," *The Weekly Herald*, January 21, 1926 through March 4, 1926.
1927	"Rambling Reminiscences," *Morgan County Herald*, McConnelsville, Ohio, March 29, 1927.
1939	"Straight Sticks from the Brush of Old Morgan County," *Morgan County Herald*, McConnelsville, Ohio, June 15, 1939 through Septem-ber 7, 1939.

Novels

1899	*Under Mad Anthony's Banner*, *Ohio State Journal,* Chauplin Press, Columbus, Ohio, 1899.
1901	*Ralph Marlowe*, Saalfield Publishing Co., Akron, Ohio.
1901	*The Sign of the Prophet*, Saalfield Publishing Co., Akron, Ohio.
1902	*In the Days of St. Clair*, Saalfield Publishing Co., Akron, Ohio.
1903	*Under Mad Anthony's Banner*, Saalfield Publishing Co., Akron, Ohio.
1904	*The Cabin in the Big Woods*, Saalfield Publishing Co., Akron, Ohio.
1905	The *Kentuckian*, C. M. Clark Publishing Co., Boston, Mass.
1907	*The Scalawags*, B. W. Dodge and Co., New York.
1908	The *Misadventures of Marjory*, C. M. Clark Publishing Co., Boston, Mass.

Children's Books

1906	*Witch Crow and Barney Bylow*, Saalfield Publishing Co., Akron, Ohio.
1907	*The Little Green Goblin*, Saalfield Publishing Co., Akron, Ohio.
1909	*Dicky Delightful in Rainbow Land*, Saalfield Publishing Co., Akron, Ohio.

Pamphlets

1907	*From Jim to Jack*, Herald Printing Co., McConnelsville, Ohio.
1911	*Across the Miles*, Rustcraft, Kansas City, Mo.
1911	*UCT Booklet*, United Commercial Travelers, Zanesville, Ohio.
1911	*Angelina's Ardent Lovers*, Advertising Poem.
1912	*For You*, Rustcraft, Kansas City, Mo.
1912	*If You Were Here*, Rustcraft Co., Kansas City, Mo.
1912	*The Old Time Friend*, Rustcraft Co., Kansas City, Mo.
1921	*Old Morgan County*, Poem, Herald Printing Co., McConnelsville, Ohio.
1921	*The Muskingum Valley*, Malta, Ohio, June, 1919.

ADDENDUM

1927	*Rambling Reminiscences*, Herald Printing Co., McConnelsville, Ohio.
--	*Flinch*, Advertising Poem.

Short Stories

1897	"Ben's Adventure," S. Q. Lapius, Copyright 1897.
1903	"Ol' Cap Mingo," *National Magazine*, V. 17, No. 4, January, 1903.
1903	"How Tom Evans Won his Wife," *National Magazine*, V. 17, No. 5, February, 1903.
1903	"The Mishaps of Ol' Andy Perdue," *National Magazine*, V. 17, No. 6, March 1903.
1903	"A Lucky Opal," *National Magazine,* V. 18, No. 4, July, 1903.
1903	"Sim Spike's Misadventures," *National Magazine,* V. 19, October, 1903 (reference to)
1903	"The Youthful Indescretions of Jim Whiss," *National Magazine*, V. 19, October, 1903 Reference to *Ohio Star*, August, 1909.
1906	"The Undoing of Old John Chaney," *Ohio Magazine*, V. 4., 1906
--	"Coming of Sawlus," S. Q. Lapius.
--	"Did It Pay?," S. Q. Lapius.
--	"Jud Trainor's Ghost," *Ohio State Journal*.
--	"Mamie's Prisoner," *Ohio State Journal*.
--	"The Diversions of Dicky Dare."
--	"The Blackmer Affair," S. Q. Lapius.
--	"The Mills of the Gods," S. Q. Lapius.
--	"One of Morgan's Men," S. Q. Lapius
--	"Spike from the Underground Railway," S. Q. Lapius.
--	"Story of a Skeleton," S. Q. Lapius.
--	"Stuff of Which Doctors are Made," S. Q. Lapius.
--	"Two Consultations at Mam Sterlings," S. Q. Lapius.
--	"Wild Tom," S. Q. Lapius

Newspaper Columns

1913	*The Ohio Star*, Marion, Ohio.
1913	"Sunshine Corner," *The Marion Star*, Marion, Ohio.
1915-1923	"Life's Vaudeville," *The Marion Star*, Marion, Ohio.
1920-1923	*The Chicago Journal of Commerce*, Chicago, Illinois.
1925-1928	*The Week*.

Political Sketches (Who's You in Ohio)

--	Allen Oh! Meyers

ADDENDUM

--	An'-drew Lightning Harris
1907	Charles Hungry Grosvenor
1907	Elmer C. Dover
1907	George Boss Cox
1907	Jon'ah McLean
1907	Joseph Beensome Foraker
1907	Kernel William Alexander Taylor
1907	May-Jar Charles Dick
--	Nickle-Us Longworth
1907	Theodore Energy Burton
1907	Tom Lofty Johnson
1907	William How-Hard Taft

Campaign Songs

1920	Republican Campaign Songs, Ohio Republican State Executive Committee, Columbus, Ohio.

Presented in Programs

1904	A Voice from the Past
1904	Down Upon the Rappahannock
1904	Flinch
1904	Follerin' the Fife and Drum
1904	My Skies are Seldom Gray
1904	The Fifer of the Buck Run Band
1904	The Girl Who Sings Popular Songs
1904	The Ol' Country Dance
1904	The Physical Culture Fad
1904	The Song in My Heart
1908	Foolin' Ma
1908	Song of the Motor Car
1908	The Cumberland Stage
1917	Old Glory, April 19, 1917
1917	Some Singers, June 4, 1917
1923	Minor American Singers, August 20, 1923
--	Boyhood Days
--	One Country, One People, One Flag
--	Pop Goes the Weasel
	Snip, A Study of a Boy and his Dog
	The Diversions of Dicky Dare
	The Jester
	The Millionaire Dude
	When You and I Were Boys
	Whistling Jimmy

Christmas Cards

Christmas in the Heart
From a Friend in Old Morgan County
Good Luck to You
Holiday Greetings
The Home Light
The Old Home Place

Broadsides

Bully Yankee
Call Him, Can Him and Cuss Him
Dr. John Goodfellow--Office Upstairs
Foolin' Ma
Gallery of the Immortals
Hands Across the Sea
My Laddie's Life Lesson
The One Flag
To Her Who Keeps My Dwelling Place
Ye Doctor's Life
Yours and Mine
What America Means

Unpublished Material

1908   Castle of Doors and Shutters, Children's story.
The Fate of the Valley Belle, (A Barefoot Avenger), Story.
Two Men and a Boy, Story.
The Adventures of the Elephant, the Monkey and the Clown, Poem.
The Cowboy and the Doctor, Comedy Sketch.
Two of a Kind, Comedy Sketch.

1916   The Little Town of Toddville, Play.
The Jackies, Play.
One Country, Entertainment Program.
When You and I Were Boys, Entertainment Program.

Acknowledgments

Special thanks to my friend James W. Mason, who shared photographs from his collection, as well as information found in his grandfather's handwritten notes in a copy of *Ralph Marlowe* that belonged to his father. In my search for period photographs, I found several in a book that I had used in researching the biography of Naylor, *Stockport, Ohio: A Compendium of Historical Information,* by Richard W. Walker, Ph.D. Although I had tried unsuccessfully to locate Dr. Walker before, this time I found him. Not only did he give me permission to use the photographs, he put me in touch with Jeff Carskadden, who provided additional excellent photos. He also connected me with Jerry and Jeannene Muse and Charles Smith, who provided information on characters and locales in the book. Rick Shriver again provided several of the photos. To all of these, I am deeply grateful.

My family continues to provide support and encouragement at every turn: my son Mike for his cover design and technical support; my daughter Vicki for her sharp eye and gentle criticism; and my husband Gerry for being there at every step along the way, providing loving guidance, wise advice and helpful support.

The Final Test
A Biography of James Ball Naylor

by
Theresa Marie Flaherty

ISBN: 978-0-9832342-4-1 Jacketed Hardcover $26.95
www.JamesBallNaylor.com
www.TurasPublishing.com
Also Available from Ingram - Amazon.com

ADDENDUM

Vintage Verse
by James Ball Naylor

Edited and Annotated by
Theresa Marie Flaherty

ISBN: 978-0-9832342-8-9 Softcover $18.95
www.JamesBallNaylor.com
www.TurasPublishing.com
Also Available from Ingram - Amazon.com

CPSIA information can be obtained at www.ICGtesting.com
Printed in the USA
LVOW061149111211

258838LV00002BA/1/P